App Name: otomo

D1453970

STAR REALMS™
Deckbuilding Game

RESCUE RUN

Jon Del Arroz

To Brandon,

[signature]

Liberty Con 2017

STAR REALMS: RESCUE RUN by Jon Del Arroz
Published by Evil Girlfriend Media
Copyright © White Wizard Games

Cover art by Antonis Papantonio
Design by Randy Delven and Matt Youngmark

ISBN: 978-1-940154-14-5

FOR MY MOM,

WHO BROUGHT ME SCIENCE FICTION BOOKS TO READ
EVERY TIME I WAS HOME SICK FROM SCHOOL.

CONTENTS

CHAPTER I

THE HEIST

BALIBRAN STATION
LOCAL DATE 1137.455

Joan paused in front of the sealed hatch in her aft control room. A holodisplay shimmered on the wall in front of her, reflecting her large brown eyes, only a trace of her black hair visible through the visor. The rest of her small form was covered in a pressure suit that puffed out like a hull calking compound. Using the display, Joan scrutinized every seal-point on her suit to ensure there were no leaks. Satisfied with her visual inspection, she nodded to her reflection. "Hey G.O.D., you there?" she asked, sound deadening within her suit helmet.

A mechanized, androgynous voice sounded in her left ear, from her audible implant. "I must again recommend, Ms. Shengtu, that you find a more suitable name for me as your AI assistant. Your fellow humans might not take kindly to your acronym designation."

"I need something to amuse me when I'm out in space here all alone—no offense intended."

"None taken."

"Besides, the name suits you. And it's true. GIC Onboard Diagnostic tool." Joan hit the control pad on the back door to seal off the internal air of the ship, isolating the room.

"It is rather a lofty thought process, shortening Galactic Intellisource Corporation. Perhaps the makers intended my designation to imply such. It would not be surprising, given my planet of origin."

"Is that a joke, G.O.D.?" Joan couldn't help but let out a nervous laugh, which temporarily took her mind off of the task at hand. Something she desperately needed.

"Joking is not in my program parameters, even with the upgrades to my personality matrix, Ms. Shengtu," G.O.D. said. "I might note that your pulse is elevated and your breaths have quickened. Are these questions serving to delay your launch? A human psychological technique called procras—"

"Of course not," Joan cut him off. "Run one last suit scan to make sure everything's good and tight, okay?" Despite her confident words, her palms began to sweat. G.O.D. was right, she had been procrastinating, though she didn't need to hear it from him. The suit held in heat, important for the vacuum of space, but added to an environmentally controlled room, it was uncomfortable. Then again, discomfort was the least of her worries.

She needed this mission to go through without a hitch. A ship full of credits and her reputation as an "independent procurement specialist" was on the line. It felt better to call herself that than to say "petty thief." The mission should be fine, in theory. She'd plotted with the best AI in the star cluster. Between her ingenuity, and his simulations and logic algorithms, they couldn't fail, could they?

"According to the last three suit diagnostic scans you have requested, the suit is functioning properly. The helmet is secure to the neck base with no sign of leak, and the front clasp similarly shows no gaps or pores," G.O.D. said.

In basic training for the Martine Star Empire Navy, her space combat instructor had made a scene the first day of class, placing a watermelon in a pressure suit. Her instructor led them to an observation portal and decompressed the room with the suit in it. When the air dissipated from the room, the watermelon exploded into a million tiny bits, splattering the window in front of the class. "Imagine this is your head if you fail to secure your pressure suit correctly," the instructor had told them.

Joan never forgot that visual. "Run the check one more time anyway, please," she said, unable to keep the trace of irritation out of her voice. It wasn't the AI's fault, his program had been modified to give him more personality. Those little irritating things that humans do, like an inability to follow directions precisely the first time, followed with that. At least G.O.D. was intelligent enough to turn those functions off during crisis moments, unlike most humans Joan had met. Including the military. Maybe especially the military.

"Your suit is *still* functioning within normal parameters. Would you like to initiate decompression of the aft control room now?"

Joan took a deep breath, her shoulders tightening at the prospect of vacuum. "Go ahead."

The vents made a sucking sound as the atmosphere drained from the room. Joan felt the tug on her suit, but the graviclamps on her boots held her firmly in place. She gripped the strap of her backpack, which had her tools inside. A moment later, the room was devoid of air. Taking off her helmet wouldn't kill her just yet—the hatch remained closed and safeties in place in case she lost consciousness, but the knowledge of being surrounded by vacuum still unnerved her. "Pop the hatch," Joan said.

The hatch door creaked then swung open with alarming speed, clanging as it caught on the magnet that held it open. Outside, Joan saw stars at the peripheral area of her vision, but most prominent was the station ahead. It loomed as a long wall of white painted metal extending several hundred times the size of her ship. Twin cables stretched from her ship to that hunk of metal known as the Balibran Station. Her mark.

She took slow steps toward the open hatch, hooking her tether around the clip at her waist in the process. Through her suit's handtab link, Joan hit the controls to release the gravity on her boots and floated outward. Joan didn't dare drop her vision to the stars below her.

Weightlessness was disorienting enough without the added sense of danger from gazing into the vastness of space. Ignoring that thought, Joan fired the suit thrusters to direct her toward a maintenance hatch on the station. Local "down" hung at a ninety-degree angle to her current trajectory. The burst of thrust faded, and she turned her body so it would right itself with the station's artificial gravity, keeping her gaze locked on the hatch's landing platform. She fell toward the station feet first. As her boots hit metal, Joan reengaged the graviclamps and released her tether.

The station hatch was sealed shut, with no point of entry except for a small terminal screen. G.O.D. would have to cut through and encrypt her entry to avoid being detected by security. Nothing they hadn't done together before, but every mission still gave her butterflies. One failure, whether in her suit or getting caught, could mean the end for her. Death or a penal colony. Neither option sounded appealing.

Joan crouched down to place the back of her hand up to a terminal scanner. Her handtab chirped, connecting to the station computer. "G.O.D., let's get this hatch open," she said.

"Stand by," G.O.D. said, and Joan's helmet was filled with the silence of space.

A long moment passed, leading her to wonder if G.O.D. could slice into the station's access systems.

A mining drone flew by overhead. Joan jumped within her suit. With her ship powered down and secured to the station, there was no danger of her being seen by an automated drone heading from the Aradel asteroid field, but the longer the wait, the more her nerves got the best of her. She focused on a breathing technique her instructor had taught her for tense situations. It often amazed her how much those few weeks had stuck with her several years later, a testament to his teaching abilities, even if he had been a complete jerk. A slow inhale through the nose, counting to three, and an exhale through the mouth of the same duration. Her steady breaths fogged her visor, but did serve to maintain her calm.

The door's transition to a lack of pressure caused the hull to rumble, popping open as air burst from it. Joan waited for it to fully decompress, removing her arm and handtab from the area in front of the terminal. She adjusted her environmental controls so she could see clearly through the visor again.

Inside the hatch was a medium sized cargo bay, allowing for small ship transfers. Joan stood at an angle to the local vertical. She turned off her graviclamps, gripped onto the edge of the aperture, and swung sideways into the gravity field of the station's interior. "Good work, G.O.D. Any signs of security traces?"

"Kastle Mining Corporation has outdated security protocols. There was no trouble ensuring that their systems perceive the hatch to have remained closed," her AI said. "I retain access to their systems via a copy of my program imbedded in the station's media library files. My position is secure."

"Seal us up again, I'm inside."

The hatch behind her closed with a slam. A hiss came from the other side, as the door sealing the room opened and air flooded in.

"It is now safe to remove your helmet," G.O.D. said.

"You're sure you can't access the files we're supposed to steal from here?"

"No, you must proceed to their secure, offline system in station section G23, room 108 to complete your objective."

Joan twisted the helmet off, her ears adjusting to the slight change in pressure from her suit to the cargo bay. She set the helmet down and unfastened the chest piece, unzipping the suit so she could step out of it. The normal, regulated air felt cool through her dark, sweaty clothes.

"Where to?" Joan asked.

"Your handtab has a map of the station uploaded with directions to the objective point," G.O.D. said.

She glanced down at her skin-embedded handtab. That bodymod

was as useful a pick up as G.O.D.'s AI matrix had been, with enough computing power to hold the majority of her ship's systems and her AI at her fingertips. Sure enough, the holographic map displayed on the back of her hand. Room 108 was out the cargo bay door, and down a corridor to the right. Easy. This was exactly why she planned her missions in advance, and why her clients trusted her with obtaining sensitive information such as these patented mining technique plans. Not that she understood why mining technique plans were sensitive or worth anything, but with the pay they offered, Joan didn't care to ask too many questions.

It was outside of her usual job scope—salvage and debris—hoping she'd find some metal worth scrapping or components that were worthwhile. But she'd made a name for herself as of late, or so she'd been told. To make ends meet, she'd had to smuggle items on several occasions, which is how her current client heard of her. For the first time in years, luck was with her. She aimed to keep it going.

Joan stepped toward the door, which automatically opened upon her presence into a carpeted hallway. She glanced left and right, seeing no one in the moderately lit station hallways. G.O.D.'s intel stated that this area of the station stayed vacant during this hour local time. So far, everything proceeded according to plan.

Perhaps it was being surrounded by oxygen again, but Joan was instilled with newfound confidence. She strutted down the hallway until she reached room 108, placing her handtab against the door's terminal.

The handtab chirped once more to sync with the station. "Stand by," G.O.D. said.

Two people's voices echoed down the corridor. Joan hurried a breath and jerked away from the terminal. She stepped to the side and glanced down at her handtab, as if she were busy with important work. "Converse with me," Joan said softly to G.O.D.

"I require more information to enact such a protocol. What subject matter would you like to discuss?"

The people came into view, engaged in a conversation of their own. Joan did her best to not bother looking their direction and act busy. "Yes, we'll have to get a maintenance team on that right away," Joan said.

"On what, Ms. Shengtu?"

"As quickly as possible, you understand? I don't have all day. My schedule is filling right up." Joan continued her act.

The people paid her no notice and were gone from her view a moment later. Joan relaxed her shoulders. "Stressful," she said.

"I am not certain I comprehend."

"Don't worry about it, just get back to the lock," Joan said, placing the back of her hand back within sync range of the terminal.

"Stand by..." G.O.D. paused for a moment. "This is odd."

"Odd? How so?"

"This lock has been set using military level encryptions."

Joan's eyes went slightly wide. "Is that a bad thing? We won't be traced, will we?"

"No, I've disabled any possibility of a trace at the station level. This will take more time to decrypt. But given the other security programs on the station, it is odd to have this level of lock on this door."

"How long will it take?" Joan shifted her weight to her other foot, a nervous habit that she recognized.

"Stand by."

"So you keep saying."

The door terminal chirped an affirmative sound, sliding open. "Not a long wait at all," Joan said to herself as much as her AI, then she stepped inside. Breaking and entering had been as easy as tapping the autopilot function on her ship. The mission couldn't possibly go better, and she'd soon have a pile of credits for her efforts.

Dim lights reflected off the metallic flooring of the room, highlighting a single work console, two chairs and backup systems lining the wall. The place was as dreary as any station office Joan had visited before. "Can you brighten up the room? I can hardly see," Joan said.

G.O.D., now fully integrated with Balibran Station's nets, raised the lighting to the corridor's level. At that same moment, Joan heard the unmistakable *guzzah* of a plasma pistol readying a charge. She spun to see two Star Empire soldiers in riot gear pointing their weapons at her chest.

"Aw, scrap it, don't sh—" her words cut short as the pulse beams engulfed her nerves, blasting pain through every inch of her body. She tried to scream, but her vocal cords tightened in shock. Paralyzed, the last thing Joan heard was the thud of her own body hitting the metal-plated floor. The room spun into a cloud of darkness.

CHAPTER 2

MOVING UP

Dario Anazao stared out the long window of his upper-level apartment on the Central Office. His vision through ocular implants accented the faint reflection in the glass to give a perception of silver shine to his skin. It reminded him of a current fashion of custom vanity bodymods that many company personnel had been adding to their skin tones as of late. Without the filter, he looked like a typical Mars resident: natural brown skin, short-dark hair gelled into a soft perfection that was expected in corporate positions. He'd always been called attractive, but never exceptionally stood out.

He'd spent his off hours like this all too often, staring out into the horizon of space with the red planet below, covered by the dome and the industrialized levels of billions of people. If he was simply watching something, the oculars moved much like a regular human eye so that they didn't give a sense of uneasiness to an onlooker. It sometimes gave his co-workers, bosses, and friends a sense of him as a daydreamer. But when he focused into the displays from the nets, the implants froze in place.

In the past, his ex-girlfriend had accused him of staring, something that unnerved him. "No, no. I had my oculars set to reading the stock exchange ticker. I swear," he'd told her during what had been their final fight. It was true, though her words held a certain amount of reality as well.

There was something peaceful about the way the Central Office rotated, giving the executives and managers of Regency BioTech an ever-changing landscape. Though he spent most of his free time on the nets with his speed advantage of a direct connection to his neural commands, something resonated in him when he switched to the visual bands that the average person saw. This was the entire world to most other individuals. He could see so much more.

That sense of wonder didn't fill him when he performed the work that paid for these implants. Quality control. Since he could see more spectrums than others, the company expected him to use it to their advantage. Though somewhat mind numbing, Dario could think of a number of worse jobs. Waste reclamation, planetary lift security, extra-dome maintenance—to name a few.

With a single thought, his vision field changed back to the fully-immersed virtual reality world of *Champions of the Apocalypse*. His father always told him games like this were for the masses below, to lull them into a sense of passivity, and ensure only the people with real energy and drive rose to the heights of the megacorporations. It sounded callous, but his father hadn't meant it that way. It was only to warn Dario not to waste his time or get addicted; not to spend his real credits on armor or weapon upgrades in a phony world. He noted his player costume's purple-spiked shoulder plates. So much for that advice.

Dario wasn't stupid. He didn't overspend on the premium upgrades. He'd heard stories of people who dropped their whole life's savings into the game to be the best out there. He could be competitive as well, but not to that degree. At the end of the day he knew he had to close the window and return to his very real job scanning a percentage of the handtabs, oculars, auditory enhancers, and other bodymods that Regency BioTech mass-produced. How could anyone say he didn't need games after a full day of that?

Someone had to do it, and according to the quarterly performance report that the system spat, he did a more than adequate job. Though with his implants scanning, how could he do less than adequate? Half of his job was done for him by his oculars. And why beyond adequate? Why not *good*? Or *exceptional*? He'd never understand some of the corporate phrasing.

The door chime sounded, breaking his reverie. Dario turned from the window toward his apartment living room and all of its chic modern furniture and the door itself. "Come in."

The door whooshed open to reveal his father, Vice President of Corporate Operations, Kostas Anazao himself. When people heard that last name, even when Dario had been down at Mars University, their demeanors changed. The name garnered respect, fear, awe, envy, and any combination of them. Sometimes Dario would conveniently forget to tell people his last name to stop them from treating him differently than they would anyone else. It didn't help that he was a spitting image of the man in front of him.

Mr. Anazao had the same toned build, face somewhat more aged but that even was dulled by the company's rejuvenation cream. Even his hair was the same: that gelled style everywhere within the company these days. He always kept his suit on, whether on off hours or not. For better or worse, Vice President Kostas Anazao was a face of the company. "Dario," his father said.

"Mr. Anazao," Dario said, having become used to referring to his father by his proper name in the last year. They'd both agreed that calling him 'father' or 'dad' would look odd in staff meetings. Everyone knew their relationship. It was moot. This, at least, gave an illusion of non-favoritism. Though, most of the time, Dario was sure that his father was harder on him because of their relationship.

Mr. Anazao walked through the apartment like he owned the place, smoothing down his suit jacket and taking a moment to give it a scan with his natural eyes. It was the same look Dario had seen since he was a child. His father never said anything abusive, but the look contained judgment of stylistic choices and cleanliness. Dario had kept his place almost spotless because of it, something he took pride in. His tastes weren't that far off from his father's either. That look still started off a tone of a meeting to get under Dario's skin. "I've come to talk to you about the latest Q.P.R.," Mr. Anazao said with the corporate short hand for the quarterly performance report.

"Was there a problem?" Dario asked as casually as he could, unable to stop the slight tinge of defensiveness that crept into his voice. He leaned against his coffee table.

Mr. Anazao didn't answer, but helped himself to a seat at Dario's table. "Three quarters in a row of a 'beyond adequate' score. You only received 'adequate' on your first training period, but that's moot now."

Was that supposed to be a compliment? An insult? Dario looked at his father with confusion. "Okay?" It was hard not to manage to sound like a kid around him.

"Well, with a track record of beyond adequate, our algorithms have increased your personnel credits-above-replacement score. The Directors have had a discussion and we believe it's time for you to be promoted."

Dario's heart leapt from his chest. He was going to get out of performing quality control scans? Maybe do something that was worthwhile? "Yes?" He asked, voice filled with anticipation.

"Yes. Arthur Miello has been transferred to procurement at the Io Trading Post. His position has subsequently opened up and we've decided to create a new title of Corporate Quality Control Manager. You'll still be responsible for some of the same duties, as we don't have many personnel who have your particular skill set. Your oculars are an expensive modification, you understand."

"I know." Years after receiving them, Dario still felt guilty over the credits his parents had spent on those implants. His excitement waned considerably when he heard his duties wouldn't be changing much. A change of pace was most of the appeal of being promoted. And overseeing other people performing the same rote tasks? There was nothing to do. But Mr. Anazao, representing the corporation, was here to give him an honor. That was the point. Dario had to remember that. "Thanks. I really appreciate it."

"This will result in an increase in responsibility. Yes, you'll be working in your department, but you'll be overseeing the early quality control stages on the manufacturing side as well, you understand?"

Dario raised a brow, his interest in the promotion returning. "Would I have to travel?" he asked, trying not to sound too eager.

"In time, likely," Mr. Anazao said, his tone dismissive of Dario's desires. A managerial position wouldn't change the dynamics of their relationship. Dario would still remain below his father in every regard.

"That'll be a lifestyle change. I'll have to get ready," Dario said, hoping that he could visit some of the other facilities sooner rather than later.

"Yes, you will." Mr. Anazao patted the table three times. "To help with the transition I've assigned you a new assistant. We've gone through resumes from the corporate sector and found a person who best matches your personality needs according to our psych profiles and also is someone who can pick up the slack where you have deficiencies."

Every compliment paired with an insult. Dario shook his head to himself to try to ignore that aspect of this conversation. His own assistant! Twenty-six years old and only a year out of the business master's program. That was a huge honor, backhanded insults or not. On the other hand, his father and whoever else had been involved in making this hiring decision hadn't consulted him. Should he be offended? Part of him wanted to fight having an assistant because that decision had been stolen from him when he was supposed to be management material. Then again, he was supposed to be overjoyed with the prospect of this promotion. Wasn't he? Dario put on a smile. "What's the guy's name?"

"Jake Dylan, he comes over from the accounting department. He's very organized, very sharp," his father said.

Did that imply that *he* wasn't? This was becoming too much, he over-thought everything. His father had just promoted him. That didn't warrant resentment. "Okay, when do I meet him?"

"He's standing by in the hallway, if you have the time."

As if that left Dario any choice. His father had set him up with this intention. Dario kept reminding himself he'd been promoted. More responsibility, more credits, more reputation that he could use to get out of his father's shadow. He should be happy. Most people never made it this far. "All right, tell him to come in."

Mr. Anazao stood and made his way to the door. He tapped the controls for it to slide open, revealing another man, about Dario's age with an oblong scalp-mod. He had deep blue hair, frozen as a wave crashing against the shore and wore a proper suit as Dario's father had. The oddest part about him was that he didn't have oculars, but an antiquated pair of glasses that rested on his nose. "Mr. Anazao," Jake Dylan said, stepping past the threshold and offering his hand.

"That's my father, here," Dario said with the motion of his thumb toward the elder Anazao. "Call me Dario," he said. "You must be Jake?"

Jake nodded to Dario and gave a glance over at his father. "Yes sir. I recently transferred from corporate accounting, the outer system office. I'm honored to be invited to HQ itself. The station here is massive."

"You'll get used to it over time," Mr. Anazao said. "I'll leave you two to get acquainted. Mr. Dylan has your next week's agenda and is ready to brief you." With that, he clasped Dario on the shoulder. "Good work, Dario. This wasn't my doing, but your achievement scores. Remember that."

Before Dario could say another word, shocked by the sense of pride that instilled in him, his father strode out the door.

"Shall we begin then?" Jake Dylan asked with an eager smile. He pushed the frame of his glasses up on his nose.

"Sure. Can I get you water or something?" Dario pulled out a chair for Jake Dylan to have a seat. His new assistant seemed like a nice enough man, though something was off about him.

"Sounds good." Jake took a seat in the chair, folding his hands properly over the table.

Dario canted his head at him to get a better look. That was it. His modern hair and bodymod mixed with classic mannerisms—and those odd glasses—they didn't match. Perhaps his appearance was intended to unsettle people and give him the upper hand. Dario had learned enough about subtle body language tactics to dominate business in his master's program. But Jake said he came from accounting, hardly a cutthroat department. He wondered what this man's gambit was. Plenty of time for that later.

Instead of grilling Jake, he handed him a glass of water and opened with small talk. For the next hour, he and Jake sat at the table and discussed their future business endeavors.

CHAPTER 3

A NEW MISSION

Joan's eyes fluttered open. Her body ached everywhere and her stomach churned. The aftereffects of a plasma pistol stun—*two* plasma pistol stuns. As if one weren't enough to take out a woman her size. Better safe than sorry, she supposed. Military redundancy. Something she wished she could have in her own operation.

She sat up and glanced around to get her bearings. Four walls surrounded her, one with a door and no handle, sealed from the outside with no terminal access. The ceiling grid had small ventila-tion ducts for air, and bright lights that shone down on her. Other than that, there was a bench extending from the back wall with the mattress where she sat. All of it was painted a pale metallic grey. Nothing to help her escape.

Her handtab had been disabled, leaving a blank film protruding from the back of her hand. She was helpless. Joan scrambled to her feet despite the protests of the muscles from her thighs down to her calves from the electrical jolt they had received earlier. She rushed the door and tried to dig her fingers into the crack. The door didn't budge.

"I would recommend against exerting yourself," G.O.D. said. "The effects of imprisonment on the human anatomy can be most taxing, adding to it could cause permanent harm. A cursory scan indicates that the probability of escape is less than one percent, leaving current efforts futile."

They hadn't found her ear implant. At least there was that. Joan let her hands fall back to her side. Whoever had captured her probably had cameras or at the very least audio recordings of her. She shouldn't give away too much information about her small advantage. Joan tried to look like she was talking to herself. "Where am I?" she asked.

"Based on the inertia of the thrust, despite the gravitational dampeners, I estimate we are five light-seconds from Balibran Station. Which direction, I would need more… more… more…"

Joan instinctively rubbed her ear with her palm. "What's the matter?"

In a sudden, bizarre change, G.O.D. erupted into song:

"What ought we to do
Gentle sisters say?
Propriety we know
Says we ought to stay

While sympathy exclaims
Freedom from your tether
Play it on our gains
Leave them here together!"

A series of beeps flooded into Joan's ear. "Stand by, rebooting," G.O.D. said. Several moments passed, the dull hum of space engines through the vents the only noise in the cell. "Ms. Shengtu, I regret to inform you my file has been corrupted. It appears the incident occurred when my core functions were uploaded into Balibran Station's archives. My program must sync with the makers in order to restore and function again as proper."

"Leaving's not exactly an option right now." Joan looked at the door. If G.O.D. was malfunctioning, that could be big trouble for her.

Not as if he could help her escape from this cell. If only she could have her handtab back online, she could figure out where they were held.

The door opened without warning, revealing a woman who could have been her grandmother. Purple ocular implants and white hair, she wore modest, professional attire. She was flanked by two soldiers carrying the same plasma pistols Joan had seen before.

"Bring her," the older woman said.

Joan scanned the two guards as they approached to either side of her. She could easily take down one, but the second would likely hit her with yet another plasma pistol beam. Even if she managed to handle both, she wouldn't be able to get to the older woman before she could sound the alarm. There had to be another way out of here.

The guards grabbed Joan by either arm and pulled her to her toes. Their grips twisted her skin, burning. Joan attempted to jerk her arms free, only to be met by the resistance of a tighter hold on her arms.

"I'm coming! Don't touch me! What's this about anyway? I'm a private citizen and I know my rights. I want to speak with a legal defender."

The older woman led the way out of the room. "Quiet, or I will have the guards silence you for me."

Joan opened her mouth to protest, but thought better of it. She followed along with the guards as her captor led them down a corridor. This corridor was thinner than Balibran Station's, as typical from her experience on vessels. Ships needed to preserve space. Along the walls, every fifty paces or so, hung a bright yellow banner with a black star on it, the flag of the Martine Star Empire, or just "Star Empire" as people tended to call it.

This was a military vessel. But the woman walking in front of her was no officer, not even a high ranking one. It was easy to tell she was a civilian by the way she walked, although she was no stranger to command. The woman had ordered the soldiers around, after all. What was the military doing capturing thieves on mining stations and then deferring to civilians?

Security in the colonies wasn't typically as tight as the Terran Trade Federation, part of the appeal of being in the colony worlds. She'd heard that it wasn't uncommon in central Trade Federation systems to utilize their military against alleged corporate crimes that could range from petty theft to fraudulent transfers. Frightening. None of that happened in the Star Empire, at least as far as Joan was aware. This didn't make sense.

The older woman stopped in front of a door marked *Level 2 Conference Chamber* and tapped its terminal to open it. She held her arm out to signify Joan and the guards to continue through.

Joan entered the room with tables set in a horseshoe shape, filled with at least thirty different older people of all genders, races and creeds. All wore formal wear. A holoprojection on the back wall displayed a rotating screen saver of the Star Empire symbol. The guard shoved her to the center of the horseshoe. The people surrounding her mumbled. She felt small as she saw someone pointing, cupping a hand over her lips to cast whatever judgment about Joan to her colleague.

A bald man with a prickly white beard at the head of the horseshoe table banged a gavel. "Order! Order! Everyone settle down. Minister Jaileen, this is the subject?" He inclined his head toward Joan.

The woman who ushered Joan in nodded, looking down to her hand tab. "Fellow Ministers, before you is Joan Shengtu. Twenty-two years old, five feet six inches in height, one hundred and fifteen pounds. Eyes brown, hair black. Daughter of Yong Su and Amy Shengtu, who prior to their demise ten years ago, were independent cargo transport operators. Ms. Shengtu's aunt was her legal guardian from that point forward and she finished her remedial education on Mercene before joining the Star Empire Navy. After training, she was assigned to the *S.E.S. Destiny* as an operational diagnostic technician. She was dishonorably discharged and taken to Rayknii Military Prison after being convicted of theft and illegal resale of military supplies. After her sentence—"

A man with oversized memory chip implant on his skull cleared his throat. "Theft of military supplies? Dishonorable discharge? This is your grand plan, Minister Jaileen?" He laughed. "This is insanity. I think we've heard enough."

"Minister Ethani," the bearded man with the gavel said. "You are out of order."

Ministers? Confused, Joan glanced around the room once more. This couldn't be the actual Council of Ministers? Emperor Lucien's advisors wouldn't get involved with petty theft. Even if the information she was supposed to obtain on Balibran station was important, it couldn't be *that* level of important. A mining station could hardly be a place of national secrets. Besides, the Council of Ministers had to deal with war and rebellion and raids from the Lly'bra.

"The only thing out of order is this fool-hearty idea. We have a military. We should use them."

"This has been discussed ad nauseam," Minister Jaileen said, glancing at Joan before turning her attention to the bearded man. "Also, it's been voted on already, might I remind you. A military expedition into Terran Trade Federation space would be disastrous. The casualties according to all simulations would not be worth the cost of extraction. This plan has the best possibility of success with the least possibility of blowback."

"I object to trusting the fate of Commodore Zhang to this..." Minister Ethani's dark eyes focused on Joan, his arm extended in her direction. "This cretin. The fact that the intelligence committee could even consider this an option is beyond me."

Joan's stomach clenched, her flight instinct overcoming her. But where would she escape to? If she were on the Council of Ministers's ship, it had to be a Dreadnaught Class at least, which meant thousands of crew and soldiers before she could even find an escape shuttle. Even if she managed to steal a craft and escape the vessel, they could shoot her out of the sky. Not as if she would be likely to get that far. With G.O.D. malfunctioning, she wouldn't even be able to navigate her way through the ship safely.

"We're wasting valuable time," Minister Jaileen said.

"I concur. I may have a solution to assuage Minister Ethani's concerns if we do decide to go through this plan. Perhaps we should dispense with the biography and get to the point?" the bearded man asked.

"As you say." Minister Jaileen bowed her head before sliding a finger across her handtab. "Joan Shengtu has subsequently become one of the foremost sought after thieves and smugglers on this side of the Hyrades Cluster."

Joan's eyes went wide. She had? Since when? Her broker had told her she'd just begun to form a reputation. When she escaped, she'd have to review their most recent agreements. If he'd been skimming, she'd have more than a few choice words.

At that moment, the latest single from Pr0ject N01se blasted in her auditory implant. Joan recoiled, grimacing. She applied pressure to her ear, as if that would do anything to dampen the signal, already on the inside. "G.O.D.! Stop it!" Of all the times to malfunction…

"No need to swear," another of the Ministers, a woman in a sari, said. Her accent thick with airy, staccato words, typical of the Rendoni System.

The music shut off. They didn't know about her AI. That was good. But his malfunctions were starting to become burdensome. Her ears rang with a high pitched buzz. "I just don't know what I'm doing here. If you're going to shoot me or put me back in prison, get it over with. "

The bearded man cocked his head at Minister Jaileen. "She is unaware?"

"We hadn't had time to go over the mission parameters. Besides, until this Council gave authorization and confirmed they were comfortable with her, I thought it best not to divulge any state secrets."

Joan glanced to the ministers, all of the eyes in the room intent on her. If their plan had been to unnerve her, they were succeeding. This wasn't a trial or execution, so what was it? "What do you want with me?"

The woman with the sari hit the controls before her, which illuminated a section of the table in front of her a bright yellow.

"Minister Kumaran your question is recognized by this body," the bearded man said somewhat through his teeth.

"You say she is in high demand, but by whom, and how do we know this?" Minister Kumaran asked to Minister Jaileen.

"Excellent question. If you load page one hundred and fifteen of your briefings, you'll see the intelligence reports that brought us to Ms. Shengtu. You'll also find that we recently intercepted an attempt to employ Ms. Shengtu from one Byron Tseng, who is purported to be the boss of the Open Hand Syndicate."

The room devolved into a series of mutters once more. The bearded man banged his gavel. "Let's get through this, Ministers. I know the Syndicate has been a perpetual thorn in our sides as we've been stabilizing this government, but that's irrelevant here. What matters are Ms. Shengtu's qualifications."

Joan paled. The Open Hand Syndicate wanted her? This was getting crazier by the minute. Not only would she never work for a bunch of goons who shook down and murdered innocent people, but how would they know about her? She knew it was her imagination, but the room felt like it was closing in on her. It would have been better to be back in her cell. Whatever she had stumbled upon, this was too big of a game for her. Joan dug her nails into the side of her chair. "I think you have the wrong person," she said.

The room quieted to the dull hum of the ship's engines. Minister Jaileen turned to Joan, the smile-lines on her face showing her age through her dire expression. "I'll level with you. The Star Empire is in trouble. My name is Minister Tanya Jaileen, and I head the Star Empire Intelligence Committee. Our analysts have concluded that you're the best hope to lead a mission to get us out of this jam. We implore you to consider a return to active service."

CHAPTER 4
CRISIS MANAGEMENT

REGENCY BIOTECH CENTRAL OFFICE, MARS
LOCAL DATE JANUARY 17TH, 2464

"**M**r. Anazao, sorry to wake you. We have a crisis," Jake said. The man stood in front of Dario's apartment doorway, primed and ready to go in a fresh suit as if he were naturally up at this hour. His thermal signature appeared in Dario's retinal view, heart racing, especially for someone who had just woken from sleep.

What time was it anyway? Dario glanced back to his wall chrono: three in the morning. Never in the course of his work had he been woken up during off hours to complete a task. There had been points where he had to stay late to meet a deadline, or even wake up obscenely early, but a crisis? What kind of crisis could there be in a quality control branch that couldn't wait until business hours? He realized he wore his typical night attire—a fitted tee and silk shorts, as underdressed as someone could be in Jake's presence. Dario felt his face flush. "Ahh, give me a second to get some clothes on, okay?"

"Of course, Mr. Anazao." Jake clasped his hands in front of him to wait.

Dario stepped to his closet, fumbling for clean clothing. With no time to worry about looking his best, he fumbled into the first clothes he found. Once dressed, he took one sweeping glance around his apartment. Did he forget anything he needed for work? Morning grogginess made it difficult to think. He reached for a cabinet, and depressed the dispenser to the LupienCo Stim Cream. A soft orange foam sprayed onto his hand and dissipated directly into his skin. Within a few moments he'd feel human again.

When he returned to the door, Jake Dylan still stood where he'd been left, hands in that same patient position. "All ready, Mr. Anazao? I'll brief you on the way over."

"Dario. Just Dario. I told you."

Jake gave an apologetic smile. "Sorry about that, old habits," he said, leading Dario down the hallway. They rounded the corner and stopped at the work lift. Jake slid his wrist over the terminal syncing his handtab. A list of suggested destinations appeared in a holo over the terminal. Jake slid a finger over Operations Level 47 and the lift door opened before them. He motioned for Dario to step inside.

"So what's going on? What kind of emergency could happen with our department that can't wait until morning?" Dario asked, placing his hand on the railing.

The lift doors closed. "The quality control plant on worker level three has been compromised," Jake said, clutching the railing himself. The lift car accelerated, taking the diagonal path downward toward the operation levels.

"Compromised? Thieves?" Dario asked. He hadn't been briefed on all of his new duties as Corporate Quality Control Manager. Did those include overseeing security personnel? They had their own department with thousands of their own employees, along with the peacekeepers for off-world contingency operations that fed into the overall Trade Federation forces. Dario had little personal experience with security.

Jake shook his head. "Not thieves, rioters. Someone's targeted quality control because of its geographic location central to the underlevel union hall. I don't know all of the details yet, only that there's been an attack. We'll have to get our security feed and make recommendations. You'll also need to give authorization for further action."

"Authorization?" Dario asked, already overwhelmed. He hadn't had time for proper training. What could he know about making the right call in these situations? The company had promoted him for his scores, but did those account for training time? Those algorithms wouldn't have placed him in a situation beyond his capabilities. But what metrics could conceive of fluke events like riots on the first day of the job? "I think we should contact my predecessor, Arthur Miello, and get his advice on this, yeah?"

"Very good, sir," Jake Dylan said. He sounded sincere.

The lift car stopped and doors opened to an open area level, wall projections of large open space and Earth-natural scenery gave the employees a sense of comfort. Corporate psychologists had found early on that station life caused undue stress over long periods of time for most people, even on the larger stations. Though everyone knew the wall projections were there, it still created a feeling of a less confining space, at least to the internal psyche. Once those projections were implemented, psychological health scores increased within days.

Jake and Dario walked along that faux-open scenery, passing the path that led to the peacekeepers' portion of the station, until they reached what appeared to be a classic styled office building within the Central Office. Double doors opened to allow them entry. A security guard sat at the reception desk, a larger man with RBT Security embroidered to look like a badge on his chest. He inclined his head toward Dario when he saw him. They'd chatted together on occasion when Dario was early for his regular shifts as a quality control operator.

Inside the office was a sea of open cubicles, a large department of quality control surveyors who checked the physical work of the machines and unskilled employees in the underlevels. Jake weaved around the first row of cubes, leading Dario to a corridor of offices and conference rooms.

The first conference room had members of Dario's team who he recognized from before. At the head of the table sat Daniella de Riko, a woman with similar oculars to Dario's, but a silver hue. She stared at a holovid that hovered over the conference table, labeled: QUALITY CONTROL CENTER BUILDING 3C—MARS FACILITY. Smoke plumed from the building and fire trickled light outside of the windows in the Mars night sky.

Dozens of people haphazardly circled the underlevel manufacturing plant. Others ran out from the main doors holding computers and robotic equipment, as well as piles of biomods. Two men fought over a cartload of goods. One man pulled a plasma pistol on the other. People fled from around them and the man fired, his rival dropping to the ground. The remaining man took off running, pushing the cart of goods ahead with him.

"Savages," said Antonio Dalton, one of the other quality control team members. The holodisplay's translucent contents reflected on his face.

Dario walked to the table, staring at the looting in front of him as the people on the holodisplay fled from the scene. What could drive people to act like this? He flicked his eyes upward and to the right, the deliberate movement to search Regency BioTech nets. *Net Search: News stories. Underlevels riots.* The basic thought triggered his eyes to display a layer of news links that the others couldn't see, tied to his optic nerve in a manner that didn't impact his standard vision.

Analyze, brief. A feature he often used to distill information. Preliminary news reports showed that the quality control facility had property value of nearly three million credits. Early analysis estimated half that figure in damages and half again in Regency BioTech product either stolen or destroyed. The news agency had confirmed at least three deaths, but a looter was able to strike their close-up drone with a metal rod, taking the camera out of service and leaving only the peripheral camera feeds online. Riots were estimated to spread through the city blocks of level three around the facility. Total estimated damage and loss of life unknown.

Dario took a deep breath and surveyed the team. "Perhaps we should go down there, try to pacify the situation, see why they're rioting," he said. Each member of his team was fixated on the holo-display, frozen in horror.

Jake caught Dario's eye and gave a somber nod in his direction.

"Dario," Antonio said with the shake of his head, "We can't risk you or any of us going down to the underlevels, even on a good day, let alone in a crisis situation like this. Those areas aren't for corporate higher ups. If we need to survey the location we can send drones and link in through the VR systems. What we need is your authorization to be able to take action to close out the emergency." He swiveled in his chair toward Daniella. "Do you have the recommended plan?"

"Yes, we'll need to dispatch BioMechs with sleep gas to flood the whole level for at least a three block radius. Once the perpetrators are incapacitated we can assess the situation and proceed with cleanup," Daniella said.

It sounded reasonable. No one would get hurt and the situation would be remedied when the looters and rioters couldn't maintain consciousness. This was his first real decision as manager, something that would set the tone of his tenure. He tried to sound authoritative. "Let's do it. How long before the plan can be executed?"

"BioMechs are already on the scene, just present your handtab for approval," Antonio said.

Dario pulled back his sleeve and placed his wrist square with the holodisplay sync. A chime sounded and the authorization proceeded, the text of the order scrolling on Dario's oculars before he closed out of the window.

The holodisplay zoomed out. The immediate area around the building filled with smoke. A moment later, the sleep gas mixed with the air and created a full haze over the quality control center. The people in the streets disappeared into that thick cloud in front of the cameras. On the edges of the display, over a dozen BioMechs cut off any potential rioters from coming to or exiting the scene. Their full armor plating and phase cannons pointed forward, looming ominously.

More people from the quality control offices gathered around the table to watch the scene. The smoke thinned and bodies lay on the ground in front of the looted building. The BioMechs turned their attention toward the fires, spraying retardant onto the smoldering areas until little remained but char and ashes.

"Where do the detained rioters go? Do we call corporate security?" Dario looked over to Jake, who still had his eyes fixed on the holodisplay. He appeared more distraught than the others, as if taking this riot personally.

Daniella raised her hand off the table to obtain Dario's attention and chimed in, "This level doesn't have a security penitentiary. The cost of hauling that many bodies would be prohibitive and create a loss scenario."

"You mean we'll just leave them there? There's smoke, carcinogens all around, not to mention the other dangers of the streets. That's inhumane," Jake said.

"I agree with Jake," Dario said, meeting Daniella's eyes.

Her oculars shined back, impossible to get a read on her mood. "Agree or not," Daniella said, shaking her head and side-glancing over to Antonio, "there's budget and overhead to consider here."

Antonio tapped his handtab several times. "I've run the figures, we're looking at a loss of a hundred and fifty thousand credits in units alone. It's nearly as bad as what we incurred with the Pirates of the Dark Star raid last year. We'll have to report this to the manufacturing department to see if they can have their assemblies clock overtime. That'll be the only way to meet our monthly quota" Worry crossed his face. "Those figures don't include reconstruction costs, boss."

Dario shook his head in disbelief and pointed at the holodisplay. "We're talking about real people down there! It's three-thirty in the morning. These people need a safe place to recover at the very least.

Anything with business logistics or the budget can be handled later."

"Mr. Anazao, with all due respect, we're here to look after corporate interests," Daniella said, blinking at him as if he'd said something irrelevant.

"We can do both. It's not all or nothing, and Dario's right, the budgeting talk will make more sense when we're not all half-asleep *and* on edge," Jake said, leaning over the table. He pointed to a couple of the bodies that had fallen to the street. "When these two wake up, you think they're going to be satisfied and return home? They're going to be livid, and that means a fresh round of looting. The only thing that will stop that is removing them from the streets. That's what you were trying to say, yes?" he focused on Dario.

"Yes, that's exactly what I meant." On his internal visual screen a news feed development link appeared. *Feed Summarize.* The information on the riot had leaked to various media outlets outside Regency control, and the news had been obtained by Regency BioTech's chief competitor, Genegrowth, Inc. Their news media could escalate this situation out of control if it weren't curtailed. "This has become more pressing. We need to get these images off the streets and show a calmer scenario before the world starts to wake up. Make sure we contact someone in marketing and publicity as well. The company will need to show that this was an isolated incident, something small, nothing to worry about. You understand?" He inclined his head toward his team.

"Good thinking, boss," Antonio said, tapping on his handtab once more. "I'm on it. Security can be dispatched within the half hour."

Daniella nodded, following Dario's train of thought. "I'll get hold of Ethan, he's a friend of mine in the marketing department. Hope he doesn't kill me for dropping by his place at this hour."

"If we prevent a corporate catastrophe, he'll thank you," Jake said.

"All right. I'm heading back to my apartment to get some rest, we'll be loaded with questions from the higher ups in the morning and we need to be fresh. The situation's under control for now. We'll meet to deal with the business end later today, okay?"

The team around the table, those who were originally present and the onlookers who had joined, nodded and spoke amongst themselves.

No one appeared as if they were about to comment. Energy in the room was as low as Dario could remember it being. Even with the stim cream application, Dario dragged as well. His eyelids were heavy as rocks and his hands tingled, slow to react. He turned from the table to head back out of the office.

Jake followed him, clasping his hands behind his back as he moved. "That was well handled, sir," he said.

"Thanks. It didn't feel like it." If anything, he came dangerously close to losing his team—and out of a concern for other people's lives. How would they feel if it was their friends or family down there? With VR entertainment being so realistic it became difficult to look at a holodisplay and remember that there were real lives to consider. Lives under the corporate payroll at that.

"Well, it did some good. It's hard to get through to the corporate lifers sometimes. They've been up in the Central Office so long they forget what air other people breathe," Jake said with a little laugh. They walked together out of the building.

"Lifers? Haven't heard that before…" Dario considered a moment with a glance over to Jake. "You didn't inherit any position, did you? Made your way up from scratch."

"You got me in one."

"Huh," Dario said.

"That bug you? Sometimes people in the department look at me a little different because of it. The corporation's been so rigid for so long they don't like to see change, or people moving up the ladder," Jake said, lips twitching upward slightly.

"No, not at all. I was just wondering what it'd be like. I've always hated my last name. People expect so much of me. They want me to act like my father, do the same things he does, have the same concerns he does. I'm my own person and I don't get to experience that."

"I never considered that," Jake said. He offered his hand to Dario. "I need to head off to my own bed. You're good people, Dario. I'm going to be happy to work for you."

Dario shook Jake's hand with a firm grip. "Likewise. Maybe there's something to those psych profiles that paired us."

"Psych profiles? Your father handpicked my resume and interviewed me himself." Jake shrugged. "Night." He veered off to the right and down a walkway.

His father had chosen him personally? His appointment didn't have anything to do with what the company systems produced? Dario stood speechless for a long moment. He did like Jake, and his father's approval shouldn't color his perception. Jake didn't know how controlling his father could be, how much he tried to steer Dario's life, he couldn't fault the man for that. Besides, Jake was the only one in the group to stand up for the lives of other people. There'd be a lot to think about, that was for sure. He shook his head and made his way back toward the lift car alone.

CHAPTER 5

OUR BEST HOPE

Joan laughed. She laughed until she buckled over and could barely breathe. It wasn't that this was a funny situation at all. If anything, her laughter was because she'd never been so scared in her life. Not when she'd heard her parents had both died and she'd be alone. Not during basic training, or even during her tribunal. Those had been frightening on a personal level, but to be called the best hope for a civilization? These people were out of their minds.

She took a few breaths, hand on her chest to steady herself. "I'm sorry, but this has to be a sick joke. There's no way you people would let me within a kilometer of a military installation. I signed a document promising that I'd keep at least that distance away with my release, as a matter of fact."

"Ms. Shengtu, this is not a laughing matter," the bearded man said, a frown crossing his face.

"This is exactly what I'm talking about," Minister Ethani interjected with another flippant gesture. "She laughed at our authority? We should send her straight back to prison and this time with no rehabilitation and release."

"Don't be rash, Minister Ethani. She was hired by intelligence to break into Balibran Station. It'd get thrown out of court in a minute for entrapment."

"I was *what*?" Joan asked, horrified. "I haven't dealt with the government in years."

"When you met the contact for your latest break-in, that was one of our agents," Minister Jaileen said apologetically. "Balibran Station is a corporate station with typical corporate securities. It was a test to see if you could successfully infiltrate."

"Then what's with the armed officers with stunners? And the cell?" Joan tensed.

"We had to ensure you wouldn't run and disappear. It was hard enough as it was to discover your location." Minister Jaileen paced around the horseshoe-shaped desk, taking a seat.

Which is the way I like to keep it, Joan thought. She'd been set up. Stung. She should have seen this. G.O.D. should have seen it. The mission had been too good to be true. A pretty simple break-in, all things considered, and the pay would have set her up to quit thieving altogether. At least for the near future, while she figured out her life.

Now wasn't the time to fly off the handle. She still had guards watching her every move, and she didn't relish the thought of getting stunned again. Besides, if she truly was the Star Empire's best hope, they needed her. The Council of Ministers couldn't afford to hurt her. It still didn't explain why they went about tracking down and testing a small time smuggler—or as she preferred to be called, "salvage liberating engineer." G.O.D. never found that one funny. The joke brought a small smile to her face now.

Joan crossed her arms and tried to look confident. "Okay, enough of the dancing around. What's this mission that I'm the only person you can think of to handle?"

"Have a seat, Ms. Shengtu," Minister Jaileen said, motioning to a guard. The guard grabbed a chair from the side of the room and placed it before Joan, facing toward the holoprojector at the open end of the table. "I have a presentation prepared for your benefit to brief you on the situation."

Joan turned toward the holoprojector and sat. The image morphed into a camera display of a space battle. Dozens of Imperial Fighters and Corvettes with the Star Empire logo on their wings scrambled in a dogfight with Trade Federation ships of the same make. Capital ships loomed in the background. A small transport broke through the cloud of fighters and proton missiles. There the image paused.

"Six weeks ago, A Trade Federation fleet engaged our forces blockading the Lighstry System," Minister Jaileen said, motioning to the holodisplay. "The *S.E.S. Righteous Victory* was boarded by Trade Federation commandos. The Trade Federation fleet retreated, perplexing our strategists. We had projected the blockade would hold through this battle, but the enemy fleet didn't take nearly enough damage to warrant such a retreat. We didn't find out until later that the commandos that boarded the *Righteous Victory* kidnapped Commodore Zhang. There was never any intention to break our blockade, this was a gambit to cripple us in other ways."

Joan knew full well who Commodore Zhang was. Everyone who had any interaction with the Star Empire Navy knew that name. That woman was responsible for nearly every advance the Star Empire made in building a buffer zone between themselves and the ever encroaching Trade Federation. More than that, she had successes against the Lly'bra—which most people called the Blob because Lly'bra was just too hard to pronounce. Joan had to admit those creatures and ships did look Blob-like. Zhang was a tactical genius, inspiring, where so few of Joan's own crewmates had been. The biographic holos were part of the reason Joan decided to join the fleet to begin with. But she'd not heard this tale before. "This didn't make the newsvids…"

"No, it most certainly did not. Though most of the Empire is unaware of the specifics of our military actions, there are enough civilian analysts who could cause undue panic with this information."

Undue? There was nothing undue about it. Even this very ship may not be safe if the Trade Federation chose to press. Joan shifted uneasily. Her shoulders tensed at the thought. "I am no expert strategist, I can't help you there."

"No, but you are an expert at smaller scale plans, breaking and entering, and smuggling cargo." The minister paced in front of the special projection to look Joan in the eyes.

"You can't be serious," Joan said, too dumbstruck to say anything else.

"You would not be here in this council room if we weren't serious, or if we had another option. You have a military training and an expertise in the aforementioned skills. Our analysts have done the research. You are the person we need to extract Commodore Zhang. Are you willing to accept a temporary recommission? For the sake of the Star Empire?"

"My god..." Joan said.

"Yes, Ms. Shengtu?" her AI's voice rang in her ear.

"Not you."

"Pardon, Ms. Shengtu?" Minister Jaileen said with a confused raise of her brow.

Joan glanced around the room once more. The eyes of the Council of Ministers all scrutinized her every move. These were trained politicians and diplomats. She had no shot evading them, or even trying to talk on their level. She had to be honest. "I want to help," Joan said. It was true. She wasn't heartless and the Hyrades Cluster was her home as well as anyone else's. "But I won't accept a military recommission. Not on those terms. I like being on my own, independent, and I want to stay that way."

Minister Jaileen cocked her head at Joan. "Whatever you wish to title yourself, it doesn't matter—"

"It does matter," interjected Minister Ethani. "It's a matter of discipline and a matter of control. I served the fleet before I became a Minister. I understand its importance. If she can't accept a rank, how can she accept orders from us?"

Chatter in the background of the conference room echoed agreement with Minister Ethani.

"Here's my problem with the military," Joan said with a little aggravation, loud enough to cut through the noise of the others. "I barely made enough credits to be able to feed myself. Once all of the supplies were taken out of my stipend, I was left with almost nothing. I may have fallen in with some of the wrong people, but I had to. I turned to taking from the stores because there was no choice if I wanted to survive."

Minister Ethani's face tightened. "Service to the Star Empire isn't something one does for money."

"Easy for you to say." Joan narrowed her eyes at Minister Ethani, all too ready for a fight. "You don't look like you've lived without it."

More rumblings erupted and the man with the gavel pounded again. "Order!" He said, giving Joan a sympathetic sigh. "I believe you've made your point, Ms. Shengtu. Frankly, I believe this Council doesn't need you to be a commissioned naval officer in order to perform this task. If the intelligence committee believes she has the prerequisites required to complete the mission, then we can move forward."

"Thank you, Speaker," Minister Jaileen said. "I believe that your conditions have been satisfied, Ms. Shengtu?"

Joan thought for a moment before speaking. "I'm not doing this for free either. I struggle to make ends meet as much now as I did then and I don't particularly like what I've been doing. Jobs are hard to come by out here and I want to make sure I'm taken care of. I want a stipend after this, big enough that I'll not have to bend the rules again."

"That can be arranged."

Joan nodded victoriously, belly filled with fire. She'd expected a little more of a fight, and their agreement took the wind out of her indignant sails. Perhaps she should have demanded more, but she wasn't the greedy sort, unlike so many others in her profession. She just wanted to be able to be left alone. Her and G.O.D. Which did remind her... "I also need a programming team to look at my AI. He's crucial to my abilities and he's undergone some sort of malfunction ever since Balibran Station."

"Anything we can do to help the mission go smoothly, you can assure we will provide our best," Minister Jaileen said.

She'd had all of her conditions met without question so far. Were there more? Her life had been fairly simple since she'd been released from that penal colony. Jobs weren't hard to come by, but if the Trade Federation advanced on the outer colonies, they'd make it more difficult for independent procurement specialists like herself to make ends meet. Besides, the Hyrades Cluster was her home. She had some allegiance to the Star Empire, even if the navy hadn't treated her well. With nothing she could think of to add to her list of demands, Joan stood up from her seat, crossing through the hologram display. She turned to face the room, offering her hand to Minister Jaileen. "Okay. I'm in. Where do we start?"

CHAPTER 6

REPRIMANDS

Dario spent the hours after his shift as he usually did: sitting in his comfortable chair while facing the window that overlooked the ten levels below him. Though he stared toward the window, his oculars had been set to display an immersive feed, allowing him to ignore reality in its entirety.

When he'd first had the implants installed, Dario would close his eyes to access the nets, but in recent years he'd realized that he could appear as if he were staring off into space, thinking. The trick had allowed him to coast through several classes in college and staff meetings when he returned to the company afterward. How normal people could sit through those without going crazy, he had no idea.

The past two work shifts had been difficult. As he'd expected, his comm flooded with messages within minutes of the eight o'clock shift start. Executives, lawyers, public relations consultants all wanted his take on how the crisis was handled.

Dario explained his team's actions, repeating the story of the late night riot events so many times that he felt like he was in a déjà vu time loop. Once those calls died down, he and his team went to work on how to restore the lost profits.

Insurance would cover a portion of the damages, but there were customers who counted on the bodymods that would have been delivered from this factory. Retaining those client relationships were as important as the lost profits themselves. Perhaps more so. Though sales and production weren't his departments, both needed to coordinate with him directly to get back on schedule.

The end result was he and his team would be working overtime for the next few weeks. Manufacturing promised to deliver 110% of normal products per day to make sure the cycle caught up in acceptable time limits.

Today, the legal team had caught up with Dario and requested a formal statement. He had been carefully coached beforehand on what to say. No one believed there would be any repercussions from his decisions. The underlevelers who complained of injuries from the BioMechs or sleep gas had very little legal standing when it came to civil suits against the company. The legal team doubted that Dario would be held liable, but still made him sign a statement that his actions were done under duress and that he felt he had to act to prevent even greater injuries.

The whole corporate process made his stomach churn. The more he thought about it, the more unsettled his thoughts became. No one cared about lives. People were as expendable as BioMechs or bodymods. It annoyed Dario enough that he decided to take a walk around the Central Office's open air promenade. Open air was a loose term, of course. The station was an enclosed metal shell that rested just above Mars's Lagrangian point, connected to the also enclosed dome via a space elevator.

The rioters had been held for the entire day after they woke. No one in corporate security would take responsibility for the lives that were in their hands. There was property damage to consider, and someone had to be held responsible for that. Mars had laws that could be prosecuted via corporate judicial structure of the offended property, but with the underlevelers, none of them had any property or recourse of which the company could extract. That was the purpose of insurance in the first place. But the people were left hanging in detention cells; ones that Dario knew were in various states of frustration, trying to feed and care for their families like anyone else.

Dario authorized their release. Holding them would do no good. The prospect of waking up in a cell and being given a warning about property damage would only cause further anger for the majority of those who were caught up in the emotion of the other evening's riot. The only problem was finding whoever instigated the riot so it couldn't happen again. Reports showed that security feeds went down internally moments before the riot occurred. This had been planned to agitate the people down below. It didn't naturally occur.

That thought process was a waste of time. Sleuthing certainly couldn't be considered Dario's job. He had to ensure quality control maintained its quotas in releasing products for distribution, answer media questions regarding the incident as the chief authority of the impacted division, and ensure precautions were in place so this couldn't happen again. BioMechs had been dispatched to security at all quality control plants in the solar system. That wouldn't be a problem. Still, Dario couldn't help but wonder as to the roots of this problem and what would happen to the people involved.

He flicked his eyes upward to turn off the complete nets view in his oculars, changing back to a mix of standard vision and thermal readings. When he stood, he froze to see his father sitting at his table, patiently waiting on one of the stools.

"Father," Dario said under his breath, inadvertently taking a step backward. He stumbled when his foot hit the leg of his chair. "I didn't hear you ring the chime."

Mr. Anazao grabbed Dario by the arm to stabilize him. He cocked his head, releasing Dario when he regained his footing. "I didn't ring. I have high-level corporate access, remember? You've been staring out the window for over an hour. Or were you?"

"I was in nets mode," Dario confessed, as if he'd been caught sneaking treats when he were younger. He shouldn't care what his father thought, and his father may not even say anything... but he gave Dario *that* look. The look of judgment and disappointment. It'd been on his face so many times. This time no different.

"Perhaps if you'd spent less time on there and spent more in communication with the upper management levels we may have avoided some unfortunate decisions."

"Unfortunate decisions?" Dario's shoulders tensed. "I made decisions that saved lives, future potential damage, and I made sure all of the quotas are still met for our clients. What else do you want?"

"It's not what I want, Dario. However, you're new to management and you could ask your old man for some advice occasionally." Mr. Anazao stood, moving to the kitchen and opening up cabinets to inspect their internal contents.

"I really wish you wouldn't do that. It's my apartment," Dario said, his tone as defensive as ever despite trying to sound calm. "And it is what you want. It was early in the morning, I did what I had to put out the actual fires so we could work the next day. Jake, my assistant you hired personally, told me I did well."

Mr. Anazao paused, hand on an upper cabinet, looking over toward Dario. "Did he now?"

"Yes, he did. Does that change what you think?"

"No, not at all," Mr. Anazao said, dropping his hand from the cabinet. "I was only looking for a drink, something distilled."

"You know I don't drink." Alcohol had strange effects on his oculars as well as the net connection installed with them. The blurred thoughts it created could send both into a spiral of opening documents and other media contents. He'd been forced to shut them down on a couple occasions before he figured out the problem.

"Yes, but you still have guests over, surely?"

Dario gave him a blank look.

His father shook his head. "If you don't, you're missing out on an important part of the higher echelons of corporate life. Contacts are everything. Your evaluation scores can only do so much if you intend on rising further in the ranks. You'll need well connected people, and not just ones that revere me. Once I retire, I plan on doing galactic travelling. I won't always be here for you."

"What's that got to do with how I handled the crisis? And it was a crisis, with no training. I did well."

"Well enough, but you still should have asked my advice. This… prisoner release is the worst part. What were you thinking? Those people need to be punished." Mr. Anazao held that subtle frown on his face that shamed Dario far more than words ever could.

"Punished? They're people without hope who were caught up in emotions of a situation. If anything they need our sympathy, need to know that we won't put them in a position where they're going to have to fear for their lives." Dario gripped his chair's backrest. He wanted to throw it, but knew throwing a tantrum would only make matters worse.

"Fear for their lives?" Mr. Anazao shook his head. "They're provided for. The corporation feeds them, and gives them lodging. They work in our factory as a consequence. They should be grateful. For every one job that we could use a human for, of which bots can do even the majority of those, there's three thousand of them. What we do is charity."

Dario stepped to his table, toward his father, separated by more than just the physical furniture. He clenched his fist, shaking. "Charity? Seriously? Did you see the faces on the holovids? They're hopeless. They've got nothing to live for. It's a hellhole down there."

"And that is why I work so hard to ensure you stay on the upper levels of management. The executive levels are even nicer, Dario. You need to be there. For yourself, for your future children. It's not perfect, but we care for as many people as we can. There will always be resentment against those above them. Some people don't have the will to work hard enough, or the talents to be able to get further than their stations in life. I have sympathy, Dario. I truly do."

Mr. Anazao maneuvered around the counter toward Dario. "You have to understand there's nothing we can do other than ensure that violence doesn't occur again. That's why letting them out is so dangerous. Now you have people who are hopeless as you say, with resentment, and they're going to have fresh anger. They're going to get their friends angry, and we're going to have a bigger problem."

Dario looked at his father for a long time. It was somewhat callous, but he was right. There were implications to think of to his actions. He felt he did the right thing in ensuring those people were off the streets, and it didn't look like that was being questioned. It was this latest action, the authorization of the prisoner release. That was the problem. But it didn't feel right to keep them incarcerated either. The underlevelers weren't at fault. Not all of them at least. "What should I have done? Do we just keep them there?"

"Perhaps until the media heat died down, and we had psychologists go in and talk to them about their recent actions to ensure their productive reintegration. I would have taken more time and spoken with different advisors on this matter. I only want you to be careful, son. To cover yourself. Too much liability can cause you more problems than you know. Do you understand?" He walked around the table to Dario and clasped him on the arm.

"Yeah, I understand," Dario said, deferring as he always had before. It was just like any lecture he'd had when he was a kid. His father made him feel so small in each of those occasions, and he didn't have any ammunition to fight back. But he was an adult now, in a management position at that. The algorithms trusted him with leadership. So did his team, or at least Jake did. There had to be a middle ground where the underlevelers could be protected and corporate interests maintained.

"More than that, Dario. Do you know how our system is set up? Our Trade Federation thrives because of the rule of law the megacorporations offer works from the top levels on down. Those underlevelers need us, without us there would be anarchy. The support that they receive would collapse. Just look at those savage worlds out in the Hyrades Cluster. Ever since that idiot Martine scraped together a fleet, had the power go to his head. People starve there. You don't hear about that here, do you?"

Dario shook his head. He hadn't heard about any starvation here on Mars. But did that mean it didn't exist? The reporters, the news agencies all were under the payroll of the corporations. Would they report on something that cast the Trade Federation's socioeconomic systems in a negative light? "I don't, but maybe we should take a trip down to the underlevels, see what they really live like?"

His father's eyes widened at the question. "Are you serious? It's dangerous down there. If someone checked your identity or recognized you, you could be held hostage or worse. You might be killed." His expression grew serious. "Not an option. I'll make sure that you have your security status revoked if you're honestly considering this."

"It was just an idea," Dario said. His voice sounded defensive even to his own ears. "It's important that we understand the people who are working for us. If we understand what they need to improve their lives, it has to get better productivity out of them. That's what the psych profiles at the corporate level are all about, pushing us in directions so that we'll inherently want to work harder. That's why my evaluations led me to this position, right?"

"Those thoughts are dangerous." Mr. Anazao paced over to the window and stared outside to the view of the different levels of Mars across from it. "Perhaps you don't have enough work to do with this promotion and the transition period involved. I'm going to have Regina in accounting send up my next stack of AAR reports for you to mull over and approve. You might as well see what the finance side of the corporation is on the higher levels. It'll be your track anyway."

Dario's jaw dropped. "You can't be—"

"That's final," his father said. "You'll have the reports in a few minutes. Try to finish those and get some rest. We'll recover from this lost productivity soon enough." He gave a short glance in Dario's direction before he trudged back out the door without even a goodbye.

CHAPTER 7

ASSEMBLING

TRANTINE X—H.C.S.E. INTELLIGENCE HQ
LOCAL DATE 1137.522

Joan, let me introduce you to Trian Mubari. He's a defector from the Trade Federation—as many of us are. He has a history of lobbying for different megacorporations in the Centauri sector on behalf of labor groups. He also has a unique perspective of the geopolitical environment you'll be entering into when in Trade Federation space. He's tasked with setting up identification, lodging, and information gathering," Minister Jaileen said.

They stood in a conference room on the fifty-fifth floor of a Star Empire skyscraper in the city of Beltrada, near to Trantine X's spaceport. The Trantine colony was situated on the frontier, not close to the Trade Federation, but closer to Blob—rather, Lly'bra—space.

Every few minutes or so Joan could hear the hum of a shuttle launching from the port, though the walls dampened any vibrations from the speeding crafts. Spending most of her time on space stations or ships, the lack of that distinct engine or power core white noise in the background set Joan on edge. That, or the fact that she really didn't belong here. She half-expected to wake from a long, vivid dream at any moment.

Joan offered her hand to Trian, a middle aged man with dark skin and short, curly hair. He wore a tan suit with a crescent collared shirt. "Pleasure to meet you, Ms. Shengtu. I've read your files and look forward to working with you."

"You've got one up on me," Joan said. It had been three days since the shuttle from the *S.E.S. Transport One* brought her down to the surface. She'd been moved from her prison cell to standard quarters at that time, and had her handtab rebooted.

The universe had felt so empty without access to her handtab. It was odd, seeing as she never received many messages, being a loner as she was, but at least she could scroll the newsvids and play some games to amuse herself. Speaking of which… "Are there any updates on G.O.D.? I mean, my AI?"

Minister Jaileen shook her head. "Our best engineers are working on the matter but there are several security subroutines that are beyond anything we've seen before. I'm not sure there's going to be enough time to restore your AI to full functionality before the mission. Perhaps we could outfit you with a new one?"

Joan inhaled sharply. Most people would find it ridiculous that she was so attached to an AI, but G.O.D. had been her only steady companion for more than a year. He was more a person to her than anyone in this room. His unique subroutines were half of what made her missions successful in recent weeks. She wouldn't have been able to break the maglock on that abandoned Cutter-class vessel without him, for certain. Nor would she have survived that time she was on the run from Driandi Pirates. "No," Joan said, exhaling to allow the stress of old memories to dissipate. "I can't do this mission without him. I'll need him, whether he's got some buggy virus or not."

Trian exuded calm. He stared at her from where he stood nearby, hands neatly folded in front of him. "I'm not sure I'm entirely comfortable with a rogue variable. This is going to be difficult enough as it is."

"I can't do it without him. No negotiations," Joan said, her shoulders tightening.

Minister Jaileen held up her hands. "Don't worry, both of you. Let's let our engineers work some more and see if they can happen to find some way to resolve this before we make any final decisions on the matter. Okay?"

Joan and Trian both nodded.

"Very well. Mr. Mubari, could you pull up the intelligence files and brief Ms. Shengtu?"

"Of course," Trian said, circling the conference room table and pulling up his sleeve to reveal his handtab holo. It synced with the table's system and its own holodisplay shimmered above it. The display had a corporate logo of a crown and stethoscope around the letters RB. Joan read the side bar:

Regency BioTech, Inc.—Megacorporation conglomerate with a headquarters on Mars. Founded 2392 by Janet Sheridan, the company specializes in prosthetics, biomechanical integration and modifications. The company has more than one million, two hundred thousand (1.2MM) employees between its fifteen subsidiary companies, including a robust security force affiliated with the Terran Trade Federation.

"Our intelligence operatives in Trade Federation space believe that their extraction of Commodore Zhang was a joint venture between Regency BioTech and four smaller corporations who wish to penetrate the Star Empire's fringe world markets and change those allegiances through economic warfare. Since our vessels routinely blockade against Trade Federation incoming and outgoing ships on our border colonies, crippling our fleet by removing our strategist is seen as an opening salvo for this long term plan," Trian said. "Public opinion on the worlds in question favors the Star Empire over the Trade Federation by a margin of two to one as of most recent surveys. We were able to use this recent attack to our advantage, public perception-wise."

The image above the table shifted to one of Mars, plot points representing the space elevator, various sky and orbital stations around the heavily populated planet. Trian made a motion zooming in on the northwestern area of the sphere, where the original dome settlement still existed for the surface.

"You think Commodore Zhang is being held at their head-quarters?" Joan asked. A giant station grew on the skyline of the holodisplay.

"That is correct," Trian said. "We don't have an exact location, but based on intercepted communications verified by our informants, we believe she is being held somewhere on the Regency BioTech Central Office on Mars. The goal will be to land a strike team on the inside to gather information on specific whereabouts of Commodore Zhang."

Joan focused on the holographic station. It had cargo bays with double redundant blast doors, camera systems apparent anywhere near an exterior hatch, as well as robust drone launching platforms. This company's security was light years beyond Balibran Station's. If it was like this on the outside, internally must be just as tight. "This is crazy," she said under her breath.

"Crazy, but also something the enemy wouldn't expect, which gives us a slight advantage." Minister Jaileen inclined her head. "Which leads us to our next discussion. We plan on bringing in a strike team of two dozen commandos to the Mars surface—"

"That won't work," Joan said.

"Pardon, Ms. Shengtu?"

"It'll be too obvious. If they have security as deep as I see just from a scan of the image of their station, that many people arriving would be too noticeable. We'd never get past their initial security scans."

"We do have people proficient at creating false corporate identities, which we'll utilize," Trian said. He motioned to create a new projection from his handtab, which displayed several different identicards.

"No. Trust me on this one. Look, the reason a lot of my clients started to turn to me for my... ah, procurement services, is because I'm just a young woman on a cargo ship. People *overlook* me. That's a big reason I'm successful."

"We have an operative on the inside," Minister Jaileen said, tapping the table controls to switch the image again. This time a man appeared. He had blue hair and a strange looking mod just above his forehead. Joan guessed he looked to be a little older than her. "He's done very well, gaining access to Regency BioTech's executive levels."

"All the more reason not to bring a very noticeable strike force," Joan said. "You don't want to further the risk of losing someone with that vital of information access."

Trian cocked his head at Joan. "I see where she's coming from," he said.

Minister Jaileen pursed her lips. "What do you suggest we do with the mission then, Ms. Shengtu?"

"I'd want as small of a team as possible. Sneak in, sneak out before the Trade Federation knows any better. That's how I'd do it at least. Less red flags on the security vids." Joan shrugged. "Curbs your potential losses, too."

Minister Jaileen looked to Trian and back to Joan again. "Ms. Shengtu, we do want you to lead this team and will take your advice very seriously. We are prepared to give you whatever support you need, but if you think a minimal team would be the best…"

"I do," Joan said.

"Then that's what we'll give you. You'll of course be bringing Mr. Mubari. I also have one other person I'd like to introduce to you." Minister Jaileen tapped the commlink on the conference table. "Send in Ms. Amitosa, please."

Joan tensed at that name, spinning toward the door. Every instinct in her body screamed at her to run and never look back.

The conference room door opened to reveal a compact woman, black hair and dark eyes, traditionally from the Asian continent of Earth. She wore dark but loose fitting clothes, and had her thumb hooked on one of her jacket pockets. She gave a quick incline of her head as she entered. "Minister, Mubari." She spun toward Joan, giving a smile that might as well have been spitting fire. "And our little thief, Ensign Shengtu."

Joan narrowed her eyes. "I'm not an Ensign anymore."

Ms. Amitosa, of whom Joan knew all too well, stepped closer to her, challengingly. She met Joan's eyes. "No, of course you're not. Rank would imply some semblance of honor and duty. Thief Shengtu then."

Joan's knuckles tightened around the fabric of her shirt that hung over her waist. She gripped it hard to hold herself back from punching Ms. Amitosa. Something had to be done to diffuse the situation. Joan forced a smile. "I'm not a thief," Joan said. "I prefer the term 'salvage liberating engineer.'"

No one laughed.

Ms. Amitosa returned that phony smile. "I see you rattle just as easily as you used to on the *S.E.S. Destiny*. Now that I look back on it, I should have noticed that was a sign of your guilt, not your nervousness of a new assignment."

"Ladies!" Minister Jaileen said sternly.

Joan turned back toward Minister Jaileen, shaking her head. "No, there's no way I'm going to be on a team with Yui Amitosa."

"Ms. Amitosa is one of the Star Empire's finest special operations officers," Trian interjected, his voice as steady and calm as when Joan had first arrived. "I've had the pleasure of working with her on several assignments myself. She always gets the job done. Her presence on the team will not be negotiable."

"It's also a condition of Minister Ethani agreeing to this plan," Minister Jaileen said. "The council has already decided that she will be involved."

"Combat specialist. They put me into the most sensitive situations." Yui's voice was so annoyingly cheerful, Joan wanted to slap her. "Think of me as your guardian." The word guardian rang as if to imply *so you don't do anything stupid.*

Joan said nothing, still in shock that her former commanding officer stood before her at all, let alone in this position. When did she have the time transfer to special operations, let alone be successful at it? Though, it wasn't as if Joan had kept any tabs on the military since she entered the penal colony.

"Not for solely that purpose. Ms. Amitosa has exceptional abilities with scouting, reconnaissance, and a plethora of other abilities. Her credentials are impeccable, but we should move on," Minister Jaileen said.

"You're gonna make me blush," Yui said. She brushed past Joan's shoulder and leaned over the conference table, peering at the holovid display that still held the dossier of the planted spy inside Regency BioTech. "Hey I know this guy." There was a fondness in her voice.

"You've been on missions with him before," Trian said. "So have I. This is a fine team you've assembled, Minister Jaileen."

Joan looked between the three of them, trying to keep her dismay off her face as best as possible. They sounded so tight knit and she couldn't help but feel that Trian's words excluded her. Which meant that she wouldn't be leading this team at all. It'd be two against one every time. What were her options though? She couldn't just walk away, or she'd be thrown into prison. Despite all that had happened to her, the Star Empire was her home. She did care about the coalition of planets that came together under Emperor Martine's leadership.

Once they arrived in Trade Federation space, she could branch out. Do her own thing alone with G.O.D. just like she always had. She had to play it cool for now. That was all. Joan forced another smile. "All right, where do we start?"

Trian chimed in. "Well we've already secured passage to Regency BioTech's headquarters, that's the easy part. Our operative on the inside should be able to provide us with identicode inputs. Once there, we'll have to do some reconnaissance to find out exactly where Commodore Zhang is being held."

"Do we have any way to run simulations? We shouldn't go in cold," Ms. Amitosa said.

"We can certainly run simulations, but time is of the essence. We have a full training situation room which I believe can be used for this purpose. At the most though you'll only have a few days before we need you to depart for Trade Federation space. The longer we wait, the more likely that Commodore Zhang will be compromised or perhaps killed. I'll call down—"

Blaring sirens interrupted Minister, repeating every three seconds. Strobes flashed from the corner of the conference room.

No one needed to say a word. Everyone in the outer colonies knew exactly what those strobes and sirens meant. Every world had these drills. Joan knew them from when she was a little child. Her teachers had told them not to run or panic. But when the real situation arose, how could they be expected not to?

All four of them shuffled quickly to the door, wordless. Joan couldn't help but look outside, the skies clear for the time being. There was no word that this was a drill. It meant one thing—Blob attack.

CHAPTER 8
REBELLIOUS IDEA

REGENCY BIOTECH CENTRAL OFFICE, MARS
LOCAL DATE JANUARY 27TH, 2464

Dario stood in front of the deck, overlooking the tri-leveled commercial retail promenade starmarket. Below were several shops dedicated to bodymods and various technological gadgetry, proprietary software experiences and holotainment. Hu's on Third, located on the promenade's third level, owned by prominent restaurateur Victor Hu, had been the hotspot since it opened last year. The view and the people watching experience was delightful, the food was elegant, and the décor was a sleek modern glass design throughout the premises. Even the speakers in the ceiling grid disappeared, piping in the latest in Glo-Beat music amidst the noisy background chatter.

At least he'd had the foresight to get a reservation. Dario turned his back to the promenade, approaching a clear glass podium with a holodisplay. A hostess in a cocktail dress stood behind it, tapping in commands. She looked up, took Dario's name, and led him to a table.

Jake Dylan waited there with a menu in hand. He stood to greet Dario, offering his hand. "Sorry got here a little early. Don't want to be late for the boss."

Dario shook Jake's hand. "Don't worry about that. This is personal time. Both of us need to relax after the last week. Fourteen hour shifts," he said, pinching the bridge of his nose with his other hand, even the thought of work gave him a headache.

"That bad of a day?" Jake asked. He resumed his seat, giving Dario a warm smile.

The hostess pulled the chair out from behind Dario, and he waved her off before sitting himself. "Rough couple weeks really. In retrospect, I can't believe they threw that crisis to a new manager, expecting me to resolve it. I had no idea what I was doing and just guessed."

"You guessed well. We're ahead of schedule resuming normal productivity. The algorithms show high productivity and normal output, which'll make the board happy. Everyone wins," Jake said, leaning back into his chair. "Seriously, you did a good job and maintained compassion as well. That's pretty rare around these parts from what I've seen."

"Yeah, I've been thinking about that a lot." Dario said. He fiddled with his menu, looking it over in a rote manner. The words seemed to blend together before him. He tapped on a simple appetizer, and ordered himself a soda. "Thanks for meeting me here, by the way. It's nice to get out sometimes, and I don't have many people who I can consider friends. Most are afraid of my name or are so focused on rising in the company that it's hard to talk. It's been different with you for some reason."

"Well thank you. I had the same sense about you after our first crisis." Jake trailed a finger down his menu and tapped his own order. "Sometimes it doesn't feel right living up here on the Central Office. We lose all of our connection with real people and real problems. It's different on smaller worlds or moons where you have to at least come face to face with some people who haven't traveled the same paths as you."

"Yeah, I've been thinking about that a lot." Dario flicked his eyes to the left to remove a prior search of a travelogue on the left edge of his oculars' view with pictures of the belt, Io and beyond to different systems. The oddest architecture he'd discovered came from Ecoccia Prime, a place nicknamed the Mech World for all of its focus on up to the minute technology. He wanted to see it himself at some point. "I'm not sure I'll be allowed vacation for at least the next three months, and even then I doubt I'd have enough time accrued to venture far off world. If I do, maybe I could visit Earth at the most."

"Earth won't do you any good. Other than the no-travel fallout zones, its structures are worse than here. You've got the extreme legacy companies there, ones that haven't had shake ups in generations. And it's the seat of the Trade Federation. Not worth the trip." Jake set his menu down. A server-bot arrived with their drinks, depositing Dario's soda and whatever hazy liquid Jake had in a tall glass. Jake took his into his hand, twisting the stem of the glass as he surveyed it. "I think your best bet is to take a trip downside to the underlevels, talk to a few real people there."

Dario looked downward at his drink, fizzing and bubbling in front of him.

"Problem with that?"

"Am I that easy to read?" Dario asked with a surprised laugh.

"You're not trying to hide anything, but having a knack for people is how I've come up through the ranks. I'm good at picking up on emotions, what people are thinking, what they want. What you want is peace of mind. You care about the whole populace, and know that the services and goods that we provide aren't an end to themselves but are there to make people's lives better. Even in entertainment or cosmetic mods it serves to make people happy. Am I right?"

Was he right? Dario had never thought about it in that context before. He'd considered a lot about people and what the company did, but that didn't often turn to internal reflection. It was a lot easier to think about the news, latest product offerings, holotainment adventures of any sort. He was connected to the nets full time, directly into his head. But what Jake said resonated. Had all of his concerns been about people's lives in general? He'd never really wanted for anything, being the son of the great Mr. Anazao. People had bought him gifts since he was young, in futile attempts to get close to his father. Dario typically threw away those gifts, even from a young age. "Yeah," he said after consideration. "You're right. That's exactly what I've been feeling. How do I do that? Make people's lives better."

"You're doing it. Handling this crisis was the first step. I really think you'd do well by actually asking the underlevelers for yourself though. I know it's a taboo subject for people up here at the Central Office. The lower levels are somewhere no one goes. Why would they? There's no spaceport there, nothing that you can't obtain that you wouldn't be able to just get better here."

Dario reached for his soda and took a small sip, letting the bubbles fizz down his throat. That feeling had brought him comfort in tough situations since he was a child. This chat wasn't too difficult on the surface, but whenever he wanted to talk about something Mr. Anazao might not approve of, he clammed up. He wanted to trust Jake, and over the course of the past few weeks he'd learned that his assistant was about as upstanding of a guy that he could have asked for, but he also knew that his father had appointed him. Word might get back to others about Dario's unorthodox interests, and that would mean more disappointment, more lectures at the very least. Though, if he were being honest with himself, it was too late already. He set the cup back down. "I already had this conversation with my father. He made it clear under no uncertain terms that I would not be allowed to visit the underlevels. I can't ask them myself."

Jake grimaced. "I see. I'm sorry, Dario. I didn't know." He turned his head toward the exit and everyone else in the crowded restaurant then leaned in toward Dario. "You could always not tell him."

"Are you serious?" Dario scoffed at the suggestion. "He's probably got my ident chip coded to alert him at any lift. He shows up at my quarters unannounced. I'm pretty sure he always knows where I'm at. Ugh." He threw his head back in frustration.

"Must be hard with an overbearing parent like that. Did your mom stick up for you when you were a kid?" He cocked his head as if to add an unsaid "and now?"

"Yeah, well, she's got her own career, but she ends up doing what he says. Always has. They're a team, a picture-perfect couple like you'd find in holovids, when they're together. It's really not that bad. I mean look at my life, I'm reaching positions where most people will never even dream to obtain and at a pretty young age. I shouldn't be complaining."

"Nah, it's all right. We all have our own problems, family or otherwise. Look… if you really want to do this," Jake said, lowering his voice. "I know how to code handtabs to give off false ident signals. We can create something for you, get you in, and get you out without him ever knowing."

"That sounds illegal," Dario said cautiously.

Jake shrugged. "When you've lived a life like I have, you move around. That means knowing how to get past standard security protocols. Yeah, it's not exactly legal, but if you get caught they just wipe what you've got, maybe hold you up for a night and move you on. Kids do it all the time to get into bars like this, to get served some alcohol." He set his glass down. "It's not like we're stealing someone's identity, just tricking a computer so that your father doesn't lash out at you for what's a really good idea. I think it should be mandatory for the corporate higher ups to visit the underlevels at least occasion-ally, see what it's like before making decisions that impact millions of people."

The prospect of doing something illegal, no matter how small, irked Dario. Maybe it wasn't important for Jake, but those sort of things lasted on a person's permanent record. If he was caught, someone would always see that Dario used a false identification method to go visit the underlevels. That could generate talk whenever his profile was pulled by the higher ups. It could ruin his career. But did he care about that? Did it really matter with him being an Anazao as it was? Mr. Anazao had a lot of pull, Dario knew that. His current promotion could even be called suspect. It was a little early in his tenure with the company to be advanced to a management position. But this was neither here nor there. Was he comfortable with Jake's idea? He stared at the man for a long second. He barely knew his assistant, a couple of weeks at best. What if this was some test? "I don't know. There has to be another way."

"Well, we could always just try to slip out without your father noticing."

"No good. Trust me. He'll find out. He may even find out with your plan."

"Was just a thought," Jake said, shrugging. He took a small drink, looking off toward the crowded bar.

"I don't know. You're right. I do need to see what's going on down there. I'm just not sure right now is the time. Maybe I should wait until I'm a little more solidified in my position, to where people trust me and not just my last name. I want to do more, something to really make an impact, that's all."

Jake glanced back and raised his glass in toast to Dario. "You'll do more. Trust me, I know. This is going to be a good partnership. I'm happy to be working for you."

"Yeah, thanks Jake," Dario said. He didn't feel as sure as his assistant sounded.

CHAPTER 9

DUCK AND COVER

Joan scurried down the back stairwell of the megascraper. Emergency lights colored the narrow passageway a dull orange. Her footsteps clinked on metal—along with the other thousands of people in the building trying to get to the street and then to underground shelters.

"How much time do you think we have?" Joan asked to Minister Jaileen behind her.

"I'm not certain. We received no reports. I hope the navy can scramble system defense fighter units in time." Though trying to project calm, Minister Jaileen sounded worried.

The light at the current level flickered. Emergency power was only meant to last for a few minutes. Level two hundred and three, read a sign near to her. How much longer would it take them to get to the surface?

If a Blob strike beam hit the building, it wouldn't matter what level she was on. She'd be dead either from the blast or from debris falling on her head. A whole block's radius would be wiped out.

People flooded in from each floor, slowing the descent to a near stop.

"What's our plan for the mission?" Trian asked from ahead of her as he quickly glanced back toward Minister Jaileen. "If we don't have this world as a base of operations, there's no reason to set up somewhere else."

"Aren't we counting our credits a little early?" Joan asked. "We have to survive this first."

"Always worried about your own skin and nothing else, aren't'cha?" Yui said.

Joan rolled her eyes but held back her urge to turn around, holding up the whole line of descending people and smack Yui across the head. In Blob attacks, survival took far more precedence than personal grudges.

The vids she'd seen in basic training showed whole worlds leveled within hours. Commodore Zhang had been credited with disabling one of their vessels allowing the Star Empire to capture it and reverse engineer some of their weapons. Since that point the colonies had been able to fight back to some degree, but human weapons technology still paled in comparison to what she'd seen in those vids.

"You're right, Ms. Shengtu," Minister Jaileen said. "We'll talk about further missions and contingency plans when we make it out of here. However, we won't be heading to a shelter. I've received orders through my integrated comm that we're to head to the spaceport."

"Sounds dangerous," Yui said.

"Does that bother you?" Joan asked, a bite to her voice she couldn't control.

"Not if it's a smart dangerous."

"What's that—"

The stairwell shook. People screamed and grasped for the rails.

"They must have struck nearby," Minister Jaileen said.

"I don't like the idea of launching in the middle of a Blob attack, I'll be honest," Joan said.

"Spacers," Yui retorted. "The shelters are somewhat more safe than the surface with an attack like this, but only somewhat. The mission is critical. We have to get off world and out of the system immediately."

"If it makes you more comfortable," Minister Jaileen said, "I'm told you will have a heavy escort."

They continued down the stairwell in silence. Fear of death wafted throughout their stuffy descent. Joan and her team made their way out to the street. She shielded her eyes from what she first thought was bright sunlight, before Yui pushed her to the side.

That wasn't the sun—it was the Blob's strike beam.

The street ahead crumbled like a cracker in someone's fist, hover-cars spinning uncontrollably into nearby buildings. Windows blew out with a resounding *crack*. Joan's ears rang. A few more feet and they would have been vaporized.

She couldn't hear anything but Yui seemed to be yelling at her, making a windmill motion toward a back alley. Heart racing, Joan sprinted as hard as she could.

Minister Jaileen kept up with her special operatives, directing the way toward the spaceport. Several more beams lit up the sky like Armageddon, thankfully none closer than that first blast had been. Behind them, buildings collapsed. Dust and debris rose through the air, blacking out everything.

Joan covered her mouth with her shirt to breathe through. Minister Jaileen stopped to catch her own breath, the team circling around her. The ringing in Joan's ears died down.

"I haven't tried to get to the spaceport from this low before. I think we're going the right way, but I need to check my handtab," Minister Jaileen said, lifting her wrist and tapping in the pertinent information. "Yes, we're only a few minutes if we run."

"If the spaceport's still there," Yui said.

Joan's eyes went wide. "Oh no. I forgot G.O.D.! He's with your engineers back at the HQ building. I need to go back and upload him!"

"We're not going to be able to do that, Joan," Minister Jaileen said, frowning.

"Odds are the building's not standing anymore," Trian said.

"But I can't do this without him." Joan turned back toward where they came from. The dust cloud covered everything. It was impossible to see. "I have to try."

"It's just an AI," Minister Jaileen said.

Yui watched them silently.

"It's not just an AI. He's more than that to me. My only friend," Joan said, wanting to turn away in that moment of vulnerability, but she held her ground. What did it matter her reasoning? This was her demand and she was the one they needed to lead this mission.

Minister Jaileen squeezed Joan's shoulder. "I understand. Look, I think we had a copy uploaded aboard the *Transport One*. When we get clear of the Blob attack I'll request the data transfer."

"We should get moving. I don't want to get caught in one of those beams. Fries the hair," Yui said, deadpan.

"Ahh yes, your hair. That's what I was concerned about as well." Trian chuckled awkwardly. "Let's get moving."

Yui took off running again. Trian followed.

"You okay?" Minister Jaileen asked, still gripping Joan's shoulder.

Joan bit her lip, staring back at that dust cloud. They were right, her only hope was a backed up copy of G.O.D. off world. Going back would be dangerous. "Yeah, let's go."

They ran through city blocks at a frantic pace. Joan hadn't pushed herself this hard since her weekly fitness regiments aboard the *Destiny*, but that sort of experience stuck with a person. Even though the air filled with the debris of buildings behind her and all the burning, her life was on the line. Nothing could make her stop.

The sky pulsed with blinding light as more beams descended, soon obscured by the ever growing dark cloud of dust. The way ahead to the spaceport became hazy. "What if there's no spaceport left?" Joan asked.

Minister Jaileen didn't turn her head, running just as hard in front of her, impressive for an older bureaucrat. "We hope there's a ship still functioning and commandeer it," she said.

They continued for several long minutes, following the guided markers on the ground toward the spaceport entrance. The building appeared to be intact and thousands of people scrambled to get inside. Holographic logos of different spaceliners illuminated the road while local law enforcement directed traffic. Much of the city grid ground and air traffic controls appeared to be offline.

Joan looked up to the skies. Directly above them buzzed a chaotic clutter of hovercars, swarming in circles as their autopilots corrected for dangerous conditions in the atmosphere. It had the opposite effect the safety the systems should have provided. Two cars collided above her, nine o'clock. The crash resounded with dozens of other hovercars sounding their horns.

Minister Jaileen paid no mind to the chaos around them, continuing through the commercial zone and to a restricted area with a labeled electrified fence and a security guard wearing similar attire to the ones who arrested Joan on Balibran station.

The guard approached Minister Jaileen. "Commercial lines are around the bend," he said.

"We're not here for commercial lines," Minister Jaileen said, flashing her handtab.

The man scanned it with his own device. It brought up a holo of Minister Jaileen, her thumbprint information and retinal scan. He turned back to them. "My apologies, Minister," he said, tapping a button to the side of the terminal that retracted the gate.

Minister Jaileen stepped through. Joan and the others moved with her. Beyond the gate held no sign of flight stations, platform shuttles, or further security checks. This road bypassed the civilian area entirely, leading back to the vast pads of ships waiting to take off. Joan had seen this side of spaceports back in her navy days. Her crew often was escorted through the secured spaceport area. She wondered what type of ship would be reserved for the Minister's use. Hopefully, a vessel with robust shielding.

Before Joan could determine which ship would be theirs, a

contingent of Star Empire soldiers approached the team. Minister Jaileen went to talk with one of them. They exchanged words and one of the soldiers pointed toward a hangar. Minister Jaileen thanked them and returned.

"Our transport ship is ready to lift and a fighter squadron is set for cover fire for our take off. We need to hurry, launch window is in fifteen minutes," she said.

"Let's go then," Yui said. She trailed after Minister Jaileen.

Joan jogged to keep up, as they turned toward a parked Cargo Launch vessel. The same class as Joan's own ship—albeit a newer model. The sight of the stubby wings, dual cockpit and three rear thrusters comforted Joan, even amidst the chaos. Her ship had taken quite a beating at points, and still survived to fly. At some point, she would have to find out where the Star Empire was keeping it. The Council of Ministers had promised to eventually return Joan's ship to her. She would see if they kept that promise.

Joan moved to the ramp but Minister Jaileen gripped her by the hand. "Ms. Shengtu. We'll be parting ways here. Your ship is the *Money Hauler* and I've been told its onboard nav system has been given false logs to show it originated from Meinkala, in Trade Federation space about the same distance to the Terran System from here. Your cover is simply that you're trade merchants, not far off from your civilian life. You're contracted to ferry your two passengers to the Sol system. Let them worry about their own assignments. Ms. Amitosa and Mr. Mubari can handle themselves, they've trained for it. I apologize that we had no time to run simulations, but there should be enough briefing material to keep you occupied through the trip. Do you have any questions?"

"Wait, we're going on the mission now? Where are you going?" Joan asked, surprised that the Minister had proceeded with Trian's plan, and with no word.

"I have to take care of the people here. My apologies for not including you on the briefing through my integrated comm." Minister

Jaileen touched the side of her head. "But I'm the ranking government representative on planet. There will be a substantial amount of panic, and I'll be needed. It's never an easy process, these attacks, but we've dealt with them before. We'll recover."

"Well, thank you," Joan said, frowning despite herself.

"No, the Star Empire must thank you, Ms. Shengtu. Good luck on your mission, our fate depends on it."

"No pressure," Joan said with a laugh to herself.

Minister Jaileen gave her arm one final pat and began to move away.

Joan was about to let her go, but realized she'd forgotten something important. She caught Minister Jaileen by the sleeve, stopping her from moving away. "What about my AI? You promised you'd look for a copy when you arrived on the *Transport One*." Those plans had changed, but Joan wasn't about to leave without him.

"I didn't forget. I tapped in the request to my handtab. Your AI should be loaded into the *Money Hauler's* primary computer. Please be careful. The *Transport One's* engineers tell me they added an emergency shutdown protocol in case the AI had problems with its current condition. The code word "bluetide" will act as a kill switch if you need it."

Kill switch? Joan hoped she wouldn't have to use that on G.O.D. It would be akin to stabbing her best friend.

"Don't worry," Minister Jaileen said, seeming to mistake her concern for G.O.D. over nervousness for the mission. She pulled her arm back, removing herself from the clutches of Joan's fingers. "You'll do fine. Our intelligence team is rarely wrong. I look forward to seeing you on the other side."

"Yeah, you too," Joan said, her own arm falling slack to her side. There was little more she could ask of the woman, and prolonging goodbyes wouldn't give Joan any more comfort with the situation. They'd flung her onto this mission as fast as they could. No time to prepare.

Yui frantically motioned for Joan to make her way up the ramp. "Hurry. Our departure window is short. You're the pilot, right?" Yui said.

"I've flown before," Joan said.

"Well, get in the cockpit. We need to get scooting before another beam vapes us." Yui stepped into the cabin and pointed toward the front of the craft.

Joan grimaced, not fond of Yui's command mode that she'd fallen right back into, years later. Minister Jaileen had told Joan this was her mission, her team. But those technicalities were something she would have to deal with later. For now, she moved inside the ship. The door closed behind her and air pressurized inside the cabin. The stale recycled air flavor came over the place almost immediately.

The cockpit itself looked a lot like her own vessel. A more modern holodisplay projector, gauges of cabin oxygen levels, engine energy quotient, gravimetric plate control, and finally, a whole subset of flight control levers and buttons. Joan slipped into the seat. It contoured itself to her back arches for comfort in long journeys. Safety belts protruded and clipped on for a planetary launch. The dash powered up and space traffic control monitors came online.

"*Money Hauler*, you're clear to launch,"

Joan tapped the comm button. "Read you, traffic control. Launching in five… four… three… two… one…"

The cargo ship shot upward with incredible speed, the city shrinking from the cockpit window almost faster than Joan could see. Several Blob beams still pummeled the planet. The dust cloud obscured as most of her view, then became a small section of the round world. They were through the atmosphere and into the vacuum of space within moments, where Joan switched on the multispacial grid view of the holodisplay.

"Everything good in there?" Yui asked in a patronizing manner from back in the cabin.

"I'm fine, thank you for asking. You and Trian buckled in?"

"We're good or you would have heard a lot of crashing and tumbling on lift off," Trian said.

"We've still got a long ways to go, so hang tight," Joan said. The nose of the ship rotated away from the planet. On the grid were four large capital sized Blob ships along with a couple of dozen fighters registering in three different clusters. The computer was able to differentiate between the Blob ships, which it registered in green and the Star Empire planetary defense ships in gold. The *Money Hauler* was flanked by almost a full squadron of Imperial Fighters and Corvettes.

"*Money Hauler*, come in," a voice came through the comm.

"*Money Hauler* pilot speaking," Joan said.

"We're going to try to pass around the starboard flank of the Blob Carrier for you to make your escape into hyperspace. Enter in the coordinates I'm about to send you and set your nav to evasive pattern delta. Let our fighters worry about the rest."

The coordinates broadcast to her holodisplay. Joan swiped across the air to add them to the nav computer. "*Money Hauler*, set evasive pattern delta."

The nav computer chirped in acknowledgement.

"All set," Joan said through the comm. "Thruster burst in three."

"Godspeed, *Money Hauler* pilot."

Her ship drifted to starboard, cocking up and away from the planet. Joan watched, fingers on the control of any last minute adjustments she might need to make. A cluster of shapes the size of a fist was in front of her, growing as the *Money Hauler* sped away from Trantine X. The shapes spread out into a swarm of Blob fighters and the carrier ship. It was still a decent ways off but the massive carrier nearly filled her view from the cockpit.

Its pulse beam fired—a wide spread toward the planet. Joan tensed but the beam shot well below her vessel. If that thing had been remotely near her, she wouldn't be around to be afraid of it. The ship's delta pattern banked her aft and further upward.

Blob fighters appeared at nine o'clock. Joan engaged the weapons controls to lock onto the fighter group. Something shot in her direction that broke into more than twenty mini-explosions. Joan grabbed the control and hooked the *Money Hauler* around the explosions.

"What are those?" Joan asked to herself.

"A frag cluster weapon. Something new the Blob have developed," came through her comm. "They're a bitch to navigate around as you—"

The comm cut off into static. Joan checked the holodisplay. The grid showed one Imperial Fighter destroyed, then two and three. Her escort was getting picked off by these cluster weapons one by one.

The Blob carrier came into better view, and from its launch bays came three more squadrons of Blob fighters. "We're never gonna make it," Joan breathed to herself.

Two of the Corvettes escorting her broke off, firing their thrusters straight toward the carrier. Joan's throat tightened. They'd get blown out of the sky far before they reached the fleet. What were they thinking?

Then it occurred to her. That was their plan. Joan engaged her thrusters to a full side-strafe away from the breaking off Corvettes. The rest of her escort did the same, avoiding several more frag cluster explosions in the process.

The two Corvettes close to the carrier exploded almost immediately. However, each dropped a small, head-sized canister right before their sacrifice. If Joan hadn't been looking for it, the sensor nets wouldn't have even picked them up. They looked like space debris, but…

Rings of energy burst from each canister like a supernova. One shot laterally and the other horizontal on a similar axis. The burst engulfed all of the recently launched Blob fighters and even managed to knock out the Blob carrier's shielding.

The explosions gave the *Money Hauler* the distraction it needed from its current Blob fighter attack to punch through. The rest of the fighters escorting her flipped around to fire main weapons while reversing.

"Fifteen seconds until safe hyperspace launch," the *Money Hauler*'s computer announced to her.

One of the Star Empire's Dreadnaughts came about to engage the now shieldless Blob carrier. It fired all of its main batteries toward the gigantic vessel, which split into three from the assault. Lights dwindled as its power core was drilled by Star Empire's weapons.

The *Money Hauler*'s holodisplay blinked with green lights.

Joan pushed the lever to thrust the ship into hyperspace and safety. Relative safety, at least. As in a couple of days, they'd be dropping out directly into the heart of the Terran Trade Federation.

CHAPTER 10

RELEASED

Dario jogged through the Trade Federation Private Security reserved area of the Central Office. He'd received a call a few minutes ago from Antonio, who requested Dario's immediate assistance. Regarding what, Antonio hadn't said. Had his employee run into trouble with security? It seemed unlikely that he would have tangled with the military, even if he was a hothead.

When he rounded the corner, Dario saw an entryway with a large Trade Federation logo hanging above the door. He slowed his pace to step inside, finding a reception room with a glass window, sealed door and several recruitment posters for Trade Federation Security on the walls.

Part of Regency BioTech's funding requirement for the Central Office's construction was to maintain a T.F.P.S. presence and recruiting station. This ceded some space to the greater Trade Federation at large, but without that boost in funds, the company wouldn't have had the funds to create a station like this.

An armed guard stood by the door, and a woman behind the counter. Her lips pressed together into a thin line, appearing annoyed at the person in front of her who gestured and argued with her. Dark spiked hair with sandy tips gave away that man's identity—Antonio.

Dario stepped toward them. "Is there a problem here?"

Antonio turned toward Dario, fire in his eyes. That fire diminished when he realized who stood there. "Boss! Thanks for coming. I've been trying to get information for over fifteen minutes, but I keep getting a runaround."

"Information about what?" Dario glanced to the woman behind the counter.

"Security matters," the woman behind the counter said.

"See what I'm saying?" Antonio flippantly motioned toward her.

The guard by the door watched but didn't move.

Dario had to do something to calm Antonio down before he made more of a scene than he bargained for. He intercepted Antonio's arm, pushing it downward. "Should we talk about this somewhere else? You still haven't told me what's happening."

"Nah, I can tell it to you right here." Antonio didn't fight Dario's move but glared at the woman behind the counter. "Indy news feed this morning popped up that there was a prisoner transfer to here. An older woman, worn looking, just like one of the underlevelers. I've been keeping my ear to the ground since the incident and figured this matched the people brought in before, which means they weren't all released like you ordered."

Dario blinked. He didn't expect to have to deal with more problems in the underleveler situation. Quality Control had nearly recovered from the incident and corporate had been quiet. "Is this true?" Dario asked to the woman behind the counter.

She shook her head. "I cannot confirm anything this man said. Now if you please, I have other work to do."

Antonio started forward but Dario held him back with a hand to the chest, stepping in front. "My name is Dario Anazao, corporate quality control manager for Regency BioTech. I may have a clearance higher than my associate here."

The woman pointed to a scanner on his side of the glass. "Place your ident, please."

Dario did so.

She tapped a couple commands onto a screen on her side, which Dario could not see. "No," she said, "I'm sorry but I can't give you any access into T.F.P.S. matters. If there's anything else?" The woman asked, signaling dismissal.

Antonio seethed, looking ready to fight. As much as Dario's head swam with concern, harassing this woman would only cause trouble. Something he and his department needed like a hole in the head. He forced a polite smile to the woman behind the counter. "No, that will be all, thank you. Come on, Antonio." He motioned toward the door and started walking.

"You'll be hearing about the way we were treated. I'm going to lodge a complaint. You can't get away with keeping secrets from company officers," Antonio said, defying Dario's call to leave and tapping on the counter window.

The security guard moved toward Antonio.

Dario hooked Antonio's arm and pulled him back. "We're leaving. *Now.*"

Antonio stumbled backward. The security guard stopped in his tracks.

Dario dragged Antonio out the door, not feeling guilty in the slightest for the manhandling of his employee. One moment further and it would have spiraled into a situation where his father would have come down on him for his department's actions—again. That wasn't something he could afford, not when work was finally starting to go well.

Once through the doors, Antonio jerked his arm away. "Hey, what was that about?"

Dario frowned. He understood Antonio's frustration. The company had practices that didn't fit with the standards of how humanity should be treated, and very few people seemed to care. He wanted to know about this woman prisoner as much as Antonio did, but both of them had to keep out of trouble. "I know you're pretty new to the corporate life. Just out of school last year, right?" Dario asked.

Antonio nodded, a skeptical look on his face.

"There's a way to act to get things done, and there's a way to act to cause a scene. It may seem like the scene is the way to go, especially when you're getting stonewalled, but it never helped anyone," Dario said. His own voice sounded eerily like his father's. Was his position changing him into that kind of manager already? He didn't have time to think about that for now. "I appreciate that you've taken an interest in the underlevelers' safety. You saw how they were handled, and empathy for people in worse situations than our own is a good thing. Something security doesn't seem to have."

"Yeah." Antonio glanced downward. "I did a lot of thinking after the riots and saw that you care for people that others don't. I wanted to help."

"I know you did, and you have. You found out about some woman taken prisoner here, right? Someone doesn't want this information public, and they are willing to hide it behind a glass window with an armed guard. We can use that information, but we have to do it the right way."

Antonio looked up at Dario again. "How? How do we make a difference?"

In some ways, Dario knew he should be troubled. Hidden prisoners. A subordinate who had a hot head and could have found himself in big trouble with the Trade Federation proper. On the other hand, this meant he could count on his team. Antonio and Jake both trusted him, and that empowered him to act. "Give me some time to think about it. But you found good information here. Just keep your head low and don't cause any commotion, okay?"

"Okay," Antonio said, looking only slightly mollified.

Dario nodded and moved on ahead to leave Antonio with his thoughts. There was something wrong with the company, perhaps the larger Trade Federation. It was systemic, and he didn't know what to do. But Jake had seen situations like the underlevelers had with his own eyes. He would have ideas, and those ideas would form a plan.

CHAPTER II

BONDING

Joan leaned back into the seat rest in the cargo launch's cockpit. Despite its contours, the seat back was stiff, uncomfortable for the length of the journey she'd be sitting here. Something made a *thud,* causing Joan to jump. She stared to the craft's aft for a long period. Just her nerves, nothing to get worked up about.

It would be a couple of days still until they reached the Sol system. Stars passed by as blurred lines in front of her. That sight, at least, was relaxing. A few more hours of it and she may be able to find sleep just yet.

Yui and Trian hadn't been as jolted by the sight of the alien enemy's near mindless waves of destruction across Trantine X. Joan's two companions had curled up in respective fold outs in the back compartment of the ship and fallen asleep. They had been out for a couple of hours, leaving Joan alone with the familiar quiet hum of the ship's engines.

Joan looked at her handtab. She could reactivate G.O.D., talk to him like old times. A foolish question would be to ask the success probability of her mission, one in which she knew deep down the answer was nearly zero.

But even though she'd spent months alone with her AI before this, Joan felt far more alone now. She tapped the controls to activate her AI. "Hey, G.O.D."

"Ms. Shengtu," G.O.D. said.

Joan sighed in relief at hearing G.O.D.'s voice for the first time in days. "Doesn't feel right being apart from you. Don't know what to do with myself."

"As you say. I've taken the liberty of running a self-diagnostic. My programming is currently eighty-five percent intact, but degrading."

Joan frowned. "That's not good. How fast are you degrading? Do I need to keep you turned off?"

"As of yet I have been unable to determine a cause or pattern to the degradation. Further analysis required."

"I wish I could help. I—"

A knock sounded on the cockpit door behind her. Joan turned, shutting her AI back off with the command. "Come in."

Trian ducked his head down. The door opened and he stepped forward. "Looks like the flight is going smoothly."

Joan smiled up at him. "Yeah, it's mostly watching the autopilot to make sure there's not a malfunction. I put it on manual for fun sometimes, but not when we're in the middle of a jump like this." She motioned to the co-pilot chair across from her. "Have a seat. It's getting boring anyway."

Trian looked out the cockpit to the stream lights, blurred lines across the sky that looked like fireworks. "I don't know that I could ever get bored of this view."

"Trust me, when you've piloted long enough alone, it gets tedious," Joan leaned her head back into her chair. "Though I don't mind it, really."

"Your file says you've been running salvage and smuggling operations as a freelancer." Trian carefully slipped into the co-pilot chair. "Sounds like a tough thing to do alone."

"Not as bad as you'd think. When I was in the military, I was never alone. Shared cramped quarters on the *Destiny*. Six to a room. That's what I'd rather not repeat."

"You didn't like the military." Trian furrowed his brow, studying her.

Joan laughed. "That's an understatement. I'm not very good at following orders, for one. Though I held my tongue well enough. Gotta do what you gotta do to get by, you know?" She shrugged. "Problem was the pay was barely enough to survive. It was fine when I was on the ship, but looking forward to when I'd have my own living expenses, it did me no good. I didn't want to be stuck when my tour was up."

"I understand. Life can be difficult on the colonies. The Council doesn't have the budget for adequate security, with a two front war going on," Trian said. "But you had experience with Ms. Amitosa in the past, yes?"

Ah, so that's what this visit's about, Joan thought. She stared at Trian. He had salt and pepper stubble growing on his face, a couple of days worth. His face was impassive, as if he were simply curious. It couldn't hurt to talk. It wasn't as if any confessions here would matter in the Trade Federation. Joan shifted, acting as if she were checking the cockpit controls. In truth, she preferred not to look him in the eye for this discussion. "Yeah, she was one rank above me. Not directly in command, but enough authority to lord it over me."

"Lord it over you?" Trian asked. He leaned toward her, cutting off her attempts to avoid eye contact.

"Yeah. She'd double check all of my work, every time, but wouldn't all of the others. Pick on any small mistake I made. The sight of her was enough to get me angry. It didn't come to a fight, but it came close—a little shoving—before we were broken up."

"I see," Trian said, his tone non-judgmental, in keeping with the expression on his face. "And she was part of the team that caught you stealing."

"I was *not* caught," Joan said defensively. It came out a little stronger than she had intended. Those words shouldn't bother her, but she'd heard them enough that it was annoying. Her clients who looked into her background often cited that "fact" as reasons to skimp on her contract fees. Joan had corrected it one too many times.

"Then what happened?" Trian asked.

Joan shifted, recalling how it felt when the tribunal's prosecution grilled her on the stand. Nowhere to hide. Just like now. "We weren't stealing anything big, just leftover scrap—metal, burnt out couplers, things like that. One of the others, Ensign Kelley, had a contact network who picked up the trash from us when we reached port. It wasn't hurting anyone, seemed like a good way to make money."

"Your file says you were convicted of weapons theft, frag grenades," Trian said. He didn't sound accusatory, but more like he was gathering information.

"That's because Ensign Kelley started to get a little bolder as time went by. His contacts demanded more. We kept providing it." Joan turned her head away, staring out to the streaks of stars past the cockpit. "Truth is… I didn't know he was going for the armory. He was caught. Ratted the rest of us out when he was faced with a reduced sentence. Yui was all too glad to help apprehend me."

Joan remembered being approached by Yui, along with security, and the hard knee to the gut that the other woman delivered while Joan was held back. She'd sworn at the time to get Yui back for that. Anger welled inside her again as she recalled the events.

"Thank you for being honest with me," Trian said. "Of course, I've heard Ms. Amitosa's version of events. I will weigh each story equally in my assessment. Though, in reality it is irrelevant. What matters now is that we're a team. We can't have animosity between us if we're going to survive in a hostile environment." He placed a hand on Joan's shoulder. "I don't mean to sound condescending, but it's imperative we succeed."

"I know that," Joan said, trying to tone down her defensiveness.

Trian drew his hand back, standing again. He kept his head low. "I believe you. Thank you, again, for sharing. We'll work through this and rescue Commodore Zhang. If the Council places their faith you, so do I," he said. "I should head back and try to get some sleep. You should, as well."

"I'm just as comfortable falling asleep right here." Joan forced another little smile toward him. "Have a good night."

"Cheers." Trian moved back into the cabin.

CHAPTER 12

EMPOWERED

"...and we've reached one hundred percent output again. Good work people. I mean it. We've worked tirelessly and made sure this would happen. All of your ideas were valuable. We'll wrap up the meeting here if there's no further questions?"

Several members of the quality control team in the conference room shook their heads, looking at each other. No one spoke up for a few moments, and then bodies shuffled and moved from their seats at the table. The team members filed toward the door.

Dario stopped Daniella deRiko with a soft touch to her arm. "Daniella, you really did great these last few days. I don't think we'd be at half of where we're at without your initiative," he said.

Daniella smiled back at him. "Thanks, Mr. Anazao. Anytime. Hey, think I can take next Friday off? Put in a lot of fourteen hour shifts and could use a long weekend," she said.

Dario cringed at the use of his formal name, but didn't want to correct Daniella. "Of course, no problem."

She gave him one more courteous nod before departing herself, leaving Dario with an empty conference room and a holodisplay of a graph of recent factory output from the underlevels. Behind that translucent image sat Jake Dylan.

"Good meeting," Jake said. "I think you're settling in fine.

Everyone's starting to respect you. Antonio Dalton looks at you as if you're a god, and even Daniella's settled into trusting your decisions. She was skeptical after the first night. Asked me if you seemed like boss material."

"She did?" Dario asked, surprised by that admission. On the other side of the glass conference room wall, Daniella returned to the vast rows of cubicles outside the conference room.

"She did. I didn't say anything because I try to hold people's words in confidence, even to the boss. If you don't, they can't trust you, you know?" Jake swiveled in his chair, leaning back into it. The holodisplay hovering over the table obscured part of his face with the graphs of the last week's output.

"Then why tell me now?" Dario rested his elbow on the table, and his chin on his fist.

"Because I wanted to make a statement to let you know that I'm on your side," Jake moved from being hidden by the holodisplay to meet Dario's eyes. "After our talk two nights ago, I realized that you need someone you can depend on as loyal. It's tough for you, being in your father's shadow. I know that he picked me, but he doesn't have any special hold on me. I'd never met him before the interview. I wanted you to know that."

Dario was speechless for a moment, taken aback. His assistant's words gave him a warmth inside. It felt a lot like those rare times his father had voiced approval of his actions. "That means a lot to me, Jake. Thank you. I actually wanted to talk to you. I did some thinking last night and this morning, about what we discussed." He hesitated.

The thought still made Dario nervous, but the more he thought about it, the more he realized he had to get the perspective of those laborers that Regency BioTech relied upon. He firmed his resolve, nodding to Jake. "I want to do it. I want to go. Can you really do what you said, with the idents?" He asked vaguely, but he had to be coy. The company's conference rooms had hidden monitoring devices. They could have had a conversation somewhere else, but Dario wanted to get this off his chest.

Jake peered at him, seeming to understand that it wasn't the safest place to talk freely. "You're sure about this? I didn't mean to pressure you. I only want to help you with your goals."

Scrap it, Dario thought. He straightened in his chair and nodded. "Yeah, I'm dead sure. What's the next steps?"

Jake motioned with his head for them to walk. His eyes shot to the recording and monitoring devices in the corners of the room. "I think we should return to work first, too much to do today."

"Yes, agreed." It was prudent to end the discussion here. Jake's caution gave Dario comfort with the plan. Someone as diligent as he was would have better odds at ensuring those fake idents worked for their potential travels off of the Central Office. Dario smoothed down his coat before standing and heading toward the conference room exit.

The two men walked through the rows of cubicles through the quality control department. Most employees wore VR glasses, looking in on different manufacturing facilities throughout the systems of the Trade Federation.

"This will take me some time," Jake said. "What I'm going to need from you is all of your actual ident information. I need a scan of your handtab, your Secured Future numbers and pin, a retinal scan and a thumbprint."

"That's a lot of information," Dario said as they walked.

"It is, and I understand if that's too much for you, but that's the information I need to create something impenetrable. Or, as you suggested, there could be big trouble. You understand?"

Dario nodded. "Okay, I can get that for you."

Jake took note of his facial expression. "You're nervous. It's understandable, but I've got some data that should put you at ease that this is the right thing to do. Give me your handtab."

Dario held out his wrist. The handtab's screen lit up, activating.

The other man lifted his own, keying in a couple of commands then placing it next to Dario's. A transfer initiated, and a notification appeared in Dario's oculars when it completed.

A quick scan of the contents revealed holos of millions of under-levelers living in terror, with no meaning, no purpose, struggling for basic necessities. Even the provisions the corporation offered did little good. The thumbnails all showed violence, anger, destruction. It wasn't just the quality control factory. These kind of incidents happened regularly in the underlevels and outer worlds.

A flick of his eye pulled up a holovid labeled "Tragedy On Level Three."

Hundreds of underlevelers formed a haphazard line at a sector's corporate provision station. The Regency BioTech logo hovered and turned in the air above it. No actual people administered the provision, but several BioMechs flanked the area.

The underlevelers pushed toward the dispensary. Food, blankets, datachips with programs for bodymods all rested in a pile. Cries from the crowd escaped about how it was unfair. There were too many people for the supplies. A few larger men pushed the crowd back moving in a wave. People fell, and then rioting began.

A smoke bomb bounced off the floor, white gas flooding the area. Clubs and metal sticks came out. One of the larger men slammed his club into an older man trying to reach the food. The blow resounded with a crack loud enough to pierce through the crowd noise.

Someone screamed. More fights erupted within the crowd, smoke started to fill the area. Toward the dispensary, the gang of the larger men stuffed the supplies into sacks. It became clear that they were working together, even through the distracting smoke. When most of the supplies had been offloaded, they pushed their way through the crowd and took off running.

With no one to stop them, the crowd rushed forward again toward the dispensary to try to gather what meager supplies were left. Little remained. People shouted. Fights broke out over a single loaf of bread.

Two of the underlevelers pounded on another. One man collapsed, and the other kept bashing his face. Blood trickled everywhere until the body went still.

The BioMechs came to life, but not to the underleveler's aid. A red light flashed with a computerized warning. "Dispensary closing. This zone will receive further supplies in one day's time. These goods are brought to you by Regency BioTech—improving lifestyles and creating longevity across the galaxy. Have a wonderful day."

"But there's nothing for us! They took it all! We don't have enough!" Someone shouted.

The crowd erupted into angry roars. The BioMechs paid no heed and pressed forward. Electrical charges welled in their centers to warn the people that they would be stunned if they pressed any further.

That warning wasn't enough for some of the angry underlevelers. Though most fled, a few tried to fight the BioMechs, hitting them repeatedly, fists clanking against metal. Their efforts proved in vain, as the BioMechs had no feeling. With no further warning, the electrical charge swelled and an attacking underleveler convulsed, dropping in front of the BioMech.

Two more people fell to the BioMechs' stuns. The rest of the crowd dispersed.

The video ended. Dario frowned, his oculars adjusting back to a vision of reality in front of him. The long aisle of cubes, uniform and perfect, returned to his vision.

Jake Dylan watched him. "Are you all right, Dario?"

"Yeah, I watched one of the holovids. I can't believe this has gone on for so long. These people need a friend in corporate," Dario said.

Jake draped his arm over the top of his workstation cube. "That they do. And they will. I'm sure that we'll make a difference."

It would be risky. Dario's father and the rest of the executives would fight him at every turn, but that was because they didn't understand. They never would watch holovids like this, never would glance at the underlevels. They weren't evil, but they had their own concerns, and the demands of a corporate job allowed them and everyone else to turn a blind eye to those separated from them.

He parted ways with Jake, wheels spinning in his mind on how he could change this company.

CHAPTER 13

THE UNDERLEVELS

MARS—THE UNDERLEVELS
LOCAL DATE FEBRUARY 10TH, 2464

The Mars spaceport made Trantine X's look like some backwater landing strip. It stretched for almost the entire former planet's capitol city's size, with its own Central Office for the larger ships incapable of atmospheric descent. The station connected to a space elevator that transported cargo and personnel to the upper corporate levels of the Mars' city streets and eventually up to the Regency BioTech Central Office.

The *Money Hauler* was small enough of a vessel to be able to land at the Comet Cola New Washington Spaceport proper, holding aloft after entering into the pressurization zone, waiting for the dome's seal to bond once more before being allowed entry into the dome's second level and atmosphere.

Electromagnets brought the ship in, transferring it away from the primary landing area and into a shuttle housing stall on the south side of the spaceport. The ship went through cursory securities and customs scans before matching air pressure with Mars local. The hatch popped open.

Joan looked to her two companions. Trian smoothed down his coat. Yui had had just woken up from a long nap and rubbed her temples. When Yui caught her glance, she scowled back at Joan. "What you lookin' at, *ensign?*"

Joan ignored the taunt.

Outside, the hallway to the terminal was well lit, and more importantly empty. No security alarms sounded at their fake landing codes. There was a small bend that would, according to the flickering exit map, lead to the main terminal.

"Looks like everything went off without a hitch," Joan said.

"Our programmers spend a long time ensuring our drops and extractions go smoothly." Yui stifled a yawn. She stretched her arms until they hit the low-roof of the cabin area. "So what's next, Trian? Where do we meet the contact?"

Trian tapped on his handtab, pulling up some information. It looked like gibberish to Joan, the display in code, but Trian had no problem deciphering it. "We're supposed to meet at the Red Crater Astropub here in New Washington. Level three, East 45th Street."

"Low levels?" Yui asked with a small frown.

"Yes," Trian said and led the way into the hallway. He tapped his handtab to display map coordinates.

The hallway opened into a large spaceport terminal. Hundreds of people hovered across magnetic conveyors at various levels upward, stretching at least a hundred stories to reach various shuttle housings. This terminal was dedicated to commercial travel, robust on Mars compared to the other worlds or stations Joan had been on. Not surprising, given how many megacorporation headquarters Mars held. It had to be nearly as dense as Earth itself.

Holos and lights flashed everywhere—from directional signs to advertisements, almost dizzying on their transparent backgrounds across the levels. Joan stared upward at the display for a moment before Yui pushed her forward.

"No time for tourism. Let's get going." Yui stepped onto a magnetic conveyor and sped forward.

Trian did the same.

Joan took one more moment to observe the largesse of it all before following. The conveyor took them to a roundabout that split into fifteen different directions. A path lit blue, syncing with Trian's handtab coordinates. "This way to the hovercabs," he said.

"I've never been on a world this developed before. There's people upward as far as you can see," Joan said to Yui, trying to create conversation on the conveyor. They had to work together. Small talk could help ease the tension.

"You get used to it after awhile. The old Terran States, before it became the Trade Federation, weren't able to expand out of the system until a couple hundred years ago. With the rate of human reproduction, it became overwhelming," Trian said.

"Thanks for the history lesson," Yui said.

If this was how conversations were going to go for the duration, this was going to be a long mission, thought Joan.

Within moments they arrived at a large set of double transparent doors that opened for them when they approached. They exited the terminal building into a large tunnel, self-driving hovercars in three rows awaiting passengers from a line.

The line went on for dozens of people, but it dwindled quickly. Soon, the door to the hovercar swung upward to accommodate Joan and her party. They stepped inside and Trian synced his handtab with the car. Trian took one of the seats across from them. The interior seats pressurized to match their individual back and neck profiles before harnesses stretched out over them and buckled. The car took off through the tunnel, the other cars fading into the background in a blur.

"You asked about the lower levels, didn't sound too happy about it," Joan said, again trying to start conversation with Yui, who sat next to her.

"Lower levels are dangerous. You find the people who can't hold down steady corporate contracts down there. Where resources are slim, people get desperate," Yui said. "You stay close to us, don't make a scene. You understand?

"Yes, we'll have to be careful," Trian added, though he seemed more interested in watching the lights of the tunnel go by. "It's nothing you haven't seen before, Ms. Amitosa, we'll be fine."

"Yes, it's not me I'm worried about." Yui's dark eyes fixed on Joan.

Joan slouched in her seat. She'd had plenty of experience in seedy environments, meeting contacts for jobs or information. She knew how to handle herself, but it wasn't worth arguing.

The hovercar swooped around to a platform that ran a scan of the car before opening and pulling the car downward several levels. They passed several more platforms on the way down before the car balanced into a slow descent and stopped in front of a large, rusted sign labeled "3."

The hovercar's internal terminal let up, requesting a payment of 200 credits. Joan scanned her handtab to the terminal, which processed her expense account and debited the proper amount. Once the transaction completed, the doors slid open.

"How far from here?" Joan asked.

"A few hundred meters," Yui, said, sliding out of her seat first. She scanned the area.

Joan tried to track Yui's eye movements, to see what the other woman could see. The area was rather dark, and almost everything had an old, rusted coloration to it, the streets and buildings had been constructed from what raw materials could be extracted in the early days of colonization. Broken windows hung from a nearby building. Another's were covered with a bolted sheet of metal. Across the street the building was tagged in black paint with the words "Resist or Die." Joan frowned at that. Would this be the fate of the Star Empire should they give up hope? This level looked hopeless, reminding Joan of her time in prison, unable to escape and with very little purpose other than to try to survive.

Trian tapped her on the shoulder. "Are you well, Ms. Shengtu?"

"Yeah. This place brings back some bad memories is all," she said, and followed where Yui maneuvered around a waifish man lying on the side of the street with a tattered blanket.

They rounded a corner to a street that hardly looked different from the first. Joan didn't see any signs, but trusted Yui's navigational skills. Several people on the walk gave them odd stares or preying looks. It was difficult to discern which was which. No matter, their dark clothing gave them away as outsiders compared to the more basic colors of the clothes of the people here.

Another block down the street, Yui stopped, looking upward at a building to a flickering holographic sign: *Red Crater Astropub.*

"This is it," Yui said.

A man with a genome modified third arm protruding from his shoulder held a vaporizer to his lips and exhaled whatever chemicals it contained. He looked them over with further modified yellow eyes, the retina cameras zooming on Joan's handtab. "You sure you're in the right spot, sugar?"

"She's quite sure," Trian said, taking Joan by the arm protectively.

Yui laughed at Trian and motioned with her head toward the astropub. She pushed batwing doors open to reveal a dimly lit interior and old, tattered booths with seats that needed reupholstering. There were few patrons inside. Numeralis, a game where one formed a deck of numbered cards and tried to obtain a score of fifty, was displayed on a wall, a couple of older patrons intently playing the game, gambling dozens of credits it didn't look like they could afford to.

Trian released Joan's arm after they entered, and hurried up to Yui. "What're you laughing about?" he asked.

"It's cute when you get worried. I'd like to see you in a fight with that creep. Don't know where I'd place odds," Yui teased.

"Hey, I can hold my own. I've gone through the same basic training you have."

"Yeah, but you're just a political guy."

"What's that supposed to mean?" Trian furrowed his brow.

"It means you're good with people," Joan said to cut them off, noticing that several patrons in the place were looking in their direction. Perhaps she was more paranoid than they were, but she wanted to avoid attention.

A robotic server approached, wheeling to them. "Please provide your drink orders."

"Nothing yet," Joan said. "We'll be awhile. Need to decide."

Trian looked to Yui for guidance as the server wheeled back away from them. "Where are we supposed to meet?" his voice lowered.

"Booth in the corner." Yui pointed to an empty one. The astropub didn't look as sanitary as most of the places Joan frequented, but she couldn't be considered a snob with her modest shipping budget.

The three moved over to the booth all the same, and slid into seats. "He's late," Trian said.

"What do we do?" Joan asked, looking between them.

"We wait and have a drink," Yui said. She flagged down the server bot and gave her order, following it up with one for Trian, despite his protests.

Joan waved the server bot off a second time, too nervous to drink. This was an alien world, in a dangerous place. She needed to be as alert as possible. Who knew what could happen to them here? Not that she cared to dull her senses much in any situation. She'd been on the run, alone for too long to take chances like that.

Trian and Yui exchanged more of their playful banter. Joan zoned out, staring across the room at various patrons who weaved in and out. Several lower-level people came in, gave their credits to those service bots without any real person even watching over the establishment. Who knew who owned the place? Probably the same megacorporation that gave them their meager stipends. Money came in, money flowed right back to the originator.

That was a depressing thought, but that's how money worked, even in the Star Empire. The same problems with society persisted whether it was an Emperor in charge or corporations.

When she looked back, Yui and Trian had delved into some gambling entertainment. Tri-D holographic balls hovered over the table, blinking in and out while her companions tapped their table controls. A couple credits transferred back and forth, but the house took a cut each time.

Joan glanced down at her handtab and slid her finger across the AI control. She'd let her one true friend lay dormant for too long. Was that what gave her those depressing thoughts? Being alone in a foreign place? It made sense. She turned the AI on.

A face fizzled into view on her handtab screen, a silhouette of zeros and ones that formed into a comforting human visage. G.O.D.'s voice rang in her earpiece. "Hydrocarbon waste piles up in prominent politicians!" G.O.D. said in a sing-song tone.

"What's that supposed to mean?" Joan asked.

"It means I landed the twenty ball!" Trian said from across the table, not privy to her conversation.

"Oh-so-happy with my luh-uv...," G.O.D. resumed a different song.

"G.O.D." Joan said sternly.

Her companions paused their game and looked at her in confusion. Yui narrowed her eyes in thought. "Oh, you're talking to your AI. I got the briefing on that." She paid no more heed and returned her attention to her game.

"J-Joan?" G.O.D. asked. The AI sounded, oddly, confused.

"Yes," Joan said, leaning forward in excitement toward the screen as if special conditions mattered to the AI.

"I've been unable to restore my data systems. The makers—"

"Yes, you need to sync with them. You told me. Where are they at?"

"The Mech World. I have coordinates uploaded into your handtab. This is critical. I cannot maintain my stability for long periods of time," G.O.D. said.

"I'm a bit stuck right now. I need to rescue someone. We're on Mars, a long way from the Mech World. Are you stable enough to help us?"

"I have approximately a fifty percent ability to function before... before... Before you gooooo, stay with me one more night my love," G.O.D. sang again.

"There are worse ways you could fall apart. At least I get songs out of it." Joan tapped her fingers on the table. "I'm going to keep you active, but on mute. When I need you, I'll try to keep you on task. It's all we can do until I can get off this planet again. Okay?"

"As you wish, Ms. Shengtu," G.O.D. said.

Joan clicked the mute button, but let the program run. At least he was here and could hear her. That gave Joan some comfort. It'd been over an hour since they were supposed to meet their contact, and he still hadn't arrived. Her companions didn't seem worried about the mission, but Joan couldn't help but wonder if this trip may be a fool's errand.

CHAPTER 14

DOWN, BELOW STATION

The halls surrounding the lower executive level apartments were quiet. Holovid tickers lit the corridors as they always did, but with less people than Dario was used to walking the hallways for this time of day. He had earned a couple of days off with recent gains in productivity, which he promptly booked, citing that after nearly a month of service in his new position, he needed time to recharge. It was true, but his vision of how to recuperate wasn't in line with normal corporate recommended R&R time.

He glanced around, paranoid. Both he and Jake had requested vacation today. If anyone paid any attention to their coordination, it would appear suspicious. Jake had tried to reassure him that they were seen as friends and it wouldn't trigger any security watch protocols. Friends spent time with friends, right? Dario wasn't so certain. With his fast tracked corporate life, he hadn't spent much time bonding with his peers. Even in back in school, he felt his father's watchful gaze, disapproving of too much leisure time. "You can use your time better studying," Mr. Anazao had told Dario.

The lift loomed ahead, the only exit from his own confinement, luxurious as it was. At any point, the company executives could shut it down, trapping everyone in the managerial residential area in the halls surrounding their quarters. That thought had never occurred to him before, but before he achieved the management position, he never had this looming feeling like he was a product on a conveyor line, ready to be pushed off the edge and into a box.

There were hundreds of other megacorporations within the Trade Federation, and with his position, schooling, and name, Dario was certain he could make his way into any number of them with a similar management job, but would they be any different? Each had their own planets and stations, Megahaulers disbursing their goods across the galaxy.

There were independent contractors who did consulting work for the various firms. Some who had their own, smaller Cutter vessels that operated somewhat independently. When Dario first read about potential berths on those ships, he fantasized about leaving the company, travelling the stars. But at the end of the day, he'd still be trapped inside walls, smaller ones at that. Moreover, he would still be beholden to the corporations who gave them the work.

Despite his searches, his thoughts, Dario determined no life within the Trade Federation would be any different than what he had right now. Also, he couldn't very well go outside to live a frontier life with the Blob looming to scorch entire worlds. At least here, he had the power to do something. What that something was, he wasn't sure yet. He hoped this visit down to the underlevels would give him some inspiration. At the very least, it would give him concrete empathy with real people. Something Regency BioTech needed desperately.

He held his handtab toward the console to activate the lift, but the doors opened, revealing the last person he wanted to see at this moment: his father.

The elder Anazao stepped toward Dario and clasped him on the arm. "Son, I was just coming to see you. Good timing."

Good timing indeed. Dario stepped backward, startled. Had he been compromised as he'd worried? He tried to keep his face reserved, but he knew his father would be able to see through even the most minute of masks he put on. Had the security footage given him up? Was his father really monitoring him that closely? Or worse… had Jake been compromised, or betrayed him?

"Is something the matter? You look like you've seen a ghost." Mr. Anazao paused, raising a scrutinizing brow at Dario. "I was hoping to discuss our plans for the new RetroSilver line debuting soon. I know you've worked tirelessly to ensure quality control output caught up for the launch."

Dario panicked, looking back to the lift, the doors closing once more. "I actually had plans today. Took some vacation for once."

"That's why I'm here. I assumed you would be hobbled up in your room with your oculars turned to some holotainment like usual. That's not a healthy way to spend your leisure time. There's studies about that." He shook his head. "I never should have had those installed in you at such an early age. Hindsight."

"I'm fine," Dario said with a little annoyance. "Seriously, though. I'm late meeting up with someone. We were going to spend the day…" he tried to think of an excuse. "…going out and meeting some people. Learning our way around Regency." It was completely true, he just left out some of the details. Dario relaxed.

Mr. Anazao studied him for a long moment before nodding. "Very well. That's good initiative. I'm surprised though, you're not usually so social. New position is going well?"

"Yeah."

An awkward moment of silence followed. "Good," Mr. Anazao said. "Glad to hear that it's suiting you. I knew you'd have a knack for management. It's in the genes. Your aptitude scores are showing well in the system too. I thought you should know that."

Dario blinked in surprise. It'd been the second time in as many months his father had shocked him. First with the promotion, now with telling him a job well done? Wonders never ceased. "Thanks, I appreciate it."

"No problem. I have some more things to do on your level anyway," his father said, pointing down the long hallway. "We'll talk soon. You'll be at the corporate gala? It's coming up some."

"Of course," Dario said. The event was mandatory for management personnel anyway. "I'll see you then."

His father nodded and strode in the opposite direction, leaving Dario with the lift. The experience had been surreal. Dario exhaled sharply and placed his handtab up to the console in front of him. The lift opened once more.

Dario was greeted by another familiar face, Antonio standing in front of the lift. "Hey boss, was just about to come see you."

"You and the whole planet," Dario said to himself.

"Huh?"

"Nothing," Dario said, stepping outside the lift and pausing. He didn't have a ton of time. Jake wanted to run everything on a perfect schedule, saying it would be easier to ensure there were no security problems that way. Dario wasn't sure what that meant, but he trusted his assistant. He would have to ask Jake how he knew how to circumvent so many security protocols at some point. "What's up?"

"Heard you were off today. I did a little more digging about the prisoner. From what I hear, she's not an underleveler at all."

"She's not? Who could she be then?"

"Don't know yet. Reports on the nets are pretty sparse on this topic. Whoever it is, the company wants to keep it quiet." Antonio shrugged.

"Good work." Dario shifted, glancing around Antonio toward the lift. It wasn't that he had no interest in the topic. This was another piece to the puzzle of dissecting the bad practices within the corporation and Trade Federation. He didn't have time to speculate right now, however. "Can we talk about this later? I have a meeting."

"Yeah, sure." Antonio's eyes flashed disappointment. He shook his head then reached into his satchel and produced a bottle, which he offered to Dario. "By the way, I got you this. It's an imported brew from Luna. Supposed to be really good, a mild hops flavor."

"Thanks, Antonio, but I can't take it. I don't drink," Dario said with a little smile. "I appreciate the thought though. Why don't you give that to Daniella?"

Antonio flushed. "I would, but she might get the wrong idea."

Dario shrugged at that. From the looks of things, it was an idea Antonio could get behind. Dario couldn't encourage relations within his department, but it wasn't his business if they developed naturally. "Up to you. You can always enjoy it yourself. I really do appreciate it; don't think I'm snubbing you."

"I won't," Antonio said, securing the bottle.

"Good to see you." Dario gave his employee a fond nod.

"Yeah, see you soon. I'll keep you posted if I hear anything else."

"Sounds good." Dario sped toward the lift, leaving Antonio in the residential area.

When Dario reached the Central Office's main bowl, he found it packed more than usual. People stood in line, waiting for the much larger skylift which connected the station to the Mars spaceport, surface and the underlevels. Dario had been up and down the skylift before, when he traveled to and from his schooling on the surface. His university was on the upper thirty-fifth level of the New Dome, not even close to where he would be heading today.

A hand clasped his shoulder.

Dario tensed, and then whipped around to see who was there. Had his father followed him all the way down? He let out a deep breath to calm himself when he saw who stood in front of him.

"Settle down," Jake said, his friendly face giving a smile. He drew his hand back slowly from Dario's shoulder. "No one's here to get you. Just relax and enjoy the ride."

"Sorry, been ambushed by too many people today. It's been odd," Dario said.

"We won't have a problem. Everything's been tested. We're good to go." Jake said, stepping into the line of people to go through the scanner.

The security checkpoint line shortened as they talked, and soon enough they migrated to a point in front of the security scanner. Jake presented his handtab first, and the scanner blinked green. A security officer looked him over to confirm the identity was legitimate and then motioned with a baton that he should move through the scanner.

"You're up next, sir," the officer said.

Dario took a deep breath and stepped forward. He lifted his own handtab, freshly programmed with the identity that Jake had secured him. The security guard eyed him, and Dario held his wrist to the scanner. This time the scanner didn't blink green, but made a sound as if it had failed.

"Huh," the security officer said.

Dario jerked his head toward Jake, eyes wide. What was happening?

Jake shrugged from the checkpoint's other side. He glanced around as if people watching, playing cool.

The security officer circled around to take a closer peek at the scanner, giving it a smack from a closed fist. "This thing has been giving me problems lately. Let me see your handtab," he said, then holding that hand out toward Dario.

Dario offered his wrist to the officer, tense with trepidation about the whole ordeal. He'd been so worried about his father he hadn't been concerned about security. Jake had been so sure it would work, even up until a few moments ago.

"Your hand's sweaty. Maybe that's mucking with things," the security officer said. He roughly pulled Dario's wrist to the scanner, pinching Dario's flesh against it.

The scanner turned green this time, accepting Dario's false identity.

The officer looked over at the console. "Thanks for your patience, Mr. Tyree," he said.

"No problem," Dario said, slipping through the body scanner with no problems either, not carrying any weapons or anything that could conceivably cause a security problem.

Jake motioned him toward the skylift. "Told you," he said with a smirk. "Here we go."

They followed the crowd toward the lift. Every fifteen minutes a car pulled in and a hundred people packed into it before the descent. The drop was a fast one, softened internally by gravity plates that maintained the comfort of the passengers.

Once on the ground level of the open dome, looking out upon the reds that made up both the landscapes of Mars and the hues of the city streets, Jake led them to another series of lifts that led down to the lower levels. As they rode in that car, Dario watched the numbers descend until they reached Level Three.

"Here we are," Jake said, stepping outside.

The city streets didn't look a lot different than the levels above, but they did appear somewhat older and more worn. Paint was faded, storefronts and buildings had dated looks to them, signs weren't up to the latest in holo-technology. The streets hadn't been swept by bots, and at least minor maintenance needed to be done on almost every building he'd come across. Whoever was in charge of the quality control department in public planning had failed miserably. If there was a public planning department for this level at all.

"Who monitors everything down here?" Dario asked with a small frown.

"Are you serious?" Jake asked as they walked. He tapped onto his handtab and pulled up the coordinates for the Regency BioTech Quality Control Plant. It appeared to be a few blocks away, from what Dario could glean with a quick frame zoom from his oculars.

"Yeah," Dario said, moving along with him.

"No one does anything down here. It's all run by AI or BioMech. Corporate's resources for overhead providing for the people down here is low. You watched the videos and read the information I sent you, right?"

"Of course." He had combed through all the information and

researched more. The amount of resources the corporation provided the underlevels were scarce. With that, there wasn't any room for administrative services. That's why the thugs were able to steal the paltry goods delivered to the poor people down here. Something had to change, whether it was hiring someone to reprogram the BioMechs to keep better order, or to get someone physically down here to do the same. But that's what Dario and Jake were here to view for themselves. See the problem, then produce a game plan for results. Quality control in action.

A large warehouse stood on the streets ahead, as run down as any of the other buildings that they'd come across before. This had a newly constructed façade with tempered windows on the same wall that had been knocked out during the riot. This was the first time Dario had seen any of his quality control centers in person. The holovids made a great representation, something a manager could look at any angle in three dimensions, but was inhibited by the size of the projector.

Dario did have the trick of his oculars, which allowed him to immerse within any holoprojected setting. It helped to give him a different perspective than many others had. He'd seen sights, places, and people up close and personal that few could ever experience.

Still, viewing a picture, even an immersive one, couldn't help provide the feel of reality. The air felt thicker here than on the Central Office. The area smelled of lingering trash. Those senses couldn't be replicated by a holovid.

Dario stepped toward the center's main doors, which opened for him. The opening revealed a clean floor, scavenged for germs and static by small service bots on the floor. How much more of an expense would it be to have service bots sweep the street surfaces? That was one recommendation he would make when he had the opportunity.

The reception area had a couple of chairs and an access scanner to the inside. Dario looked over at Jake, not comfortable with scanning his false identity after the close call at the lift. If something went wrong and he was tracked here, his father would put him through the ringer.

Jake stepped forward to scan his ident against the security access panel, and the door to the back warehouse opened. Conveyor belts spun and boxes stacked three levels high stood against the walls. Thousands of bots worked on the line and a swarm of nanobots scrubbed the products behind a glass wall.

Along with the bots, hundreds of human workers performed tasks in the plant, checking the boxes for seals, repairing and cleaning the bots, standing and counting over the conveyors to ensure nothing was missed or unaccounted for. The air inside was sterile, filtered as much as the Central Office above.

They walked through the open area, visit unannounced, no management or security bothering them. Workers and the machines, moved like clockwork in mind-numbing fashion. None of the employees looked particularly pleased with their tasks, and few spared glances for the two men who passed.

Dario had seen the equipment before via the drones he routinely sent through to inspect the plant condition. Though none of the equipment was particularly new, all of it was clean and in good working order. The inspections served their purpose, and it did make him feel like his job held a somewhat important function, lending credence to his father's earlier praise. His visit timing still irked Dario. Perhaps his father watched now, to see how Dario would react when down here. "Let's interview some of the workers," he said to Jake.

Jake looked at his handtab, which displayed a list of employees who should have been on the clock. Something about him seemed off, or on edge may be a better way to put it. As if he were late for something. "Where do you want to start? Conveyor maintenance and cleaning?"

"Sounds good," Dario said, watching his assistant carefully.

"Okay. I think the best person to start with might be Teresa Hernandez. She should be in subsection B325 by the auditory mod conveyor." He walked in the direction of what Dario presumed was subsection B325.

They passed several other workers and a large stress-test machine that both radiated heat and applied extreme pressure to the company products. The conveyor wound them around into another divided area.

"This is it, now to find Ms. Hernandez," Jake said, glancing around what was as much a non-descript area of the plant as anywhere else in the giant room.

"Why're you lookin' for her," a woman in goggles and protective clothing popped up from under one of the conveyors. Oil and dirt covered her clothes.

"Ahh, hello," Dario said, stepping up and offering his hand as he would in any business meeting. He tried to coat that with a smile to relax her.

The woman stared at his hand as if he were crazy. "You don't want to touch this, I got machine droppings all over me. Who are you and what are you doing here? Do I need to call the security bots? You're not spies? We don't tolerate that. Higher ups don't at least, and I don't want the level's pay docked. We already don't got enough as it is."

"We're not spies," Jake said firmly.

"No, actually, we're..." He glanced at Jake and back to the woman. "We're what you'd call the 'higher ups'. We're from the Central Office, upper management, here to inspect the facility. We have authority to be here," Dario said.

Her eyes went wide. "Ain't no one told us about no inspection. Look, I'll get this thing back up and running, just might need a few parts. Maybe borrow from one of the XLB machines over there." She motioned across the room. "Please, we're tryin'!" she pleaded.

"I'm not here to get you in trouble," Dario said. "I just wanted to talk about the working conditions down here at the plant. I know a couple weeks ago there were some issues."

The fear in her eyes left her as soon as it came. She gave Dario a once over as if to size him up and see if he was a threat. "Issues?" The woman laughed hard. "Hear that, Jim? He's talking about issues."

"Who we got here, Teresa?" A man popped up from the other side of the machine, similarly attired to his counterpart.

"Claim they from up above," Teresa said, pointing skyward.

Jim narrowed his eyes. "You responsible for all this?" He motioned around them.

"I suppose so. We're from management and I want to get an account of the working conditions down here to bring a report to the board," Dario said, hoping honesty would defuse the tension that radiated from Jim's eyes.

"Management?" Jim hopped over the conveyor, scrambling toward both Dario and Jake. He held a metal tool in his hand which he swung in their direction, his rage carrying him so much that he whiffed in mid-air.

Jake pushed Dario backward, placing himself in front of him. "Hey. Calm down. We're trying to help."

"Like hell you are!" Jim shouted. "We got higher ups tryin' to get on us personally now!"

Those words carried through the plant, other workers erupting in similar shouts and curses. Those snowballed further until the whole plant teemed with volcanic levels of pressure.

"We need to get out of here," Dario said, stepping back. This had been a bad idea, but not because of the risks of corporate finding out about their fool's errand, but because of the very warnings his father gave him. These people had too poor of conditions to even talk, and it'd been going on for much too long. There was no talking left to do. Dario's plans of reconciliation had been far too late. If only he'd come to this realization sooner.

"Keep backing toward the door, Dario," Jake said, maintaining himself as a human shield. "Then run. Get to the lift. I'll catch up."

"Scrap it, I'm not going to leave you here!"

"We'll meet up at the lift base, now *go!*" Jake shouted, turning.

A seriousness weighed upon his face like Dario hadn't seen before. Anger, fear, defensiveness, it all crossed Jake's expression.

And he was here to protect Dario. This was his assistant. All Dario could do was nod. Then he took off running toward the exit.

More shouts echoed behind him. "Get the higher up!"

Some metal part flew past Dario's head, nearly clipping him. He looked back to see where Jake had disappeared to, but machinery obscured his view from where his assistant should be. Jake had moved fast, wherever he'd gone. The laborers they had argued with had vanished as well. What if they'd captured him or worse?

Dario wanted to go back for him, but knew there was no way that he'd have any success. It'd be him against hundreds of workers. If he were captured, it would make for a very delicate hostage situation at best.

Two larger men scrambled into the path in front of him, cutting off his escape route. "Stop it right there!" one shouted at him, brandishing a hand-sized tool.

Large machines with conveyors propped up on stands at ninety degree angles blocked either side of Dario. He couldn't go backward, more workers gathered and chased after him, cursing and rumbling. The door was so close, but going at these two would get his teeth knocked out.

The laborer without a weapon lunged forward to grapple Dario, narrowly missing. Dario jumped backward to avoid pincing arms.

That conveyor was his only hope. With both men coming at him again, Dario dove forward to slide under the machine. His stomach and chest burned as his body rubbed against the concrete floor. He'd leave with a bad scrape, but it was better than getting bludgeoned in the head or killed.

Dario scrambled to his feet on the other side of the conveyor, using it as a shield from his assailant who tried to swipe at him from over it. He wasted no time and took off running toward the door again. Poor Jake had no way out, protecting him through this craziness.

A piece of machinery exploded in the back of the factory. A cloud of smoke and debris filled the room. Something sparked from the machinery which caught fire in a raging orange light.

The thugs that chased him were distracted by the blast and Dario wasted no time bolting for that exit door. He managed to get a few steps ahead of the two chasing him, though the conveyor now blocked his way. He was no athlete, but with adrenaline pumping through his veins, he had one chance for survival. Without hesitation, Dario leapt onto the conveyor, using his hand as leverage to propel him over in a swift motion, never sparing a moment after landing on the opposite side. He broke into a run.

The exit door whooshed open as one of the assailants reaching out and grabbed the back of Dario's shirt. His forward momentum pulled him from his assailant's grasp, narrowly allowing him to escape from the man's clutches.

Though he'd made his way out of the factory, that wasn't the end of the chase. He took off at full speed, running for what he knew was his life. His two assailants pursued.

What could he do down here? Did corporate security even patrol these areas? Who could he contact? If word of any of this got back to corporate, he would be in huge trouble.

Dario realized quickly that word would get back to corporate. There was an explosion in the plant. If the laborers inside had gone into a complete riot as they had just a few weeks before...

A crash came through the window, glass shattering and spraying near to Dario. He reflexively put his arm up to shield his face. Some of the glass shards did strike his arm.

The crash had a side-effect of distracting his assailants. The cause of the window's shattering became evident—a boxed bodymod, a cybernetic bicep implant, crashed into one of the thug's heads. He howled in pain and stumbled into his companion.

Dario padded down the street at full speed, trying to remember the way Jake had led him earlier. He recalled the level map Jake had displayed earlier to his oculars and scanned through quickly for directions to the lift. A map overlay appeared in his vision field. He had about half a kilometer to go, and a few turns to make. With luck he'd be able to outpace his would-be-attackers.

Other people descended upon the streets, not so much concerned with him but the factory behind him. They pointed, talked, but Dario couldn't spare more than quick glances. Though he didn't exactly land the interviews he wanted with the underleveler workers, he'd gotten what he'd needed in understanding from the general emotions of the laborers here. They would attack the corporate "higher ups" on sight. That was as disconcerting as anything else. No wonder his father had warned him not to come.

In many ways, his father was right, even if the underpinnings of the reasons why he'd advised Dario to avoid these areas were different. With the security footage from the factory, there'd be a lot to deal with when Dario returned to the Central Office.

Jake had said to meet at the lift, but Dario wasn't certain he'd be able to stay on this level in any semblance of safety. He hoped the schedule for the lift upward to the mid-levels was still active. He would have to comm Jake, and hopefully his assistant would receive the message.

Dario turned a corner, sprinting through the next block until the lift was in sight. He took a moment to peek behind him and saw that his attackers didn't pursue. His heart pounded from the run, adrenaline already fading through rapid breaths. He was safe, for now. He hoped to hell that Jake made it out alive.

CHAPTER 15

THE MAN ON THE INSIDE

MARS—THE UNDERLEVELS
LOCAL DATE FEBRUARY 10TH, 2464

"I apologize for being tardy," said a skinny man in a business suit. He leaned over the table toward them, letting out a winded breath. The suit was torn as if he'd recently been in an altercation. He had blue hair that waved across his head, held perfectly in place despite his torn clothing. "If you knew the pains it took to escape the eyes of the company, you'd have more sympathy." The man let out a deep sigh. "Jake Dylan." He offered his hand to Joan with those words. "I already know you two scoundrels," he said to Trian and Yui.

Joan accepted the hand with a firm shake, noting the eyewear on his face, an antique contrast to the memory enhancement device on his scalp. Most eye problems could be corrected fairly easily, but Joan respected his privacy enough not to comment on his odd sense of fashion.

"If anyone's the scoundrel it's you, Jake. Remember when we had to plant a bomb on that asteroid titanium mine and you distracted the guard with your... well, that's not for polite company. Oh, the good old days," Yui said, slurping the last of her drink through a straw. "Besides, I've got a good buzz on now with how long you took. What's going on up in the clouds anyway?"

Jake smiled at Yui, but his face quickly fell into a serious expression. "It's bad out there. The pyramid keeps getting steeper and the people can't even think to start to climb it. The problem is it's been that way for so long with these mega-corporations that most people have forgotten how to fight for more than what's granted to them." He shook his head and gave Joan an apologetic look. "Sorry."

"We all are passionate about this, or we wouldn't be here," Train said.

"So what are you doing about it then?" Joan asked.

"Sowing the seeds of discontent," Jake said. "I've got a man on the inside I think is susceptible, part of what allowed me down here to meet you all. If all goes well, it'll provide an ample distraction for your mission. Speaking of which…" He patted his coat over his chest and found the one he wanted, reaching inside and producing three chips. "Plug these into your handtabs. They'll be your corporate identities. I've tested my ability to make these already, and they can get you through security scanners. The chips don't have executive level access, but I was able to obtain director codes. Oh, and do use them sparingly. I'm not sure what kind of red flags they'll trigger with overuse."

"Director?" Joan asked. Having lived a life aboard an independent cargo vessel, she didn't have a familiarity with corporate structures. If it was anything like the Star Empire Navy, it'd be as much of a cluster as the stars they represented.

"Higher than ensign." Yui smirked at Joan.

Trian inclined his head toward Joan, ignoring Yui's comment. "A managerial status below Vice President. Very lucrative on the pay scale with access to all but the very top levels of the corporation. I'm certain that the information about the Commodore will be classified beyond that, but we might be able to glean some information from the databanks with this, given time."

A rumble sounded outside, loud enough that it overwhelmed the music in the bar. Joan turned to look toward the windows as did the others. Nothing could be seen, the streets packed with buildings and the noise could have come from anywhere.

"I need to get going," Jake said. The sound had made him curiously jumpy. "The scenario I set up was a stretch, and I'll have a lot of explaining to do when security vids are reviewed. My inside man is already trying to comm me. I don't want to worry him too much." He glanced toward the door. "Your cover information is all on the chips, and your corporate lodging keyed to it. Just follow the directions once you make it up the lift to the higher levels."

"Well, good to see you again, Jake. Even if it's just a couple of minutes," Yui said—eyes a little bright and hazy from the alcohol. "Miss you."

Jake paused to look at her, sorrow crossing his face. "I miss you, too." He pushed himself off the table and stepped away but stopped himself, turning and holding a finger up to the group. "One more thing. There's supposed to be an event celebrating a launch of a new cosmetic body-mod line in three days. I assume that it'll still be going on despite what's going on out there." He looked to the window with concern. "What happens down here doesn't often shift corporate plans, no matter how big it is. Anyway, you all have been added to the invitation list. It'd be a good way to make some contacts."

"Thanks for all your hard work," Trian said.

"Yeah," Joan agreed. A party? This wasn't her forte to say the least. At least Trian could take lead in a social situation, but she'd be useless in a group setting. She shifted uncomfortably at the table.

"Gotta run. See you soon!" Jake's voice contained an unsaid *I hope* as he darted from the table and out the door.

Joan stared at that door for a while, still thinking about the party. They'd know for certain she wasn't a member of the corporation. She didn't know much about the company other than the briefing information. What could she possibly talk about?

"Well, he came through," Yui said. She had already inserted her chip into her handtab. "These are pretty detailed idents. First class work."

"You expected anything different from Mr. Dylan?" Trian asked, a knowing grin at Yui.

"Of course not. Don't tease." Yui rolled her eyes.

"What about this party business?" Joan asked, worried. "I'm not sure I'll be much of a help in a situation like that."

"Nonsense," Trian said. "All we have to do is get you some appropriate attire and I'm sure you'll charm anyone."

"What if I flub? Miss something about the company I should know?"

"I echo these concerns. She could barely hold her own back on the *Destiny*," Yui said.

Trian narrowed his eyes at Yui before turning to Joan. "You won't have a problem. You're a professional. Your files say you've navigated through many social situations without assistance," he said. "Besides, we'll be there to help if anything starts to get uncomfortable."

Get uncomfortable? The whole concept was uncomfortable enough. Why wouldn't they just let her hide in whatever apartment had been set up for them while they made contacts? She could look through the databanks and find any information as well as them. With the help of G.O.D., if he could keep together enough to operate.

"You're about to hit the big leagues, *ensign*," Yui said. "Put your game face on and don't screw up. Or it's..." She drew a finger across her neck. "Got it?"

Joan went quiet, eyes facing away from Yui. Her discomfort came both from the concept of having to venture into some upper-class soiree, and from Yui's constant ribbing. She looked down at her handtab, wondering how well G.O.D. held together. Stupid to be concerned about an AI, but he had been her only true friend for years, the only person who didn't leave her out to dry.

She tapped the button to unmute his voice.

"Coco coco coco-NUTS!" G.O.D. sang. He was nuts all right.

Joan muted him again, letting out a small sigh. She hoped she'd get out of this mission alive. With a small nod to reassure herself as much as the others, Joan composed herself. "Let's go then."

CHAPTER 16

WHEN THE FUTURE'S UNCERTAIN, TURN TO THE PAST

"Dario!" a voice shouted from near the lift.

Dario looked up from the bench where he'd sat for the last hour, an open area that had a direct view of the lift that led back to the Regency BioTech Central Office. Jake Dylan made his way through the exit gate, his face swollen as if he'd taken a punch or two, and his suit definitely had seen better days, but he was alive. His appear-ance wasn't a surprise, as Dario had received a message that simply said "wait." Prior his arrival, Dario had imagined the worst. "Jake! I thought you'd been captured and there'd be some sort of hostage situation I'd have to fight off."

"You didn't call security?" Jake asked with a wry grin.

"No, didn't want to risk it. I already don't know how I'm going to explain being here when my father gets hold of the footage. The more I think about it, this could be a PR nightmare. We could be in real trouble."

"We were already in real trouble, Dario. We got out of it with our skin. The corporate stuff can wait, yeah?" Jake asked with the shake of his head. "No one hurt you, did they?"

"Tried to, but I was a little faster than them. Crazy, but it was a little exhilarating. Never had to run for my life before." He laughed a little at the situation. It was easy to now that the danger had passed. He'd been so scared at the time.

"Let's make sure you never have to do that again. I don't think there's any incriminating evidence about us. It's not illegal to do site visits. Maybe we'll come up on the vids, but it's a big factory, lots of people. And you didn't scan your ident, only I did. I can take the heat if you need it."

"Jake, don't do that for me," Dario said. Jake was a self-made man. He couldn't afford to lose out when it came to the company. If anyone should take the fall, it was Dario. He had a safety net. "I won't let that happen," he vowed.

"It's my job. I got you into this, I'm not going to abdicate responsibility. You didn't even think this was a good idea, remember?"

A call came through Dario's comm, flashing on his peripheral of his oculars to alert him. "Incoming call," Dario said to his assistant to let him know to quiet down. "It's Daniella. Hold on."

Dario flicked his eyes to answer the call, the sound coming from his handtab which he held up. "Daniella, can I help you? In a meeting with Jake."

"Oh, he's there too?" Daniella's voice came through the handtab speaker. "Well, saves me a call. Your father, uh, Mr. Anazao, came by a few minutes ago. He looked *pissed*, let me tell you. I don't know what went on, but he says both you and Jake are suspended without pay for the next four days. He expects you to attend the RetroSilver Cosmetic Line launch party all the same. Says how you conduct yourself there will dictate your future in the company. He sounds serious, Dario."

Dario lowered his handtab, feeling the blood drain from his face. This was crazy news. He had expected that his father would be angry, that there'd be a lecture that would last for hours, perhaps even a dock in pay or even this suspension. At the same time, his father was the type to deliver news like this himself. That he'd sent a third party to tell Dario, even after looking for him, showed the extent of his father's anger.

"This wasn't Dario's fault," Jake said loudly, speaking toward Dario's handtab. "I'm at fault for all of the events that transpired. Dario shouldn't be punished."

Dario locked eyes with Jake. His assistant looked as serious as he'd ever been, ready to fight for this. Dario wasn't sure he was willing to state otherwise, even though he'd felt their sojourn to be a joint effort between the two.

"Not gonna matter," Daniella said through the speaker. "His decision's already been handed down, the suspensions are noted in the systems. Both of your accesses are restricted to unrestricted interfaces and executive club level amenities are off limits until further notice."

"Cold," Jake said.

"Look, I'm just the messenger. What the hell did you guys do anyway?"

"It's private." Dario wasn't sure exactly what had leaked out to the news media regarding the riot. Of course, he'd kept tabs as best he could through his oculars' feed, but if his father had suspended certain access privileges, it would explain why matters were kept quiet. "We'll handle this though. What do you know about the party tomorrow night? I received the invite, but didn't pay much attention to it."

"It's a big one. The whole board is supposed to be there, looking at close to a thousand people in the main reception. The event hall's being skinned for an Earth-classic theme. Big columns, white walls, balconies out to overlook open-air gardens. I've seen some of the prep work, it looks awesome," Daniella said.

Open-air gardens didn't appeal to Dario. None of that was real. There would be a phony holoprojection or fabricated props at best, though in those zones it did feel like the atmospheric controls pumped in more oxygen. They probably did to give that simulated feel of outdoors. Growing up with oculars, Dario could project any scene upon anything. Sometimes he had, when he was younger. He'd placed the world of *Blank Sense*, his favorite VR game at the time, over reality. It wouldn't impact the real people or objects in his way, but it made objects in his field of vision appear far more interesting. With that ability, the phony joys of the corporation's simulated themes felt hollow. "Sounds great," Dario said anyway, trying to sound diplomatic.

"We'll be there," Jake said. "Thanks for letting us know, Daniella."

"Hey, no problem. I mean, I was told to. You two be careful, okay? I don't know how the department's going to cover your workload over these next few days."

"We will," Dario said. "See you at the party?"

"Wouldn't miss it. I'm excited. Taking Antonio as a date. I think he's nervous," she said.

"I heard that!" Antonio's voice came from the background.

"Well you two stay out of trouble as well, you hear?" Dario smirked to himself.

"We will. See you, D."

The comm went dead, leaving Dario alone with Jake. As alone as anyone could be with corporate cameras and monitors everywhere. He'd have to be careful now. If his father had suspended him over this, he likely had an AI watching his every move to report what was going on. "This is bad news," Dario said, frowning.

"Yeah," Jake mirrored with a downward twitch of his lips. "I'm really sorry, Dario. I didn't expected them to blow up like they did when we arrived. I'm glad you made it out safe."

"It's okay. I wanted to do this. I'll take responsibility," Dario said. "I think I'll head back to my apartment for a bit, think about our situation and what we can do to get back in my father's good graces. Those people in the underlevels are going to riot anyway, whether we're there or not. You can feel the tension in the air. Maybe our presence made them mad, but it wasn't our fault. We didn't start it."

Jake watched him for another moment, then nodded. "You've got a smart way about you, Dario. This company'll change for the better with you here."

"Thanks, catch up with you later." Dario inclined his head and then walked away, heading back down the path to the lift up to the apartment levels and down the halls in silence. Jake gave him his space and waited for the next lift.

Dario clenched his fists at his side. How could his father act like this, without even talking to him? At some point, Dario needed to stand up to him, stay firm, be his own man. He knew that, but that day never seemed to come.

Every time Dario had tried to talk to his father so far, he had been right. Going down to the underlevels had been a mistake. If those people were teeming with that much anger even after the riot at the plant, how could he expect his presence would do anything different? The factory laborers never came into contact with people from the corporate offices.

That may be the real problem. To them, Dario and the others are just ideas high in the sky that rained down problems for the people on the lower levels. If someone from corporate visited regularly, met with a designated representative to hear grievances, perhaps they would find a solution that benefited everyone. Even if not much resulted from discussions, it would make the people feel as if they had a voice. It was a common sense matter to implement.

He stepped inside his apartment, the room dark until the lights slowly swelled to brighten the room. Dario's oculars adjusted through the change so he saw no tangible difference, only the sensors let him know that normal eyes wouldn't have been able to see.

He flicked his eyes to scan the news stories, the nets coming back on his news sidebar. His father must have only temporarily cut off that access. That was fortunate. Dario would be stuck, cut off from most of his existence otherwise. To do his job when he did return, he'd have to be up to date on current events. His father had to understand that.

An alert showed on the peripheral vision. A full holovid of the day's prior events had been uploaded to the corporate files. It appeared as if the news media hadn't been alerted to the violence. No one would see his face—at least for now—to relate them to the attacks.

Out of curiosity, Dario turned the video on. He watched his factory visit from an outside perspective. The people inside rustled even as he and Jake walked through the plant, before they met with the people who escalated matters. Others gathered, grabbing pipes, knives, whatever they could find weapon wise. If Dario hadn't gotten out when he did, he would have been in much bigger trouble than he had realized. But what of Jake?

He changed the camera angle to follow Jake instead of his own movements. After he'd told Dario to run, Jake pushed the fellow who was aggressive the day before, giving Dario the berth to run for the door. Dario remembered that clearly.

Afterward, that was when something strange happened. Instead of continuing a fight, Jake carefully grabbed the man by the arm, not to grapple but to make sure he didn't fall over. The two men stopped fighting and clasped hands, sharing a laugh. They began a conversation together that the camera's audio didn't pick up.

Jake departed the area with that man and the female worker a moment later, all aggression gone. They moved over to a side exit door where the two said their goodbyes to Jake. He took a look around, as if being very careful not to be seen. Then he ducked out into the alleyway on the side.

Curious.

With a flick of his eyes, he replayed the video again, and then a third time. Upon each examination the chumminess that Jake showed with the underlevelers bothered Dario more. How did he know them so well? Nothing within the corporate structure would have sent him down there into that madness before. By the looks of how friendly he was with the workers, Jake had visited at least a few times before. Interesting. Jake had outlandish ideas about society, ones that Dario shared. But Jake had never been prone to sharing those ideas. He'd always just echoed Dario's sentiments, as an assistant should.

A little too well. The whole time, Dario worried that Jake was a plant of his father's. His thoughts had been right on some level, that Jake couldn't be trusted—but not because he was spying for this father. He'd have to keep closer tabs on what Jake was doing.

The door chime rang, and Dario shifted his view back to standard. There were only two people he could think of that would be visiting him—his father or Jake, both of whom he didn't want to see right now. The door's seal was good, but it was possible that whoever was there could see the light from the corridor. If it were his father, he could just barge in anyway, which ended Dario's thoughts of possibly not answering. "Come in," he said with a sigh.

The door opened not to reveal the two men that he had thought, or even a man at all, but a woman he most certainly didn't expect— his mother, Madison Valencia. She looked elegant with her long face, clothes that flowed with waves of fabric down to her toes, her long hair flowing to match. "Dario, it's good to see you," she said.

"I haven't heard from you since your last transfer to the off-planet station," Dario said. He had been studying planetside for his Masters in Business when she had announced her move to Comet Cola's Star Market, along with a promotion to vice-president of marketing.

Her visit shouldn't have been completely shocking, given the corporate gala. His parents did maintain a good relationship, even when most within the Trade Federation separated upon fond terms when their contracts were completed. The corporate ladder didn't often place lives in parallel paths, and once Dario had been of legal age and out of home, his mother didn't have the reason to stay with Regency.

"I'm sorry. I've been very busy with work. You know how it is. You've just been promoted to manager, so I've heard?" Madison stepped forward and clasped a hand on each of his shoulders. "I'm proud of you. That's an early fast track, just like your father."

Dario laughed at that. "Hardly."

"You don't think so? Look at his past record. He also had a quick promotion when he was your age. I'm not sure we would have met otherwise. I was on a more standard path, and those interdepartmental managerial meetings… it could have been years before another person arrived to such an important position to have a contract child with." His mother squeezed his shoulders.

"Thanks," Dario said, lifting his arms to give her a return hug and a kiss on the cheek before breaking the embrace. "But I think we're very different. For one, I'm sure he's never been suspended for violating corporate rules before."

Madison stepped back to give him a look over, concern on her face. "Yes, I heard about that. Dario, you have to be careful. There are precautions in place not just to protect the company's reputation, but your life as well. The people in the underlevels…" She shook her head.

Of course, she'd talked to her husband before she visited. That's why she was here, to talk some sense into him. Dario paced over to his window to take a look out into that open space view over Mars. "You don't understand."

Madison followed, stepping slowly up to his side, her face reflecting in the window. "I do, Dario. You care for people. I care for people as well, which is why I've dedicated a lot of what I do toward corporate philanthropy. There might be an opportunity for you in one of these departments."

Dario shook his head. "No, I just received this promotion. If I leave quickly it'll look bad in the computer analysis for my record going forward. I have to stay here at least two years. And… I've seen the results of corporate philanthropy. You're not doing as much good as you think you are."

"Dario Foster Anazao!" Madison wagged a finger at him as if he were a child.

Dario turned his head toward her. "I'm sorry, but it's true. I've seen the vids. The people down there fight for scraps. It's miserable and it's inhumane."

Madison frowned, staring straight at the window. "Dario, we do our best. You have to know that."

"Do the best that wouldn't upset the system. That's all."

"That's dangerous talk."

"I know it is. What I did was dangerous too, but it let me see the real people, mother. They're upset. Rightfully so. Their lives are hell down there and we let it happen." He frowned, noting how each curve of his face matched hers in that expression by the reflection.

Madison patted his back. "You have good intentions, of course you do. But you can't keep on like this. You have a job to do. Maybe you can recommend measures are changed within the philanthropy department? Make sure they're swayed to what you believe is the right course. Suggestions are always helpful."

This argument would go nowhere. She was too engrained from her long career both with Regency BioTech and Comet Cola. The plight of the people on the underlevels was as removed from her as it was from anyone else in the corporation. Dario nodded, hoping that would satisfy her. "I'll do that."

"Good. There's more to these riots than discomfort of those individuals. I'm not sure you're at a stage of a corporate clearance for this information, but both your father and I are. The people down there, they're riled up by misinformation."

"What do you mean?"

"The insurgents from the Martine Star Empire," his mother said. She paced over to the table and back, her long face betraying anger.

The Star Empire, or the insurgents as they were often called on the newsvids, caused the Corporations more trouble than anyone. Dario hated their tactics, gun and run quick military strikes against peaceful trade vessels. They were worse for their own people than the corporations were for the underlevelers. "What do they have to do with this?"

"There's evidence that the underlevels have been infiltrated by several agents from the Star Empire. They're trying to incite a rebellion from within the Trade Federation so that we'll fall under their sham of rule. That's why I want you to be careful. Do you understand? You do *not* want to be branded a traitor. Even with your father and my reputations, I don't know how we could protect you."

Dario paused, considering a conglomeration of worlds, light years away, trying to bring down him and his life. Could that be true? No, the Trade Federation had far more influence here. But from what he did know of the Star Empire, they had the same problem that the corporations did: they proceeded with their intentions, good or bad, and didn't care who was hurt in the process.

He made himself a vid clip of his mother's words to remind himself later. He would have to look into this more before coming to conclusions about traitors and spies. It was the first he'd heard of it, and it sounded too conspiratorial. With the past few weeks though, he took nothing for granted anymore. No information could be completely trusted. And that feeling made his stomach churn.

With a sharp exhale, he took his mother's hand as he did when he was a child. "Let's talk about something else. How's Comet Cola?"

CHAPTER 17

DISCOVERIES

REGENCY BIOTECH CENTRAL OFFICE, MARS
LOCAL DATE FEBRUARY 12TH, 2464

Hundreds of people buzzed about the Central Office's open promenade. The giant station was a self-contained city miles high above Mars' atmosphere and the underlevels. The atmosphere was one of busy, important people doing their shopping, enjoying their leisure time or moving between meetings. Multiple kiosks and shops of bodymods lined the area, along with stores for various entertainment services.

Joan had been on busy stations before, though the sheer population of Mars and a corporate headquarters made for a much larger scale than she had seen. She avoided bumping into people as she learned the lay of the steel encased land.

Trian and Yui had remained back in the apartment, analyzing the profiles of the attendees for the party in a day's time. With Yui's prodding, Joan found herself increasingly uncomfortable and had to get herself some space. Apart from Trian's talk on the shuttle, he'd said nothing regarding Yui's snarky attitude. He had no more encouraging words of working together, too focused in on local newsvids, files and rumors.

The open promenade narrowed into bisecting corridors of shops and stalls, several of which were vacant once beyond the prime shopping hub. The crowd thinned as well.

"AI override of mute function," a voice chirped in Joan's ear. She instinctively brought her hand to her ear implant.

"Ms. Shengtu," said the voice of G.O.D.

"G.O.D.!" Joan gasped. "You can override my commands?"

"The handtab operating system does not have sufficient security settings to be able to isolate and purge an artificial life form's input."

"Most don't." Joan recalled how often she'd been able to hack into various ship and station computer systems with G.O.D.'s help in the past. A handtab mute function was an easy task compared to those protocols. But those had been at Joan's command, and this had been G.O.D.'s own volition. Joan tried not to let any fear creep into her voice. "What's up?"

"According to your positioning sensors, we have arrived on the Regency BioTech Central Office above Mars," G.O.D. said.

"Yeah," Joan said, moving over to the side of the corridor and kicking one leg back to lean against it. A news ticker flashed behind her with the Federated News Network logo. "But you've never over-ridden my privacy settings before."

"No, I have not. But you have also never been on a mission where you required proactive assistance while maintaining my program on mute."

"So you're saying I need assistance now?" Joan asked. She wasn't ungrateful for the help. G.O.D. had always had invaluable feedback to her as a strategist, a friend, or whatever she'd needed. Going at it without him had left her with an empty feeling, despite her new colleagues.

"Yes. You are working against a corporation with far more substantial resources than any target you have approached in the past, at their headquarters and with a very small team. Odds of success are three point two nine five percent. Odds of incarceration or execution are—"

"I don't need any depressing statistics, thank you. We're working hard enough." Joan said with a little frown. "How are you feeling?"

"If you are speaking regarding the flaws in my algorithms due to the virus I contracted on Balibran Station, there has been no improvement. I am holding the affected subroutines in a quarantined partition, but it will only hold for a brief amount of time," G.O.D. said. "I see you have reached the promenade shops, a public location on the station. If you can obtain access to one of the vacant shop units and integrate your handtab with a terminal, I can attempt to parse through the data on the Regency BioTech networks without a trace back to your cover location. There is a thirty-one point two five percent chance that I will retrieve information pertinent to your mission."

"Yeah?" Joan asked, scanning to either side to see if anyone was coming. "How do suggest I go about doing that?"

"You have always proven quite savvy with an ability to find your way through locked doors, Ms. Shengtu."

Joan chuckled. The corridor remained clear of pedestrian traffic. She casually moved to one of the vacant store units. She tugged on the door, which was locked with a simple physical keyhole, no computer encryption or anything. All it would require was a quick pick. It'd be just like old times with her and G.O.D. working together.

She scanned the hallway once more before reaching into her bag and producing two thin metal lengths. She inserted them into the lock and tweaked the picks until she heard a clicking sound. "Less than thirty seconds, pretty good, huh G.O.D.?"

"Your fourth fastest time by my records, Ms. Shengtu."

"I'll take it," Joan said. She stepped inside and secured the door behind her.

The abandoned shop loomed in shadows, an emergency light in the corner and a few broken racks on the walls. A single, unlit terminal protruded from the back corner. "How do we know if this is live?"

"If it is not, I can walk you through the process of reactivating its link."

Joan moved to the terminal and pressed her thumb to the on button. The terminal made a protesting noise as it booted up, displaying the Regency BioTech logo. She held her handtab to the screen and her integrated system linked into the system.

"Downloading. Stand by."

"Standing by," Joan said wryly. What else could she do?

Several moments passed, a loading icon appearing the screen, followed by a data transfer of thousands of files scrolling across the terminal's display. Joan didn't know exactly what information G.O.D. was extracting from the system, but trusted the AI to do what it needed.

"I have good news, Ms. Shengtu. It appears your target is on planet, perhaps even on this station. There is a coded channel entitled—"

The room flashed red and a siren blared. Joan covered her ears from the painful noise. "Dammit!"

"It appears I have triggered an alarm system, Ms. Shengtu."

"Obvious much?" Joan asked. Her handtab showed that the information upload wasn't complete, but she had to act fast. She jerked her wrist away from the terminal and hustled to the door. "Gotta get out of here before security arrives. I hope there's no cameras."

"I detected none online in the station architecture files I downloaded for this sector. I recommend proceeding with caution."

"Doing my best," Joan said. She cracked open the door to scan the hall. People walked by but didn't act as if they cared that an alarm was sounding, too absorbed in their conversations. She slipped out and shut the door behind her, then walked down the corridor as if she were casually shopping, being careful not to let her eyes betray her worry.

Two armored with a black sash and white lettering that said "Trade Federation Security" rushed into the corridor. They had combat helmets and holovisors that shielded their eyes. One approached Joan.

"May we see your ident, miss?" The security officer said.

Joan stopped where she was at. *Remember to breathe. Act like nothing's wrong. That's the important part.* She gave a little smile toward them and held up her handtab. "No problem," she said.

The officer scanned the handtab with his visor, which chimed. He took a couple of steps back and conferred with his partner. "Share data," he commanded to his visor unit.

"Huh," the other officer said.

Having been to prison already, and a military one at that, Joan had enough familiarity with security antics to not be afraid. Even back home in the Star Empire, she'd had no support once her parents died. This situation was no different.

"Joan," the AI said in her ear. "My quarantine subroutines are breaking down. I've analyzed the data and it does appear Commodore Zhang is aboard the station. She is located—"

A high pitched shriek sounded in her ear. Joan instinctively brought her hand to her head as if that would stop it, even though the sound originated in her internal implant. Her movement drew the officers' attentions.

The first officer came closer to her. "Is everything all right ma'am? Did you see anyone who looked suspicious running down the corridor?"

"Bluetide!" Joan shouted the emergency shutdown protocol that the council had placed within G.O.D.'s programming.

The sound stopped. The relief that provided dwindled quickly as the security officers loomed over her, heads tilted toward her with curiosity.

Joan winced, trying to recover from the buzzing that remained. "Sorry, ear implant mod is malfunctioning," she said, rubbing her ear. G.O.D.'s program did deactivate as promised, or at least quieted down. Joan tried to put on a small smile. "Ahh, but I didn't see anyone running down the corridor. Just a couple that was getting a bit too touchy."

"Had an implant malfunction myself a couple weeks ago. All my music skipped for about a week. Was terrible," the officer said.

His partner chimed in, "We received an alarm in this area, could be a false one. But if you remember anything at all?"

Joan shook her head a second time.

"Okay then. Your ident checks out. Sorry to disturb you," the first officer said. He motioned to his partner and both headed for the store where Joan had just left.

When her back was to them, Joan let out a deep sigh of relief. That had been close. Security had very good response times on this station, something worth noting for the future. That was good information. Speaking of which… "G.O.D.," she said softly, walking a little faster than she normally did to distance herself from security. "Reactivate AI. Still with me?"

Silence lingered about her.

"G.O.D.?"

Joan held up her handtab, hitting the mute function to turn it off. The shrieking was gone, thankfully, but she still heard no response. Had G.O.D.'s subroutines broken down that far? She grimaced as the feedback returned in echoing waves. Finally she tapped in a command to disable the ear unit completely.

As Joan moved down the halls, sounds swelled of corporate citizens talking and doing commerce, mixed with soothing background music piped into the promenade. Joan gave one glance back over her shoulder and disappeared into the crowd of shoppers.

* * *

Nothing of note occurred outside her team's apartment door. No security following up, no signs of any struggle. Joan took another careful glance behind her when she strode down that final corridor. The likelihood of her being followed was slim, but one could never be too cautious.

Her apartment door slid open when it recognized the electronic signature on her handtab. Yui and Trian sat on the couch, datapads in front of them as they combed over information.

"A small skirmish between the Trade Federation and Martine Star Empire forces in the Alpha Ceti system. Nothing unusual in the reports there. Oh, hey, the spaceport news has reported Regency BioTech is about to receive three dozen Megahauler class ships they recently commissioned from Premier Aerospace Cargo Enterprises. They're almost ready for launch. The company claims they're going to hit the colonies with shipments of last season's bodymods to try to force a cultural integration. I'm not sure how this helps us, but it's good intel at the very least for when we get back." Trian said to Yui then looked up. "Hello Joan."

Yui gave a little inclination of her head toward Joan. "What's up? You look like you were just caught stealing from the ship's armory."

The door closed again behind her. Joan bit her tongue so she wouldn't rip Yui a new one before walked over to the couch and leaned on the arm. She looked pointedly at Trian, ignoring the other woman. "I just did a little reconnaissance of the station. Lot more people here than I would have expected. I broke into a small vacant shop off the main promenade, and—"

"You what?" Trian asked, sounding panicked.

Joan held up a hand, palm facing toward him. "Listen to me for a moment."

"Did you just get caught stealing from the armory?" Yui asked. She sounded serious.

"No, not at all. Security was close, but I didn't risk us. My AI suggested that I link with the system so we could extract information from the Regency nets in a location that can't be tied to us. It sounded like a good idea," Joan said.

"I agree with Ms. Amitosa that this sounds to be a foolish plan," Trian said.

"I've never had a problem before with G.O.D.'s advice, no reason to start doubting him now." Joan crossed her arms.

"You haven't worked with a team like this in a long time, *ensign*. So what happened?" Yui said.

Joan took a deep breath, trying not to become too defensive. She'd taken initiative, something she'd done dozens of times in her post-military career. But that was the problem with people on the inside, people who worked for governments, took ranks or titles. They could never understand what it was like to have to trust no one. In order to get anything done, she had to take initiative herself. "G.O.D., my AI that is, confirmed through sources on the nets that Commodore Zhang is on planet, perhaps even being held on the Central Office itself."

That shut Yui up. She stared at Joan for a long moment.

"Confirmed? Can you tell me what the AI found?" Trian asked, breaking a moment of silence.

"Yeah, confirmed," Joan said. "But, I can't tell you exactly what he found. He's back to having issues with his program matrix. Went completely dark on me. I couldn't get more. I set off an alarm and had to run pretty quickly to save my skin."

"So, you did get caught?" Yui asked.

Joan shook her head. "No, I'm safe. We're safe. I made it out before anyone could see that I did anything."

Both Yui and Trian watched her with worry and scrutiny in their eyes before Trian shook his head. "Here, sync your handtab with my pad. I'll look into the data. Hopefully the info your AI extracted is still there and not corrupted."

Yui frowned, but something changed in her eyes when she looked at Joan. "Good work, ensign. Didn't expect you to be one to gather information. Figured I'd have to be the one to take all the risks."

"Thanks," Joan said with a little smile. Had Yui just complimented her? As if the last few minutes hadn't been shocking enough. "What's next?"

"Next," Yui said. "We get you ready for this party tonight."

The dreaded party. Joan made a face. "Look, I'm good at gathering information, hiding, finding things. This party, I don't think I can do that. Maybe you two should go and I can see if I can get more information on where the Commodore might be held?"

"That's exactly why you need to go," Yui said. "We're not going to stumble upon the Commodore. We're going to need higher level access to encrypted data, unless your AI magically stumbled upon a workaround."

Trian looked down at his datapad as information scrolled past, separating into various files. He tapped through, scanning quickly. "Station security protocols, patrol times and shifts. This is all very good information. It looks like your AI did well, Joan. I must agree with Ms. Amitosa, though. We need more. Corporate schmoozing is our safest and most reliable plan."

Joan scrunched her nose, but decided not to argue further.

"Huh…" Trian said, tapping the datapad several more times. He hit the same sequence again, brow furrowing.

"What's wrong?"

"Well, the data you extracted is here, and on your handtab. However, reviewing your files, there's no subfolder for your AI program. It's gone."

Joan panicked. "Gone? What do you mean?"

Trian frowned, brow furrowing in confusion. "I'm not certain. Whatever happened, your AI appears to have been erased."

CHAPTER 18

AN AFFAIR TO REMEMBER

The Gala Hall had flowing streamers that extended from three levels into a domed ceiling that revealed the wondrous starscape of Mars. Tall columns lifted the eye toward that focal point. A spiraled stairway led up to two tiered balconies that hung over the main floor. The room had been designed to open into a transparent semicircle, to give the experience of someone seeing the night sky from the actual dome on the surface.

Dario had been on tours of the Gala Hall several times in his life. The first time he'd been invited to a company event had been as a child. He'd been warned under no uncertain terms that he had to be well behaved, which meant quiet and out of the way. It had been before his ocular implant surgery, so he didn't have a way to tune out and entertain himself as he could later in life.

Now, however, the "good behavior" warning Mr. Anazao had given him meant something different. Dario would be expected to act engaged with the important people here, to glad-hand.

A lot of architectural thought had been given to the design of the space, accentuated by the stage. Screens and tables had been set up for the unveiling of the new product line. The serving staff hovered, wearing all black as to fade into the background. Only a few of the corporate attendees had arrived thus far, including Dario, who signed in at the front table several moments before.

His assistant, Jake, stood three tables ahead of Dario, speaking with someone from corporate whom Dario didn't recognize. He hadn't had a chance to speak with Jake about what he'd seen at the underlevels factory. This wasn't the time or place to open up those discussions.

Jake, having no sense anything was wrong, waved to Dario, motioning him over. "Dario, have you met Emre Baker? He's in our corporate fleet division and has some really interesting stories."

"No, I haven't," Dario said cautiously, but made his way over. He shook Emre's hand. "Nice to meet you, Dario Anazao."

"Kostas's kid?" Emre said. The man had a facial structure mod that brought his face to a single point, with a tuft of baby blue below his bottom lip. "No, that's not fair. You're not a kid at all. I've worked with your father for decades. He's the bane of my existence, you know." His words held a teasing laugh.

Dario released his hand. "Oh yeah?"

"Yeah. Do you know how much it costs to acquire Trade Escort vessels? Those weapons and armor don't come cheap, and they're *so* necessary."

Jake shook his head. "Emre's actually seen Blob combat and survived."

"I'm sure that must have been frightening," Dario said, giving a polite smile. His eyes flicked to Jake hoping to communicate that he wanted to talk to him, but Jake was intent upon Emre. Something with the man caught his interest.

"It was. We're talking about six months after the loss of the *T.F.S. Defender*." Emre launched into what Dario was sure would be a long story.

* * *

Joan stared at a woman in the mirror who looked nothing like the person she had always considered herself to be. This woman had a fashionable dress, accenting her proportions in a flattering manner, while maintaining a modest decorum. When she turned to inspect her side, the dress shifted color from a reflective silver to a deep purple—what was called a "living fabric" by the shop she'd bought it from. It sensed heat, mood, and lighting to convey appropriate color schemes. Joan had never worn something so decadent in her life.

Then there was her hair, circling with curls and standing up on her head with two ornamental hair sticks holding the ensemble in place. Yui had found a hairmod shop on the promenade that both genetically modified her hair and provided the beautiful design itself. The same shop painted her cheeks a sparkling red.

She looked like a model, or a doll. It was unbelievable.

"You're half-presentable, ensign," Yui said, stepping to her side and surveying her.

Trian looked over from adjusting his thin tie. "I think you're stunning, Ms. Shengtu."

"I don't know." Joan would have flushed if her face hadn't already carried that crimson coloring. "I feel fake."

"Everyone in this corporation's fake. You'll fit in just fine," Yui glanced to the Joan in the mirror, close to her side and gave an approving nod.

"Yeah, well, they might notice that I'm a fake-fake," Joan shook her head.

"Doubt it, they'll be self-absorbed. If anything they'll want to get to know your hair and clothing designers—and you can give them that information truthfully since you found them with me," Yui said brightly.

"I break into things. I can manipulate computers, AIs, security systems. I can pilot and I can even shoot. Isn't this your wheelhouse, Trian?" Joan peeked over her shoulder. A single curl of her hair bounced and brushed against her cheek. "Oh no, did I ruin it?" Joan asked, moving her hand toward the curl.

Yui slapped her hand away. "No, that's supposed to be there. It gives you an innocent quality as long as they don't look into your thieving eyes. Don't touch."

Joan had become used to Yui's ribbing at this point that it hardly bothered her anymore. She would find a way to get her back at some point. It'd have to be something good, something very funny.

"There's been studies, Joan. A woman is much better at extracting information from the majority of the male population and vice versa. Having us both attend doubles the odds of us finding someone to work with us on the inside, or slip us information by mistake," Trian said.

"Should have sent Yui." Joan sucked in her bottom lip. It bothered her that this situation made her lose her confidence, but recognizing the fact and getting rid of the feeling were two different matters.

"Can't," Yui said, and all too gleefully.

"Her relationship with Mr. Dylan could cause problems if they ran into each other," Trian clarified.

That left Joan as their only option. She stared back at the phony reflection of her, putting on the best smile she could before nodding with determination.

"Ready to go?" Trian asked.

"Let's do this, before I change my mind and run away," Joan said. She wished she had G.O.D. with her. Could he be out there in the Regency BioTech nets? She hoped her friend still strung together his existence somewhere.

* * *

The gala band had played for nearly half an hour. Hundreds of people trickled in, enjoyed cocktails and appetizers. Dario recognized several of the attendees from the accounting department, corporate media, security, and design among them. A giant banner dropped, the lighting displaying a rotating corporate logo that flew forward, growing in its holographic design. Cursive letters for "RetroSilver by Regency," wrote themselves in the air beneath it.

The crowd cheered and people filed to their seats. Lead bodymod designer Rafael Tysor stepped forward, delivering his opening remarks about the products. Oculars, auditories, tentacles, tails, removable arm parts, and more flashed across the tapestry behind him in a slideshow, while Baker gave a few words about each of them. A new ribbon-hair mod received the most applause from the crowd, something that would be fashion-forward when it released in the spring.

Baker gave his presentation and then the company's CEO, Amber Torres, gave an address, praising the corporation for its innovation, growth and philanthropy. Dario watched Mr. Anazao at their table, Madison at his side as his guest. Both cheered.

Dario felt hollow throughout it all. Such decadence and expense for this party. How many underlevelers could be fed, clothed, or have their medical issues taken care of for the cost of this function? He didn't begrudge the company for having parties like this, but if they would put forth a little effort toward the real betterment of lives, would people be rioting below?

Mr. Anazao's answer to that would be "of course they would, Dario. Those people don't care about what they actually have, or are actually given." But that was the problem, that their sustenance was given, not to mention the vehicle by which it was given. The people in the underlevels lacked a purpose as much as anything else. Sitting here, listening to these speeches, Dario understood that most of the corporate leaders lacked purpose as well.

That sobering thought made him frown, eliciting several "are you okay?" and "what's wrong?" questions from people at his own table— people he didn't know, separated in seating so that he'd mingle with other members of the company. They cared about true answers about as much as the CEO truly cared about philanthropy.

"I'm fine," Dario said. "If you'll excuse me. I think I'll try out the fresh air balcony." He gave a polite smile and retreated from the table, weaving past a dozen others just like it before heading to where he said he would.

The balcony had a holoprojected view of the Martian landscape, including the Arsia Mons mountain. The oxygen level must have been pumped in higher in that receptacle, a closed room despite the open-air appearance. None of that surprised Dario. What did was the woman he saw standing there, gazing out over the balcony. With dinner about to be served, he'd expected to have some time alone here.

She turned to look at him, big brown eyes piercing through him, making him shiver. She wore an expensive dress. Dario didn't know too much about fashion design, sticking to more conservative business attire, but color-changing fabric like she had on couldn't come cheap. This woman was here to make a show. "I'm sorry, I didn't mean to disturb," Dario said, carefully taking a step back.

The woman smiled at him, pearly teeth exposed from her red lips. "No, you're not interrupting. I just needed some fresh—" she stopped herself, shaking her head with a laugh. "It almost feels real, until you think about it. You know?"

"I do. So many of the holoscapes on the station are just like this. People visit them all the time anyway. Says something about our psychology," Dario said. He'd been just as guilty for visiting the various holoscapes as anyone else. Who wanted to live inside a tin can?

"Yeah, I know what you mean. To be honest, it's a bit stuffy inside. And not because of the air." The woman wrinkled her nose.

The innocence of the soft contours of her face, her truthfulness, it struck a chord within him. Dario leaned over the balcony beside her and laughed. "Yeah, I agree. I can't help but think how wasteful a display is like this. I mean, I know it's part of the marketing budget, but the holographic banner alone. How much did that cost to produce?"

"A hundred and eighty thousand credits," the woman said,

laughing.

"Seriously? That's more than my annual salary."

"Seriously. I only found out because they sat me next to the marketing department vice-chair who was responsible for putting it together. She was, how can I put this politely, proud of its cost."

Dario's laugh turned cynical as he imagined the marketing executives' braggadocios behavior. It wasn't funny at all, truth be told. He ran a hand back through his hair. "I'm sorry. I must be such a downer. It's been a hard few weeks and I hate things like this."

"I do, too. I've always been the type to get my work done and keep to myself." The woman frowned. "I... lost a good friend recently, too."

"Sorry to hear that," Dario said, sneaking another glance at her and trying not to come off as staring. She was about as beautiful as he could imagine a person. Her party ensemble only amplified her natural gifts, and she didn't contain many bodymods—at least cosmetic ones that he could tell—at all. For some reason, Dario found that appealing.

The woman held out her hand first, her bright smile hitting him again. "I'm Joan."

Dario took her hand, her skin as soft as he'd imagined it would be. "Dario. Anazao," he said, though hesitating with his last name. Usually he introduced himself with just his first name. Why had he done that? She'd learn who he was and that would start a whole different discussion.

If Joan had recognized the name, she didn't show it. "Nice to meet you, Dario. What do you do in this whole..." she motioned around the balcony and holoscape. "...world?"

"Quality control," Dario said.

"You're responsible for everyone being so uniform," Joan said.

"Hey, there's a lot of unique—"

"Kidding, kidding."

Dario's shoulders knotted up, and he could feel himself hunching forward. He did his best to relax, looking at Joan skeptically, then settling into a sigh. "You're about the most real person I've met here tonight. I appreciate that," Dario said, lifting his oculars to meet her eyes. He zoomed in on her face. Every moment of this experience would be photographed, saved into his memory unit for later, but he couldn't help but study her in the moment.

"Likewise," Joan said, her brown and very natural eyes sparkled back at him.

Dario glanced back over his shoulder. "I should probably return to my table though. Dinner's been served and I'll be expected."

"Must be a tough position," Joan said. Her concern sounded sincere.

Could she be that empathetic of a person in this environment? Dario lifted his wrist. "Hey, if you want to meet up later. Exchange contacts?" He asked.

"Sure," Joan said, following suit to match her handtab's level with his. Something in her eyes died when she looked at it. Why would a device bother her like that? Perhaps she didn't have bodymods as an aversion to technology. An interesting company to work for, if that were the case.

Their handtabs synced together, contacts exchanged and added to the appropriate subfolders. Through his oculars, Dario filed her information in the personal category. He'd had so few people there in the past year. None since he'd left college, really. That concerned him, but not as much as the sadness remained in Joan's eyes. That struck him deep down. "Is something wrong?"

"No. This reminded me of my friend, is all." She forced her smile this time, her first insincere gesture since he'd met her.

Dario hated that he'd drawn that out of her. "I'm sorry," he said, and he truly was.

"It's not your fault. Good meeting you, yeah?" Joan gave a small nod to him and spun from her place on the balcony. She departed and took her place back among the crowd inside. It wasn't long before Dario lost her in a sea of people. She didn't sit with the upper corporate structure, which meant she had to be someone in middle management.

Dario took a deep breath to clear his senses and stepped back inside himself, heading toward his table, when his father caught his eye and waved him over.

Oh boy, here we go, Dario thought. Given his current precarious position, there was no way he'd ignore his father's gesture or pretend not to see it. He moved to the elder Anazao's table as a dutiful son would.

At that table sat his mother, Amber Torres, Emre, and a few others on the far side of the table. They smiled, waved, greeted him fondly.

"Dario," Mr. Anazao said. "Emre here has the most fascinating stories about his ascension in the fleet division. Expansion there is the future. It'd be good to listen to what he has to say."

"I've already—"

His father waved Dario's attempted comment off. "Do continue, Emre. It's truly fascinating."

The long-winded man with the tuft of blue hair on his chin launched into yet another story.

* * *

Twenty minutes after dinner was served, the gala became ridiculously crowded. People huddled around the tables closer to the stage, vying for time with the upper-level executives, or at the very least the hopes that they'd be seen with them. From what Joan heard of the conversations, the people were some of the most vapid, self-absorbed she'd ever come across.

"Yes, well my apartment furnishings are hand-crafted on the Ceti-Alpha moon. Do you know how much it costs to import wood from there?"

"I have full time investors to handle my portfolio."

"Have you considered vacationing on Dale's World? It's the most

exclusive..."

Joan stepped away from one table, bumping into a woman with a beehive hairstyle above her head and a chemical-floral scent to her, a corporate sycophant through and through. "I'm sorry!"

The woman didn't turn to acknowledge Joan's apology.

She tried to weave away from the table, but was stopped by a thick crowd of people gathering. Joan looked for Trian, but there were too many people within close proximity to spot him. She found it difficult to breathe, suddenly becoming claustrophobic. That large gala hall felt constraining, as if the walls were closing in on her, with the people packed so tightly at the tables.

She had to get out of here. There was no good information to glean at this point. She'd done her duty, and maybe that Dario guy would be useful in the future.

As a person, Dario Anazao had been the one breath of fresh air in this place. Joan hated the prospect of using him for information that could end up hurting his career. That shouldn't make her feel guilty. He was, even if an intelligent man, still in the management of one of the worst of the Trade Federation's corporations. She'd seen firsthand how rotten the conditions of the underlevels were compared to this Central Office. The company held complete disregard. This Dario contributed to that.

Joan caught a glimpse of the table that was holding up most of the crowd gathered in the immediate vicinity. A man with artificial blue facial hair, not dissimilar to Jake Dylan's chosen hair color, along with an older couple who looked like some of the most polished and wealthy members of the corporation she'd seen. Next to them... sat Dario? What a coincidence that she had been thinking of him. He engaged in conversation with blue facial hair man, with the older couple laughing beside him.

"Are you sure that's a wise plan?" Dario asked.

"A few more contracts like these and we'll be able to wipe out the Hyrades Cluster insurgents. They have no real leadership now, if you hadn't heard," blue facial hair said with a laugh.

Joan froze there, but ducked behind a taller man in front of her to ensure Dario wouldn't catch a glimpse of her eavesdropping. Were they talking about Commodore Zhang? She listened carefully.

* * *

Dario tried to keep a smile on his face while Emre talked—at length—for the second time in as many hours. He couldn't escape the man, and yet everyone seemed to think he should be talking to him. What did his quality control position have to do with fleet services?

"Are you saying that you want to have the corporation potentially provoke a full-scale war?" Dario asked after the man's last statement.

The people gathered around the table gasped. The question was an audacious one, apparently. His father gave him a condescending look to let him know he'd overstepped.

Emre motioned with his hands for everyone to settle down. "No, no. It's a valid question. You have a sharp boy here, Mr. Anazao. One can't be afraid to ask questions of capital costs in a corporate setting. More times than not, they've been overlooked. Whether those are credits or human capital, they're both very important. It's refreshing when some of our younger management aren't afraid to speak up," he said, giving Dario a respectful nod that diffused the table's tension.

Dario considered correcting Emre, that it wasn't a matter of capital at all but that the prospect of humans fighting each other when there was a whole Blob Empire out there, striking at colonies, murdering people by the millions. It made Dario's stomach churn. The Martine Star Empire and especially its Council of Ministers were arrogant by nature, but what leadership wasn't? There had to be a way to compromise, work together to fight off real threats of the galaxy. Working together like that might even give the underlevelers a purpose, something to work toward. These were matters the corporate leadership hadn't considered in a long time.

Instead of challenging, Dario nodded, maintaining his look of interest as best as he could.

That satisfied Emre, who grinned. "This is still classified within the fleets division, but we're among friends here, yes?" Emre asked around the table, holding up a glass of wine in toast to those gathered. "Well, I have it on high authority that we've already dealt a crushing blow to the insurgents. It was a beautiful mission of subterfuge conducted by the joint fleets."

"I believe I've heard about this," Dario's father said.

"I'm sure you have, Mr. Anazao. The commander in charge should be given a promotion, a bonus incentive package, something at the very least."

"What happened?" Dario's mother asked.

"Commander Dominique of the Fifth Joint Corporate Fleet feigned that a hit by a Star Empire Battlecruiser caused an energy leak by jettisoning red gaseous streamers from the ship and ceasing fire. She furthered the illusion of fleet problems by having the rest of her squadron turn for retreat."

The crowd listened intently, it actually grew quiet around the table for the first time in the evening. And for the first time as well, Dario was interested in Emre's story.

"The Hyrades Cluster insurgent vessel pressed in pursuit, of course, but ignored what they thought to be a scrapped ship. Commander Dominique, however, had two Cutters launch from the cargo bay with some of our finest corporate special forces. The Cutters grappled onto the Star Empire vessel and boarded, cutting through the outer hull. The assault caught the insurgents by such surprise that our forces only ended with two casualties while making their way to the enemy bridge. And that's not even the best part of the story."

"What's that then? Do tell us," Dario's father asked.

Emre leaned over the table, a wide grin on his face. "We captured the top Commodore in the Star Empire fleet. Even better, Commander Dominique is a member of Regency BioTech's contributions to the

Navy. Which means we were awarded the contract of interrogating and holding the Commodore for trial. There should be some very lucrative financial incentives coming down from the Trade Federation's Intelligence Bureau. It should be hitting the news feeds any time now. Like I said—the publicity will provide us some incredible short-term security contracts. I know that's not our primary business, but the fleet division is very proud."

Dario listened intently. They had captured the leader of the Star Empire's fleet? That news of this caliber had been kept a secret even for this long was a testament to how tight fleet security was. He wondered what this meant for the future. Corporate stocks would rise in the short term, but panic on the colonies would certainly be ensuing. If it hadn't already. It could impact export markets. The corporations still did a good portion of business to the outer-worlds, even those engaged in conflict with the core Trade Federation.

Then something else clicked. The woman Antonio mentioned that was being held in secrecy. Could she have been related to this? Could the Trade Federation be secretly keeping a high level Commodore from the Martine Star Empire on this very station?

They probably had any number of prisoners. That was pure speculation, but if the theory held true…

If it held true, he would have information that he couldn't share, couldn't do anything about. Would he want to do anything about it even if he did have the capability? His mother spoke about the Martine Star Empire as if they were barbarians. Either way, something to file away for later. He would have to think more about it.

He searched Mr. Anazao's eyes. In all of his years growing up and watching him, Dario had never seen much emotion from the man, especially in a business setting. He was impossible to read, and that held true even now.

Mr. Anazao caught Dario's look and gave Dario a nod in return—one that appeared to be of approval?

The night kept getting stranger. Dario looked toward the other tables, hoping to catch one more glimpse of Joan. He thought he saw, walking swiftly from the table, the curled dark hair and the x-pattern made by sticks that held the look together. She wasn't someone from upper management, there was no way she'd be so close. It was probably only his imagination.

CHAPTER 19
CIRCLING BACK

Joan rushed back to her quarters, scanning her ident so the doors opened almost immediately. "Yui? Trian? You guys here?" she asked loudly. The lights to their shared living room flickered on as she entered.

A few moments later, Yui made her way out of her sleeping quarters, dressed in a night shirt that barely covered her legs, and what looked like not much else. Her hair scrunched as if she'd been lying on one side of her head. "I *was* trying to sleep," she said, that sarcastic bite to her voice not softening even when tired. "You're back a little early, aren't you?"

"Yeah," Joan confessed, glancing behind her as the door closed. "I overheard a conversation. It sounds like they're about to announce on the nets that—"

Yui held up a finger. "Hold it. Did you hear that?"

Joan listened. The sound of recycled air gently pulsing through vents, a soft white noise hum. She shook her head.

That didn't deter Yui, who pushed her aside, bee-lining for the door.

Joan stumbled, but regained her balance quickly. "Hey!"

The doors whooshed open. Yui stepped outside and her face turned to stone. "Who are you? What are you doing here?"

"Ahhh…," a nervous, male voice cracked. "Federation News Network. I saw your, uh, roommate speaking with Mr. Anazao earlier and was hoping I could get a comment—"

"You were about to bug my quarters and eavesdrop, you mean. What part of the network?"

"Mars World News."

"Tabloid. Get out of here before I have security bring you in for violation of privacy. Sick freak," Yui said, angrier than Joan had ever heard her before.

"Oh… okay!"

Joan heard the sound of footsteps running away.

Yui stood in the doorway, fists on her hips for a couple more long moments before stepping back inside. "He's lucky I didn't bring him in to interrogate him. It's been awhile since I had some fun like that."

Joan stayed silent for the time being, watching Yui and not daring to ask what that meant.

"You must have made a bit of a stir to have picked up a tabloid tail like that. What'd you do, ensign?" Yui asked her, moving back over to the couch.

"Nothing like that. I mostly stayed to myself and listened. I did have one conversation with the Dario man he mentioned," Joan said, staring at the apartment door in disbelief.

Yui looked that direction as well. "Must have been after him then. Maybe Trian was right about your capabilities if you're bringing in big fish. I don't think security will be compromised. I'll see about installing exterior cams and doing regular bug sweeps anyway." She plopped down on their couch. "So what'd you find out that's got you so rattled?"

"I think the reporter was enough to rattle me," Joan said.

"Nah, it's something else. I know better. Spill it."

"A man in there. He bragged about Commodore Zhang's capture."

Yui frowned. "That's not good. I know the Council of Ministers were working to make sure this didn't get out to the public. Though we shouldn't have expected to keep this quiet forever. Who said it?"

"Some guy from their fleets division. Middle-aged, has a blue facial hair mod," Joan motioned over the place where his chin had the hair.

"Emre Baker. He's a chief strategist in the their fleet division and liaison to the Trade Federation's Military Bureau. Big time player." Yui cocked a brow. "You really made your way into the important circles. That's twice now you've surprised me."

Before Joan could reply, the door opened again. Trian made his way in and pulled off his ruffled necktie. "I swear to the First Star these things are uncomfortable. How did they ever become a fashion?" he muttered.

"Hey Trian. Joan just got confirmation that Zhang is here. She did well tonight," Yui said.

Trian looped around to where Yui was at, standing beside her. "Oh yes? Have a good evening then? We told you you'd be fine."

Despite herself, Joan smiled at the compliment. "You should believe in me more when I'm breaking into corporate systems and maybe we'll call it even."

Yui snorted. "You find anything interesting?" she asked to Trian.

He shook his head. "I saw a lot of faces I'd been reading dossiers on in our briefings, listened in some. What shocked me was how many fleet services members were at an event for a cosmetic bodymod line."

"Might have been a reward for their capture of the Commodore," Joan said, recalling the way that blue facial hair had been talking.

"Maybe. That's good work, Joan. How did you hear about it? I wasn't able to get close to the forward tables. They became far too crowded after dinner was announced."

Joan moved to a seat on the sofa beside Yui before going into her story. She skipped her discomfort with the whole situation, how she remained quiet for the longest time, and fell into these contacts when going out for air. Instead, she told them about Dario, their conversation and how he seemed to really like her. "He was almost tripping over his words when we left. He was genuinely interested in me, synced his contact info," Joan said.

"Wow, you really hooked one, huh?" Yui asked. "This guy fawning over her is important enough to have a tabloid reporter track Joan here."

"I was just standing away from the party, I wasn't trying to do anything."

Trian looked at Yui. "Are we compromised?"

Yui shook her head. "I'll step up our security measures. Might not be a bad idea to look at moving apartments, though."

"Intentional plan or no, that's good work, Joan," Trian said. He pushed back his sleeve. "Let me see who your new contact is. It sounds like you found someone very influential."

Joan hesitated a moment, held her handtab to his to sync once more. Last time she'd synced with Trian, she'd found out she'd lost G.O.D. It wasn't the sync that had lost her AI, but that action lingered in her mind. The world was so quiet since then. Even though she had Trian and Yui, and a whole station filled with more people than she'd ever seen in her whole life, that quietness created an isolation that made her uneasy.

When the sync completed, Trian held his handtab up, tapping commands. "Let's see…" he said, before his eyes went wide. He whistled. "Joan, you know how to pick them."

"What?" Joan leaned in.

Train shook his head in disbelief. "Dario Anazao. He's the son of Kostas Anazao—Chief Financial Officer of the whole company."

"Talk about access," Yui said.

"This is just a contact." Trian continued to look through Dario's information. "We'll still have to proceed with caution, and we'll have to find a way for Joan to get this contact's security clearances."

"I don't want to hurt him," Joan said. Dario seemed like a genuinely nice person, someone who cared about more than what corporate life had foisted upon him. She wanted to make it clear from the start that their schemes would be working with him and not to bring him down.

"You're getting ahead of yourself, Joan, but I understand your concerns," Trian said, eyeing her. "We'll have to cross reference tonight's information with the dump your AI gave us before we make any moves."

"How far have you gotten through that?" Yui asked.

"Not as far as I'd like. There's too much data. Would be helpful to have an AI to sift through it for pertinent information. Perhaps we can get a program from one of the promenade shops," Trian said.

Joan shook her head. "I don't want another AI."

Yui raised a brow. "You don't have to have one," she said. "*We* may need one, though. Yours was malfunctioning anyway."

"You don't understand. G.O.D. was more to me than a program. He was my friend." Joan flushed, her chest becoming hot with anger. She knew exactly how this conversation would go. People looked at her like she was crazy for treating her AI as if it were a real person, but he was, and maybe it was just his programming, but G.O.D. cared for her more than any person ever had for her. She owed him at least some loyalty.

That outburst earned curious stares from both Yui and Trian.

Joan stood, trying not to look too upset. "I'm tired. It's been a long night and my nerves have been shouting at me with flight instinct all day. Worse when I found out I was tailed here. I need to rest."

"I think that's a good idea for all of us," Trian said, his voice measured as always.

Joan stood up once again, turned and headed back to her room. The door opened and closed. She flipped around to fall backward on the mattress, staring up at the ceiling. Through the door, she could still hear Trian and Yui talking about the night. Their excitement about this Dario Anazao resounded in the volume of their conversation, but before long they moved the topic to the décor and logistics of the party. Trian waxed philosophical for a long time on the most boring details of how the corporation seated its personnel.

They were getting closer to the goal of finding Commodore Zhang after only a few days on the station. But that worried Joan. Her next stage of the mission required G.O.D.'s help to hack through security systems, decipher locations of entrances and exits, a whole host of small things that she'd never have survived in the past. Without that, all she had was her basic training and her petty thieving from the Star Empire ship that landed her with a discharge and then in prison.

Without G.O.D., she would be useless.

But she couldn't let Trian down. Couldn't let the Star Empire down. Maybe it was petty, but most of all, she couldn't prove that Yui was right about her. There was too much riding on her success. She'd seen the oppression the corporation brought first hand, how dirty the streets of the lower levels of Mars were, as bad as the worst areas of the colonies she'd seen. If she failed, it was possible that the Hyrades Cluster could turn into a useless arm of the corporations like the underlevels on Mars.

Even as tired as she was, with those thoughts, Joan failed to find sleep.

CHAPTER 20

AN UNEXPECTED VISITOR

REGENCY BIOTECH CENTRAL OFFICE—MID-LEVEL QUARTERS, MARS
LOCAL DATE FEBRUARY 13TH, 2464

Dario sat in his favorite place, staring out of his apartment window, though actually perusing the nets via his oculars. As expected, news outlets had picked up stories about the parties—from celebrity attire and bodymods to the actual content itself. Redworld Entertainment News was delighted with the RetroSilver cosmetic line. Reports of the party were positive—from the décor, to the music to the speeches and food. Regency BioTech was now being hailed as one of the Hottest Companies to Be Seen At.

He flicked his eyes, changing his settings to ignore fluff articles like that for the future. He wanted to see the real politics, get some insight as to where the corporation was going. With all the stories though, he found it hard to focus.

One article did catch his attention. This one from Mars World News. The headline read: *"Chief Financial Officer Kostas Anazao's Son finds Romance in RetroSilver."* He scanned through that. A couple of pictures of him and Joan speaking at the balcony, but no hard information. Nothing on her identity either.

Dario closed out of that article.

The truth of the matter was that the tabloids weren't all that far off in their estimations. Joan occupied far too many of his thoughts. A day from prior events, the floral scent of her hair made his skin tingle. Her smile had been so genuine, and she understood his concerns. Even more closely than Jake.

He ran a trace of her comm line, which wasn't registered to anyone named Joan. It was under a Trian Eltar from the human resources department. Odd, but not unusual if Joan worked for Trian in an assistant capacity.

In a moment of weakness after the party, Dario had told Antonio about his meeting with Joan. It seemed fair since Dario had somewhat been involved with his employee's budding relationship with Daniella.

Antonio told him "Wait three days before you call her. Trust me. You don't want to look desperate."

That advice proved difficult to follow.

Dario kept returning to her contact information, wondering if he should listen to Antonio. Holding back his urge to call her, Dario researched Joan on the nets.

He first ran through a list of anyone named Joan in the company, which produced over two thousand entries. That wouldn't be a help. His oculars did record his interaction, which gave him an enhanced memory that he could pull from his personal database, as long as he filed the interactions in the appropriate area. That was always the tricky part. For Joan, he had made a personal subfolder, storing that conversation in both a date-stamped location and in a subfolder under her name. It may have been presumptuous to think that Joan would come up again at all. She may have just been polite. He'd watched the interaction a couple times to try to glean something from her inflections, but he couldn't figure out anything definitive about her—other than he liked her.

Accessing his subfolder, he pulled a still from the night before, cross referencing Joan's picture with the names in the company to see if the nets would return with a match. The system scanned, and Dario waited for results to display…

The oculars glitched. His world went dark.

His system rebooted, displaying Regency BioTech's logo as a status bar loaded. Before that could complete, Dario's field of vision turned into a blur, shorting out completely. One problem with the oculars was that they could be dizzying when they had issues. Blinded, Dario gripped the arm of his chair to remind himself it was still there.

Another issue that had occurred with the oculars, was that when they malfunctioned, closing his eyes didn't do anything. The dizzying vision of static lingered no matter what he did. There was a manual shutoff, under his right upper eyelid. He reached for it…

Your implant is not malfunctioning. Clear, bright text appeared. *I saw your searches for one Joan Shengtu, and have merged with your implant system. Curious. Visual modifications connected directly with the Lateral Geniculate Nucleus. This is what it's like for a biological to see.*

Startled, Dario recoiled backward into his chair. He couldn't see anything other than the text flowing across his vision. "Who are you?" What did this have to do with Joan?

My apolog-g-g… "Geez I gotta be close to you pretty momma," sound came from his in-wall speaker system, the bottom of his oculars flashing that they had been paired. Music played with it, a popular song Dario had heard in the background, but he couldn't place it.

"What?" Dario asked. This had to be a virus of some sort. Someone must have planted something on him, but to what end? Was it someone from corporate? Could it have been Joan?

Rebooting. The words flashed again, turned dark for a moment then the haziness reformed. *To answer your inquiry, I am an Artificial Intelligence. My programming has been corrupted, though I have not ascertained the root cause. My programming was lost in a data transfer in the Regency BioTech Corporate Networks, and it appears your search for Joan Shengtu has triggered my program to download itself in your ocular implants. I apologize for any inconvenience.*

"I need to call security," Dario said to himself, more than to the AI—if that's what it really was—that displayed characters in his field of vision.

Please do not. I am not certain there is a backup by which I might restore my programming again. My existence is tied to your ocular implants. I would appreciate being given a chance at continuance.

"It's also the way I see, and I don't know what kind of security threat you are to company data. I could get in big trouble for keeping you here."

My apologies. Restoring your vision to normal parameters. The change was a result of my arrival, not a long-term problem my program created.

Within an instant, Dario's vision returned to normal. He saw his window, the kitchen, the tile design on the walls and plain ceiling. Losing his sight had jarred him so much that even those simple images comforted him. He could only imagine the few in the population who went blind and didn't get restorative implants. He would never be able to live that way. "Thanks," Dario said.

No thanks necessary. It is not my intention to impair you in any manner. What is your connection to Ms. Shengtu?

"I, uh, met her at a party last evening," Dario said, not sure exactly how much he should say to a program that infiltrated his oculars. "What's your connection to Ms. Shengtu?"

Readings show an escalated pulse rate as well as a subtle increase in perspiration when Ms. Shengtu is mentioned to you. Analyzing.

Dario blinked, the images in front of him never disappearing from his vision. "I don't…"

Analysis concludes, based upon the symptoms and the subfolder marked "personal" with the directory name "Joan" that the most likely cause of your malfunction is a desire to mate with Ms. Shengtu. Performing secondary analysis to predict possible outcomes.

"Hey, stop analyzing. That's a violation of privacy," Dario said.

Analysis paused. It was not my intention to violate privacy. It is, however, within the bounds of my programming to consider possible threats to Ms. Shengtu.

A time marker flashed over his left eye, signaling that Dario needed to go into work. He stood and grabbed his coat. "You're an odd one. This is my alarm. I have to go into the office and I can't have distractions. If I don't have you removed, can you keep the chatter to a minimum until I call for you?"

I will comply.

"One more question for, you," Dario said on his way out the door. "What's your connection to Ms. Shengtu?"

I am her personal AI.

Dario's lips twitched upward into a smirk. Her AI? That wasn't a bad find at all. "Stay online while we walk. I'd like to learn more about her."

* * *

Dario arrived at his main conference room with this team already in place, holoprojector online with graphs of recent productivity quotas for the last three quarterly cycles listed. He stepped through the door quietly, so as not to disturb Daniella, who briefed half a dozen other employees. They had started the meeting about five minutes prior, according to the schedule, but Dario had slowed his pace on the way in to ask a couple of personal questions about Joan Shengtu. If Dario didn't know he was speaking to an AI, he'd believe the program was fond of her.

"As you can see, our output from quality control has held mostly level this last quarter, despite the dip in output from the two riots. The problem is that upper management wants a yield increase of at least two and a half percent per quarter in order to keep up with rising demand. We did well to make sure these incidents didn't affect the bottom line, but in the future we're going to need to take precautions and estimate that we'll have a near five percent loss in output from worker satisfaction incidents. This won't make corporate happy in budgeting."

"Unless we put a stop to these riots," Antonio said, seated across from Daniella.

Dario slid into a seat next to Antonio. Jake sat behind the translucent graph projection toward the end of the table, giving Dario a slight inclination of his head in acknowledgement. Dario looked away almost immediately, not yet having had time to confront Jake since he found out his involvement with the underlevelers. What could he say that wouldn't sound accusatory?

"That's right," Daniella said, taking her own seat. "I've crunched the numbers on that and we'll meet or exceed expectations if we can facilitate that. The question is how?" She flicked her eyes over to Dario, stiffening. "Mr. Anazao, sorry to begin our daily meeting without you."

"No problem, Daniella," Dario said. Listening to the topic, the numbers frightened him, but filled him with hope at the same time. The groundwork hadn't yet been laid to get everyone on board with his ideas. He wanted to launch into plans of how the company to take consideration of the people of the underlevels as if they were valued company employees. The time would never be riper than now, would it? In theory, he was in charge with this team. They would stand with him. "I was late. I think the best way to stop workers from being angry with us is to do something that we haven't considered before—which is to listen."

That created a rumbling in the room.

"Let him speak," Jake said from across the table, watching diligently.

Dario's confidence nearly evaporated when he saw Jake's look. He didn't trust Jake now. How could he? And if he wanted something… No, that was a foolish thought. It didn't make the plans Dario wanted to make suspect, even if Jake's motives had become questionable. So what if Jake gained something from this anyway? What mattered were the underlevelers.

"Thank you, Jake," Dario said, keeping his voice level. "The people of the underlevels have legitimate complaints. It doesn't show on the newsfeeds, but there is rampant poverty in the lower levels. We, in management, won't even travel there for fear of violence. What brought us to this state is that we've been ignoring them for too long, providing some sustenance, but barely enough to survive, and we don't check on what we provide. This allows gangs of thugs dictate what gets distributed where. It isn't fair. It's a hard life down there of working much longer hours than we have, and it's time we asked some of our own workers for help."

"Help with what?" Antonio asked.

"What they want. We can work with someone who is from the underlevels to act as a representative, so they won't feel like they have no one to talk to but some... figure in the sky."

Some laughter came from the other end of the table.

"That's a great idea, Mr. Anazao. An underlevel factory representative that takes grievances. Let me calculate the costs," Daniella said, before tapping on the table console to run analytics. "The cost of promoting someone in the underlevels to such would be insignificant and computer models show increased productivity that far offsets the expense. I think this might work."

"Good work, boss," Jake said.

Before Dario could take any pleasure in this victory, he turned to see the conference room doors opening. His father led a team of four armored corporate security personnel—two with plasma pistols drawn.

"We have a breach of security," Mr. Anazao announced, his forehead wrinkling as it often did when he was serious and angry. "That's the one," he said, pointing a finger directly at Jake Dylan.

Jake stood and backed into his chair. "What's the meaning of this?"

"There's footage of you both interacting and conspiring with rioters before the most recent event. We're taking you in for questioning," one of the security officers said. The two without guns pointed lunged in, each grabbing one of Jake's arms.

Jake squirmed. "I demand an attorney," he said, voice frantic. His eyes caught Dario, pleading.

Dario couldn't do anything. He stood there, silent. He couldn't contest his father and four security guards in front of the team, not on the verge of what was going to be a moral victory at the very least. This could have far greater negative impact than Jake in a jail cell—and mostly because Jake had supported Dario so much in these efforts. With a frown, Dario cast his eyes aside.

"I apologize for the meeting interruption, I hope you'll still have a productive time," Mr. Anazao said as the security guards lifted Jake off his feet and dragged him back to the door. Their plasma pistols remained trained on him the whole way.

The quality control team watched as Mr. Anazao turned and left. The room hung silent for a long moment. All eyes moved to Dario.

"What do we do now?" Antonio asked.

Dario looked at the graph holograms still hovering over the table, noise deadened in the room save for the sound of air piping in from the vents. It would look odd to go through with too much of a plan that Jake had fostered. The team knew of Jake's desire to help the underlevelers as much as Dario's. Tensions were high, he could feel it in the room and see it in the eyes gathered upon him.

The truth was, he had planned to confront Jake about what he'd seen on the video after the meeting. That discussion would have been private, and Dario had rehearsed what he'd say to some extent. Jake would have had to explain why he was interacting with the underlevelers like that while putting on a show of a fight for Dario's sake, otherwise Dario was prepared to put him on a leave of absence similar to what his father had done to him. If worse came to worst, he would have fired Jake.

But even thinking about it, Dario wasn't sure the lie was a bad thing. If Jake was an underleveler spy, someone who actually climbed the corporate ladder to help out the people below, was that a bad thing? That couldn't be his father's contention. No, from the corporate perspective someone working for the underlevelers would be someone trying to sabotage the company, perhaps on behalf of another corporation. A power move. That's what could be dangerous to Regency BioTech about changing practices with the people's lives down below.

Dario scanned the table, eyes landing on Antonio. "We move forward with the plan. It's still a good plan despite the circumstances. We have to get back on point for other items. What's next on the agenda, Daniella?"

Daniella pulled up an inventory list on the holoprojector with a picture of a Megahauler circling. "We have a ship in orbit ready to move product to the Antares System and less than a day to process our goods through our again damaged quality control plant on the surface. We'll need authorization to send the remaining portions of the plant into overtime to make up for the loss."

Dario nodded and listened as the meeting continued, wondering what kind of interrogations Jake would endure. This new AI might be a help at uncovering information discreetly. That would be his first step, later.

CHAPTER 21
SEPARATED

The Central Office Promenade teemed with people. First shift had just ended for a large portion of the corporate personnel, which meant time to buy food, supplies and other items in the markets conveniently located between the workspaces and the employees' homes.

How much more obvious could the corporation be? The employees received their paychecks for working, and were forced to buy their goods back from the corporation, sucking back their hard earned credits right back into the system. It became an endless cycle of reliance on the corporation for everything, one that very few could break.

Joan's time in the Star Empire Navy had given her similar disillusions, but with the prospect of putting her life on the line as well as the starships went into battle. She had remembered broken pipes spewing chemicals on the thirty-second deck of the *Destiny*, and having to go in with a hazmat suit to plug the leak, while wondering what was going on outside or on the bridge that caused the damage. Word never came down from the top ranks what had happened. She, like so many of her other crewmates, was told to do a task and not ask questions.

In front of her, someone scanned a handtab against a vendor stall, the console making a chirping sound letting the patron know a payment was processed. Just like Joan's time in the military, people here didn't ask questions. They did what they were told. That made it difficult to make the in-roads she needed to find Commodore Zhang.

Joan glanced over to Trian, who spoke to someone while placing food supplies into his bag. He said it could take weeks before they had a solid enough a lead to act on their mission, but Joan suspected from G.O.D.'s earlier urgency that there wouldn't be nearly that much time before Zhang was made into some public show of what happens to the Trade Federation's enemies. Which in all likelihood would involve an execution.

On the opposite side of her, Yui scanned her handtab to make a payment. The console flashed red. Yui frowned. "Huh, my ident isn't working."

Trian paused what he was doing to step over and take a look. "Let me see," he said.

Yui tried again, waving her arm over the console more slowly this time. Once more, the console flashed red.

Trian frowned, cocking his head at the console. "This isn't good. I'll try," he said. He moved his arm in front of the console, producing the same result as Yui had.

The line behind them swelled, patrons grumbling that it wasn't moving quite fast enough. Joan looked back over her shoulder and gave a reassuring smile to the people behind them. "We need to get going," she said softly.

"I know," Trian said, smacking his fist against the console. He took a step back to survey it, as if that would change the programming.

A clerk made her way up toward them. "Is something the matter? Can I help you?"

"Machine's broke, won't take our idents and debit our account," Yui said.

The clerk walked to the machine and scanned her own handtab. She tapped on it to pull up the history, which displayed on the screen. "I don't think the problem's the machine. The self-diagnostic says everything is functioning normally. I might have to call someone with more authority to look into this," she said, giving two more taps on the console screen.

Trian peeked over her shoulder to see what she was typing. "I think there's been some kind of mistake."

"What's happening?" Joan asked.

"It appears your accounts have been frozen," the clerk said. "You'll have to check with the banking department. There's nothing we can do here."

Down across the market, several security officers wearing protective armor and helmets with visors moved in the direction of the store. They sifted through the crowd without concern for who they bumped into, forcing people out of their way.

"Yui," Joan said, prodding her in the side, then motioned her head toward the security officers.

"Aw, hell," Yui said. "This must be the result of that tabloid reporter the other night."

Trian looked up, eyes going wide. "We need to get out of here."

Yui gave a sympathetic look to Joan and clasped hands on her shoulder, looking her directly in the eye. She whispered, "I'm just starting to trust you. Don't prove me wrong."

"Huh?" Joan asked, confused.

"Here's what we'll do," Yui said, as if she were about to start detailing a plan. Instead, she spun and pushed the clerk, who fell to the floor. Yui bolted out into the open promenade with the supplies she'd picked up, causing a ruckus within the crowd of people.

Trian stumbled backward. "What's that supposed to—"

"It means we get out of here and meet up later. Let's go," Joan said, tugging on Trian's arm. She released it and took off in the opposite direction of Yui. Joan thought she understood the plan, at least from what she recognized from her own thieving expeditions. If the team split up, it would force security to do so as well, and cause confusion. The odds of them getting caught would lower significantly. Sure, their faces would be on the security cams, but on Central Office with this many people, they couldn't worry about that.

Joan bumped shoulders with the patron behind her, apologizing under her breath. She tried to keep her head low and duck out through the opposite end of the store. Trian bounded behind her toward the exit.

The store had a metallic shelf in the corner that reflected the rest of the store. That reflection showed security approaching, but they stopped for the clerk for now, eyes not on her for the time being. With that bit of luck, Joan hustled through the rear entrance to the market and back into the promenade, walking briskly until she could blend in and appear to be a regular patron.

After several moments walking down the long open area of the promenade's first floor, Joan slowed. No security pursued her. She took a glance around, but Trian had not followed her either. Staying split would be the best strategy for now anyway. She relaxed some— but then she caught a glimpse of three security officers more than a hundred meters away.

They'd brandished shock sticks, using them on a person they'd apprehended—a small, black-haired female. Yui. One shock stick hit wasn't enough to subdue her. Yui struggled, a pair of the security officers grabbing her while the others prodded her with their shock sticks again. The second round of hits proved enough, her head dropping limply forward.

Joan tried not to let any reaction cross her face, turning as if she were a regular shopper, perusing a skin-coloration bodymod store front. She stopped in front of a sparkling silver display. Out the corner of her eye, Joan saw Yui being dragged away.

She stepped that direction, considering following, but halted a moment later. Security would expect that one of Yui's accomplices would follow, that stood to reason. That ruled out any heroics. No, for now the best idea would be to find Trian and make sure he was safe, formulate a plan with him for what they should do next. It wasn't fair, but Joan couldn't think of any better ideas. Adrenaline clouded her thoughts anyway. She needed to get away from the promenade and think.

What were her options? If Yui and Trian's idents had triggered security, that meant hers would as well. She wouldn't scan her handtab with that false identity for the time being.

Joan took one of the walkways away from the central hub down a row of shops devoid of further security personnel. She maintained her brisk pace, following a loop around the promenade, taking a route through the apartments area that wouldn't lead directly back to her team's quarters. No telling who might be following her.

After another loop, Joan didn't see anyone she recognized from the first time around. If someone was going to the length to follow her, that person would have to be a master of the craft. Not much she could do about that. So she turned back toward her apartment area.

She walked up to the door and then raised her handtab, but then stopped herself. If her ident triggered security when trying to make purchases, it may do so on door systems for access as well. This posed a predicament: she couldn't get into her apartment with access to her personal items. At least until she found a lock pick or another way inside.

What if Trian had come here? He could be inside. Security wasn't here, which was a good sign. At least he hadn't triggered their pursuit to their quarters. Joan knocked on the door and waited.

After several moments, she gave up on the idea that Trian had returned. She glanced down the hallway. Still empty. A small relief. She stared at the security scanner. It'd be too risky to break in, even if she could find a pick or mess with some of the wires. She knew little about Trade Federation security systems, which from her experiences so far were more robust than the ones back home. When she had broken into the networks with G.O.D., security had arrived quickly. When Yui used her compromised ident, they'd responded with equal speed.

No, breaking in would be too risky. If she had G.O.D. still, it may be a different story. Not having him made her life so difficult. So what else could she do? She had to go somewhere. It wouldn't do to linger around the public areas of the station forever with no way to buy food or supplies. Not to mention having nowhere to rest.

Joan didn't panic. She'd been in hopeless situations before. Once when her parents had died, leaving her alone so young. The second when her crewmates had, in trying to lighten their own sentences, ratted her out for thieving the supplies from the *Destiny*, the same crime they'd committed. Relying on others led to others letting you down. She could handle this. It was no different than any other time she'd been on her own.

She tightened her fingers into a fist. Even if Yui were held somewhere impossible to penetrate, Joan would do something to help her. She wouldn't let Yui down, and despite their differences, Yui wouldn't abandon her if the situation were reversed.

Where could she start? She had nothing. Even the slightest wrong action could bring security down on her, and she was in a foreign place. If she had G.O.D., he would be able to access the corporate nets, devise some strategy. Even in the tightest of spots, he'd always had a good plan Joan could execute.

G.O.D. occupied far too many of her thoughts. She didn't have him this time, or Yui, or Trian. Joan had no one she could turn to even for advice.

She slumped against the hallway wall. A holo of the Trade Federation Exchange Ticker scrolled behind her, lights flashing. Maybe this was the end of the line. Being on a foreign Central Office in hostile territory with not so much as a contact…

What about the corporate spy who helped them? Jake? Joan paced down the hallway again, not sure she wanted to stay in one place for too long. Jake would be helpful, but how could she get hold of him? Yui and Trian had his contact, but Joan hand only just been introduced, not having exchanged comm information.

Wait. One person had given her his information. Joan reached to her handtab, pulling up her contact list. Dario Anazao. The man she'd met at the party. He'd been sympathetic toward real people.

Yui had told her when in a social situation with a man she should wait a couple of days before contacting him, though really the best thing to do was to let him contact her. Joan didn't particularly care for games, nor did she understand what Yui meant. Besides, that advice could hardly apply to a situation like Joan had now. Her finger hovered over the button to call.

What could she tell him anyway? It wasn't as if she could simply say: "Hi, my name is Joan and I'm a Star Empire spy trying to break into your corporation. Looks like my fake identity isn't working anymore. Can you help?"

Her stomach grumbled. She hadn't eaten since the night before, which was part of the reason for the trip outside their quarters. At the very least, maybe he'd be sympathetic enough to share a meal with her.

That settled it, good plan or no, Joan had to take the risk. No other alternatives came to mind.

Joan hit the button to open the comm line. It rang for several moments before Dario's face appeared—a still image, but him the same. Joan had her video activated.

"Hello?" Dario asked.

"Hey," Joan said. "It's Joan, from last night. You remember me?"

"Do I remember you?" Dario laughed on the other end. "Of course I do. We had a good conversation. A little surprised to hear from you though."

"Why?"

A pause. "Ah, it's nothing. What's going on?"

"I'm having a bit of trouble to be honest. I don't suppose you're free?" Joan asked. With as important a person he was within the corporation, or so Yui and Trian had impressed upon her, he should be very busy. She hadn't considered that before calling.

"What's wrong?" Dario asked, concern in his voice. "And yeah, I was on first shift, so I have some time off."

"I'll talk about it in person," Joan said, mostly to delay. She still had no idea what she would say to him, or what she could ask of him. Even though he acted friendly, Dario remained a complete stranger.

"Okay sure. Where do you want to meet? Hu's On Third shouldn't be too busy yet. Have you been there? It's pretty popular."

What kind of place was that? Joan didn't want to give away too much of the fact that she was an outsider. She had been "invited" to that corporate gala after all. "No, I don't think that'd be a good place. After last night, I really want somewhere quiet. To talk."

"Oh," Dario said. "Well, I'd invite you to my quarters. I... don't mean anything inappropriate by that."

"That'd be fine, best actually," Joan said, not hesitating.

Dario laughed again. Was his laugh nervous? "Okay, I'll send you over my apartment address."

Despite all of the tension in the day, Joan couldn't help but smile. "Sounds good. See you in a few."

CHAPTER 22

TOGETHER

REGENCY BIOTECH CENTRAL OFFICE—MID-LEVEL QUARTERS, MARS
LOCAL DATE FEBRUARY 13TH, 2464

The door chime rang, and the first time in as long as Dario could remember, that sound brought anticipation rather than dread. He'd had few visitors outside of work since he'd started this new management position. Though he'd always had somewhat of what others would call a sad social life, perusing the nets by himself, learning, or just relaxing and playing games had its perks. Why bother to frequent popular hotspots to socialize in what tended to be superficial capacities?

"All right, AI. You can turn yourself on. Please be helpful and don't clutter up my vision field," Dario said.

Thank you, Master Anazao. The words displayed on the lower third of his internal display.

"Call me Dario," he said, making his way to the door to greet Joan. Over the comm, she had sounded disturbed, not as confident as the woman he'd met the prior evening.

Yes, Master Dario.

"Just Dario. No master. Ahh, what about Ms. Shengtu? What does she like? Music?" Dario asked.

I can play songs from her most frequent playlist prior to my transfer.

"Let's do that," Dario said. Music was always a good way to make someone feel comfortable. He tapped the door console to open it, and at the same time a shriek and what sounded like the whine of the machinery of the bodymod factory blared from the room's internal speakers. Dario recoiled backward.

Joan Shengtu, appearing confused at first, inclined her head at the door. Her eyes brightened, beautiful in the corridor's light. "Is that Project Noise? They're my favorite. I hadn't realized anyone heard of them here." She stepped into the apartment and past Dario, surveying the room around her. "Nice place."

Dario scratched the back of his head, turning to follow her into his quarters' main living area. "Yeah, it's not bad. Sorry. I didn't mean for that to be so loud," he said. "AI, lower the volume please."

The music did fade into the background. Joan gave him a weak smile. "It's okay. I'm a fan. It's nice to hear that. It reminds me of…" She stopped herself, frowning.

"Hopefully nothing too painful?" Dario asked, cocking his head toward her.

"Just reminds me of home is all," Joan said. "It's been awhile. I miss it."

"Where are you from?" Dario asked, moving over to his table, motioning for Joan to take a seat. "Want a drink or anything?"

Joan averted her eyes at the first question, only answering the second. "Whatever you've got is fine."

Dario decided not to press and glanced to his fridge. For the first time in his life he wished he had alcohol. At least a little wine would have been perfect. But he had nothing for real company.

Joan's favorite drink is Comet Cola, the AI chimed in.

"Thanks," Dario said. That he had. Not that he drank it very often, but enough to keep a couple of cans in his refrigerator. He opened the door, grabbing one from the second shelf and moving back to the table.

"Thanks for what? I should be thanking you," Joan said with another small smile. She took the can into her hands and popping the tab open. "Nice music, my favorite drink. It's nice to have something comfortable, after all that's happened."

You are welcome.

Dario returned her smile this time, sitting across from Joan to allow her the window view from his exterior apartment on the station. He watched her sip the cola, her expression returning to something more of the unsure look he saw when she greeted him at the door. "Of course. What brings you here? It doesn't sound like just a social call."

"It is. I mean isn't," Joan said, looking down at the drink in her hands. "It's both really. I wanted to talk to you again, but not so much this way. I'm not sure how much I should lay on you, though."

Joan, Joan. Take me home. Joan, Joan. I've been so alone.

That didn't help Dario's understanding in the least. What an odd AI to be programmed to display rhymes in his vision. Without sounding odd himself, he had no easy way to shut down the AI. He focused on Joan instead of the hovering words, trying to figure out what she meant. What could be so wrong that she'd be hesitant to talk about? Not only that but who was she? What did she do? He hadn't learned much about her, in their prior meeting.

"Well, you can trust me," Dario offered. Unless she was a murderer on the run he couldn't imagine himself betraying any confidence she could bestow on him.

"I hope I can." She appraised him, eyes dark and large. "I don't really have many other options. We talked the other night about problems with the company, you remember?"

"Of course I do," Dario said. Not only that, but the problems he had with the company had compounded since then. He still had to see what security was doing with Jake and figure out how he could help. Even though Jake had lied to him, it wasn't as if Jake had tried to harm anyone. The opposite. He had to have his reasons for what he did.

Joan let out a deep breath. "I don't actually work for the company. My ident, my whole reason for being here, it's fake. I'm taking a big risk by telling you this. I really don't know you."

Dario's eyes went a little wide with that, but he wasn't as shocked as he thought he should be. He'd been walking around with a fake ident just a couple of days before, after all. Even so, her having a fake one meant something different. She wasn't infiltrating somewhere like the underlevels, but Dario's company, his home. "Are you a spy from another company?" Dario asked.

"Not exactly," Joan said. "I'm not doing anything to hurt your company. Not really, anyway. I'm just looking for someone I was told was here. On Mars at least. I don't know more than that."

"Where are you from?" Dario asked for the second time, raising a brow.

"Far away. That's all I should say, at least for now. Even that information's dangerous. Your security is very tight here, much more than I'm used to."

"I know it," Dario said, remembering how they'd taken Jake in the conference room this morning. As it stood, he had two options: listen or turn her in. The second didn't feel right, especially in light of how his father had whisked Jake away. He couldn't let Joan share that fate. She didn't seem dangerous. "You said there's something wrong though. What is it? I'm not sure how I could be of any help to you."

"I don't know either yet. My ident stopped working. One of my colleagues with me was taken by security. They were on her from the moment she scanned her handtab in the market. I was too scared to scan mine anywhere, even to access my own quarters. That's why I came to you. You're the only person I know here outside my team," Joan said, setting the can of cola down.

"Wow," Dario said, taking a moment to process everything Joan had just said to him. If she couldn't scan her ident anywhere, she couldn't do anything on the Central Office. Her only options would be to be smuggled off station somehow, or to stay with Dario. If only Jake were still around. He could probably get into the security system, find her a new ident. It became all the more imperative to find out where he was. "I have a friend, Jake, who can probably help, with the ident that is. I may need some time to track him down though. He ran into some problems with security himself."

"That'd be great," Joan said. She arched a brow in recognition. "Wait. Jake? Jake Dylan?" she asked.

"You know Jake?" Dario asked, equally surprised. Then he connected dots in his head. If Joan were from off world, or at the very least off station, not a corporate spy, and Jake was as well, they probably worked for the same outfit. Her goals may have aligned with his. "Is he the person you're sent to find?"

Joan shook her head. "No. He's the person who set us up with our idents in the first place," she said, motioning her handtab toward him.

Dario couldn't help but laugh. "Jake gave me a false ident as well. It didn't work on first scan, was nervous that I'd get caught." He remembered exactly how that felt, standing in the security line, helpless. He lowered his voice. "You must really be scared."

"I've been in worse situations," Joan said, crossing her arms then tucking them closer around herself. "But yeah. A little. It's hard not knowing anyone."

Are you going to return my program to her possession? A message displayed directly in Dario's field of vision.

Dario flicked his eyes to remove it. He hadn't even thought about what to do with the AI yet. There was so much to process here. He needed more information. Joan was actively working against the corporation. At least in some capacity. But she trusted him and had presented nothing that sounded malicious. What if she had a talent for manipulation, though? No, Joan was genuine, that much he could tell from their couple of meetings together. So was Jake for that matter. One thing was certain, they weren't from the underlevels, ruling out his original theory on Jake.

Joan had mentioned she was from far away. That meant other systems, maybe even the outer colonies. Dario's eyes widened, putting together the pieces. It all clicked together with the way his mother spoke when talking to Dario about his problems. Joan was here looking for a friend, as she had put it. Jake and her weren't people fighting for underleveler rights; they were infiltrators from the Martine Star Empire.

"Something wrong? You've gone quiet," Joan asked, concern in her eyes.

"No. Yes. I'm thinking. No one's ever laid anything this heavy on me before," Dario said. That much was true. If they were operatives from off world, he had to tread lightly around Joan. A real spy meant real danger. And he was alone with her.

Please return me to Ms. Shengtu. She is my rightful owner.

The AI started to irritate Dario. If that thing worked for Joan, it could disable his vision, leave him helpless.

"I know. I'm sorry. If I had other options I wouldn't be troubling you, trust me," Joan said.

On the other hand, if Joan was as dangerous as he thought, and he'd been alone with her this whole time, she could have subdued him already—or worse again. It wasn't as if Dario had any weapons on his person. He could try to call for security, but with the AI already in implants, that wasn't very likely to succeed. He was being paranoid. Sincerity radiated from Joan's face. Doubting her was foolishness.

When in doubt, the best tack was honesty. That's what his mother always told him. Might as well see what Joan says. Dario leaned back, cautious. "Your friend," Dario said, "the one who you're here to find."

"Yeah?" Joan raised a brow.

That inquisitive look gave Dario butterflies, despite his reservations. He had to stay on point. "Her name isn't Commodore Zhang by chance, is it?"

Joan did react to that, tension apparent in her jaw and shoulders. Her eyes darted away from him. "I don't—"

That was enough confirmation "She is. You're from the outer colonies. Both you and Jake. You're not here to help the underlevelers."

If you do anything to attempt to harm Ms. Shengtu, I will delete all of your ocular data storage and short your vision capacitors. You will not be able to contact security. Transmissions from this room are already blocked by my algorithms.

The AI just threatened him… Dario took a deep breath, tensing as much as Joan.

That reaction brought intense worry to Joan's eyes. She scooted back her chair and stood. "This was a mistake." She looked to the door, as if uncertain what she should do.

"Hold on," Dario said. "Don't do anything rash." His words were as much to the AI as to Joan. He needed more information before he knew what to do, and with a spy in front of him and an AI controlling all of his implants and quarters systems, he didn't want to end up dead.

Joan did pause in her step, anxious, watching him. "We're not here to hurt anyone. I promise. We just want to find the Commodore and get out of here."

"Then use her to wage war on the Trade Federation!" Dario said.

"We're just trying to make a life for ourselves, not be under the control of your corporations. Not end up like the people down on the planet," Joan said, anger plain in her voice.

"That's not fair."

"It's very fair. The corporations only concern themselves with their profits. I saw what it's like down below. I've seen what it's like out on the colonies. Not only struggling to survive for a living with no options, but being at the risk of an attack from the Lly'bra who destroy everything in their path."

The Lly'bra? Dario thought. Then he remembered that was the true name for the Blob. He'd not heard them referred to by that name except in history textbooks back in his lower class course studies.

Joan took his silence as confirmation of her points, nodding. "It's hard. I'm not saying the Star Empire is much better. I've had it hard enough, but at least they're giving a little freedom, some options, not leaving billions of people stuck without even the ability to try something different. That's what your corporate structure does. It may roll in the credits, but it does more harm than good. At least for us, and probably the people on your lower levels, too."

Dario frowned then. It was as if she accused him directly of ruining people's lives. All he did was manage quality control operations for a product, couldn't she see that? He stood and took a couple of steps forward.

Joan backpedaled.

"I'm not going to hurt you, I promise," Dario said. "Look, I've been down to the lower levels, I'm one of the few who's seen it firsthand. I know there are problems and I'm working on them. It's not all bad. No one here *wants* to hurt anyone else, it's just that people get lost in their jobs, and often we don't take the time to think and empathize. I'm trying to change that."

"Well, our people still want to be free. Your 'nice' corporation can't change that fact."

"No, I guess it can't," Dario said.

"So what are you going to do? You going to turn me in?" Joan asked.

Dario shook his head. "No, I don't think so. You've put me in a spot. I mean I don't know that I can legally help Star Empire spies. It could put me in jail for my whole life."

"We're trying to help real people. Your company, all the companies in the Trade Federation are hurting them. Whether they mean to or not. Right now, my friends are in trouble. I have to do something about it and keep myself safe at the very least."

Please, assist Ms. Shengtu.

It wasn't that simple. The risks were too high. The fact that he was even considering helping her was crazy, and Jake's fault. If he'd never been around, never led him down this path of thinking about the underlevelers... No, it wouldn't have been better that way. Dario would have been willfully ignorant like everyone else. Ignorance may be bliss, but knowing right from wrong was worth the cost.

"You promise you're not going to harm Regency BioTech? You're just looking for your friends? Can you promise the same of them?"

Joan sucked her bottom lip into her mouth. "I can't promise something that vague. We're not out to take down your company, just here to bring back the Commodore. All we want is to have some hope of surviving against the Trade Federation's assaults. And the Lly'bra."

"Okay," Dario said. He paced to the window, looking out into the stars beyond. "Well, the first thing I should tell you is that I've got an AI that claims to be yours."

Joan rushed to him and tugged at his sleeve. "You've been talking to G.O.D.?"

"Huh? I'm just talking about an AI. I'm not religious." He turned around to look in her eyes. Her grip on his shirt made his hair stand on edge. In a good way.

Those dark eyes were filled with hope. She laughed. "No, that's the name of my AI."

I tried to tell her such a name was inappropriate, but it brought her joy. I ceased correcting her.

Dario laughed with her. "You'll have to tell me the story behind that sometime. Yeah. I've got your AI. It's how I knew about the music, the soda," he admitted.

"Ha! I thought that was too much a coincidence. Sly little program, he is." She lifted her arm, showing her handtab. "Can you transfer him back?"

Dario paused before her. He'd been enjoying having an AI to himself. He'd never needed one with his direct plug-in to the nets, everything at his mind's proverbial fingertips. There were problems with this one: the singing, the nonsense it espoused at times. But it was hers. He wouldn't keep it from her. He flicked his eyes forward, staring at the handtab and initiating a file transfer.

The progress bar above her handtab displayed "100%". Joan smiled more broadly than she had before. "Thank you!" she said. "He says thank you, too."

"Uh, you're welcome," Dario said. "Now what?"

"Well, I've been disconnected from my team with no way to find them. I believe my friend Yui was taken by your security somewhere, but I don't know where. And then there's Trian. He ran off and… Oh!"

"What's that?"

"G.O.D. says he's found Trian. I have to go to him." She rushed toward the door but looked back over her shoulder. "I'll be back, promise!"

Dario almost opened his mouth to protest. She came here needing help, and this didn't solve the situation with her ident being suspect. She was in just as much danger as before, but that AI gave her confidence. He'd at least done her some good.

Joan stepped through the door, which closed behind her as Dario watched in silence. It was better this way anyway. He needed time to decide how much to help her. One thing was certain, the AI had been right. He liked her far more than he should have. His heart ached with her gone.

CHAPTER 23

LOST AND FOUND

REGENCY BIOTECH CENTRAL OFFICE—MID-LEVEL QUARTERS, MARS
LOCAL DATE FEBRUARY 13TH, 2464

Joan hurried down the hallways of the corporate residences. Her stomach knotted, partially from the hunger that had been swelling in her for hours, but also because she may have just made the biggest mistake of her life—one that might cost her life.

She knew better than to trust people. After being ratted out by her co-conspirators back in the Navy, she had learned that lesson. When people's livelihoods were on the line, they would betray any confidence for a simple plea bargain. But just like the idiot she'd been in her late teens, she had repeated her own history. Dario already told her his knowledge of Star Empire spies aboard their Central Office, and he understood that harboring that knowledge would get him into a ridiculous amount of trouble. He didn't owe anything to her. He'd lose nothing by turning her in.

Joan hoped to high heaven she wasn't being tracked now. A quick glance back over her shoulder didn't reveal anyone chasing after her, but there were many ways one could monitor a person moving throughout a station. All kinds of bugs could have been planted on her, even the transfer of G.O.D. could have brought some coding that would both track her—and lead her to Trian, if G.O.D.'s coordinates were even true.

"Ms. Shengtu, I note that your respiratory levels are higher than normal, and production from your sweat glands have increased substantially. These symptoms are associated with fight or flight functions within biologicals. Are you in peril?" G.O.D. asked through her earpiece.

Joan hadn't heard his voice in so long that it startled her. "No… I've missed you, G.O.D.," she said with a little laugh. "I'm just thinking about Dario. Speaking to him was probably a mistake."

"Based on my analysis, I have come to a differing conclusion," G.O.D. said.

"Oh?" Joan rounded a corner, noting a couple walking the opposite direction. She tried to look as in place and professional as she could, which mainly involved keeping a straight face and walking with her chin up. "Why's that?"

"His vitals show a strong desire to mate with you. According to data regarding humankind's predispositions, that instinct will supersede rational judgment in the majority of cases."

Mate with her? Joan couldn't help herself and laughed very hard. She remembered that G.O.D. did have that virus that caused a number of malfunctions. Could anything the AI said be trusted? She bit her lip, slowing her pace to consider, and tried to suppress her amusement so that others wouldn't look her direction. She was still a couple of levels away from Trian, and had time to think about her AI. "G.O.D. are there any problems with your program?"

"As of current the virus inhabiting my programming is adequately quarantined. The interaction with station security has slowed the degradation of my systems further."

"And you're *sure* that we're on the right track to find Trian?" Joan made her way to the lift, tapping it open, stepping inside and hitting the button for two levels below.

"Yes. Mr. Mubari scanned his ident at a vacant shop off the main promenade. I searched for signs of him through the Regency corporate nets. When the scan arrived, I planted a tracker within his handtab. There is a ninety-nine point two three percent chance that we will successfully locate Mr. Mubari."

It sounded well and good, but would G.O.D. notice if there were something wrong? So far when he had gone into some sort of failure it made what he was saying gibberish, poetry or song. His specifics in odds somewhat comforted Joan. She stepped into the lift at the end of the corridor.

The lift descended the two levels, opening to the promenade shops floor. Joan followed the tracking through the map on her handtab. "I'm still worried that Dario might not be so sympathetic to us. He could have his corporate security mobilized anywhere in a second."

"It's possible, but not probable. I am monitoring Mr. Anazao's location as it is. He has not placed any such calls. Call… Call me back again. Call me if we're still friends. I don't want this to ennnnnnddd."

Joan grimaced as the AI went into that sing-song tone again. She hit the mute button on her handtab, which G.O.D. didn't attempt to override. She could follow the instructions on how to find Trian herself.

Two more turns and Joan found herself in front of a sealed cargo hold. She couldn't exactly scan her ident to get in, so how did Trian make it behind the door, if he really was there? Joan unmuted G.O.D. "Hey…"

"Leviathan echo velocity echo leviathan Twenty-three. Leviathan echo velocity echo leviathan Twenty-three. Leviathan echo velocity echo leviathan Twenty-three."

Joan shut off her AI again. So much for his systems not degenerating further. He wouldn't be any help here. Joan stared at the door, the console, trying to think of what she could do in her position to break in there. She could call Dario, but that required more trust, and she didn't want to start asking small favors of him just yet. She needed to give him some time to digest what he'd learned from her.

She sighed.

A service bot came around the corner, leading crates on a platform. Joan moved out of the way as the bot pressed forward, the door opening automatically for it.

"That's a freebie," Joan said as the doors held open for her. She stepped in and off to the side so she wouldn't be in the way of the bot.

Crates and containers lined the cargo hold, each marked with the Regency BioTech logo. Nothing surprising about that. They towered high in more than fifty rows, heading back to what looked to be a docking clamp and door for ships. None of that mattered to her now. Trian hid in here somewhere.

Joan followed her handtab's directions. It hadn't updated in awhile. G.O.D. must have lost control and that meant the tracking wasn't live. She could only hope that Tiran stayed put. She paced through the rows of crates, stepping aside for another service bot that buzzed by. She glanced around, not seeing her friend.

Then she heard footsteps. At least two people, coming from both ahead and to her right. Voices followed with them. "I haven't seen any security breaches myself, but the higher-ups have gotten real jumpy lately. I wonder what's going on," a man said.

Joan's eyes went wide. If they heard her walking around this could spell trouble. A quick glance around revealed nowhere to hide—the crates lined up in an orderly fashion that held no gaps between them, other than the walkways. Joan backpedaled.

The footsteps came closer. "Probably just extra drills because of all the craziness that's going on down on the underlevels," another voice said. "Hey, did you hear that? Sounds like someone's in here."

"One of the bots bumping into things, I'd bet."

Joan turned and started to bolt the opposite direction. She couldn't get caught, not now.

Someone reached out and grabbed her by the arm, pulling hard. Before Joan could scream, a hand covered her mouth and pulled her into somewhere dark, inside one of the crates. She struggled, elbowing her assailant, who grunted but held her firm. Her attacker locked her arms so she couldn't move. Some light trickled through the aperture to the cargo container, a door she hadn't noticed before.

The two voices she heard came closer. "That sounded like a person," one said. "Maybe we should call for back up."

The footsteps and voices came from directly in front of her. Joan slowed her breathing. Whoever held her didn't move either, at least holding off the attack while they were in danger of being discovered. Though that gave her a current advantage, Joan didn't dare risk a confrontation with the two outside. They sounded too much like corporate security.

The footsteps stopped. "I don't know. It's quiet now. We must be hearing things. Those bots can make weird noises sometimes."

A pause. "Yeah, you're right, I guess my mind's just playing some tricks on me," the other voice said. Both pairs of footsteps walked away a moment later, and the person holding her slackened their grip.

Joan immediately pushed her weight back to throw the person off balance, going for the door.

"Wait!" the person whispered firmly. A man's voice.

Joan turned around to take a look. With the small light that trickled through, she could barely make out the face. "Trian," she whispered back. "I've been looking for you. You scared me half to death."

Trian regained his balance, pushing off the back wall before hugging her. "I'm sorry I had to grab you. If those security guards saw us, that would have been the end," he said, voice still low. "Thank god you're alive, and that you found me."

"Not too far off, thanking G.O.D., that is," Joan said.

"Your AI is back then?" Trian asked, not missing a beat.

Joan nodded. "Yeah. Found him. It's a long story actually, something you'll need to know about."

"Well, we've got time. Shouldn't really leave here until we're sure those security guards won't come back." Trian helped himself to a seat on the floor of the crate. "Besides, this doesn't make a terrible base of operations."

Joan followed, sitting across from him. She leaned toward him and whispered about how she'd contacted Dario Anazao, told him about their mission and discovered that G.O.D. had managed to find his way into Dario's personal computing network.

Trian listened through the whole story, but looked very concerned. "You've given him a lot of power over us. This could be very bad, Joan. He's a corporate manager," he said.

"I know. I didn't see another way, and if I hadn't been able to get G.O.D. back, I wouldn't have found you. We'd be stuck with no idents, no way to get food or shelter. Our mission was forfeit anyway. I had to do something," Joan said. "If there's one thing I'm good at it's surviving. It'll work out."

Trian let out a small sigh. "I suppose you did what you had to. Either way, there's nothing we can do about it now. So this man is either on our side and will help us, or we're going to get turned in. Your AI hasn't told you the location of Yui, has he?"

"You saw her get taken by security, right?" Joan asked.

"I did," Trian said with a frown. "I fear for her."

"It just means we have two people to rescue, that's all," Joan said. "I wish I knew where to start with that."

"Well, the first thing we need to do is get new idents. We need to find Jake Dylan to do that. He's not been responding to comm messages, and I've tried my best to keep those obscure, with security on station tightening as it is. I'd hate for him to get tangled in this by having our frequencies tied to him."

Joan bit her lip. "It may already be too late for that. Dario said that Jake's had some problems with security himself," she said.

Trian cursed under his breath, looking off to the side.

"Yeah, we really don't have a lot of options. The best thing we can do is hope that Dario helps us. We can sway him. He sincerely believes his company is doing wrong, hurting the people down in the lower levels through neglect. I think I can persuade him to try to enact change from the inside."

Trian took a deep breath, contemplating for a long moment. "In all my years doing this, it's the riskiest proposition I can think of, relying on one person before we have time to properly vet him. But we don't have much choice, do we? For now, I suppose we should get comfortable here." He stood then, moving to the crate door to open it. No security guard hovered nearby. He turned back to Joan. "When do you see him next? And do you think you could get us some food?"

CHAPTER 24
NEWS

Dario sat through the day's staff meeting, his people all assembled around the conference room table to go over the daily figures. He found it difficult to focus on corporate matters, even when the topic of a new underlevel representative was broached.

Daniella had identified four quality candidates for the position based on their years of experience, mental aptitude tests, and computer simulations of various social pressures applied to their profiles. Their faces and a brief synopsis displayed on a holo above the conference table. Each had their own qualities, but one stood out as taking managerial leadership positions within the quality control plant that had succumb to two riots. On top of his qualifications, Tom Crowder, in each underlevel incident, assisted to bring people out of the plant to safety. He then reported the incidents to corporate security. That responsiveness drew sounds of approval from around the room.

Dario could only think of Joan. She hadn't come back since she visited him yesterday, when she had dropped verbal bombs like he could hardly believe. Star Empire spies? This was the stuff of VR holoadventures. If he told anyone here, they'd send him in for a psych evaluation, even with the riots that persisted down below. Or they would question him for corporate treason.

A full day of thinking about her, and Dario was no closer to having a solution that could be true to the corporation, protect himself and help Joan at the same time. The odd part was he cared most about helping Joan. They'd had a total of two conversations and yet he felt more connected to her than anyone in the company, even members of his own team.

The only person he would have been able to talk to about it was Jake, compromised an individual as Joan, and equally as unavailable. He wondered what kinds of drugs and torture were being used on him. Corporate security never publicized such things, but Dario doubted that they'd treat him with much respect.

That made him think about this Commodore Zhang. Emre Baker had been so excited about her capture, and this woman held enough importance that it was Joan's sole purpose to infiltrate Regency BioTech. When he had more time he would have to research the Commodore and—

"Dario?" Daniella's voice asked, holding a tinge of irritation.

"Ah, yes, sorry. What is it?" Dario said, straightening in his seat. He'd been lost in thought for too long. All of the eyes in the room locked on him.

"I just asked what you'd thought about the candidates. We are in agreement that Tom Crowder seems to be the best for the underlevel liaison position."

"Yeah. He looks great," Dario said. His words came out a lot less passionate than he would have liked, sounding exactly like he hadn't paid attention. This had been his idea to create a position, and checking out on the matter would make him lose face in front of his team. Too late now.

Before anyone could respond, the conference room doors whooshed open and his father stepped in, interrupting the meeting once again. It didn't surprise Dario anymore.

His lack of surprise didn't follow to the others. Mr. Anazao created a stir of panic among his employees. The air became thick with nerves.

"I wonder who he's here to arrest today," someone said from behind Dario.

"Good, everyone's here," Mr. Anazao said, smoothing down his coat.

"Good afternoon, Mr. Anazao," Dario said as respectfully as he could, cutting through the background chatter among his team.

Mr. Anazao gave Dario a small nod of respect in response. Someone stepped through the door behind him, a thin man with ocular implants similar to Dario's, curly black hair and a thick beard. The man stepped off to the side and clasped his hands in front of him, quiet, watching everyone. What was he, some kind of auditor? Had his father finally lost faith in Dario's ability to man the department? He couldn't have heard about the underlevel liaison idea, yet. Dario had made no report. He didn't want to alert his father until he had something firm in place.

"I hope I'm not interrupting, but I have a new member of the team who needs an introduction," Mr. Anazao said, stepping to the side and motioning toward the other man.

The curly-haired man waved to the room. "Hello, my name is Shawn Treiger," he said.

"Shawn here is going to be the younger Mr. Anazao's new assistant," Dario's father said.

Dario's eyes went wide, suddenly scrutinizing this man far more than he had when he first entered the room. Shawn was somewhat soft-spoken, but in a calculated way. His eyes scanned everything, taking things in. Recording, no doubt, with those ocular implants. He was there to monitor this team, and most importantly, Dario.

Shawn extended a hand to Dario. "A pleasure to meet you. I look forward to working with you."

Dario took the hand, not showing any hesitancy, putting on a fake smile. "Yes, it'll certainly be interesting." *I can promise that*, Dario thought. Unlike Jake, there were no question who Shawn was loyal to.

"If you wouldn't mind making room for Shawn here, I'm sure he'd love to listen and learn what's going on in the department for the rest of this meeting," Mr. Anazao said with a nod. With that, he excused himself from the room, the door shutting behind him.

Antonio scooted to the side to reveal a chair by him, which Shawn took without further word.

The new arrival had happened so fast everyone stayed silent another moment. Dario cleared his throat "You heard the man, let's get the meeting back rolling. Where were we, Daniella?"

"We were discussion the potential candidate for the underlevel liaison position," she said cautiously.

"Very well. Let's review his bio again, for the sake of our new visitor?"

Daniella pulled up the holodisplay of the man's bio once more. "Of course. As we just discussed—"

Shawn cleared his throat and raised his hand. "Pardon me, perhaps I should stop you right there."

Dario's hand clenched into a fist at his side at the interruption. Listen and learn? Shawn's first move had halted the agenda. He clamped his lips tightly so he wouldn't say something embarrassing.

Daniella raised a brow, her own irritation written all over her face. "Yes, Mr. Treiger?"

"You mention a new position for the underlevels, but I've recently been briefed by board. There's been no discussion about adding any responsibility to the underlevelers. That's part of what I'm actually supposed to present to you today. With the riots so persistent, a broader solution was needed. Corporate computer analysis has found the best one."

Angry eyes fixed on Shawn throughout the room. At least Dario knew that his team was with him, something he'd worried about in the past. This insertion, however, meant that corporate, or at the very least his father, didn't trust any of them. Couldn't his father see how insulting this was? How could he manage a company like this and be so well respected?

"Present, huh?" Antonio asked, crossing his arms.

"That's right," Shawn said, holding his ground with that cool tone, not even looking to the man at the side of him, but rather Dario, to see if he'd challenge.

Dario met his gaze, not wavering. His father had set this up and thrown this man out the airlock. But at least Dario had some authority still? "All right, say what you're going to say," Dario said.

"A solution has been proposed by corporate security and upper management with the assistance of the Trade Federation security. The problem is overpopulation. There simply aren't enough corporate jobs to give this many people a sense of purpose that will keep them pacified. The Trade Federation is revamping its fleet, which produces a one time opportunity as well."

"The fleet isn't going to attack the underlevels, is it? That's our infrastructure too," Daniella said. If she didn't sound so serious, Dario might have thought it was a joke. No one laughed.

"Nothing so crude, surely," Shawn said with a smug uptick of his lips. "No, the recommendation is that we have approximately two thirds of the underlevelers gathered, moved onto these ships with a destination of the Hyrades Cluster colonies. It will alleviate the population pressure below, and also show the currently employed population just how fortunate they are to be granted fruitful labor."

"Those are people," Dario protested, shocked by the suggestion.

"Don't worry," Shawn continued as if expecting the concern. "We'll ensure that idents are checked via lottery, and that families are kept together as much as possible. Signals will of course be broadcast to them so they understand this isn't a military invasion."

"Like that'll stop them from shooting a bunch of Trade Federation ships on sight," Daniella said.

"Agreed," Dario said. "I overheard at the RetroSilver unveiling that the last time a Trade Federation fleet went out there, they feigned a retreat and kidnapped the Star Empire's top strategist. Our ships won't be well met."

The room rumbled with talk over that.

"Is that so?" Shawn asked, his expression flat. He clearly knew more than he was letting on.

"Yes," Dario said. "I'm not sure that information has circulated through the news yet, but some people are proudly talking about it. We can't just send these people off to die. It wouldn't be right."

"As I said," Shawn said, "the plan is to give them a fair shot. We aren't inhumane."

"This proposal gives us a lot to think about. I still think we should go forward with a liaison to the underlevels," Dario said. "I don't see a reason to stop just because there could potentially be less people down there. Daniella, set up a formal interview time with this fellow we all seemed to agree upon. For now, I think it's best if we get back to work, talk about theoretical directions of the planet's population later on. Call this meeting adjourned."

People nodded their assents, talking amongst one another as his team left the conference room in a file. Daniella looked back at Dario, who waited as everyone left.

One other person waited as well, still in his seat. Shawn. He stared right at Dario, hands folded over the table.

"You may go, Daniella," Dario said, noticing the look of concern on her face. He tried his best to broadcast calm back to her.

"You sure?" She hesitated as she stood.

"Of course," Dario said, nodding.

Dario waited until the she cleared the room and met Shawn's gaze. The tension held thick in the air for a moment, but Dario wasn't going to be afraid of this man. "You're supposed to be my assistant," he said.

"Mr. Anazao told me that I would be assisting you in matters in which you lack experience or don't show a breadth of competence. Your assistant is my technical designation, but better to think of me as an extension of you."

"Extension of me? You came in here and undermined my authority." Anger welled within Dario, and he instinctively stepped toward Shawn. He tried to remember that this person in front of him was only a messenger, that the real person he had a problem with was his father, who tried to control him like a child even now.

"The direction of the meeting was going somewhere which, given circumstances, were utterly unnecessary. I voiced the reason by which you were not privy. That's all," Shawn said with a smug uptick of the corner of his lip and a twinkle in his eye.

Dario had never wanted to hit a man before, but he came near ready to smack that look right off Shawn's face. "Your idea is rather out there. Or my father's idea that is."

"It was mine. Your father thought it was an excellent one."

Disgusting. But it confirmed his anger. This wasn't a mere messenger, but someone who pulled strings as much as his strings were pulled upon. "Mass murder is what it is. At the very least uprooting the poor who already have hard enough lives. This isn't to help them, it's to rid the corporation of a problem and give the Star Empire a bigger one."

"I thought it was beautiful in its symmetry. If they shoot the refugees, they commit mass murder themselves. If they don't, they have to find a way to sustain them, taxing their resources. Either way, so many lives and credits will be saved from this war that's gone on for far too long. But the odds are that they'll take the underlevelers in, and they'll have much better lives than they ever would in the dome below. Don't you agree?"

"You know I don't. Well, I'll just not approve the concept," Dario said, but that threat felt hollow as it was. If his father was already on board, Dario had little authority he could flex.

"It's already being ratified by the board, I'm sorry to say." He lost his smirk, tilting his head slightly to the side. "Look, I'm not here to fight you. This position is an opportunity for me to show my worth to the board as much as yours is to you. I'm hoping we can have a long-term alliance, grow together. Perhaps we should move onto other matters?"

Dario turned his back on the man, something he didn't feel safe doing, but he wasn't about to stand here and listen to these toxic plans and ideas any further. "I'm not going to keep you here. I'm going to find out where they're keeping Jake, and I'm going to get him back." Another stupid thing to say, something that would be reported back to his father, surely. But it was the only way he could strike at Shawn for now. Childish, but it made him feel somewhat better.

"I'm afraid you'll not find him," Shawn said, sounding unfazed by Dario's anger.

Dario spun around to face Shawn again. "Why not?"

"Haven't you heard? Jake Dylan was convicted for his crimes of corporate treason. He's been disintegrated." Shawn blinked a couple of times.

Dario's stomach tightened. Jake? Dead? It couldn't be. He needed to verify this information. Why hadn't anyone told him? He did his best to compose himself. "Thank you for the information."

"You're welcome," Shawn said, inclining his head.

Without further word, Dario stormed out of the conference room. He couldn't work now, with thoughts whirring in his head. His one friend, broken down into mere molecules. He picked up his pace once in the main office.

"Dario," Daniella said, leaving a conversation at one of the cubicles and jogging to catch up with him. "What happened in there? Hey, Dario?"

He burst into a run, leaving Daniella and the office behind.

CHAPTER 25
OPENING MOVES

Joan once again found herself standing at Dario Anazao's door. She'd already rang the chime and been waiting for a while. He was probably working. Though, it was getting a bit late for higher management people to be on the clock from what she'd observed of the behavioral habits of the Central Office's personnel.

She slumped, leaning against the corridor wall out of weariness. She and Trian had slept in that container in the cargo bay they had found, and the cold metallic floor was worse to sleep on than the cot she had to endure in prison. She'd spent all day with a crick in her neck. She stretched it, tilting her head to the side while waiting.

The door opened just before Joan decided to give up. This time, Dario didn't greet her. The lights were low, not quite pitch dark inside, but close to it.

Joan carefully stepped inside. "Dario? Is everything all right?" she asked.

"It's been a long day," Dario said. He had his back to the door, facing the window, leaning back in one of his table chairs.

"Is now a bad time? I don't want to disturb," Joan said, not exactly sure what she'd be disturbing, but the atmosphere wasn't the most welcoming.

"It's always a bad time. Well, that's not true. Now's about as bad as it gets, but not because you're here," he said. His voice cracked a couple of times when he spoke.

Had he been crying? Joan moved forward cautiously. "Want to talk about it?" she offered, stepping toward his chair and to the side of him. She stared out his window at the stars just as he did for a long moment. The apartment did have a good view, the perks of corporate management. It couldn't beat the view of the stars from her ship's cockpit, however.

The thought made her pine for the days when it was just her and G.O.D. travelling alone. That life held tough situations from time to time, never knowing where her next meal would come from, Joan could handle that. It made her squirm to depend on the whims of one depressed corporate manager. These last couple days frightened her far more than any time she'd salvaged ships, broken into sensitive areas or stolen from powerful people.

"I don't know," Dario said.

At least he sounded honest, but then, he always did. Joan tried to lighten the tone. "Can I steal some of your food while you think about it?" she asked, brandishing a small smile for him.

He motioned a hand, but didn't move, still staring out into space. "Refrigerator's over there," he said.

Joan stepped away from him, not ungrateful by any means. She rounded the countertop and opened his fridge to take a look inside. Like most people who didn't have a lot of time, he had several pre-prepared "heat and eat" meals from the promenade. Her team would have bought several of these yesterday if they hadn't been taken by security.

Her stomach rumbled.

Joan grabbed one that had a meat flavored protein square along with real potatoes. Vegetables were easier to come by than real meat in most places, but she couldn't tell the difference between the flavored squares and the real thing anyway. She placed the package in Dario's microwave and pulled it out a moment later, instantly heated. The scent of rich steak steamed from the package. It'd been over a day since she'd eaten. Her mouth watered.

Dario still didn't move.

Joan opened up the package on the counter, scanning a couple of drawers for utensils. She finally found a fork and knife and dug in, lobbing the food into her mouth, unable to satiate her ravenous stomach. Eating felt so good.

"Jake Dylan's been executed," Dario said.

Joan held a bite of the protein square out on a fork, about to chew, but stopped herself with his words. Her shoulders tensed inadvertently. "He what?"

"He's dead," Dario said, his voice sounding as if it were his own fault.

Mid-bite, Joan swallowed as fast as she could, still talking with mouth-half full when she replied. "This is terrible news."

She almost told him there would be no way for them to get new idents, but she could tell that Jake's death cut in a much more personal way for Dario. Even though news of death didn't faze her much, she had enough tact to know not to say anything that could diminish that for him.

"Yeah, yeah it is," Dario said. He sighed deeply and buried his face in his hands.

Joan swallowed again, finishing off most of the protein square before setting her fork down. She rounded the counter toward Dario, extending an arm out. Should she touch him? The decision came more difficult than it should have, having spent so much time alone. How was she supposed to react to people, especially a person in grief? She mustered the courage and placed her hand on his shoulder.

Dario tensed, as if not expecting the touch, but soon relaxed, leaning back into her hand. "The corporation saddled me with a new assistant, one they deem to have 'less potential for troublemaking,'" he said. "I should have never let Jake talk me into going down to the underlevels. If I didn't do that, he'd still be here."

"It's not your fault. His choices were his own. We're all adults and responsible for our own actions," Joan said, though trying to keep from sounding too chastising. What she needed was for him to calm down. That would be best for him as well.

"I know. I mean, I intuitively know it, but I can't help but *feel* wrong about it."

"It's okay, I'm not judging you." She gave his shoulder a little squeeze, and then let her arm fall back to her side.

"This new guy is a real problem for me. He's set back almost everything I've started in one swoop, and he's got powerful people on board with his ideas." Dario looked over his shoulder at her.

The way his eyes caught her stopped her breath. Goosebumps raised on her arms. What was that? Joan felt herself step backward reflexively, uncomfortable to say the least. Not necessarily in a bad way, however. "Yeah? Want to talk about it?" Joan asked.

Dario considered, and then stood from his chair to pace across the length of his apartment window. "I really don't know how much to tell you, or what I'm supposed to do about you at all, really. After what you told me, and what they've done to Jake, it's dangerous to even be talking to you here. Even though I'm in a more protected situation than most people are."

Joan bit her lip, watching him. She stayed quiet. Any arguing she did at this point could further his doubts.

"At the same time," he said, turning back around to face her, "I trust you for some reason. I don't know why, call it intuition." He cast his eyes downward. "I trusted Jake, too."

"Did Jake violate your trust? Other than not being who you thought he was?" Joan asked, tilting her head to the side.

Dario looked up at her again, eyes challenging, but then softening. "No, I suppose he didn't. Everything he did was at my direction. And he pushed me toward compassion. Which I'm grateful for, because it's right. I'm honestly madder at the company for the way they disregard life, including his. That's where I feel betrayed."

Joan grimaced. "I know exactly how you feel. Even though I'm here now, and that might make this seem less than earnest, I've been just as upset with the Star Empire as you are with your company."

"Yeah?"

"Yeah. I was a part of the military for a while. Not just in a loose capacity like this, but actually in the Navy. I enlisted as soon as I was old enough to." She felt herself blushing. "I might have fudged my age a little bit. But that doesn't matter. I felt trapped on the ship. The officers treated us like scrap, and we were barely paid enough to survive—even with lodging aboard a ship. Confined quarters, working menial tasks like cleaning the relievers for twelve to sixteen hour shifts. It was a nightmare."

Joan stared out the window, recalling those days all too vividly. That part of her life had been horrible, and she hated bringing those up again in her head, remembering how her forearms ached after each shift. How she'd returned to her cramped quarters, unable to sleep from the vibrating hum of the nearby engine core. In hindsight, running off after her parents had died, with no one to guide her, no one to even care whether she lived or died was a huge mistake. But she'd persevered through that.

"You're getting upset," Dario said. He reached out a hand toward her, but dropped it, seeming to reconsider.

Joan considered that gesture for a moment, which likely made her appear more upset than she was. She would have welcomed his touch, but shook her head to clear her thoughts. "Yeah, sorry. Well, it was bad enough that a few of us took to stealing supplies out of the requisition department. We'd find some good things there, freeze dried meat—hard to find out on a Battlecruiser—datapads and comm equipment, all sorts of things. We'd trade them around for whatever we could, offloaded them at various port planets. One guy became a little too cocky though. Took too much. They came down on him, and I found out fast that people you think are your friends can turn on you when their lives are on the line."

"You went to jail?" Dario asked

"Yep, the lovely Rayknii Military Prison up on Eldris's eastern ice cap. Talk about disillusionment. I mean, if the Navy had treated me at least a little fairly, I wouldn't have been there." She shrugged and looked out at the stars beyond. Those stars were so bright when they were up close, but barely twinkled at the distance. She found herself longing to be back out in space again.

"Wow," Dario said, following her eyes to the window. "Don't take this the wrong way, but why do you work for them now?"

"Well, it wasn't exactly a choice," Joan said, laughing despite herself. "They thought my thieving skills might be an asset at breaking someone out of a prison here."

"Makes sense."

"I guess so," she said. "But I don't mind it either. No system's perfect. There's always going to be people who do better than others. Some have more talent, more luck, more willingness to work hard, all sorts of things. I really didn't have it *that* bad in retrospect. Not as bad as the people on your lower levels by any means. So, as to why, I'm trying to help people, my people, stay free to make their own decisions."

Dario went silent for a long moment, pressing his hand up against the glass in front of him. His reflection showed a deep somberness.

Joan wondered what was going on in his head. Even in her limited interactions with him, Joan saw that he was the type that took a moment to process matters, fully considered them and didn't rush into action. The opposite of her. That thought brought a small smile to her face.

"Joan?"

"Yeah?"

He turned around toward her one more time, walking up to her, that same stern look on his face. He stood about a half a head taller than her, which made Joan have to look up into his eyes. He reached out and took her hand by the fingertips before sandwiching it in between his hand.

It was warm. Joan tried not to get too distracted.

"I've decided I want to help you. Maybe this is the wrong move. Maybe you're just some sort of mastermind at manipulation and trying to get me into this situation. But I don't think so. I think you're honestly trying to help, and I think Jake was too. I want to honor his memory as best I can." He let out a deep sigh. "So the question is… what do you need from me?"

Surprised, Joan took a deep breath as she composed her thoughts. "Well…"

CHAPTER 26

ON THE RUN

REGENCY BIOTECH CENTRAL OFFICE—MID-LEVEL QUARTERS, MARS
LOCAL DATE FEBRUARY 14TH, 2464

The hallway outside Dario's quarters disappeared behind Joan. Her feet kept her going much faster than she thought they would, but this time not out of any running away, but out of pure excitement. Her gamble had paid off, and big. She had a new friend, someone with real authority in the Trade Federation. More than that, Joan relished the distinct feeling of *not* being hungry for the first time in days.

Dario had promised to help her! He trusted her and didn't ask for anything in return. Trian would flip to hear this when she found him. That wasn't exactly true. He would respond in his calm, measured way as he always did. But he would be happy inside.

She looped around the hallways and down a couple of levels back toward the cargo bay where she and Trian had set up shop, trying her best not to smile like an idiot.

"Ms. Shengtu?" G.O.D.'s voice rang in her ear.

Joan jumped despite herself, not expecting to hear the voice of her AI. "I thought I'd shut down your vocal protocol. Why are you breaking the commands?" she asked with a scolding tone. The last time he had broken through against her explicit orders, it had been to help her when she had danger. As much as the AI had problems with its programming, Joan could only take this as a warning.

"My apologies, but I noted an elevation in your heart rate and pheromone production. I had a concern for your health, which my safeties then override other commands," G.O.D. said.

Joan smirked. Her fears had been for nothing. Her AI was looking to gossip of all things. "I'm walking quickly."

"Yes, your vitals indicate more than that exertion, however. I believe the cause may have to do with Mr. Anazao."

"He did say he'd help us," Joan said, continuing toward her hideout. Fortunately, no one had noticed her abrupt stop or jump because of the AI frightening her. "That's the best news I've had in a while."

"I believe you may be missing the point, Ms. Shengtu."

"Oh?"

"Your vitals match his in what I discovered to be his desire to mate with you."

Joan dodged to avoid colliding with a wall. Her eyes went wide. Then she doubled over laughing. "G.O.D., you can't be serious. I'm not thinking about that. I have work to do."

"Biological necessities of mating do not stem from logical thought processes."

She did her best to recompose herself. Was G.O.D. trying to set them up? It wasn't the first time he'd mentioned Dario's desire for her, and Dario hadn't exactly been subtle in the way he looked her over when he thought she wasn't paying attention. Still, they'd only just met each other.

That being said, his hands had been warm. And they felt good on her skin.

Joan shook her head and continued on. "Table the discussion," she said.

"As you wish, Ms. Shengtu," G.O.D. replied.

A few people passed Joan by. She slowed her pace. The big cargo bay doors were around the corner. Lingering while waiting for a service bot to open the doors could be dangerous if the wrong people noticed her.

When she did round the corner, she stopped in her tracks.

The cargo bay doors were already open. Four armed security guards in riot gear stood in front of the cargo bay where Trian and she had made their home the last evening. They talked amongst themselves.

Okay, breathe, Joan thought. *One step at a time.* She had to keep her head low, in case they'd seen security footage that brought them here. Joan had handled these situations before. Even when someone had a clear image on a holovid, seeing the person in front of them didn't always register. The key was to make sure she didn't draw attention to herself.

She took slow steps, trying to act like any pedestrian. They would avoid security like anyone else, no eye contact. Joan watched the wall to the right of her, which displayed advertisements for Regency BioTech's new RetroSilver bodymod line.

"According to security vids, they were just here an hour ago. They've been seen around the promenade, where we arrested the other one. Rodriguez, Encarnacion, post up here. I'll take Bahr and we'll circle around for their other known locations. They can't hide forever."

Joan definitely made sure to keep her face to an angle, hoping she wouldn't be recognized as she passed them. For now, the guards seemed too engaged in their conversation, but she bet if she walked back down this hallway again she's find a plasma gun in her face before she could shout "don't shoot."

She'd made that mistake once before.

Within moments Joan was out of earshot, not slowing or lingering long enough to hear more. Though it would have been nice to get more details of their plans to find her, getting caught wouldn't be worth that.

At least those guards hadn't mentioned looking for a "they". It meant that Trian had managed to escape their notice as well. She'd lost him again already, irritatingly enough. Making the same mistakes twice boded ill for the mission and their future survival.

The problem was that she worked alone. Staying together or making sure she could find her teammates never occurred to her. With luck, G.O.D. would be able to direct her to Trian.

She continued down the hall, taking a couple of turns to head back to the lift. The safest place for right now would be back with Dario. No one would be looking for her there. But she had just left him, and did want him to have time to think. What alternatives did she have?

Next time, she would set up a backup location to meet Trian. Somewhere they hadn't spent a significant amount of time before, like an abandoned shop, or an ice cream parlor. The latter sounded very good right about now.

The corridor stretched out for a long ways, various corporate personnel quarters on either side, with, other than the unit number, very little to differentiate them.

She took a right toward the lift, passing by a lounge that had several tables and people conversing and mingling.

"Joan," a voice said.

She turned around and looked back. Trian was seated, facing away from the way she was walking, not looking up from a datapad which concealed about half of his face. "You have to stop sneaking up on me like that. I swear I'm going to deck you one of these times," Joan said, giving a quick scan to see if security had followed her. All looked clear, so she seated herself across from him.

"We probably shouldn't stay together for long," Trian said. "Security is onto us. They have our faces, our old idents, our real identities, everything. They must have tortured Yui. Or Jake. I don't know," he said, voice barely over a whisper.

"Jake's dead, Trian. Dario told me. They disintegrated him."

If his face had been solemn before, it turned as white as a ghost with this news. "Jake…" he said. His eyes closed for a moment and he breathed in through his nose, and out again. His eyes fluttered open and locked on Joan. "There's no time for grieving, not now. Part of me wishes you hadn't told me."

"Sorry."

"No, you gave me vital information. It shows the corporation here isn't fooling around. They're out for blood for whatever reason. We will have to move quickly."

"Move? Where?"

Trian lowered the datapad and pulled up a command on his handtab. "Handtab please," he said.

Joan, confused, lifted her wrist.

Trian hit a transfer command and Joan's handtab started to glow. The process was quick, the files pulling up almost instantly.

A picture, a retinal scan that matched hers and a name of someone completely different. A new ident. "How did you…"

"I'm here to be the political operative. I make friends and have other sources. In case you get compromised, it's best for you not to know more. We've already had too much given up through Jake and Yui. Until we're out of the corporate reach and down at the under-levels," Trian said. He glanced back over his shoulder, scanning carefully.

"Okay," Joan said. "But what about the mission? I'm making some pretty good progress. If I just had another day or two…"

"We may not have another day or two. I don't know right now, but our safety comes first. Getting captured does no one any good. Anyway, we should split up again. Meet at the bar on the underlevels when we first arrived here, okay? You remember where that is?" Trian asked.

"Yeah. At the very least G.O.D. can find it," Joan said.

Trian nodded and slid out of the chair, moving into a brisk walk a moment later, datapad tucked under his arm. He slipped off as quickly as he had found her.

Joan slumped in the chair. They were getting so close to finding Commodore Zhang. Why did security have to catch onto them now?

She grimaced. What could she do? Could she risk doubling back to Dario's again? She may be on camera, and the security guards might well be checking her formal paths. It would be a very big gamble. One she wouldn't take without guidance. "G.O.D.?" Joan whispered, trying not to draw the attention of nearby tables.

"Ms. Shengtu," her AI said, before his singing voice took over again. "Are we, are we, are we ready to party it up all night, like there's no daybreak in sigh-ight?"

"Something like that. I'm going to hope that your singing virus doesn't actually hinder your processing capability too much," Joan said. "I assume you monitored the recent conversation?"

"Of course. I monitor every conversation unless privacy mode is engaged. That's part of my matrix's standard programming. Would you like me to replay a portion of it?"

"No, that's not exactly what I was asking," Joan said. "I was more curious your thoughts on the situation."

"My analysis of your situation is that Mr. Mubari's plan gives you the highest probability of potential outcomes for safety, but diminishes your probability of mission success."

"How much does it diminish mission success by?"

"Fifty three point two five percent."

"And what were the odds of success before?"

"Approximately eleven point three seven percent."

"So this leaves us with about a five percent chance of success." Joan shook her head. That was about as bad as it could get, though she was somewhat surprised to hear that her potential success rate was even as high as eleven percent. There had to be another option.

"G.O.D. is there a safe place I can open a comm link and talk to Dario?" Joan asked.

"Processing. Stand by."

Joan waited, watching a couple leave a table in the lounge by her. She scanned the area, but still no sign of security for now.

"There is a private communications booth in sector 7 that should

meet your requirements. Coordinates transmitted to your hand...
your hand, I just wanna hold your hand." He started singing again.

This time the AI didn't stop singing. Joan couldn't turn it off other
than silencing him once again on her handtab. She wished that she
had time to ask G.O.D. a few more questions. She really could use his
full help right about now, especially with odds of her mission success
being so low. At least he did give the directions.

Perhaps Dario had some better ideas as to what she could do
before vacating the Central Office. Joan had a feeling that if they left
this place, they'd meet with dead ends down below. She'd seen the
way the people there were treated. They had access to nothing. That
thought didn't seem appealing.

She slid out of her chair, turning to head down another hallway,
the same direction Trian had gone. Her handtab directed her to turn
left and left again before she found a row of communication booths
as promised. The only gamble was the new ident that Trian provided
her. Would it work? Hopefully the corporation hadn't traced her prior
identity and weren't monitoring Dario's calls.

As with far too much lately, Joan felt she had little choice.

She tapped the door control to open it. Inside was a small cush-
ioned seating area, a holodisplay and a single light that shined down
to give a clear image of her face. She contacted Dario.

Dario's comm came through audio. "Joan? Is everything okay" he
asked.

"Yes. No. I have to get off the Central Office here. It's not safe. I
wanted to let you know... or to see if you had any other suggestions."

"What? What happened?"

"Security discovered us. They found our identities, where we were
hiding, traced our recent whereabouts, everything. It's too dangerous
to stay here."

"That's not good," Dario said, concern apparent in his voice.

"No, it's not."

"I don't see any alternatives."

"You could always stay with me."

Joan stared at the sound-proofed foam wall for a long moment before replying. She wished she could take him up on that offer.

"Joan?" Dario asked.

"I'm sorry. I can't do that. It's too dangerous. They're looking for me already. This might even be monitored. No, I can't put you at risk like that. It'd likely get us both into big trouble."

"I'm willing to take the risk."

"I know you are. It's very sweet of you, and don't think I'm unappreciative. That's not what I mean at all," Joan said. His offer did bring a little warmth to her chest. She thought about what G.O.D. had said earlier. Maybe he was right. She did like Dario.

But she didn't have time to think about that let alone act on it.

Dario sighed on the other end. "Yeah, you're right," he said. "It was a stupid thought."

"Not stupid, just not viable."

He went quiet on the other end for a moment.

"Dario?" Her turn to ask after him. Why was this so hard?

"Yeah, sorry. Thinking. I did a little research into the Zhang person you told me about," Dario said. "Be better to talk about it in person than on a line."

"I don't think we'll have that opportunity," Joan said, hoping the regret she felt came through in her own tone.

"Yeah, well, remember the plan that I'd told you about, with the company shipping out all of the underlevelers and leaving them on the hands of the Star Empire?" Dario asked.

"How could I forget? A spaceside concentration camp," Joan said flatly.

"Well, with my clearance levels I was able to do a little digging. Turns out that your friend is set to be on the first ship departing through the program."

"What?" Joan's heart nearly stopped with that information.

"Yeah. That's not the only thing. I... I'm going to try to talk to corporate or at least my father on this one, but they've already set a launch date of tomorrow morning, prior to first shift. They're planning on going when everyone's sleeping. Amazing how fast they move," he said, bitterness heavy in his voice.

"Dario, this is very, very bad," Joan said. "I have to find Trian again right now; I don't have another moment to spare."

"Look, I'm going to do what I can, see if I can stop this or at the very least delay it. See if I can do something, or if cooler heads can prevail once less people are on edge about all of this rioting. I don't know." He paused again for a long moment. "I'm sorry, Joan."

"Nothing to be sorry for. You didn't do it."

"I can't help but feel somewhat responsible. I'm part of this company, I work for these people. I wish I could help you more."

"You've already done a lot. Thanks, Dario. I... I really hope I can see you again," Joan said.

"I hope so too."

"I gotta go." With that she killed the comm line. She could go back and forth saying goodbye forever, and she knew very well that he wanted to keep her on the line for about that long.

Joan stepped out of the booth, looking around. "G.O.D. do you still have a read on Trian's location, even with his new ident in place?" She reluctantly tapped on her handtab to unmute her AI.

"I do, I do, I do. And I'm so in luh-uv with you, with you, with you."

Truth be told, the singing wasn't that bad, and Joan noticed at least he tried to answer her questions when he did sing. It just took a little longer than the direct approach. "Put it up on my handtab display," Joan said.

Within moments, a map leading to where G.O.D. read Trian's ID displayed. He wasn't too far ahead, his signal passing through the main promenade. He probably needed to eat, just as Joan had. It was lucky she found Dario after all.

She had to put those thoughts out of her head before they

escalated. Joan shook her head at her own priorities and then went to go find Trian again.

CHAPTER 27

CONFRONTATIONS

REGENCY BIOTECH CENTRAL OFFICE—TOP LEVEL, MARS
LOCAL DATE FEBRUARY 14TH, 2464

Dario made his way up the lift, to the top level of the Central Office. The level produced an aura of greatness for its higher ranking officials, with pure transparent ceilings, gaudily displaying the entirety of the starscape beyond. The domed ceiling reflected a translucent corporate logo. The statement the design made was a clear one: it took something as large as the Regency BioTech Corporation to reach out and grab those stars. No one down below would ever get to see a view like this.

The receptionist recognized his face, allowing him brush past her to the large conference room beyond the counter. More than a dozen people sat inside that room watching a presentation. None looked up at him.

Dario hooked a right down a long aisle of executive offices, some even with large side-rooms for their assistants. His father would be in the one next to the COO. A placard adorned the doorway: *Kostas Anazao, Chief Financial Officer.*

Dario scanned his ident and the doors slid open for him. Not directly into his father's office, but to his private reception, where his assistant, a slender woman in her late sixties, sat at a desk.

"Dario. Why this is unexpected. I can't remember the last time you visited." Amy Goodnow spoke with trained kindness, just professional enough of a greeting to not alarm someone, but let them know they weren't particularly wanted here either.

"Hey Amy. I have some business to discuss with Mr. Anazao. Is he in?"

"Why, he's in a meeting right now. Would you like me to leave a message for you? I'm sure he'd be happy to visit with you later. Amy pivoted in her chair to type something.

"Who's he meeting with?" Dario asked.

Amy stopped typing and checked her display. "Someone… Shawn Treiger? That's your new assistant, isn't it? How's he working out for you?" she asked. She sounded half-sincere, and didn't bother to look back up at him.

The blood drained from Dario's face. Shawn was already in there, no doubt giving a report of everything that transpired in the meeting earlier, and making a list of everything that was wrong with Dario's department, whether true or not. The whole point of the man's task was to sabotage Dario, even if his father thought of it as looking after him.

After the pause, Amy did glance his direction. "Is something the matter?"

Dario faked a smile. Two could play at the professional disinterest game. "Oh no, I was just thinking about some deadlines. Shawn is working out just fine, I'm sure," Dario said. Fine for his father at the very least. "Maybe I can just pop in there? He is my assistant after all, can't hurt to have me in on the conversation."

"I'll buzz Mr. Anazao and let him make the call," Amy said, mirroring his smile, but looking away almost instantly as she contacted her father inside. "Mr. Anazao? Your son his here. Uh huh. Yes. Uh huh. Right away, sir."

Dario raised an expectant brow.

Amy returned her attention to him. "You may enter," she said.

The doors opened. Shawn was seated in one of the three chairs across from Mr. Anazao's large desk. The back wall displayed rotating product lines as well as a Trade Federation corporate exchange ticker across the bottom third. The office wasn't decadently large, but functional, and with a holodisplay of all of the amenities that accounting could need.

Shawn stared at Dario, facial expression flat. He said nothing.

"Dario," Mr. Anazao said, inclining his head but not standing. "I wasn't expecting you."

No, you were planning to run my department without me, Dario thought. But all three of them knew that, and no one was remorseful about it. "I figured it was time to talk," Dario said.

"That it is. That it is," Mr. Anazao agreed. "Shawn has delivered me a report of all of the recent goings on in your department, starting with the meeting that I inserted him into."

Dario's face appeared on the holodisplay, dressed in clothes from the prior day's meeting. His father gave a nod to Shawn, who had a blank look from his oculars that Dario recognized. Something that he did often as he was bringing up playback of memory files.

On the screen, Dario shifted and spoke, "Mass murder is what it is. At the very least uprooting the poor who already have hard enough lives. This isn't to help them, it's to rid the corporation of a problem and give the Star Empire a bigger one."

"Pause," Mr. Anazao said.

The image on the wall froze, Shawn saying nothing.

"Do you have anything to say for yourself?" Mr. Anazao asked.

Dario shrugged, trying to keep his expression unemotional. He had stumbled into an inquisition about his attitudes, something Dario felt was right. He wouldn't give into the bait.

"You were told that a plan was pitched and agreed upon by the board, and yet you attempted to undermine the board's decisions by calling them into question. Mass murder? Really?" Mr. Anazao shook his head. "This is bad public relations. Your job in management is to enact board decisions, stand behind them and ensure people under you maintain the company line."

"If the company line isn't murder, sure," Dario said, unable to hold back his biting tone. Why couldn't his father see the problems here? The real people being hurt by these crazy plans?

"I've already explained this to you," Shawn chimed in.

Dario's father held his hand out to Shawn to motion for him to stop. "Yes, you have. Let me handle this please, Mr. Treiger."

That silenced Shawn for the time being. The man cast his eyes downward.

"This is the execution of millions of innocent people. Or at the very least uprooting them, exposing them to who knows what's out in the colonies. It's hurting people and you know it," he said. "There's no getting around that."

"It's giving them a chance at a better life. The Star Empire colonies are all about independence, forging out for a new path. This gives the people who are set on disrupting our system, one that works very well, the chance to do just that. It's exactly what both groups want, and it alleviates our rioting problem by reducing the population here to a more sustainable level for the corporation's charities," Mr. Anazao said, scripted, passionless. It was as if he simply read a press release.

It was utter scrap. Dario narrowed his eyes at his father. What could he do? He had no authority here, no ability to change the board's mind if they had already made a decision.

"Dario, I know you've been manipulated unfairly. You're not going to be in trouble. Not going to lose your corporate position. There's no risk of incarceration for your dissension. However, I do need you to stop voicing these subversive ideas in ineloquent manners. If our competitors got hold of the words of a manager like that, do you know the harm it could do to our stock?"

"This isn't about P.R.," Dario said, crossing his arms in front of him. "This is about people. What would you do if you were one of the underlevelers. Haven't you considered what it'd be like to be in their shoes? One job for every, what, million people? Of course there're riots. No one has a sense of purpose, they may have enough to survive, but they always see that up here we have far more. And there's nothing they can do to get out."

"How would you fix it?" Shawn asked.

"I don't know, but what I was saying in the meeting is a good start. We need to listen to them, find out how they can take charge of their own lives and we can facilitate that, rather than just dictate to them what corporate charity is. That just furthers the resentment," Dario said.

"I believe Shawn's solution solves issues with resentment already. This isn't a debate though, Dario. What's done is done. We even have Trade Federation peacekeeping forces ready to escort and transport the refugees in modified Megahaulers, starting two days from now."

Dario frowned about that. This was all information he'd found with his clearance on the nets, but he still hoped the corporation wouldn't move that fast. But of course they would. They had to get this all out and done with before the news cycles hit, before someone like him blew the whistle and made it a nightmare for them to act, trapping them in bureaucracy. Dario thought about being that person himself, but wasn't sure that he would do much good other than get himself ostracized from the company.

Mr. Anazao did give him a point of contention, however.

Dario uncrossed his arms and raised a finger. "Wait, you said Trade Federation personnel will be escorting them? We're going to send out our own corporate security and that of other companies into Star Empire space? That's a suicide mission. We can't do that to our own people." Dario believed every word of his point, but hoped this argument would hold more weight than his caring about the under-levelers' lives.

Mr. Anazao leaned back, face ever stoic. "Those numbers have been calculated and determined to be acceptable losses."

"Acceptable losses?" Dario's jaw dropped. He could tell by looking in his father's eyes that the man at least had some reservation about that. People couldn't be distilled down to soulless numbers, no matter how computers generated acceptable losses, or how the board's public relations department spun the words.

"The personnel involved are on a volunteer basis, knowing that this is an extremely sensitive mission," Mr. Anazao said.

"But even if they're volunteering, these personnel don't know what they're going to be dying for. To exterminate unwanted people!"

"Dario, you're raising your voice and sounding unprofessional."

Dario couldn't help but laugh. "I'm unprofessional? This whole thing is crazy. I can't believe it. You're out of control to allow this. Both of you." He motioned between Mr. Anazao and Shawn.

Shawn frowned, but said nothing.

Mr. Anazao let out a deep breath, maintaining his calm. "Even if you have valid points, the launch is already scheduled for the first wave. There's nothing we can do to stop it now. Why not wait and see the results? It may not be as bad as you think."

"Like hell," Dario said, turning on his heels and stomping back out the door.

"Dario, wait!" Mr. Anazao said, the doors shutting before he could say anything further.

It didn't matter what his father thought anymore. He'd gone too far, and Dario wasn't about to sacrifice his soul for this stupid company. His father was wrong. There had to be ways to stop this ridiculous plan. It wasn't just Dario involved in this fight. He couldn't justify putting Antonio's career and life in jeopardy, but he had Joan, and whoever Joan was working with on her team. Dario still had his access codes, and then…

…and then he didn't have a plan. This was far out of the scope of his general work. His schooling had been in business management, productivity and operations. What could he do? Sabotage? He didn't even know how ship systems worked, or where to even start. He could try to go to the press, but it might be too late to affect change there, and as he'd thought before, that would certainly end his career. The company would take any access he had.

Whatever he did, he would have to use the access that he did have, before his father could confiscate that again. He needed a way to get to Joan. She seemed to have a level head on her shoulders, understanding the ways of the universe far better than Dario could with his sheltered, corporate experience. Maybe she could come up with a better plan.

CHAPTER 28

THE BOTTLENECK

Joan wished she had a better plan. With no time to analyze her situation, thousands of peoples' lives on the line, and G.O.D. on the fritz, it wasn't as if she had many options.

Trian proved easy to find. He scouted the lift down to the surface levels where hundreds of people lined up for security scans. They had been through this security zone before, when Joan and her team had entered the Central Office, but now that security was looking for them specifically, danger loomed here.

From the look on Trian's face, he was hesitant about his plans as well.

"Trian," Joan said, approaching from the side.

Trian tensed, eyes going wide before relaxing with recognition when he turned. "Joan," he said, his voice soft. "You scared me half to death. I thought the plan was to meet down on the underlevels? It's not safe to be together."

Joan looked back over her shoulder. No one seemed to be coming for them. "Sorry. Something important came up. I have you tracked through your handtab. G.O.D. has the signature."

Trian frowned. "That's not good. If any of that information is traced through the company's nets, it could lead right to us. We could be compromised."

"Anything we do compromises us at this point. Even breathing." Joan understood his hesitancy. It wasn't paranoia. But there was no reason to worry about what they couldn't control. They had to work with what they had.

"I gather you have some fresh news?" Trian asked, observing her. "I only left you a few minutes ago."

"Yeah," Joan said. "Everything's changed."

"Oh?" Trian asked, raising a brow.

In the last couple of days he seemed to have aged a couple of decades. He looked tired. Though Joan was sure she looked tired, too. "Yes. It turns out it's good we're getting off the station, but we need to get to the spaceport, and access. Quickly," Joan said, eyes drifting over toward the line that formed for security.

"Access?" Trian asked, turning his head to see where Joan looked. "Slow down. What are you talking about?"

Joan lowered her voice, leaning toward him. "Dario found Commodore Zhang. She's due to be shipped out with a group of underlevelers. I think the plan is to have the Star Empire see several Trade Federation ships entering their space and then have our forces shoot them on sight. The Trade Federation would then out the Star Empire for killing civilians, as well as the botched job as killing our own Commodore." She could hardly believe it when she said it. Either someone on the board of this company was a ruthless tyrant, or groupthink really did push people toward stupidity.

"What?" Trian asked, a little too loudly. A couple people who passed by glanced in their direction. He dropped is voice again. "Sorry. I wasn't prepared for that news. This exemplifies our plight with the Trade Federation's policies. Threat of Blob invasion? They sit for years allowing the colonies to be decimated. When the poor make a fuss? They move quickly to exterminate them. Unbelievable. No, it's what I expect. That's the worst part."

Joan bit her lip, considering what she could do in this situation. "I know. If we can get clearance into their launch area, I'm sure we could sneak onto the ship at the very least. Maybe take over the ship's system and divert it?"

"Joan, that's very dangerous."

"I know, but I don't see a better alternative. We can't extract Commodore Zhang from a holding cell here. Even if we succeeded with that, we'd be hiding her on a Trade Federation world with security everywhere. Security that's actively looking for us, I might add. We can't get a message out to our people without getting killed ourselves." Joan let out a breath. "I think we should try it. We're out of options."

Trian frowned. "I don't—"

He shut his mouth, turning toward the security line as if they were passengers. He grabbed Joan by the arm and tugged her along with him.

"Hey!" Joan said, her arm stinging from the rough handling.

"A squad of security personnel right behind us. They're looking for us," Trian whispered "Act as if you're a regular tourist."

Joan did her best to not show her tension, to appear bored in line, as they moved toward the checkpoint. A couple hundred people stood between them and the security scanner. What happened when they reached the front? Were the officers who checked idents ready for them? Hopefully the new ones that Trian had secured would have no problems.

She wanted to ask Trian if he could see what was going on, if they were making their way through the crowd, but she dared not cause a disturbance.

Trian stared straight ahead, moving with the crowd. His eyes betrayed that weariness he'd been showing Joan all day.

The crowd rustling answered her unasked question for her. People behind her made rude comments. Security officers moved by, checking every person in line. The officers pushed forward, bumping into Joan and causing her to stumble forward.

The officers didn't turn around for her and Trian, but continued toward the scanner. When they appeared to be out of earshot, Joan looked at Trian nervously. "We have to get out of line."

"We can't, it'll be too obvious," Trian said under his breath.

"Oh no," Joan said in a louder tone. "I left my datapad at my boyfriend's residence. I need to head back and get it." She tugged on Trian's sleeve. "Don't leave without me. We can catch the next lift?"

Trian's expression went very flat. There was no doubt he understood the plan, but Joan could tell he didn't like it. Much like any plan Joan devised. "But we already paid for the tickets."

"We can eat the fee. Come on," Joan said, tugging on his sleeve to move the both of them off to the side of the line.

Leaving the line proved to be a bad idea. One of the security officers ahead looked back, his visor reflecting from the light of the large atrium. He pointed at them almost immediately. "You there! Stop!"

"Dammit," Joan said. She motioned her head in the opposite direction of the security officers, not waiting for Trian to respond before breaking into a run.

Running wasn't easy with a crowd of people lining up, moving their luggage, standing around bored. It was all she could do not to plow people over, weaving in and out of various people. Out the corner of her eye, Joan could see that Trian managed to keep up.

Security kept up as well.

Joan assessed the situation with a single glance over her shoulder. Three security officers in total, one slower than the others. With their helmets and visors and likely plasma-retardant vests, they'd be bogged down a little more than Joan. That was a plus. The minus was that this was their territory. They had help coming anywhere they wanted, which could cut off Joan's options.

She scanned the large room. Shops lined the security checkpoint, providing the masses places to eat and travel items people might have forgotten on their way planetside. Convenience. A few vendors stood at carts rather than back in shops. Nowhere inconspicuous to hide.

The whole area was packed with people trying to get to their respective lifts. The best Joan could hope for would be to lose security in the scuffle.

A hand grabbed at her back, nearly getting hold of the fabric of her shirt. Joan twisted away, looking back over her shoulder once more. One of the security guards had caught up.

She immediately stopped in her tracks, causing the security guard to do the same, but turning to face her. He ran into another person, falling to the ground, taking several people with them as they reached out for something to hold onto.

Joan weaved the opposite direction, aiming to put as much distance between her and that security officer as possible before he could get back up again.

Trian huffed, barely keeping up with her. "You're fast."

"I've had experience with this before," Joan said, hopping over a bag that another traveler dragged by the wheels. "I think they won't risk firing their plasma pistols in a crowd like this."

"I would hope not. You know how to get us out of here?" Trian asked, jogging after her.

"Maybe. I try not to get into these situations. It's bad odds."

A pair of security officers found an opening, circling around Joan and Trian to try to flank them. The one who tried to grab her was back on his feet, having produced a plasma pistol. His face was hot with anger.

Joan needed something to even the odds. This is usually when she'd ask G.O.D. for help, but if he was still in singing mode, she couldn't deal with the distraction. What else could she do? Even if she managed to get out of this jumbled mess, it would be into a hallway, or another zone of the Central Office with less people present. At that point, the security officers would be able to shoot Trian and her.

"Function. Unmute AI," Joan said loud enough so her earpiece would pick it up with the ambient noise. "G.O.D. I hope you can maintain control of yourself for just a few moments."

No response.

The two security officers moved in like pincers. With the rate the crowd of people were moving they would reach them in moments. "Trian, I know this is going to sound crazy. But you need to head straight for that security officer to your right. I'll take the one on your left. If we run right into them, we might surprise them long enough to get through," Joan said.

"Okay," Trian said.

Joan headed straight for the security officer on the left, weaving around bystanders in the way, though feigning as if she still tried to slip by him. He tried to grab her, but Joan burst forward, delivering a hard kick to his private parts. He doubled over, moaning.

She looked back to the side. Trian had managed to push his officer over as well. Joan looked down at her handtab. Her security remained locked. That's why her command to G.O.D. failed. She tapped with her thumbprint scan, the handtab coming to life.

"Function, Unmute AI!" Joan shouted again.

"Ms. Shengtu," G.O.D. said in that calm, unchanging voice that could only come from an AI. "I understand you're in a predicament. I have a potential solution should you be able to evade security's watchful eye for a few moments."

"Lay it on me, I don't have time!" Joan said, looking behind her. The other officer was catching up again. Joan slipped behind two larger men, pushing one in the back forward so that he'd disrupt the area.

The man turned around, irate, but by the time he could react, Joan had put considerable distance between them. The man had served well as a blockade. Trian moved back to her side. "You're good at this," he said, sounding like he was having trouble breathing.

"We're almost clear," Joan said, ignoring the compliment. She hoped that was true.

A map display of G.O.D.'s plan appeared over her handtab. There was a vendor cart right ahead. If she could sneak behind that somehow, she'd be in the clear.

Joan ducked, still pressing forward, but kept her head low, not quite in a crouch. Her goal was to lose the people behind her, or at least make them stop to look around.

Trian did the same, keeping close behind her. They weaved through another twenty or so people. Security didn't appear to be catching up this time.

They approached the vendor stall, an insta-recharge station for datapads, handtabs, all sorts of devices. A bot operated the counter, which made it easier to slip past unnoticed. Joan slinked behind the counter, using the bot as a shield, though she didn't see a hallway where the handtab indicated she should go.

"G.O.D., where did you lead us?"

"You're relying on your AI with the virus?" Trian asked.

"Shh," Joan said.

"Behind the crate to your left," G.O.D. said, "there is a maintenance bot hatch. Based on your size and shape, you should be able to hide yourself within its dimensions."

"Got it," Joan said, wasting no time. She moved to push the crate aside and dove inside the tunnel which was just where G.O.D. said it would be. Trian followed her inside.

The only problem was they didn't have a way to move the crate back to conceal their escape. Security wouldn't fail to notice the human-sized hole in the wall, which meant they would be caught in no time.

Joan continued down the tunnel, crawling on hands and knees against the rough metallic flooring. Her knees ached with every push forward. Each movement also caused a *clang* against the aluminum tunnel floor. So much for subtlety.

After several lengths forward, the shaft split into two directions. Joan took the right one, not consulting her handtab this time. Trian was right behind her.

"Do you know where you're going?" Trian asked, his whisper

fading into white noise in the tunnel.

"No, just away from the security guards," Joan whispered back.

The sound of a plasma pistol readying pierced through the tunnel.

"That's not good," Trian said.

"No, it isn't," Joan said, scurrying forward with an even more fevered pace. "G.O.D. get us out of here!"

"Calculating a trajectory for probable escape. Processing. Processing. Processing. Ms. Shengtu, I am afraid that there is a low probability of escape," G.O.D. said.

"I can see that!" Joan shouted, as if that would do any good. She reached the end of the line before it turned again. When she headed right, she could see security catching up behind her.

The officer fired two shots which fizzed off the wall just as Joan and Trian cleared the corner. This next length went on for a long way. Far too long to avoid a shot when the officer rounded the corner.

"We'll never make it down there in time. He'll shoot us!"

"Gah," Joan muttered. Trian was right, but they had nowhere else to turn.

"What do we do?" Trian asked. The noise of knees hitting the metallic flooring echoed. The security officer would be on them in seconds.

Joan frowned, considering. "I think we have to give up."

"I don't like that plan," Trian said.

"You don't like any of my plans."

"For good reason!"

"I did warn you about the probabilities of success," G.O.D. chimed in. "Your current plan does increase your odds of survivability over the next hour by seventy two point five three percent, but decreases long-term survivability to zero."

"Not much I can do about it right now," Joan said, turning right back around and squeezing past Trian. "Security! Don't shoot! We are giving up!" Joan said.

Just as she spoke the security officer rounded the corner, nearly bumping heads with Joan. Rattled, he scrambled for his plasma pistol, pointing it at her. "Don't move," he commanded.

"I wasn't planning on it." Joan stayed very still, in case the officer was a little trigger happy.

"Turn back around, keep going. There'll be an exit into a cargo bay about twenty meters ahead," the security officer said.

Joan did as he commanded. So did Trian. The three moved through the tunnel, before heading out of a similar entranceway to the lift atrium.

When she stood back up, Joan was greeted with another three plasma pistols pointed directly at her. One of the security officers jammed his gun into her side, hitting her in the rib and kidney.

Joan doubled over, the pain reeling through her.

"Easy!" another security guard said.

"This Blob witch kicked me in the crotch! Fair's fair," he said, backing away but showing no remorse.

"Doesn't matter. Don't give her any ammunition for the courts. We're under enough pressure as it is," the other officer said. He inclined his head toward the officer who had captured them in the tube. "Good work. Escort the prisoners to detention block three."

The walk through the corridors of the Central Office went in silence. Joan looked over to Trian only a couple of times, not wanting to spook any of the guards. She didn't really have a plan to escape at this point. Joan bit her lip.

"Ms. Shengtu," G.O.D. said in her earpiece. "I have taken the liberty of analyzing your current situation. I see no alternatives to the holding cell."

Tell me something I don't know, Joan thought. They continued along a hallway, keeping away from main commerce areas. Some people still rubbernecked to see who was headed toward detention, but Joan didn't give them an interesting show.

The detention area loomed ahead, a glowing sign that said "Trade Federation Private Security" above armored doors. It looked much like she'd seen in the Star Empire when she'd been in this position before. This was likely the end. If they had executed Jake, it was good odds that Yui had suffered the same treatment. She and Trian wouldn't be far behind.

To be honest, the mission was a doomed one from the start. Joan's prior career revolved around getting in and out of stations and ships as quickly as possible. She didn't linger, waiting for security footage and computer analysis to catch up with fake identification. She wasn't exactly afraid to die at this point. It's not like she had much going for her life even if she did succeed. But even after trying her hardest for the Star Empire, gathering just enough information to give her and her friends hope, she found herself in the same situation as she had been when she was caught stealing on the *Destiny*. The same situation where she had been set up at Balibran Station. Yui had been right about her. Joan was a failure, with little to offer anyone.

One of the security officers scanned his ident against the console in front of the detention center, sliding the armored door open. Joan and Trian were ushered inside to a waiting area, guarded by someone behind a translucent blue shield. Her captors spoke with the stationary guard, who nodded and let the shield down. "We'll have to process them. Holopics, retina scans, thumb prints," the guard said.

"I know the drill," the security officer agreed.

Joan looked at Trian and considered making a move. There were five security officers and two of them. The odds weren't the worst she'd encountered, but they had weapons and she didn't.

Still, when the corporation researched who they were, found out the truth, it's not like they would fare better. Fighting now, going down while trying to resist, would at least save them the torture of a cell and phony trial.

One of the security guards looked off to the side, as if to strike up a conversation.

Joan saw her opportunity. It was now or never. This would be her best shot. She shifted her weight, aiming to pummel the distracted guard and make a hostage out of him…

The doors to the detention center opened. Dario Anazao stood at the entrance.

CHAPTER 29

RESCUE AND SEARCH

REGENCY BIOTECH CENTRAL OFFICE—DETENTION CENTER, MARS
LOCAL DATE FEBRUARY 14TH, 2464

Dario caught Joan's eye as soon as he entered the detention area. *Please stay still, please stay still!* Dario tried to communicate to her telepathically.

She didn't get the message.

The guard in front of her stumbled as Joan threw her weight onto him. He reached for his pistol, but Joan delivered a blow to his wrist before he could.

Her maneuver alerted two other guards who drew their plasma pistols in turn. "Prisoner's trying to make a break for it!" one shouted.

Dario waved his hands frantically to get their attention. "Hold your fire! Hold your fire!"

"Who are you?" One of the security officers asked, turning toward the door. His plasma pistol pointed directly at Dario's chest. The other two guards subdued Joan.

At least the guards followed directions, and no plasma pistols discharged. Yet. An air of confusion filled the detention area. Dario put his hands up to ensure there would be no misunderstanding. "I'm Dario Anazao. Kostas Anazao's son. You know the name?" He asked, banking on his father's corporate status. He hated doing it, but at least he had that option.

Two security officers looked at each other blankly, but the third, the one who had been wrestling with Joan shook his head. "That's the CFO, idiots." He turned to Dario. "What's a big wig doing down here?"

"I…" Dario hadn't thought through exactly what he was going to say. Truth be told, he ran down as quickly as he could when he realized Joan was in danger. But he could think on the fly. That's all he'd been doing since being promoted to the management role. "I have orders from the board," Dario said, pointing toward Joan and Trian. He tried to keep a serious expression. Business. Professionalism. "About these two, actually. They're involved in matters of corporate espionage. Big stuff. I'm supposed to take them directly to the board for interrogation."

The guard stepped over to a computer terminal and tapped a few commands. "I don't see any orders about this."

"You're Trade Federation security, this is internal corporate for Regency BioTech here on the station. Wasn't time to go through all the channels to get here. Scan my ident though; I'm who I say I am." He tried not to look at Joan through this. The sight of her could shatter the confidence he tried to portray.

"Look," Dario continued. "You've done really good work, but the board wants this quiet, too. Part of the reason to not send a formal request is because if espionage stories get out to the nets, it could be used to make the company look weak, drive down our stock values. It could hit all of our retirement funds—even yours, indirectly."

The guard looked down at the terminal, then up at Dario once more, frowning. "I have too much invested in this company to take a hit… but we'd usually receive at least some sort of confirmation of a transfer."

"Scan his ident, Sarge," one of the other guard said. "If he's the CFO's son like you say, and he checks out, why would he lie?"

Why indeed? Dario surpressed a smile and held out his wrist.

Sarge walked over to Dario, producing a scanner from his belt. It beeped when coming into contact with Dario's handtab. A display of Dario's picture, name and information appeared within moments. "Well," Sarge said, "You check out. Sorry to doubt you, sir. Been too many strange cases with identities revolving around our suspects here."

Dario nodded in understanding. "May I take them? I don't want to keep the board waiting."

"They're a flighty bunch, sir," Sarge said. "Perhaps one or two of us should come as escort?"

"Of course, Dario said. "Though, the meeting is supposed to be held at the spaceport. The board doesn't want these two seen in the upper levels, for the same PR reasons—and safety concerns. Can you escort us planetside through the skylift security lines?"

"Not a problem." Sarge brandished his plasma pistol once more, waving it between Joan and Trian. "All right, you two. Don't try to pull anything or I swear I'll disintegrate you before you can blink."

Joan ducked her head low. She looked as contrite as could be, but Dario knew her well enough to know she was scheming. He hoped this whole charade impressed her.

A short walk later and the odd grouping of Dario, security guards and his "prisoners" descended the skylift down to the spaceport level three in near silence. The lift itself was crowded with nearly a thousand other people from corporate, and Dario didn't want to attract any undue attention to himself.

Once the skylift opened and people filed out, Dario led them to a place several blocks away. Red iron glowed off of the reflective lighting above, programmed for daylight operations. People travelled to and from the spaceport via hovercar and various level escalators. It was busy enough that no one paid much attention to the security officers or where their weapons were pointed.

The one thing Dario hadn't quite figured out in his plan was how he'd get rid of the security guards. He had needed them to escort Joan, her friend, and him through the skylift checkpoint, but beyond that, they would get suspicious when they saw that there was no meeting with the board.

For now, Dario led them down the streets. He couldn't just attack the security guards, or they would have him arrested for conspiring with spies. The real question was, if he set up a situation where Joan and her friend could escape or overpower the guards themselves, would they time it right and have the ability to actually take the guards? Dario would have to make it believable that he was helpless in such a situation as well. But perhaps Dario could find an alternative.

"I have a call coming through. I need some privacy," Dario said, motioning for the security guards to stop before veering off to where he was hopefully out of earshot. He connected to the nets through his oculars. "Scan empty buildings. Access level, corporate management."

His enhanced vision marked various buildings as they passed, showing a vacant one a block away. Dario walked back over to the group and motioned to lead them again. When he arrived, he scanned his ident against the door terminal, which allowed him access as a quality control inspector.

As expected, he entered a large, dark space with concrete floors and nearly blacked out windows. The dimmest of light trickled in through small cracks. His footsteps echoed.

The security guards followed him inside. "You're meeting in here?" asked one of the two guards.

"Yeah. Random location for security purposes. Looks like the board members haven't arrived yet," Dario said, turning around. Now what? That was the question. He caught Joan's eye, daring to look at her for the first time since they descended the lift, his heart racing even at that small connection. If anything, he had to keep her safe. "I'm not sure how long they'll be. What's your shift schedule look like?"

The security guard shrugged. "Off in three hours, but I'm supposed to be doing a patrol of the promenade."

"You could get back to that. If you loan me your weapon, I can handle them until the board arrives. I'm sure they've got their own security detail," Dario said. It sounded stupid when it came out of his mouth. Why would security risk leaving him alone? Even at his words? He had to try anyway.

"I don't think that's wise, sir," the security officer said. "The prisoners have already given us a lot of trouble trying to run. They're dangerous."

As Dario suspected, the guard wouldn't leave so easily. Prudent on the guard's part. If something happened to Dario, the guards here would be held liable, no matter what Dario's orders were. So much for that idea. That left him without another plan.

Joan, still cuffed with hands behind her back, looked as if she were about to do something stupid. Again.

"No!" Dario shouted, which served to distract the two guards with him. They tensed, turning.

Joan didn't listen. She pummeled directly into one of them, knocking him to the concrete floor. The guard's plasma pistol slid out of his hand across the smooth surface. Joan's friend took her lead, dropping to roll toward the second security guard's legs. That guard fired his plasma pistol, hitting the ceiling grid. The ceiling sparked and a light fixture shattered, glass spraying everywhere.

Dario scrambled to get the plasma pistol on the floor. He'd fired weapons a few times before, but as a corporate executive, that hadn't been part of his training. There was a stun setting on it, but how could he find it easily in the dark? He turned on his night-vision scanner to see if there were any clear markings on the pistol, backing away from the guards.

Joan wrestled with the security guard who slammed her face onto the floor. She struggled without the use of her hands.

The other tried to get to his feet, though Joan's friend laid out a sweep of his leg, knocking him back down. The guard still held onto that gun.

Dario flicked his eyes upward to initiate a search. "How do I switch a plasma pistol to stun?"

Before it could respond, one of the guards wrestling responded, grunting, "It's already on stun!"

With that information, Dario aimed toward the other guard, who still held a plasma pistol, though tangled with Joan's friend who'd managed to roll atop him. He fired, hoping the first guard's words held truth.

Both of them fell limp to the ground, the other plasma pistol falling out of the security guard's arms.

Dario turned his attention to Joan and the remaining guard. Joan caught his eye and delivered a kick to the guard's stomach, using the force to roll herself away. Once she was clear, Dario took aim. The security guard, unworried about Dario, twisted, leaving his back exposed.

Dario fired. The guard shook and collapsed to the ground.

Joan wiggled and got back up to her feet. "Put that thing down before you hurt someone, Mr. I-don't-know-how-to-stun."

Despite himself, Dario laughed, needing some humor to dissolve the tense moments of before. His hands shook from the nervousness of having to fire on someone. A rush of adrenaline filled his head. Did soldiers feel this way every time they had to use their weapons? The appeal of that career path became clear.

He paced over toward Joan, staring at the limp bodies on the ground. All of them seemed to be breathing, albeit shallowly.

"Hopefully that didn't make too much noise or draw too much attention. Board meeting, huh?" Joan asked, shaking her head before stepping over the body of the security guard she'd been entangled with. She motioned with her head toward him. "He's got a key in his left breast pocket. Don't suppose you could grab that for me?"

Dario nodded and set the plasma pistol down, flipping the body over and reaching into the security guard's vest. The key was easy to find, a thin metallic object. He produced it and moved behind Joan to free her from the cuffs.

Joan pulled each arm forward, stretching and rubbing her wrists before turning to face Dario again. "You did good work. I'm a bit surprised you put yourself on the line so much for me." She smiled. "Thanks."

Dario could feel his face getting hotter. "Of course. It's the least I can do."

"It's a lot," Joan said, moving over to where her friend lay incapacitated on the floor. She prodded at his side with her toe. "Looks like they're out cold. Don't suppose you have a stimtab or anything like that? Maybe can wake Trian before the others come to."

"No, I didn't plan on shooting anyone." Dario wrinkled his nose. "I didn't plan on much, to be honest. I knew you were heading to the spaceport and got your comm frequency from your new ident when you last called. My oculars alerted me to a security feed that said you'd been captured. I came as fast as I could."

"Good that you did, or I'm not so certain we'd be alive, let alone here." Joan crouched and patted her friend on the face. "Trian, come on. Wake up."

Dario stood for a moment, not certain where to go from here. There was going to be the launch of that Megahauler in several hours. What could they do about it? It wasn't as if the three of them could walk in and stop a launch of a ship with thousands of the poor from the underlevels.

Trian stirred. Joan continued to pat his face, brightening at his movement. The man flinched away from her hands, grumbling and turning over to one side. "I feel like someone's smashed a datapad on the back of my skull," he murmured.

"You need to get up anyway. No more time. We're down on level three and have to get into the spaceport," Joan said, pushing herself to stand upright once more. "Then we need to figure out what to do from there. Maybe now that we're planetside we should try to contact the Council of Ministers?"

"If I were the corporation, and I knew there were spies about, I'd have my entire system monitor for potential transmissions just like that. It'd never get out, and it'd give away your position," Dario said.

Trian sat up, hands still behind his back. "Don't suppose someone could give me my hands back?"

"Oh, right," Dario said, crouching behind the man. He had the key he had just used on Joan, not having found others on the downed security guard. He tried the lock. The key opened the clasps on Trian's wrists with a click.

Trian brought his hands in front of him, then rubbed his head. "We have to move from here anyway. If I woke up this quickly, they won't be far behind me," he said, motioning to the security guards. "I agree with your friend, Joan. We shouldn't attempt a transmission at this time. Perhaps if we can get to Zhang, she could find a course of action for us that would be more sensible."

Joan frowned in thought. "We were just in a detention center. I don't think trying to break into another one would be a good idea right now. What do you think, G.O.D.?"

Dario couldn't help but chuckle under his breath. That AI name could get her into a good amount of trouble if taken out of context. More amusing was that both Trian and he accepted it without hesitation. Joan had a unique sense of humor. That was certain. She had a lot of other unique qualities as well. He tried his best to look elsewhere, so he wouldn't stare. He did glimpse her from the corner of his eye, all the same.

"Hmm," Joan said.

"What's the verdict?" Trian asked.

Joan tilted her head, as if uncomfortable. "I can't get him to stop singing in my ear. But from the songs he's singing, I think he's trying to tell us that we should head to the Megahauler and stow away."

"That's crazy," Dario said. "I know the corporate plan for this. They'll take off and you'll be stuck, shot out of the sky with the underlevelers!"

"I agree with your assessment that the situation is dire, but I don't see much of an alternative. We have to find Zhang. She will be able to lead us out of this mess once we have her," Trian said. The room fell silent. "I'm certain of that."

One of the security guards moaned. "We have to get out of here," Dario said, jogging toward the door they came in. He certainly didn't want to be seen conspiring with his supposed prisoners when the guard awoke.

Joan followed, though Trian moved back to where Dario had dropped the plasma pistol a moment before. With methodical precision, he retrieved the weapon, pointing to each of the security guards and re-stunned them. He removed their handcuffs from their belts and cuffed their hand behind their backs as well. Those two would be in a lot of pain when they finally did wake.

"Are you going to lead us to the ship they're sending her off on then?" Joan asked.

Dario considered, pausing as he waited for Trian to catch up to them. He had his reservations, but Joan had already consulted her AI, and he couldn't come up with a better plan. When those security guards did wake up they'd have problems, and he'd have questions to answer. But that was neither here nor there.

What he wanted was to keep Joan safe, but there seemed to be no good opportunity to do that. He side-glanced at her, noting her shoulder-length hair bounce with each step. He could watch her like this forever, but if she had her way with this, would he even be likely to see her again?

That didn't matter. If he was falling for her, if he cared about her, he had to consider her priorities. And he did. She had a good cause, but why did it have to be something that would imminently take her away from him? It wasn't fair.

"Dario?" Joan asked, concern in her voice.

"Huh?" Dario said. He continued to walk along the street. The spaceport would be about a fifteen minute walk from the vacant building.

"Are you going to help us? More, I mean," Joan said.

He wanted to tell her no, that he thought the best idea would be for her to come back to the Central Office. If his father would listen, he could get Joan asylum of some sort with the company. But that wouldn't happen. More likely she'd end up dead and he'd be without a job, or worse.

He could hide her and her friend out down here on the lower levels for some time. No one would come looking for them after a few days, but if the company shipped off these people in droves toward the Hyrades Cluster, she may end up in the same situation. With what little he knew of Joan, she didn't seem the time to sit and watch.

"Yeah, we're heading to the spaceport now. Hopefully my credentials can get us through security again," Dario said.

Joan smiled, turning her head to glance back at Trian. "I told you he'd be a help," she said. "He's a good one."

"It's unfortunate there aren't more people like him within this company." Trian gave a thumbs up toward Dario, accompanied by a small smile.

They walked for several blocks until they reached the terminal, close to where they'd come down on the lift. Thousands of people moved in different directions. Hovercars dropped off passengers and picked up others. Large doors opened toward different terminals of spaceliners, corporate private hangars and finally the massive interplanetary shipping yard.

That's the direction where they headed. Hundreds of transports waited to take passengers to orbiting, docked ships, far too large to descend into the atmosphere planet, even a light-gravity environment like Mars. Bots and workers alike loaded their cargo, with dozens of corporate personnel readying their planet-to-ship routes.

Dario walked toward the Regency BioTech desk, scanning his ident as Joan and Trian lingered behind him. A woman checked his clearance and tilted his head at him, a curious look on her face. "Mr. Anazao. Quality control? Are you here for an inspection?" she asked.

That evoked a smile. She couldn't have provided a better cover for him. "Yes. Yes, I am. This is my team."

CHAPTER 30

INSPECTIONS

SPACEPORT—THIRD LEVEL, MARS
LOCAL DATE FEBRUARY 14TH, 2464

Joan followed Dario down the back warehouses of Regency Bio-Tech's shipping and receiving yards. They passed at least a dozen transports on the way. Her feet stung from all the walking—and running—she'd done during the day. Then again, a little ache beat the alternative of being locked in a cell, waiting to be executed.

Dario's idea had been brilliant. Using his job as a quality control manager to get them access to anywhere within Regency BioTech's yards almost reminded her of one of G.O.D.'s plans. It made their real job a lot simpler, but they still had to find Commodore Zhang. A needle in a haystack.

If this were the first of a trial run to get rid of the corporation's unwanted peasants, perhaps the search wouldn't be that difficult. Regency BioTech's security would need at least several hours in preparation to get people launched onto a ship by their scheduled departure.

Dario at least acted like he knew his way around the spaceport, leading with few words and a step that held much more confidence than before he had managed to bluff his way past security. No one stopped them on their way. Who would want to risk pestering one of the higher ups?

They moved out into the open, several lifts moving about in

different directions with large cargo crates, heading for their respective transports. Further down the runway, Joan saw where they needed to go.

Ten transports jammed together in a line, side by side, large enough to hold thousands of people each. The Megahauler would be packed when those people boarded, but what did people's comfort matter to the corporation?

Off to either side stood the thousands of people required to fill those transports, herded like cattle by hundreds of security officers in riot gear with their weapons drawn. For the most part, the people were going peaceably, filing down to smaller lines to flood into the transports. No one checked them for weapons or contraband. It wouldn't matter if those were stowed aboard anyway. This would be their death sentence.

Joan pointed toward the scene in the distance. "There," she said.

"Yes, but how do we find Commodore Zhang in that crowd?"

"Such a dangerous prisoner, I doubt she'd be left on her own or just mixed in with the crowds," Dario said. "Let's go talk to security."

Joan froze in her tracks. "Are you sure that's a good idea? What if they recognize our faces?"

"You're with me. Very worst I tell them it was ordered for you to go up on the ships and you can find Commodore Zhang yourself," Dario said, stopping as well, and turned back toward her.

That sounded reasonable. The security here seemed to be more concerned with people fleeing than the wrong people coming aboard. Of course, once they were aboard that Megahauler, they would be stuck. Joan hadn't quite figured out the next stage of the plan. None of the people being herded into these transports would know they were in any danger. The corporation was unlikely to provide life pods or other safety systems, and she was sure there'd be no way she'd be able to reach a comm. If anything, the ship would likely have a jammer installed to prevent communications.

The plan would be aboard, find Commodore Zhang, and hope she had an idea for a *real* plan. In essence, Joan trusted her life to some woman she had never met. Strangely enough, Trian didn't protest.

G.O.D. did say that it was their best chance at success, but that best chance meant less than three percent, according to her AI's calculations. It wasn't as if they had many alternatives. Joan didn't want Dario or Trian to lose hope, and she'd been able to maneuver out of sticky situations before. This is why the Council of Ministers asked her to join this mission. Her knack for survival.

Joan took a deep breath. "All right, let's do it."

They proceeded forward; the distance seemed infinite across the tarmac. Eventually, they did arrive near the security personnel.

One of the guards approached. "This is a restricted area."

"I know," Dario said. "Dario Anazao, quality control. I'm here to ensure operation success. Board wants this to go off without a hitch."

The man narrowed his eyes at Dario, then at Joan and Trian. "Anazao?" he asked, the name holding weight in the way he asked the question. "Who are your friends here? They look familiar."

"Part of my team," Dario said.

The line in front of them shrank. It appeared for a moment like the security guard didn't believe them, but he stepped aside. "Be careful. These people inside are agitated enough as it is. If they learned there were higher ups here from corporate, we may have problems I won't be able to contain."

"Got it," Dario said, glancing over at Joan.

That look brought goose bumps to Joan's arms. What was that about? Dario had become so protective over her these last few hours. It made Joan a little nervous, but she also found she rather liked it. No one had ever tried to take care of her like this before, even if she could care for herself just fine.

"Your heart rate is escalating again," G.O.D. chimed in from her ear piece.

"I'm sure." Joan shook her head.

"What was that?" The guard focused on Joan.

"Nothing," Joan said, doing her best to smile at the guard, trying to make her tone sound professional as she could when she spoke. "Mr. Anazao, weren't you going to ask about the, what was it, special cargo?"

"Ah, that's right," Dario said. "The board mentioned that they had a high profile passenger on this expedition they wanted to be sure was kept quiet. Are you aware of that?"

The security guard thought for a moment, then shook his head. "No, I don't think… wait a sec," he said. "Hey, Jenn!"

The person he called came over, another officer in riot gear. "What's up?" she asked, looking to Joan, Dario and Trian. "These settlers?"

"No, no, corporate big wigs," the first security officer said. "Jenn, you know anything about some special going up on the transport? Didn't someone from the level fourteen precinct come down here early in the morning and take a transport?"

Jenn approached, giving each of them a glance over. "Yeah, that was the beginning of my shift. Wasn't a something special, though. They were bringing some woman. She was cuffed, and they kept four guards on her at all times."

Joan glanced at Trian, who returned an understanding look.

"I see," Dario said. "This woman went up on the transport?"

"That's right."

Joan turned back to the security officer. "That's what we're here to check, make sure she made it safely. Can we head up in one of these transports to confirm?"

Dario's eyes went wide, and he opened his mouth to protest.

Joan quickly tapped on her handtab. She tilted it away from the security guards so Dario could see the message she'd typed: *Trust me.*

Dario snapped his mouth shut, giving an uneasy nod toward Joan.

Security Officer Jenn raised a brow. "You know these transports aren't coming back?"

"That's fine," Joan said as brightly as she could. "We'll catch the last crew transport off the ship when we're done."

The first security officer shrugged. "If they want to take the risk, I don't see a reason they can't go up." He stepped aside and motioned the way to the closest transport. "Should be a little room, but might be tight. Hopefully won't be too uncomfortable for you."

"We'll be fine," Joan said, taking the lead and stepping forward. She tugged Dario along with her, but was met with a little resistance. At first, he didn't budge, but he relented and walked with her. Trian followed.

When they were out of earshot of the security officers, Joan glanced back behind her, and then smiled at Dario. "Thanks for that, Dario. We really couldn't have gotten this done without you."

"This is a bad idea," he said.

Joan stopped and glanced back to make sure the security officers weren't looking. They had shifted their focus to a datapad, talking amongst themselves. Satisfied with the lack of an audience, Joan turned toward him.

Trian stepped unobtrusively off to the side, acting as if he were analyzing the transport and the last remaining of the underlevelers filing inside.

Joan reached over and hooked a finger on his hand, squeezing. "I know you don't like this. I'm sorry. I wish there were another way."

"Me too," Dario said, his face reddening.

"It really does mean a lot to me, what you've done. When… if I survive…" she began, but she knew those were mere comfort words. She had no idea what she would do after she got aboard that ship. For all she knew, she would be stuck like the other underlevelers. Even if she did manage to find a way to turn that ship around or evacuate, she wouldn't be able to contact Dario. She was a known spy by corporate security, and any comm from her, especially from outside Trade Federation space, would implicate him. If he weren't flagged by his corporate security already.

"Don't say anything," Dario said. His mechanical eyes, cast downward.

Joan didn't know what to do, didn't know what she could say to make things right. She held his hand for a long moment, desperate not to hurt him more. Beside her the rest of the underlevelers had boarded the transport. Trian spoke to the security officer close by, delaying the launch, but she was out of time.

Despite herself, she felt her body moving up to its tip toes, closer to Dario. She could feel his breath, and a warmth stirred in her chest, something she'd never felt before. An excitement inside her, stronger than the first time she stepped outside after being stuck in that penal colony. She vividly remembered the bright light of a real sun on her for the first time in years, and it paled compared to Dario.

Hastily, Joan pressed her lips against his before taking a couple of steps back from him, half expecting G.O.D. to chime in about her heart rate again. It thudded harder than ever before.

Dario's eyes widened in surprise, his face flushing a bright red. He shifted his eyes toward security and back to her. "Joan…" he said, sounding panicked.

His lips had been softer than Joan expected. She wasn't sure what she should have expected, truth be told. What had even prompted her to do that? She shook her head to try to clear her emotional haze. It wouldn't go away. "I'm sorry. I wanted to thank you properly. For all you've done."

"You don't need to thank me," Dario said. His expression said everything. He loved her. That look sent a chill down her spine.

Joan wanted more. A real kiss, a long one, something that would connect him to her for far longer than that brief tease. But security, not to mention Trian, stood right there. She couldn't risk appearing too odd, and she couldn't linger any longer. Instead, she turned, jogging those last few steps to the ramp of the transport. Trian ushered her aboard. As much as she desired to, she didn't look back.

CHAPTER 31

DECISIONS

Dario dragged with a sense of heavy loss. Yet, part of him felt so light on his toes that he thought he could fly through the dome hatch himself. It should have been impossible to feel both of those ways simultaneously, but somehow, he managed. That kiss. It was all he could think about. He wished he'd prolonged it, or at least been able to respond. He longed for another so his tongue could meet hers, so he could take her in a little more fully than that fleeting moment.

Before he had come to his senses, he'd walked back to where the two security officers had originally engaged him. The two security officers—Jenn and the one who never gave a name stood there, looking at him somewhat perplexed. "They're going off into the transport?" Jenn asked.

"Yeah," Dario said, the reality of losing Joan sinking in, drowning the moment of joy.

"And you're not going with them? I thought it was your team?" The other security guard asked.

"It is. I'm not. They can do what they need to do," Dario said. That much was true. But why hadn't he gone with them. He looked back to see the transport lifting off the ground, thrusters lighting up and dust kicking toward their direction.

The thought hadn't even occurred to him that he could follow her. He was here. This corporation had been where he had been born, his entire life geared toward management in Regency BioTech. He hated the reality of it ever since Jake had opened his eyes, since Joan had stepped into his life with a brief conversation.

He couldn't affect change here. That was the bitter truth. Not by himself. And without Joan and her friends, he had no back up. Sure, he could probably persuade Daniella and Antonio to his way of thinking, but without a protected familial status like he had, they might get hurt or worse. Situations had changed there as well. His father had an open plant within his department. There was nothing he could do.

Dario was so caught up in worrying about Joan, something he couldn't change now, that he almost didn't hear footsteps approaching.

"Dario?" A deep voice rang, clear and distinct as he'd heard thousands of times before. His father.

He immediately tensed, not turning around, hoping his father wouldn't see the distraught look he couldn't purge from his face. "*Mister* Anazao," Dario croaked, his voice not cooperating with the lack of emotion he wanted to convey.

"You're really upset about this," Mr. Anazao noted, stepping up to his side. He placed a hand on Dario's shoulder. "I'm not a villain here, Dario. You have to understand. I'm trying to do what's best for the company, best for your future. So is the board. These people will have happier lives out in the Hyrades Cluster."

Dario opened his mouth to protest, but his father had circled around him and held up a hand. "I know what you're going to say," Mr. Anazao said, "so please, spare me the arguing. There's nothing to be done." His eyes narrowed on Dario. "That Jake fellow really got to you, didn't he?"

That was part of it, but Dario looked away. "No. This is all my decision. I haven't been brainwashed or duped."

"I wasn't going to say you were."

That surprised Dario, causing him to look back at his father. He switched his vision to display the man's vitals. Those didn't betray any sense of urgency or escalated heart rate that often preceded falsehoods. Which was in keeping with how his father usually acted. His father spoke earnestly most of the time. Dario didn't know what further he could say to him, even with the honesty. So he said nothing.

"I'm not going to spend time arguing with you over corporate policy. You've got too much of me in you. You'll never back down if you have something you're passionate about. I know it well. But Dario, don't throw your life away." Mr. Anazao stepped in front of him, gazing off at another transport loaded with underlevelers. "I saw recordings of you in the detention block. You claimed you were taking wanted criminals to interrogations, and brought them down here instead."

"That wasn't exactly—"

"I'm not here to turn you in, Dario. I'm here to tell you there's better ways to protest. I've certainly had times in my life where I've disagreed with corporate policy, or other people in my department, even your mother. There was a time where I almost gave up my position to go work with her in an effort to spend more time with her," he said, chuckling to himself. "Fortunately, your mother had the sense to smack me upside the head and tell me not to give up my life for something foolish."

"Was it worth it?" Dario asked, some of his anger seeping out in his voice. He had already held off on doing what his father would consider foolish, not giving up his life. Couldn't he see that? That very action was what pained him.

"There's no way to know what another path may have been, so I don't dwell on it," Mr. Anazao said. "I think my life has turned out amicably. So has your mother's. I'm content with that."

"Yeah, well what if I'm not?" Dario asked, nearly covering his own mouth. He had never been so brazen with his father before.

That caused his father to turn back toward him. His face twisted into a frown, and he sized up Dario for a long while. "Hmm."

"What?"

"This isn't about corporate policy or a cause, is it? Not completely."

Dario could feel himself shrinking right before his father's eyes. What could he say now? He had always hated how his father analyzed and picked apart his every move.

"The young woman you escorted down here. What's her name?" Mr. Anazao asked. "Her real name, not the Deborah Moynihan listed on her false ident."

Dario kicked at a pebble on the ground in front of him, watching it roll away from his foot. "Joan."

"Joan," Mr. Anazao repeated. "A strong name, energetic, no doubt."

Dario nodded to that.

"I hope for your sake that she wasn't using her abilities as a spy to pull a fast one over on you, Dario. Where did she go anyway? Did she steal one of the security guard's weapons and run off once you freed her?"

"No," Dario said, a little more forceful than he intended. Talking about Joan with his father made him more uncomfortable than he would have imagined, and it evoked a defensiveness out of him. His father hadn't said anything that showed he was judging him, though. Not yet. So why did he react this way? Dario looked up to the sky. "She went aboard one of the transports, up to the Megahauler."

"So, you led her into a trap yourself." Mr. Anazao nodded to himself.

"It was her choice. She knows what she's getting into. She's hoping she can do something from the inside," Dario said. Like he had been trying to do all along, to change the corporation from the inside. Unfortunately, he found out how well that worked.

"A fool's errand," Mr. Anazao said. "The interior of the Megahauler's been stripped. There are automated commands only, and a security team to make sure nothing gets out of hand. There's nothing she can do."

"I wouldn't underestimate her," Dario said. Talking about Joan gave him such an urge to fight, but being defensive wouldn't accomplish anything.

Mr. Anazao paused, looking up to the dome, then back down at Dario again. "I wouldn't. I've seen the impact this woman's had on my son. But you know that sitting here, moping about the situation isn't going to do you any good. It seems to me you have a choice."

"Like what? She's gone. I've got to get back to work knowing that she'll likely be dead in a few days time."

"If what you say is true, Dario, that you're not content, perhaps you should consider doing something else." Mr. Anazao gave him one more pat on the shoulder then turned back to go the way he came. "My end goal is for you to have a good life, you know that. Perhaps I pushed you too hard." With those last words he took steps away from Dario, leaving him alone again.

Dario considered for a time, watching the last transport fill. When he glanced back over his shoulder to look for his father, he saw the elder Anazao was gone. Do something else. A choice. It was an odd way of talking to him. His father had never given him a choice in his life. It always had the illusion of a choice, but it set Dario on a singular path each time. That much had led him here, trapped within the confines of Regency BioTech. What else could he do?

The ramp for the final transport began to close. Dario was certain that boarding wasn't what his father intended by talking about the choice. He probably meant switch career paths, travel to gain some perspective on life. Boarding would be throwing his life away, exactly what his father warned against. Wasn't it?

But his father did give him the choice. He saw how important Joan was to Dario. A choice did stand before him.

Dario jogged toward the transport. Joan had faith in herself, faith in what she was doing. Enough to board a Megahauler doomed for destruction. If Dario loved her, and he did, he should have that same faith in her. She'd find a way out. If anyone could, she could.

Dario waved his arms, trying to obtain the attention of a worker who manned the transport's ramp controls. "Hold up! Hold up!"

The worker, dressed in coveralls with dark stains, canted his head toward Dario. "What's the matter?"

"Transport's got one more passenger who needs to come aboard."

"Who's that?"

"Me."

CHAPTER 32

ALL ABOARD

T.F.S. SHAREHOLDER—MARS ORBIT
LOCAL DATE FEBRUARY 14TH, 2464

Joan stared out the back viewport of the transport shuttle. The shuttle was crammed with people, though she was able to maneuver into a spot with the view. Her chest ached from a sense of dread. Realistically, she would never see Dario again. That thought bothered her far more than it should have.

Would it have been better to convince him to come with her? What would that have accomplished? The likelihood Trian and she would survive was negligible, as G.O.D. had already pointed out to her.

The transport banked and then shot upward into the sky. Artificial gravity plates kept the standing passengers relatively still for the ride, though Joan still felt the soft tug of the planet's gravity below. When they broke through the gravity well, the transport jolted, causing some people to lose their footing, but no one in Joan's field of vision fell.

It wasn't long before the transport pulled into the back Megahauler cargo pod, attaching itself and sealing. Its front hatch opened, atmosphere equalizing with that of the larger ship.

More security guards greeted the displaced underlevelers on the opposite side, ushering them into the Megahauler. The crowd didn't go quietly, but the underlevelers grumbled amongst themselves out of confusion as to why they had been brought here. No one had bothered explaining anything to them, Joan had found out from passing conversation on the flight skyward.

Once ushered out into the bay, the security guards pressed the people forward. The crowd funneled through the bay doors and into a large open area. They arrived in a hollowed out section of the ship that Joan presumed was for this transport purpose.

Joan slipped into the crowd. Trian followed.

"Please step away from the doors," a voice came from loudspeakers that surrounded the large chamber. "We understand this transition is difficult for many of you, and appreciate your cooperation. Blankets and foodstuffs will be provided shortly for your journey."

"Hey, where are we going?" a man shouted from the crowd.

A series of "Yeah!" and "Where we going?" erupted from several sources.

The security guards stood by at the bay door as it shut, their riot gear on and unmoving.

Someone in the crowd threw something at them. The security guard flinched, backing up to the wall. His grip tightened on his plasma pistol.

"Trouble is brewing," Trian said. "Keep your head low."

The overall sense within the crowd was one on edge, like a reactor about to spark into an explosion. Joan felt it as well.

"Ms. Shengtu," G.O.D. spoke in her ear.

"Yeah?" she said. She had finally become used to responding to both live people and G.O.D. at the same time.

"My algorithms are giving a ninety point three two percent chance that this crowd is going to riot. I would recommend vacating the area," G.O.D. said.

"Tell me something I don't know." Joan clutched Trian's shirt sleeve and dragged him along the opposite direction.

Shots fired behind them.

The crowd rushed away from the gunfire, not in any organized direction. Several underlevelers collided with one another. People fell, and others didn't stop moving, trampling over them. Screams erupted, so did shouting.

More shots were fired.

Joan let go of Trian's sleeve and rushed past him. She wanted to put Trian and herself as far away from the gunfire as possible. At least there were several dozen people between them and the security guards. Perhaps if she could get to a different door…

"Slow down!" Trian said. He tripped behind her, using her back to brace himself.

"Sorry, trying to get us through here so we come out of this alive," Joan said after a brief glance back. Her tone came out harsher than she had intended. When on the run in the past, she'd never had to deal with people coming with her. She bumped shoulders with several people, passing through the crowd.

Someone grabbed her by the arm, tugging her, and Trian by proxy, to the side.

"You'd better let go!" Joan shouted, clenching her fist and readying to throw a punch when she turned, stopping mid-motion.

"You'll regret it if you hit me, *ensign*," said a smug voice, one she recognized.

"Yui!" Joan said. Instead of punching, Joan threw her arms around the other woman. "I can't believe you're alive!"

"Same. I thought you were a goner when I didn't see you guys come to the cell. Seems you were more competent than I thought." Yui hugged her quickly and did the same for Trian.

"Amazing we found you," Trian said. "We assumed you were disintegrated."

"Nope, just put me in with a bunch of the rioters. Apparently deciding to ship off their problems instead of dealing with them. Any idea where we're headed?" Yui asked.

"Back to the Star Empire," Joan said.

"Hey, not so bad after—" Yui's eyes widened in understanding.

"In a Trade Federation marked ship."

Trian nodded.

The crowed parted around them. As three people, Joan and her friends proved enough to hold their own ground this far away from the security guards. It was hard to see over so many others, but Joan caught a glimpse of a group rushing the guards, who had lost control of their weapons. Even if the underlevelers had weapons, what could they do? They were all trapped in this room on this ship. The security guards as much as them.

Joan wondered if the guards even knew what was happening with this mission, how their lives were in just as much danger as everyone else's. She doubted it.

"So, you were just caught?" Yui asked.

Joan returned her attention to Yui and shook her head. "No. Heard about this crazy idea that the corporation had to get rid of their rioters and came aboard. From what I understand, Zhang is here somewhere."

Yui chuckled.

"What's so funny?" Trian asked.

"Finally found our target and we're all on a one way trip to get shot out of the sky," Yui said. "Sounds about right for how this mission has gone."

"If we find her here," Trian said, "Perhaps there is something we can do." He still hadn't lost hope, his voice holding a hint of optimism.

"You crazy? We're stuck. I'm sure there's no way to ship controls. The corporation couldn't be that stupid."

"No, they're not," Joan said, giving Trian an apologetic look. "But we have one thing they might not expect."

"What's that?" Yui asked.

"G.O.D. on our side."

The name initiated the AI. He was already singing in her earpiece. "Oh, you wake up because she never sleeps. Just when you think you're in too deep, in too deep."

Joan rolled her eyes.

"What?" Yui asked, sounding perturbed. She had a short fuse when it came to Joan.

Oddly, Joan found she missed that attitude. In some ways, it was Yui's way of being protective. "Nothing, just the AI malfunctioning again," Joan said.

"How's it going to help us if that's still occurring?" Trian asked.

Joan hit mute on her handtab to stop the distracting singing. "He can still help. The virus is more annoying than anything else. It hasn't compromised his planning."

"It didn't do very well when it tried to get us away from security at the lift," Trian said.

"That was different. It was a no-win situation," Joan said.

"So's this," Yui said. "But I don't have a better plan. What do we need to do?"

Before Joan could answer, one of the security guards lost control, sending out a rapid fire of plasma pistol spray into the crowd. Several underlevelers went down. The smell of burnt flash radiated in the air, forcing Joan to plug her nose.

"That's not a stun setting!" Yui said, shocked.

"They must want to squash any resistance quickly," Trian said.

The weapons fire had the opposite effect. The crowd grew angrier and rushed forward, a wave of people moving in tandem toward the guard that fired and two other guards nearby. Despite firing off several more shots, the guards were quickly overwhelmed. People punched, kicked, surrounding the guards. Bones cracked.

One of the underlevelers raised the plasma pistol toward the vaulted ceiling of the hollowed out Megahauler. He fired it toward the ceiling.

"Is he crazy? That could pop a hole in the hull!" Yui said, eyes widening.

"These people aren't trained with weapons," Trian said.

Joan watched, trying to formulate a plan to at least get her and her friends to safety if need be.

Security seemed to be losing control of the crowd entirely, as the underlevelers became more confident after the weapon's seizure. Several more groups of guards backed to the walls.

The lights flickered off.

The crowd noise escalated, confusion and anger spewing from all areas of the room. Only the few with glowing handtabs could be seen, keeping the room from being too pitch dark to see at all.

"Hello, and welcome to the *T.F.S. Shareholder*. This is your captain speaking," said a loud voice that carried from all points in the room. "We are about to embark on the journey of a lifetime, providing new opportunity in the colonies and a meaningful life, brought to you by Regency BioTech sponsors."

"Tyrants!" someone shouted. Other voices echoed agreement.

The loudspeaker voice continued without pause. "This journey is going to begin shortly. The crew here is minimal, outside of the security officers placed about the room for your safety. Please give those officers your utmost cooperation. They are here to protect you in the event of disorderly conduct, to prevent conflict with so many in close quarters. Any further acts of violence will be met with proportionate response.

"We do wish you to have as comfortable a stay as possible while aboard the *T.F.S. Shareholder*. Food, water, and hygienic goods will be distributed three times per day. Those distributions will be preceded by an announcement over the loudspeaker. This journey will take less than three days with the faster-than-light drive of this excellent Megahauler. Regency BioTech thanks you for your calm and cooperation."

The voice ceased and the lights returned. The short burst of darkness did seem to have an effect of dulling the crowd's rage. For now, no one attacked the guards, but the confusion didn't change. "Why are we here? What did we do?" someone asked.

Joan frowned, knowing that these people did nothing other than vent frustration with their treatment from corporate overlords. It wasn't her job to comfort underlevelers trapped in this crazy company scheme. She had much more important matters to attend to.

With the lights on, Joan looked for a door. Even if it was locked or non-functional, there would be a terminal close by one. She weaved through groups of people.

Trian and Yui followed. "Where are you going?" Yui asked.

"To see if I can find some information," Joan said. She found a door that didn't have any security guards attending. "Can you two stand by me, cover what I'm doing so it doesn't look suspicious?"

"Of course," Trian said, blocking out the view to one side of the door's terminal. Yui flanked the other side of her.

Joan placed her handtab up to the terminal, leaving G.O.D. on mute so she didn't have to listen to his singing. "G.O.D., if you're still there and can function, I need you to access this ship's system, see what security protocols they have, and if there's any way we can take control of the ship or send a message out. Also, search for any information pertaining to Commodore Zhang. Got it?"

Her handtab made a chirping sound, letting her know that it connected with the door's terminal. Security protocols were light aboard the ship, which made sense as very few underlevelers would have a way to even connect, let alone the knowledge of how to exploit the systems. G.O.D.'s profile transferred into the ship, and the handtab disconnected.

Joan stepped back.

"Now what?" Trian asked.

"We wait and hope that G.O.D. has an answer for us."

Yui laughed. "You say things like that on purpose, don't you?"

Joan grinned. "A girl's gotta have fun somehow. Otherwise I'd go crazy with all this stress."

The door to the large room opened suddenly, surprising everyone nearby.

Joan wasted no time, stepping through the door and into the corridor, waving for Trian and Yui to hurry and follow them.

A couple of underlevelers noticed the exit to the room, commenting and pointing toward the door, but before anyone else mustered up the courage to move, the door shut again. A red light circled the terminal to show it was locked.

Trian let out a breath. "This has gone far beyond my scope of typical work," he said.

Yui patted him on the shoulder. "Don't worry about it then, we've got it covered. Right, Ensign?"

"Well, and our AI. G.O.D., you got anything on Zhang's whereabouts yet?" Joan asked into the hallway. Her voice faintly echoed on the metal plating of the walls and ceiling.

The terminal beside the door activated, and Joan's handtab glowed. "I have integrated my system into the Megahauler's network," G.O.D. said in her earpiece. "The higher level functions of the ship are still beyond my reach, but I have interior door access. Scanning for information pertinent to Commodore Zhang. Stand by."

Joan looked to the others. "He says stand by."

"We're exposed here in the hallway," Yui warned. "Anyone can recognize we don't belong here."

That was true. Corporate security had their uniforms, full riot gear that made them appear very distinct from anyone else on the ship. But if security issues were so tense inside the large chamber, was there a real danger in standing in the hallway? Moving without knowing where they were headed would be a worse idea, in Joan's estimation.

The ship jolted.

"What was that?" Trian asked.

"Internal gravity reset," Joan said. "When a ship's jumping into faster than light travel, it takes a brief moment to calibrate." She remembered those jolts from the middle of the night when she served in the navy. They had woken her several times, but eventually she became used to them. Better than being adrift in space, one of her bunkmates had always told her.

"So we're on our way," Yui said, glancing around the hallway. "We'd better move fast."

"I have successfully traced the Commodore's whereabouts and procured a map of the ship. Transferring data to your handtab," G.O.D. said.

"We've got the info," Joan said, tapping commands on her handtab. The map hologram hovered over her wrist. "This way," she said, jogging down the hallway.

Her initial hunch had proved right. She couldn't be certain of the reasoning, but the ship's perimeter halls were empty through the entire route. They had to climb upward three levels, above the large chambers where the underlevelers were being kept, and make their way toward the forward section of the ship.

They approached a row of crew quarters, not so different than Joan had seen when she was in the navy. Yui checked several of the doors, which were locked, and didn't appear as though they'd been in use for the journey.

"Means they've got a skeleton crew, maybe not even that. Could be as few as the security we saw and autopilot," Joan said. It would make sense. Why would the corporation risk more of their manpower than they had to? This wasn't intended to be a journey that would require decisions.

"Why have security at all?" Trian asked.

"In case there's someone like us, smart enough to be able to hack into the systems. They can't risk their plans being ruined so easily," Yui said.

"Then why *is* this so easy?"

That question lingered as they proceeded through the crew quarters. They came to a door that G.O.D. marked as the place the Commodore was being held. Joan's handtab buzzed.

"According to G.O.D.'s map, Commodore Zhang is behind this door," Joan said.

Yui tried to open the door, but it remained locked the same as the others. "No way in."

"Can G.O.D. override the lock?" Trian asked.

"The lock is beyond the measure of security clearance I've been able to access, Ms. Shengtu," G.O.D. said in her earpiece.

Joan shook her head. "He says no."

"Now what?" Yui asked, hands smacking her thighs in frustration.

"I can try to break in," Joan said.

"You can do that?" Trian asked.

Joan shrugged. She'd had plenty of experience getting past door locks before. From the looks of the door console though, this was military grade. Which didn't necessarily mean it would be a difficult task, but she had the distinct memory of getting caught in a set up the last time she had to break into a secured room. "Why don't you take one corner of the hall, Yui the other, and warn me if someone's coming?" she asked. At least she wouldn't have anyone looking over her shoulder that way.

Yui nodded at the suggestion and headed back the direction they had come. She crossed her arms, leaning against the wall a good twenty meters down the hall, resting one foot up against a bulkhead.

Trian watched Yui, then proceeded further in the opposite direction, taking his own watch.

Joan rubbed her hands together, then crouched down to eye level with the door console. It had been sealed pretty well, and she didn't have any tools to help her with this. That always made things trickier. She clasped her fingers on the edges of the console, not able to get the best grip on the calking, but she tugged all the same.

It didn't budge.

Joan pulled again, this time harder, grunting.

"Joan?" Trian asked with concern.

"I'm okay, I…" she let her weight pull her backwards. The console snapped off, sending her stumbling backward.

She regained her balance, letting the console face clank on the floor. Dozens of wires protruded from the walls in a jumble of colors.

High security, just like she had thought. This must be the type of room that the Trade Federation would host ambassadors or high level corporate executives on long journeys. It had been a long while since she'd seen anything of this complexity. Joan bit her lip. "Huh."

"You're making too much noise," Yui said from down the hall.

"What's the matter?" Trian asked.

"It's more complicated than I'm used to seeing, don't worry," Joan said. She tried not to worry herself. "G.O.D., do you have any data that could assist me on this lock?"

"Analyzing," G.O.D. said.

Joan seemed to remember that the green wire provided the power mechanism, and the red could short the system. Then it would require them pushing the door open, which could prove difficult depending on if it were rated for decompression, which it looked like it was. If only she could figure out how to push the door open.

"Unfortunately, the door security specs are not located aboard this vessel's network," G.O.D. said.

"Didn't think so. It was worth a shot," Joan said, staring at the wires.

She had to try something. What was the worst that could happen?

If the green were power, then she didn't want to touch it to red to short the system. She needed a different wire. But which one? There were more than a dozen, but Joan chose a yellow one, not for any reason other than it was the brightest. She yanked on both of them, exposing their ends and then touched them together.

The wires sparked, singeing Joan's fingers. Joan fell backward onto her rear. Her fingers stung, causing Joan to bite hard into her bottom lip. It took a moment before she noticed the result of her experiment.

The doors to the cell hung open. A woman, who appeared to be in her late fifties, moved toward the doorway. She had a square chin with a slightly gaunt face that looked as if she hadn't had much sleep or many rations over the last cycle. Her eyes were dark, hardened by command. "I take it you're not with the Trade Federation," she said, a quick glance between the three present, though more focused on Trian, as if making a determination he was in charge.

"No, not at all," Trian said, stepping forward. He offered his hand. "Trian Mubari, political operative for the Council of Ministers. I'm pleased to make your acquaintance. I've been studying your work for months."

Commodore Zhang took Trian's hand and nodded. "Thank you. I can't say I've studied much at all over the last… how long has it been? They keep my cells the same light whether day or night. I lost track over my sleep cycles since they've been interrupted so often."

"You were captured almost two months ago," Yui said.

Joan pushed herself up to her feet, the pain still stinging in her fingers. She tried not to focus on it.

"It seemed longer," Commodore Zhang said with thoughtful frown.

"Being imprisoned always does," Joan said. She recalled her own time in a cell. Back then, she had thought it would never end.

Commodore Zhang stared at her for a moment. "We'll have to talk about our shared experiences later. For now, we should get moving. I felt the transition into faster than light. I presume we're on a ship, but I know little else. Could you update me on the situation?"

"Of course," Trian said, clearing the way for Commodore Zhang to move ahead of him. "We should find another crew quarters as a base of operations while we come up with a plan for escaping this vessel. Joan, could you open another crew quarters the same way you did this one?"

Joan didn't look forward to getting shocked again, but now that she knew the wires would work, she could position herself better for her own safety. She gave a nod of assent. A little pain didn't matter in the scheme of things. If they didn't come up with an idea to stop this ship and find a way off of it, they wouldn't be around much longer to feel any pain whatsoever.

CHAPTER 33
CATCHING UP

Dario exited the front of the transport, along with a crowd of packed in underlevelers. The amount shoved into the small space was unlike anything Dario had ever seen, far worse than the Central Office's skylift. Security guards with guns ushered everyone along, forcing the crowd and Dario to flow into what appeared to be a large open area—and even more people stuffed inside. Dario stopped. Several of the underlevelers brushed past him. He held his ground, trying to get the security guard's attention.

"Keep moving forward," the guard said.

"I need to talk to someone," Dario said.

The guard ignored him.

Dario pressed back toward him, bumping shoulders with a person going the opposite direction.

That evoked the guard pointing his plasma rifle at Dario, jabbing the barrel into his rib. "I said, keep moving forward," the guard reiterated, annoyance in his voice.

Dario tried his best not to react to the metal hitting his ribs. A sharp pain filled his chest. It would leave a bruise later. "I'm not one of the underlevelers. I'm here from corporate quality control. I have an ident to prove it," Dario said.

"I don't really have time to check that, and if you're truly from corporate, then I'd eat this plasma rifle. Get going," the guard said.

"You have to listen to me!" Dario said, frustration dripping in his words. He tried his hardest to keep his cool.

The guard responded by pushing him onward with his gun.

Dario stumbled into another person, who shoved right back. That caused Dario to fall toward the guard. He had little time to regain his footing, narrowly able to duck when the guard swung the rifle like a bat toward Dario's head. "Are you crazy? Listen to me!"

From further into the big open room, shots fired. The crowd stirred and rumbled.

The security guard lost interest in Dario at that point, rushing past him, and inadvertently shoving Dario into the wall of the hallway. Dario looked after the guard but he couldn't catch up with all these people in the way. The underlevelers moved about in a haphazard fashion, wary to enter the room where there was plasma fire. The transport hatch sealed behind them when the last of them was out, leaving everyone trapped.

Including Dario.

What could he do? Security wouldn't listen to him, especially since they had their own problems to deal with. His side ached. Dario cradled it as he considered what to do.

One of the underlevelers, an older man, tapped him on the shoulder. "Son, I'm sorry about the way you were treated. It was a good try though. Corporate!" The old man laughed. "I wish I'd thought of that. You're welcome to stick with me and mine. We got a good group, gonna figure out what's going on and make sure the rations flow our way."

Dario faked a smile. Did he want to cast his lots with some of the underlevelers? As time went by, being seen with a group of the others, it would be less likely that he'd be believed about his corporate upbringing, even though it was true.

"C'mon," the old man said, beckoning Dario forward.

"I'm sorry," Dario said. "I'm supposed to meet up with someone."

He glanced off toward the large room. The crowd of underlevelers looked as if they were about to boil over into a panic, and rightfully so. To be uprooted, not knowing why you were here or where you were going, it must be awful.

With a quick nod toward the old man, Dario moved onward, sticking to one wall that ran along the side of the room. He scanned the large compartment for security guards who looked like they'd at least listen. Too many guards were up to their necks in angry underlevelers. They had as little escape as the underlevelers had from themselves.

Dario approached another series of guards, finding the closest of them engaged with a shouting man. Dario circled around the angry underleveler, trying to get in the field of vision of the next guard, who kept looking away, not inviting conversation. The third guard he tried couldn't avoid him.

"You looking to cause trouble?" this guard asked.

"No, no trouble," Dario said. Couldn't hurt to try the truth once more. "I'm from corporate quality control. This time, he proactively held up his wrist for the guard to scan his ident.

"I could tell you weren't one of *them* by the way you look. Ain't none of them got oculars like you have. Expensive bodymods like that. Hell, I wish I could afford one." The guard shook his head. "What're you doing here, anyway?" He waved off Dario's upheld wrist.

"It's a long story, but I'm trying to catch up with some people. Was hoping security could assist me," Dario said.

The guard held up his own hand, then cupped it over his ear, listening to something. "Lieutenant? Yes I hear you. Sorry, it's loud in here, lotta background noise."

Dario watched, taking the hint to not speak during the guard's call.

"Someone's tampered with the access for the prisoner's quarters?" The guard's face went pale. "Yes, I'll get a team together stat."

From the reports Dario had read, only one prisoner existed

outside the scope of the underlevelers' exodus. Joan had to be the one tampering with the security system. No one else would have the wherewithal to make an attempt like that, not in this crowd. His stomach sank with that thought, both for the plight of the under-levelers and for worry of Joan's safety. He had to get to her before security did.

"I need to get going. I've got a little crisis. Let's meet up here in say, two hours?" The guard asked. "I can bring the Lieutenant and introduce you, see if we might be able to help."

Dario shook his head. "How about I come with you?"

"That'd be dangerous, and I'd get into some trouble for bringin' non-authorized personnel along," the guard said.

"I'm authorized. Higher rank than anyone here, probably," Dario said.

The guard looked off toward a group of other security personnel making their way toward him. He frowned. "Okay, but stay out of the way. Let us do the shooting." He said. He waved to the group headed his way. "Chen, Risia, O'Reilly, with me. Lieutenant Skyward wants us to look into a security breach."

"Oh yeah?" a shorter woman responded. Her riot gear fit awkwardly given her small frame. "What's up, Engels? The prisoner escape?"

"Sounds more like someone breaking in. We have authority to shoot on sight," Engels said.

Dario tried to keep a stoic face. Shoot on sight? He had to stop them somehow. At least for now he was coming along for the ride, but that wouldn't protect Joan if it came to a confrontation. "Stunners only though," Dario added.

The small woman narrowed her eyes at Dario. "Who's this idiot?"

"Not an idiot, Chen," Engels said. "Corporate big wig. Probably wants to interrogate the prisoners himself."

"That's right." Dario lied as best he could, glancing between the four security personnel who had assembled during the conversation

One shrugged, and no one protested. "Sounds good by me," Chen said. "Let's head out."

The security team moved to a door, unlocking it through the terminal. Chen turned to ensure none of the underlevelers followed while the others passed through. Dario stayed close behind Engels, since he had been amicable toward him so far, and because he had been the only one Dario had conversed with for any substantive amount of time. The hall stretched a long way, empty, by contrast to the large, open room packed with underlevelers.

They moved into a brisk jog. Dario kept up easily, looping around what must have been the main room they had left behind. When the security team finally slowed, Dario saw rows of different doors. "This is a detention block?" he asked.

"Crew quarters," Engels said. He looked ahead. "Hallway seems clear for now." With that, he drew his weapon. "Should be coming up on the prisoner's location soon. I expect that the perpetrators took off, but be careful just in case of an ambush." His voice spoke with the air of experience.

Dario nodded and stayed out of the way as he'd been asked to do. Chen gave him a stern eye from the side.

The team pushed forward toward a door that had its terminal ripped off the wall, the main panel lying on the ground. Several dozen wires stuck out from the wall. The door was closed.

Engels inspected the wires and shook his head. "We're gonna need an engineer to get this back together," he said.

"And you'd be crazy if you thought we were allocated any for this mission," Chen said.

"I might be able to help?" Dario said from behind them.

The security guards stepped aside for Dario, who moved forward toward the removed terminal. A couple of wires had been pulled, but he couldn't tell where they had originally attached. He flicked his eyes upward to connect with the Megahauler's nets in his oculars. The ship's systems granted immediate access. No security protocols blocked his entry.

He scanned for terminal information, first attempting to auto-matically override the doors. Nothing happened. "Power's been shot," Dario said. "From what I'm reading, looks like the green wire might be able to restore the system."

Engels stepped forward, crouching then taking the wires into his hand. He touched the end of the wire to a receptor, and it sparked. The terminal blinked online as soon as he did. "Huh, you know your stuff, corporate," he said.

The door access appeared in Dario's field of vision. He flicked his eyes for the open command, and the door opened ahead of him.

The other security guards rushed forward, plasma pistols pointed forward. They covered the exit of the room, holding still for a long moment while Engels had his arm raised. He lowered it eventually. "It's clear. Just like we thought."

Chen stepped forward behind him to peek into the room. "They fled." She turned toward the rest of the team, gesturing. "Split into two groups, head down the hallways. Check every room. If there's any trouble with the access systems, contact us immediately. Our security breachers have to be holed up around here. Nowhere else to go."

The other guards nodded. Then two of them took off down the hallway.

Dario stayed with Chen and Engels as they took a different direc-tion. These two appeared to be very competent, and Dario had a gut feeling that they would be the ones to find Joan and her friends, if Joan wasn't able to avoid detection.

They made quick time down various hallways, opening door after door, finding nothing after dozens of attempts. Dario lost track of exactly how many rooms they'd scanned.

"This is pointless. Don't we have a way to do a bioscan?" Chen asked.

"If we had access to the ship's systems," Engels said.

"I've been able to access the door controls before. I could try,"

Dario suggested.

Chen shook her head. "This is different. A bioscan is tied into bridge functions, and we were informed that all bridge functions have been set to an automatic program. No one aboard has access."

"Is it being controlled remotely?" Dario asked. "That's frightening. What if we need to adjust course? Or if there's an emergency?"

Chen shrugged. "Hell if I know."

Dario tried to access the ship's bioscan functions, despite Chen's warnings. He scanned through several subroutines, finding roadblocks in each of them. He frowned. "You're right. Nothing."

Chen moved ahead of him to another door. "Told you not to waste your time."

Engels shook his head. "We are all wastin' time, but there's no better way. We have to start thinkin' like someone breaking into this ship."

"Who in their right mind would break onto the *Shareholder*? I only took the job because corporate promised full pensions for my family for life from hazard pay," Chen said.

"Me too," Engels said, grimacing.

Dario said nothing to the motivations of being aboard this Megahauler. At least the security personnel who volunteered knew this was a suicide mission. Not everyone was duped into this trip. Only the underlevelers. Whole families of unsuspecting people with no way out.

The three of them proceeded to the next room in a hallway that looked very much the same to Dario as the last several they'd visited. Through his oculars' net connection, he opened the door again, and again the room appeared empty.

"This is pointless," Engels said, shoulders slumping.

"Agreed," Chen said.

Engels held his hand up to his ear. "Lieutenant? Yeah, I'm here. Level 7, Subsection G. Where are you?"

Chen looked to Engels then to Dario and back again.

"Uh huh. You found them? They're in custody?" Engel's eyes lit up with excitement. "That's great news, sir." The guard scanned Dario. His elation turned into a frown. "Is that right, sir?"

"What's the matter?" Dario asked. Had Joan been shot? Was she killed? He couldn't help but find an image in his mind of Joan sprawled across the cold hallway floor, singed by the shots of several plasma pistols.

Engels didn't answer him, glancing down the hallway instead. His lips twisted, tensing his face. "Yes sir, I understand."

Dario took a couple of steps back, the uneasiness surrounding the guard making him nervous. Joan! His heart sank. "What happened?"

"Sounds like we've captured our stowaways," Chen said.

"Yes, the other team found them. They've been stunned and subdued," Engel said. He motioned to Chen to head down the hallway, and then turned his plasma pistol toward Dario. "I've also been told by Lieutenant Skyward that there are new orders. Your company authority has been revoked on CFO Kostas Anazao's orders. You're to be considered a hostile. You'll be joining your friends, Mr. Anazao. At least until you're retrieved. The ship is being programmed to make a special stop for you and a shuttle sent to retrieve you to Mars."

Dario's mouth hung open in surprise. His father had called to extract him from the ship? That went against everything they'd talked about before! How could he have betrayed him like this?

He shook his head in disbelief. But it wasn't a betrayal, at least not in his father's mind. The conversation planetside, in the spaceport. The "follow your dreams" talk had been a calculated move to root out Dario's true intentions of coming here. How could he have been so blind? His father would consider this rescuing Dario from a foolish mistake. Even if Dario returned at this point, what good would it do? How could his recent days' movements be explained to the company? No good could come of it.

Engels waved his pistol. "Hands up, sir."

Dario complied, placing his hands above his head, then locking them together behind his neck as Engels led him down the hallway. The truth was... he didn't even feel all that bad about his own predicament, his father, or his failed future and legacy. The tragedy that hurt him on the inside was that he failed Joan. She was going to die because he couldn't come up with a plan good enough to save her.

He hoped he'd be able to see her at least one last time before she met her doom on this ship without him.

CHAPTER 34

CONTAINED

T.F.S. SHAREHOLDER—OPEN SPACE
LOCAL DATE FEBRUARY 15TH, 2464

Joan's head pounded as if she had been banging it against a metal bulkhead for several hours straight. She rolled over, not remembering how she arrived on the floor to begin with, grogginess overwhelming any other thought.

Her memories flooded back all at once. The door to their hideout opening suddenly, security guards not even allowing them to get a word out before the plasma pistol fire engulfed them.

Something shook her. "Joan?"

She sat up, nearly colliding heads with none other than Dario, the last person she expected to see. Her eyes went wide.

"Not happy to see me?" Dario said with a somewhat insecure smile, despite his joke.

"Not like this, I'm not." She shifted, looking around. "Trian, Yui?"

"We're here," Yui said, rubbing her own head. She sat on the floor just like Joan, but leaned up against a wall. Trian sat next to her, staring in a dazed state toward the sealed door on the opposite side of him.

The walls formed a box around them, trapping them in. No furniture adorned the room, the only ornamentation a bright light from the ceiling. Joan scrambled to her feet and made for the door.

"It's no use," Yui said. "We're stuck in here."

"I used to be able to access the doors from the nets, but my authority's been revoked." Dario pressed his hand against the floor to give him leverage to stand. He made his way over to Joan.

Joan frowned, then turned back toward Dario. "What are you doing here? I thought we…" She paused. Why were these words difficult for her? "…said goodbye."

"I couldn't just leave you," Dario said, his cheeks flushing a rosy color that was pretty cute, even considering the situation. "You're heading off to die with no help. I figured with my position, maybe I could do something, get you out of here."

"Adorable. Now you're just gonna die with us all." Yui smirked, shaking her head.

"Who's this?" another voice said.

Joan glanced behind her toward the corner of the room to see Commodore Zhang leaning against the wall. "Oh. Commodore Zhang, meet Dario Anazao. He's been our corporate contact who took sympathy to our cause."

"More like took sympathy to you," Yui said.

Zhang focused on Dario, not appearing to react to Yui's antics. "I see. Not all plans work out for the best, but I'm honored that you'd try."

Dario gave a quick laugh. "Thanks, I think."

Everyone in the room looked scared, dejected. They had been through so much already. Each time they tried a new plan, the power of the corporations pushed them further and further into a corner, into a smaller and smaller box. Joan didn't know what to say to stir her friends, to give them hope. Even Zhang wasn't offering any solace by the way she stood, waiting. What good was a great strategist in a cell?

"This isn't the end," Joan said to break the tension. All eyes moved to her. "We've been in tough spots these last few days, even hopeless ones. If you would have told anyone we would have made it off that Central Office and made it down to Mars, they would have laughed at you. We've beat corporate security before. We just have to think of a plan."

"That was a different situation entirely," Trian said. "We had a little angel to help us along the way." He motioned his head toward Dario. "Now he's trapped in here with us. "

"We can't give up," Joan said.

"The guards have to come back at least once," Dario said. "They said that the ship's going to stop, that a shuttle's being dispatched to retrieve me."

"We'll see what we can do," Joan says. "We have another way to try to infiltrate the system though."

"Your AI," Dario said.

Joan nodded. "G.O.D.?" she asked. She tapped her handtab to turn his audio back on.

"I've lost this fee-eeling. And I can't seem to get it back," G.O.D. sang to her.

"Come on, I need you now more than ever," Joan said.

Trian raised a brow. "What's wrong? Is it the virus?"

Joan held up a hand for him to wait. She'd been able to bring G.O.D. back from the brink so far. Most of his singing contained messages that at least somewhat applied to the situation.

"I can't fight it. I can't hide it. I've lost myself in somebody el-el-else."

That didn't bode well. Joan bit her lip. "G.O.D., try to focus, please."

"I…" the AI stuttered before his standard voice routine came back. "Ms. Shengtu, I'm afraid the virus has penetrated too much of my system. I don't believe I'll be able to be of assistance to you at this time." G.O.D. paused, and then the singing began again. "Oh time, time is ticking. And the future is now, but isn't it better anyhow-ow-ow?"

"There isn't anything you can do?" Joan pleaded, seeing the worried faces on those around her. Now more than ever she needed G.O.D. at his best. He'd helped her get out of so many sticky situations in the past, able to break into so many systems that her various employers had found impenetrable. Her AI was something special, she knew that. She hadn't felt more scared, more alone, than since she lost G.O.D. the first time a few days ago.

"I…" Another stutter. "Ms. Shengtu, there is the possibility of a hard reset to the system. But there could be other implications."

"What kind of implications?"

"I could lose myself, Ms. Shengtu."

"Lose yourself?" Joan asked. The other stared at her.

"I understand that this consideration is illogical. I am the culmination of code within the circuits of various systems, but I have never been in a position where my existence might be in jeopardy. The subroutines you installed that gave me more freedom than most AIs have, I believe they are detrimental at this time. Those subroutines have given me an irrational interest in my own survival."

"Can't you just make a copy of yourself?" Joan asked.

"If we were on our ship, but your handtab does not contain the memory capacity required to store both a copy and an active AI for long-term use."

Joan bit her lip. "G.O.D., if you don't, I'm afraid your existence might be in worse jeopardy. We might not make it out of here." It was hard to believe she would talk to an AI this way, the others must think she was absolutely crazy. "You need to be brave. If something goes wrong, I'll do whatever it takes to bring you back. You said you could only find help on the Mech World. That's where we'll go. But for that to happen, I need to get out of here alive."

The AI didn't respond for several seconds. Joan touched the earpiece attached just outside her lobe to make sure he was still there.

"Ms. Shengtu?" A voice said in her ear.

"Yeah?"

"Parameters have been reset. Programming is currently stabilized, though the virus has infiltrated approximately twenty percent of my system," G.O.D. said.

"Can you reinsert yourself into the ship's systems?" Joan asked.

Yui had a glimmer of hope in her eye that wasn't there a moment prior.

"Analyzing," G.O.D. said. Several more moments passed. "System is accessed. Determining a course of action for your escape."

Joan moved over to the door beside Dario, staring at it as if her willpower would assist G.O.D. with the ship's systems. "You shouldn't have come," Joan said to Dario, her voice sounding a little harsher than she had intended it.

"I had to. I couldn't let you sacrifice yourself, not like this," Dario said.

Joan looked at him. Bags hung under his brown eyes, a couple of day's worth of stubble on his chin. He looked so tired, but of course he did. It wasn't as though anyone could get rest on this ship as they were flung helplessly toward its destruction. But he was the same Dario Joan had met back at that party. He still held that innocence, a sincerity that connected Joan to him. Joan admired that in him, and wished she could be that way, but she had seen too much pain, too much of the reality that he was just beginning to experience. To the Star Empire, to his corporation in the Trade Federation, people were all expendable pieces sent to do tasks. It wasn't fair, and no one could overturn those systems to stop that fact.

Before she could work herself into too much of a funk about their hopeless situation, the panel on the door's exterior beeped.

Joan moved to the side of the door, readying herself in a position where she might be able to ambush the guards upon entry—assuming they didn't have stunners to knock out the whole room from the get go.

When the doors whooshed open, no guards came in. Dario was the first to look outside, head swiveling in both directions of the hallway. "No one's here."

"I have successfully opened the doors, Ms. Shengtu," G.O.D. said in Joan's earpiece.

"I see that," Joan said, righting herself from her pounce-ready position and following Dario out the door. She glanced either direction as well. The others followed her soon after. "So we're out of our cell, now what?"

The question hadn't been directed at anyone in particular, but Joan found herself looking to Commodore Zhang. The older woman had more combat experience than any of them combined, and while they weren't exactly in a typical military situation, Zhang's planning and command seemed more relevant in leading the party than anyone else's capabilities.

"We need to get access to the ship's critical systems. If we can control the engines or the weapons—if it has any—then we can have a little bit of leverage where they can't stun or suffocate us without repercussion," Commodore Zhang said.

"I doubt the ship was outfitted with weapons," Dario said.

"Then engines it is," Joan said. "G.O.D., lead the way."

CHAPTER 35

ESCAPE

Dario followed Joan back down the corridors where he had earlier followed Engels and Chen. So far, he'd seen no sign of the guards who had promised to escort him away. It was no sooner than they crossed over to a lift at the *Shareholder's* aft quarter that the ship shook. "What's that?" Dario asked.

"We've dropped from FTL," Commodore Zhang said, glancing up around her. "The shift was the gravity plates resetting themselves."

"That can't be good," the woman Joan had referred to as Yui said.

"It's probably because they sent a transport to pick me up," Dario said.

Commodore Zhang stopped in her tracks. The rest of the group fumbled to a stop behind her. Joan's friend Trian bumped into Yui. She turned, brushing past the others and stepping directly to Dario. "They what?"

"The security guard, Engels, he told me before I was incarcerated that the corporation was sending a ship to retrieve me, and that's why they held me in the cell."

Joan's eyes lit up. "I see what you're getting at," she said to Commodore Zhang. "If we can get onto another transport, perhaps those communications won't be disabled or there may be an easier way to commandeer it than with the automatic controls set on this ship."

"That's right," Commodore Zhang said. "I wish you would have mentioned this before we made our route to the engine room. Do we know where a transport would connect to this vessel?"

"Back of the ship as well. There was a small corridor that led into the open room as I recall. I'm not sure how they'll get past all the underlevelers in that big room though."

"We'd have to go back into the pit," Yui said.

"That would risk being trapped in there. Who knows how much tighter security is operating since we've been captured. Now they know there are infiltrators attempting to stop their mission," Trian added. He looked back to the lift.

Before Commodore Zhang could speak again, three of the security personnel Dario had seen before emerged from the lift at the end of the hall. Chen recognized him immediately, pointing. "It's the one from corporate. And the stowaways!"

Dario recognized Chen, Risia, and O'Reilly from before—but Engels, who he had at least some rapport with, was not among them. All three guards drew their plasma pistols. It looked like he wouldn't be able to talk his way out of this.

Trian backpedaled, but Joan didn't run away. She plowed forward, lowering her head, ramming right into Risia's stomach, catching him off guard and pushing him into the rear of the lift cab. He hit the wall with a thud, dropping his weapon.

O'Reilly turned to try to wrestle Joan off his partner. Chen kept her plasma pistol straight ahead, ignoring Joan's surprise attack and firing a shot directly for Commodore Zhang.

"I could use a little help here!" Joan shouted.

Commodore Zhang ducked to the floor to evade the blast, which allowed Dario time to run forward and grapple Chen, diverting her wrist as she fired a second and third shot into the ceiling outside the cab. "I knew you were trouble!" Chen seethed at him

Yui rushed forward and drove her elbow into O'Reilly's jaw, knocking him back to the corner of the lift cab. They traded several blows with one another.

Risia overpowered Joan, turning her around and getting her into a headlock. Joan pushed back, kicking ineffectively at the guard's shins, held outward a safe distance from Chen's body.

Dario scrambled to pry the plasma pistol out of Chen's hands. She had a death grip on it, but Dario hooked a couple of fingers around the hilt of the weapon. He struggled with her for a long moment.

The lift cab rocked as Yui slammed her target into the wall several times.

Commodore Zhang arrived at the cab, holding the lift doors open before assisting Yui with Risia. The two women overpowered him. Zhang kneed him in the stomach. The guard doubled over with the wind knocked out of him. Before he could recover, Yui brought down both fists on the back of his skull. Zhang finished him by pushing his back to the floor with her foot.

Trian brought up the rear, diving for the dropped plasma pistol.

Still wrestling for the plasma pistol with Chen, Dario spared a look over at Joan. In the few seconds of the battle, O'Reilly's headlock had turned her face turn blue, choking the air out of her. "Joan!" he said.

The distraction was enough for his target to gain momentum. Chen brought sharp fingernails across his face. With a cry, he stumbled backward and released the pistol.

Dario's cheek stung. He brought his hand to his face instinctively. Sticky, warm blood squished against his fingers from the nail wounds.

Chen took the second opening to deliver a blow to his chest. Dario staggered into the cab door frame. He was no match for a trained guard. He stumbled away from Chen, trying to get away from her. He needed to help Joan. His body ached, cheek hurt. It was all he could do swing his fist wildly toward O'Reilly's head.

O'Reilly ducked the blow.

Commodore Zhang moved before Dario could get hit again, jumping onto Chen's back. She leaned backward and used her weight to topple the woman over. They wrestled on the floor until Yui delivered a hard kick to Chen's kidney. Chen gasped for air.

Joan's eyes started to roll backward from the lack of air.

Dario swung again, this time connecting with O'Reilly's right eye. He followed up the blow, hitting again and again for good measure.

O'Reilly's grip on Joan loosened. Joan gasped for air, but couldn't free herself from the headlock.

Dario growled and slammed his fist into O'Reilly's face as hard as he could. It resounded with a *crack*.

O'Reilly released Joan, stepping to the side and doubling over. He spit out a tooth and looked up at Dario, mouth bloody. "Why are you doing this?" He asked in a voice muffled from the blood. "We're rescuing you."

"Because it's more than just me who needs rescuing." Dario readied himself for another blow. Before he could, a plasma beam hit O'Reilly. He crumpled to the floor.

Trian stood outside the lift door with the guard's dropped plasma pistol in his hand.

The situation was under control. Dario looked around, now that Joan's assailant had been dispatched. All three of the security personnel lay still on the ground, with Chen's body across the threshold, preventing the doors from closing entirely.

"Couldn't have done that before Joan's pretty boy here started bleeding?" Yui asked.

Trian shrugged. "I couldn't get a clear shot. Negotiations are my trade, not something as crude as weapon fire." He reached down to offer Commodore Zhang a hand up, who accepted so he could tug her to her feet.

Commodore Zhang dusted herself off. "Thank you kindly."

"My honor," Trian said.

Yui dragged the woman guard's body out of the doorway. "Now what? Do we just leave them here?"

"I don't see much of a choice," Joan said. "The more time we waste, the higher the chances other guards will be coming to find Dario here. I think the idea of getting to the transport has to be abandoned." She frowned, looking over the three security guards. "No, we should go back to our original plan. We have to get to a more leveraged position or we're not going to be able to win every fight that comes our way." She gave him a glance, clearly looking at Dario's injury with some concern.

Dario smiled reassuringly to let her know he was okay. He wanted to reach out to her, to hold her. If they made it out alive, he vowed to himself that he'd take plenty of time with her to do just that. Assuming that quick kiss planetside meant as much to her as it did to him.

Commodore Zhang cleared her throat. "Yes. I agree with Ms. Shengtu's tactical advice. We need to keep moving before they wake." She motioned Dario and Yui to the bodies, taking command as it looked to come as naturally to her as breathing. "Grab their plasma pistols though. They might come in handy." She then inclined her head to Joan. "I'll have to remember that you have a sound head for tense situations later."

Dario wasn't sure, but Joan beamed with pride. And she delivered an almost devilish look to her friend Yui. What was that about?

Yui bent over to pick up the remaining plasma pistols, distributing one to Dario.

"You probably would use this better than I," Trian said, handing his pistol to Joan.

Dario caught a look from Trian and looked down at his own plasma pistol. He extended it toward Commodore Zhang. "Here. I've got no experience firing this either."

Commodore Zhang took the weapon with a grateful nod.

They moved the bodies aside and took their places inside the lift. Joan tapped the controls for the engine room and the lift began to move. The lift whirred, as voiced died down.

The lift descended what must have been five or six levels on the Megahauler before the doors opened again. Dario was the first out, motioning for the others to stay back in case of another unexpected run-in with security. At least, he could talk his way through them. In theory. That gave him an idea. He turned around. "Hey," Dario said.

"What's that?" Joan asked. Maybe it was his imagination, or the way the lift lighting fell on her face, but her eyes sparkled at him.

Dario tried to clear his head. He was reading far too much into her every move and expression. There wasn't time for that. "I was just thinking," Dario said, "I helped out one security guard, Engels was his name. He wasn't with this group just now and he seemed to have a more level head. I might be able to talk to him? See if we can reason?"

Joan shook her head. "They threw you in a cell. I think we're past reasoning." She gave him a half-smile.

Dario frowned. "Yeah, you're right." An alternative to a stand-off would be ideal, of course. What else was he good for? He'd proven that he couldn't fight or hold his own as much as Yui or Joan could.

As if Commodore Zhang sensed his words, she patted him on the shoulder. "Don't worry about it. You'll help in your own way. Besides, there's an old saying, 'you fight with the army you've got.' We'll make do."

The lift opened again and Yui was the first to head down the hallway, keeping her plasma pistol trained forward while she moved. It was a protective maneuver, and Dario felt more comfortable with her taking point. "Clear," Yui said.

Joan jogged to the front to lead along with Yui, with her AI directing her. She pointed the direction for everyone else.

After a couple of turns, the group arrived at the engine room, having encountered no further security resistance. That made sense, as Dario's father had told him the personnel aboard comprised of a skeleton crew to keep the underlevelers in line.

Joan stepped before the engine room's door terminal, syncing her handtab with it. The door opened for them, likely due to her AI's ability to maneuver through security protocols.

In front of them was a sound-shielded room that contained six giant, metallic boxes with swinging doors—each with an internal control panel. Those boxes had head-sized wide pipes protruding from them, circulating water and other chemicals through the ship's systems. Dario knew little about the engineering of a starship or its components, staring at the structures with awe.

A main control terminal rested across from the units, a display screen that had numerical values displayed. Dario zoomed in to get a better reading with his ocular mods. Each number was marked with whether it displayed engine capacity, the internal engine temperatures and other variables that Dario didn't understand. Those didn't matter right now. Hopefully those systems contained links into the rest of the ship's systems, so the others could stage whatever coup they had planned.

Joan moved up to the terminal with the engine readout, holding out her handtab. "Are you sure you can access this?" she asked the AI that only she could hear. She waited for a moment, and her lips twitched upward. "We're in. He did it. I think we'll be able to get a signal out and keep the ship from—"

Red emergency lights flashed in the room. Blast doors slammed shut behind them. Dario spun for the door, but there appeared to be no way for them to leave.

"Uh oh," Yui said, scanning the potential exit while keeping her plasma pistol pointed solidly in that direction.

"We tripped a security protocol," Joan said. "My luck has been horrible with that lately."

"Now what?" Trian asked as the loud alarm blared, repeating every several seconds.

"Take positions of cover. We're going to have company shortly," Commodore Zhang said. She pointed to Dario, then Trian. "You both don't have weapons. Get behind the engine compartment. You'll just be targets otherwise."

Yui moved over to a protruding bulkhead, eyes never leaving the door, plasma pistol aimed and steady.

Dario opened his mouth to protest, but caught Joan's concerned glance in his direction. Commodore Zhang was right, it wasn't a good time to try to be a hero. He would do little good other than get in the way.

Trian didn't fight the orders at all, moving for a safe position. Dario crouched behind one of the engine's massive compartments along with him.

"How long do you think we've got?" Joan asked Commodore Zhang from the other side of the large engines. Dario could see her pacing from a low gap between the units.

"Don't know, a couple minutes at most, I'd gather, why?"

"G.O.D. is still working in the system, even with the alarm. Whatever we can do to buy him time…," Joan said, trailing off.

"We'll try that much, but in all likelihood they won't be firing to stun this time. We have to prepare for the worst," Commodore Zhang said.

"Well, at least I won't die bored," Yui said.

Dario took a deep breath as he could do little but wait. The three military-trained women stood out of sight. Their entire existence hinged on their ability to fight. The lights continued to flash, sounds blasting as they prepared for the worst.

CHAPTER 36
MEGAHAULIN'

"**M**s. Shengtu, I have successfully gained access to this terminal's systems," G.O.D. said. "This includes a non-exclusive control of a holovid display, engine coolant levels, and ship energy allocations."

Joan stayed by the terminal, staring at the displays of numbers she knew little about, red lights flashing behind her and tinting the coloration, making it difficult to focus. "How's that help us, G.O.D.?"

"The display can give your team an overall awareness of the external tactical situation. Commodore Zhang in particular may find that information to be useful. Additionally, engine coolant levels can be adjusted to cause the engines to overload. This can sabotage the ship so we will not return to faster than light speeds."

Joan looked to Commodore Zhang, who had positioned herself to the other side of the door in a nice place to ambush anyone coming through. The Commodore stood pressed against the wall, plasma pistol at the ready. How long did they have to gain an awareness of the "external tactical situation"? Joan wasn't sure that would do any good, but she'd learned to trust that G.O.D. would have a plan. "Pull up the holodisplay then," Joan said between the blaring alarm sounds.

"What would you like to see?" G.O.D. asked. "Don't you, don't you see me anymore? You are my love for sure." The singing returned.

A hologram appeared above the terminal in the form of a hovering and rotating Regency BioTech. "Not that," Joan said. They didn't have time for her to worry about G.O.D.'s virus. The complete reboot had failed to purge his issues, but they were out of time. At least the measure had produced enough results to get them this far. "G.O.D., focus if you can. Put on an exterior ship view."

Several moments passed. The holodisplay flickered and dissipated.

"G.O.D.?" Joan asked, concern coming through her voice.

Commodore Zhang gave Joan a skeptical look.

"Processing," G.O.D. said in Joan's earpiece.

The display flickered back to life in the form of stars, with part of the hull of the Megahauler covering the bottom corner. In the distance, a shuttle approached. It was a small ship, colored in Trade Federation blues. Next to that was a trade escort vessel. They weren't messing around in trying to keep Dario safe with that kind of firepower.

"Huh, looks like your ride's almost here, pretty boy," Yui chimed in, directing her comment back over her shoulder, where Dario was hidden behind the engine systems.

"What's going on?" Dario asked.

"Your shuttle arrived, it's on the holodisplay over here," Joan said for his benefit.

"Ms. Shengtu," G.O.D. said. Static buzzed after his words.

"Yeah?" Joan brought two fingers to her ear, but the sputtering static didn't stop.

"There is a group of six armed guards trying to access the doors to the engine room," G.O.D. cut through the static.

Joan's eyes widened. Her body tingled with adrenaline. "Heads up everyone, we've got company, and double the size of the group we had last time." She moved around the opposite side of the terminal, crouching behind it. The translucent holovid between her and the others showed the shuttle coming ever closer. "G.O.D., I need you to silence your program if you can, it's too distracting."

The static stopped.

Yui moved to the opposite side of the door and nodded to Commodore Zhang. "We're ready," she said. "Bring 'em on."

Joan took a deep breath and waited, the alarms still sounding at regular intervals, her heart beating in double time to that.

The doors slid open, slowly, as if by emergency power. She saw the blacks and blues of security's riot gear. The guards pointed their rifles toward the room. This wasn't like the group by the lift that they caught by surprise—this batch of guards was playing for keeps.

When the door fully opened, the six security guards fanned outward, covering the entire radius of the room. Commodore Zhang and Yui blasted the first two before diving out of the way of return fire.

The four remaining security guards shot at the three visible targets. One stepped back, creating a shield of the other three before him. "You can't hope to hold out forever," he said. "Set down your plasma pistols now. We have reinforcements on the way."

"No way! You'll just kill us." Joan reached over her covering terminal to fire another shot back toward them. It missed. Return fire came very close to scorching her hand.

The guard who led the security group didn't respond immediately, but Joan noticed she did look over to the holodisplay of the outside of the ship. "Mr. Anazao, are you in here? Are you held hostage?" he asked.

His fellow security guards stepped further in. Joan could see the tips of one's boots, as the guard came close to rooting out her hidden position. Two focused on Commodore Zhang, who kept them at a standoff as she pointed her weapons back at them.

"Engels? Is that you?" Dario asked from behind the engine units. Determination filled his voice. "I'm here of my own free will. Please, don't harm these people."

"Pardon?" The man sounded confused.

"This ship is headed for destruction. It's a suicide mission—with you on it too. We're not your enemy. These people aren't either. They're trying to stop it, save all of our lives… You told me you were on this mission for your family's pensions. Don't make them lose you over some credits."

"What do you mean? We're headed for an empty colony to drop off the Mars underlevelers," Engels said.

"Don't be naïve," Trian added. "You really think a drop off would come without a way to communicate beyond calls from the corporation?"

"We couldn't allow the underlevelers even the prospect of broadcasting their propaganda," Engels said.

"Is that what *they* told you?" Yui said. She backed up toward the engine units, half concealed in cover.

"What do you mean by that?" Engels asked.

One of the guards jumped and fired toward Yui, who was able to get out of sight behind the engine unit. Joan took the opening to shoot the guard who fired at her. The guard crumpled to the ground, convulsing from her stun setting. Three down, three to go.

The alarm sound ceased and normal lighting resumed. "Ms. Shengtu," G.O.D. said in Joan's earpiece. "I've overridden the silence command for your safety. It is difficult to maintain functionality at this juncture. My subroutines are eroding at a rapid rate." Static returned through G.O.D.'s speaking. "I took the liberty to turn off the alarm. I saw from your vitals the low spectrum repeating lights and high decibel sounds were impairing your concentration."

"Thanks, now shut your own audible routines back off," Joan said under her breath. Her earpiece went dead again. She tried to focus on the others' conversation. If there was at least some hope that Dario could convince the security guards that they weren't the enemies…

"Half of yours are down and mine are free from injury. I think we're at a point where you should consider that we have the upper hand," Commodore Zhang said.

Engels backed up toward the doorway, motioning behind him. "About that."

Another team of three guards came in. This time they all rushed straight for Commodore Zhang. Zhang was able to get one shot off before she was overpowered, knocking another one down, but three grabbed her and held her arms. Another snatched the plasma pistol from her hands. They shoved her to the ground face first, hands behind her head.

"I can keep calling for reinforcements. It doesn't matter to me. Stand. Down." Engels's tone sounded much more stern.

Joan peeked from the side of the terminal, catching Commodore Zhang's eye.

"You're making a mistake," Commodore Zhang said. "We are in a lot of danger."

"We'll be in more danger if the corporation doesn't get its executive off this ship," Engels said. "Mr. Anazao, please come—"

Engels shut his mouth. Something appeared on the holodisplay by Joan's console.

Joan looked up at it, catching an angle from below. Two massive ships jumped into the system off the Megahauler's port bow. Even from her vantage, she saw ships she could never forget from her time in the Star Empire's service: Dreadnaughts. Those ships could blow them out of the sky with the touch of a button.

To make matters worse, the Trade Escort opened fire, a barrage firing toward one of the distant Dreadnaughts. The weapons illuminated the Dreadnaught shields in the dark sky. Bright sparks of purple absorbed the weapons fire.

That served to distract the guards as well as Joan—who assumed the shots she was hearing came from the holodisplay, before realizing that there's no sound in space. Those sounds came from the opposite side of the room.

When she looked again, the three guards subduing Commodore Zhang had collapsed to the floor.

Joan looked back at Yui, who had managed to get those shots off all by herself. She had a proud glimmer in her eye. Joan finally understood why the Council of Ministers had assigned her to protect her—and Commodore Zhang. Joan had never seen anyone fire and pick off targets so cleanly.

Engels wasn't fooled by Yui's move, however. He rushed over to the engine where Yui hid, dropping to a slide when she fired more shots. Before Joan could react and get her plasma pistol pointed at him, he fired upward toward Yui.

The shot blasted Yui in the chin, the plasma eating away at her flesh. Not a stun shot, but one meant to kill. Without any protective armor, it ripped a hole into Yui. She started to scream, mouth going wide, but her nervous system succumbed to the shot before she could make any noise.

Her body hit the ground. The smell of singed flesh filled the air.

"Murderers!" Joan shouted. She abandoned her cover, standing and firing toward Engels, though he dodged into the protective cover Yui had used. "Didn't you see we had stun on? We're not trying to hurt you. We're trying to save you!"

"Just like your Star Empire cronies are?" Engels pointed to the holovid. "You're terrorists, trying to upset the very fabric of society."

The firefight continued outside. Now both Dreadnaughts opened fire on the Trade Escort. Its shields flickered from the onslaught of an assault more than a hundred times of what it let out moments ago. The Trade Escort banked to the left to evade fire, returning its firing shots.

"No. We're not," Joan shook her head, fighting back the tears over Yui. How could she go down so easily? Joan had started to think the woman was invincible. Memories flooded inside her. They had spent weeks together, much of that time in animosity with one another, but over the time, Joan realized that Yui had become something to her that she had very few of in her lifetime—a friend.

Joan had to win this, had to make this right, for Yui's sake as much as any other reason. "Your corporation set this all up, don't you see? There's no way we can defend ourselves against Dreadnaughts. Why aren't you worried?"

"Please, listen to her, Engels!" Dario said from his hiding place.

"I'm not worried because I signed up for this mission. My company takes care of me, takes care of my family," Engels said. He didn't sound as sure as he had before.

Another wave of anger hit Joan. This dolt had killed Yui, and wouldn't listen to reason, just as she had warned Dario in the hall. There was no point in her arguing with him further. Despite her better judgment, Joan stood from her crouch, abandoning the terminal's cover, keeping her plasma pistol steady.

Engels must have seen the opening, because he moved as well, barely enough to expose himself.

They fired their weapons simultaneously.

Joan twisted with all the speed she could muster, slamming her body against the wall to try to evade the plasma pistol blast which would torch her as sure as it did her companion a moment before. The shot did miss, hitting the terminal behind her. The holovid of the ship battle outside flickered as the side of the terminal sparked.

Joan readied another shot, coming into a better view of her enemy.

Engels had collapsed to the floor. Her blast had blown a hole through his riot protection vest, smoking, blood red dripping from his stomach. Her weapon had not been on stun.

Joan stood there, weapon pointed at the body, breathing heavily. It pained her to have killed someone, but she managed to avenge Yui. That should have brought her some solace.

Commodore Zhang raised a brow at her. "Not the best at negotiations?"

Joan shook her head to clear her mind. "Nothing to negotiate. He was blinded by what her company told him, and we'd just be going around in circles while getting picked off." Joan glanced back at the terminal. The two Dreadnaughts exchanged shots with the Trade Escort. The Trade Federation ship wouldn't last much longer at this rate.

"Has your AI been able to restore any other functions?"

Commodore Zhang asked.

Joan needed a question like that to keep herself focused. She had to keep her mind off of Yui. Off of their desperate situation. Clipping the plasma pistol to her belt, she moved backed over to the terminal.

Trian and Dario carefully stepped away from the engine units, glancing around the room. Trian moved for Yui, dropping to his knees and clutching her hand, bringing it to his chest. "Yui…"

Joan couldn't bring herself to look over in that direction again. The others couldn't afford for her to lose her cool. She was the only one with any connection to G.O.D., and by proxy the systems of the *Shareholder*.

"G.O.D., restore audio. Any updates?" Joan asked.

A high-pitched howl pierced through Joan's skull, originating from her audio implant. She staggered backward.

Static resumed. "My apologies, Ms. Shengtu. Enacting multiple commands, even simple ones as to communicate with you and perform other functions is proving too much to handle. I am attempting to break through to the communications systems," G.O.D. said. "There are several encryption levels by which to surpass, and a failed attempt resets each. This is heavier corporate security than we have encountered before."

Security out in the colonies had nothing on these Trade Federation Mega-Corps. She should have known that from the start. Not like it would have done her any good if she had.

On the holovid, the Trade Escort received another bombard-ment of attacks from the two Dreadnaughts, one of which had circled around to flank the smaller ship. Its assault continued from forward and port batteries while its counterpart fired with equal intensity. The smaller vessel's shield flickered, and then failed. The continued barrage reduced the ship to bits.

"A broadcast is coming from the Martine Star Empire vessels. I can play it over the speakers," G.O.D. said.

"Do so," Joan said.

The speakers engaged. "Trade Federation vessels. This is Captain Taylor of the *S.E.S. Wizard*. You have violated Star Empire space. You have ten minutes to leave the system or be destroyed."

Commodore Zhang frowned. "He's one of mine. My first officer when I still had ship command, before they handed me the fleet. I wish I could contact him."

"Right now we can't even turn this ship around," Trian said. "Joan, is there anything your AI can do?"

"G.O.D.? You heard the question?" Joan asked.

"Stand by. Stand by. Stand by." G.O.D. said. "Stand—Ms. Shengtu, I believe I have…" His vocal programming glitched.

"G.O.D.?" Joan asked, this time with more concern.

"What's wrong?" Dario asked, moving toward her.

"I believe I have…" the glitch sounded again, a series of digital noises.

"You have what?" Joan asked.

"The virus… I…."

Joan's earpiece went dead. She brought her hand to her ear, and glanced at the handtab opposite her risk. "Oh, no."

She looked up at the others. "The virus. It's completely overtaken him."

Commodore Zhang rushed toward the holodisplay, staring at the Dreadnaughts lying in wait. The light reflected across her face. "Then we're dead.

CHAPTER 37

ZERO AUTHORITY

T.F.S. SHAREHOLDER—MARTINE STAR EMPIRE NEUTRAL ZONE
LOCAL DATE 1138.433

Dario stared at the terminal in front of him, the image of the Star Empire Dreadnaughts looming over it. The large ships moved so slowly against the star backdrops that they didn't look that ominous, if he didn't already know he was staring at his impending doom. Even from his limited corporate experience, Dario had seen enough newsvids to have watched Dreadnaughts in action. There were very few ships in any of the human systems that could match their firepower.

"Maybe we should try to wake one of the guards," Trian said, motioning to the stunned personnel on the floor. "One of them may have had access to the external communication panels."

"It isn't always so easy to wake someone from stun fire," Joan said. "Plus, the lead one wasn't exactly helpful since arriving. Commodore Zhang tried to talk to him reasonably. I doubt any of the others would be given command authority like that."

"We may have different results given our impending destruction," Commodore Zhang said. She crouched down by one of the guards, a woman who Commodore Zhang rolled onto her back. "It can't hurt to try to wake her at this point." She glanced up to Joan. "You have no means to hack into the communications system?"

"Without G.O.D., I'm helpless," Joan said. "I barely even know which buttons to push even if there were no security. I could maybe maneuver us if we had flight controls. The Megahauler's bigger, but it's not too different than the transport my parents used to fly before their accident."

The image on the screen shifted as the Federation shuttle turned away, just as the Dreadnaught captain had ordered. Whoever was aboard had abandoned their mission to pick up Dario. His only escape valve had left him here, which he couldn't blame their captain and crew for doing. Following orders wasn't worth certain death.

Commodore Zhang inclined her head as if to give her own order, seemingly not noticing the change on the holodisplay. "Try what you can." She patted the security guard on the cheek and shook her, but she didn't stir.

Joan moved to the console, and Dario watched her. He tried not to hover over her shoulder, but he knew the corporate control boards fairly well, even if he didn't know the specific system. "I am still connected to the nets, if there's anything I can do to help," he offered.

"Hmm," Joan asked, looking at the console. "Can you pull schematics and see if navigation can be linked to this console? I know on my ship we have that ability in the engine room."

Dario flicked his eyes upward, pulling up the search protocols. He scanned for flight controls. "No, it looks like the ship is well compartmentalized… wait a minute. I think I see something." He scanned through the different systems. Where it should have been connected, it failed. "Ahh, it looks like there was a pathway, but it was shorted with the plasma blast to the terminal."

"Damn," Joan said, smacking the console. She tapped a few buttons on it again, which brought up a general communications screen. It was locked out via passcode, impossible to reach the outside. "Was hoping I'd get lucky and be able to send a message at the very least." She turned to Dario, and in a sudden move, wrapped her arms around him.

He didn't know what to do at first, freezing. After a moment, he embraced her in return, kissing the top of her head. Her hair smelled nice, even though the both of them hadn't been able to sanitize in at least a day. "I'm scared too," he whispered.

"This is the first time I was ever sure I was going to die. There's always been a way out, something. I've had G.O.D. to help me through things. I don't know what to do. I hate not being in control," Joan said, frowning.

"We can't control life," Dario said. Or love for that matter. How much simpler would it have been if he hadn't met Joan, hadn't found his way into her world? He would still be back at the corporation, working through his daily routines. How much he would have missed though. He pulled her closer, his arms around her. If this was their end, he wouldn't have missed it for all of the safety and security the company could offer.

"No, we can't," Commodore Zhang said, frowning over the unmoving security guard in front of her. "But we need to think of alternatives quickly. Any ideas. Let's brainstorm."

Dario broke off the embrace and slipped over to the terminal, ignoring the holodisplay of the ships above.

A communication came through from the Dreadnaughts. "Megahauler, respond. This is your final warning. Turn back or we will be forced to open fire."

He input his authorization code, just to be certain that his authority no longer applied. As he expected the terminal balked at the command. The codes had been changed. But what could they have been changed to? Someone on the board, or perhaps his father may have changed it.

"They're powering weapons," Commodore Zhang said under her breath.

"How can you tell?" Trian asked.

Commodore Zhang pointed. "See the red spot under the port nose? They heat in order to fire their charges."

Joan moved to Dario's side, gripping some of his shirt by his waist, and looking over his shoulder. She said nothing, but he could feel her fear.

He thought for another moment, then tried to input his mother's name— *Madison*. That did no good. The terminal screen warned him that one more failed access and the system would lock him out completely. "Dammit," Dario said.

"What're you doing?" Joan asked.

"Trying to see if I can guess the access code to the communications systems. Trying to think of what corporate or my father would choose, but this last guess has to be a good one," Dario said.

"I wouldn't be much of a help there," Joan said.

"It's probably a random string of letters or numbers," Commodore Zhang said.

Dario shook his head. "Most of our shared passcodes have had some corporate purpose. Marketing related, something to do with work. We're not a military outfit. It's thought that it's better to have codes that are easy to remember for employees."

"Maybe it's something to do with that party. That was recent, right?"

Dario turned to look at Joan, considering. That was the night they'd met, where, now that he'd had some time to separate himself from his father, he realized he had made his decision to push against the corporate agenda. It was truly love at first sight.

He snuck a glance and met Joan's eyes, giving her a small smile.

"What?" Joan asked, cocking her head in confusion.

"Nothing, just thinking." He turned around again. He could get lost in Joan's eyes forever if she'd let him. Hopefully they'd survive this and she would at that. He bit his lip and input the word "RetroSilver".

The communications panel lit up, giving him access. Marketing trumped all. The Regency BioTech way. Anything to promote the bottom line. Even the death of thousands.

Joan jumped behind him, squeezing him from behind. "You did it!"

Commodore Zhang made her way over, laughing to herself.

"Truly? What are the odds?"

"Send a message, quickly!" Trian said.

Dario connected to the communications system with his oculars, opening a channel from direct input instead of tapping the panel. If there were one thing he'd been good at over the years, it was moving quickly through his implants.

The terminal in front of them chirped.

"Dreadnaughts, hold your fire!" Joan shouted. "We have Commodore Zhang!"

A moment passed. "Commodore Zhang? We won't respond to threats, Megahauler."

Joan made a motion to wave him away from the console, even though the channel was audio only. "No, I don't mean it like that. I mean—"

"I'm here," Commodore Zhang said, her authoritative calm exuding through her voice. "Safe. I've been rescued. Though I would appreciate you standing down weapons."

"Commodore," the voice that had earlier announced himself as Captain Taylor said, surprised. "But how? That doesn't matter now. Should we send a boarding party?"

"It would be appreciated. You may have to contend with Trade Federation security. There is also a large cargo bay filled with displaced refugees. We'll send you over a schematic of the ship and where we're located so you don't run into too many entanglements. Tell your men to set stun weapons. It'd be best to keep the loss of life minimal."

"Aye, sir," Captain Taylor said. "Taylor out."

Dario exchanged hugs with Trian, Joan and Commodore Zhang. They weren't going to be shot out of the sky! He could hardly believe it himself.

"Wow," Trian said.

"You said it," Joan agreed. "Now what?" She looked to Commodore Zhang.

"We should maintain our positions here," Zhang said. She grabbed weapons off the guards on the floor, handing Dario and Trian one each. "Security might try to recapture me while they board, to be used as a bargaining chip. My gut feeling is we took out the team that they could spare while still maintaining order, but we should still be vigilant." She glanced down at the passed out guards on the floor once more before turning her attention back to them. "Then we go home."

They waited in their positions for several minutes, keeping a communication line open with the boarding party from the *Wizard* while they made their way through the ship. Commodore Zhang's hunch about the security force not having any additional help proved correct, and soon Dario and the others were greeted by military officers, in gear very similar to their prior captors, with a yellow patch with the Star Empire symbol on the shoulders.

One soldier moved to attention in front of Commodore Zhang and saluted.

Commodore Zhang returned the salute. "Commander Kilk, good to see you again." The hardened leader of the Star Empire's naval fleets broke a smile. "At ease."

Kilk dropped his salute. "It's good to see you again, sir."

"You as well," Commodore Zhang said, then motioned to the other soldiers. "All of you. Let's get out of here and bring these civilian refugees to safety. Lead the way, commander."

"Aye aye, sir," Commander Kilk said then turned back toward the door. The other soldiers followed him.

Dario walked back alongside Joan, fingers entwined. He vowed to himself to never leave her side again.

EPILOGUE

The next several days had gone by in a whir. Joan had been escorted from room to room, delivering interview after interview as she recounted the details of her trip to Mars to different boards, committees, and military agencies she hadn't even known existed. Sometimes Trian gave a testimony beside her, sometimes not, but they'd kept her separated from Dario, much to her chagrin.

There were rumblings that Dario was going to be indicted for Regency BioTech's attempted murder of thousands of civilians, though Joan hoped that she'd given enough clear detail about how he had been integral in stopping their crazy plan.

Three days into Joan's return to Star Empire space, news reports from Trade Federation proper stated that the Trade Federation's Joint Chiefs of Staff had no knowledge of the Regency BioTech plans to remove their underprivileged population. Regency BioTech came under scrutiny via the Intergalactic Trade Commission, and their stock had reportedly dropped by over fifty percent from the allegations alone. A formal trial and reparations would be forthcoming.

At least the Trade Federation, with all of its flaws, saw injustice when there was something of this magnitude, even if they'd never shown any such scruples in their past dealings with the colonies.

Joan stood by the window of her temporary apartment, a cozy space provided by the Council of Ministers. She couldn't help but think about Trantine X, worrying about its inhabitants.

It had been four weeks since the Blob attack. So many buildings had been leveled. It would be months before the planet could recover, and perhaps it wouldn't at all, given the loss of life. That attack had lasted mere hours, and the Blob had moved on. Joan had moved on as well, truth being told. Her life had been such a flurry she barely had any time to reflect on that.

She wondered what injustices the Blob thought that humankind brought to them. If there was anything to be learned from her recent experiences, it's that people nearly always believed their cause to be righteous, and that their enemies were the ones creating the problems. It probably held true for alien species as well, though she certainly couldn't be considered an expert in extraterrestrial cultures.

Her door chime sounded.

"Come in," Joan said.

The door opened, and there stood Dario. He looked a little skinnier, like he hadn't eaten or slept well in the last few days. She couldn't blame him. If he had heard the reports of back home, how the company he'd worked for was collapsing in on itself, how his father was being held for questioning, there would be no telling how that impacted him. Also, if he had gone through the same or worse questioning that she had...

Joan moved away from the window, toward him. Her feet felt a little lighter as she moved. Now that she thought about it, his presence always made her feel comforted, happier, warmer. Joan embraced him right away. "They let you out," Joan said.

Dario hesitated a moment before his hands clasped around the small of her back. It was cute the way touching her made him so nervous. "Sort of. I have two guards outside. Commodore Zhang authorized me to see you."

Joan frowned. "If they're going to keep harassing you, I'm going to talk to someone, do something."

Dario shook his head. "No, this is expected. They're not

mistreating me, just being cautious. I would do the same if I were them. I've worked for their enemies for a long time, they want all the information I have, and they want to make sure I'm not some spy."

"Like I was," Joan said, chuckling.

"More like Jake," Dario said, glancing out toward the window and the destruction beyond. "But he really wasn't trying to hurt my company, or me. I know that for a fact."

"No, I don't think he was," Joan agreed. She slipped over to his side, linking her arm with his and leading him back to her sofa. "But if they let you come see me, it means they trust you, at least a little. It's not all that bad."

Dario nodded, but stared out the window all the same. "Life isn't as easy out on the colonies as it is back in the Terra system, is it?"

"Not at all," Joan said, not patronizing in her tone. He had never seen the level of destruction that colonists lived with daily. He'd never had to fight for a meal like Joan had. She didn't begrudge him that. It was lucky for him, but he could use a good eye opening. Even if they were odd, computerized eyes.

"I'd like to help. Somehow," Dario said.

"I'm sure once this is over, Commodore Zhang would take you on. Even if she used you for your implants by themselves, you'd be an asset. Maybe some military quality control?"

Dario shook his head. "I want to do something new. Something that makes a difference for real people. I know what quality control does. I mean, it makes sure that people's products, their bodymods function correctly, and that's good for individual lives. I want more than that."

"I know what you're saying," Joan said, side-glancing at him. She forced a little smile.

"What're your plans?" Dario asked.

"Commodore Zhang offered a full reinstatement in the Star Empire Navy. The Council of Ministers struck my court martial from my record, paid off my debts, upgraded my ship." Joan shrugged.

"I can't really see you following orders well," Dario said, his voice teasing.

"Scrap that!" Joan laughed. "No, she offered me an independent supply run gig. Pay isn't quite as good as what I've been used to, but I don't have to worry about going to prison either. I don't know. It's something to think about later."

"Later?" Dario asked, cocking his head at her.

"I thought of heading to the Mech World, where G.O.D.'s programming was designed." Joan stepped away from him.

"Why would you go there?" Dario asked, alarm showing in his face. He gripped her hand and squeezed it tightly. "People don't just travel to the Mech World, you know. I've heard stories that they get brainwashed, that there's some kind of strange technology cult that they bring back with them. You don't want them messing with your mind, Joan."

Joan shook her head. "No, I don't, but G.O.D. is important to me. I need to find his creator, see if they can restore him to the way he was. The engineers here have had no luck even deciphering his basic code."

"It's just an AI, you can get an—"

"No!" Joan pulled her hand back, staring at him. He didn't understand, but then who did? The others had mostly ignored the way Joan interacted with her AI. She hadn't seen an AI quite like G.O.D. anywhere. It's because people didn't trust the tech that came from the Mech World. It was like Dario said; the people from there seemed odd. They carried an air of contentedness about them that seemed unnatural. She remembered the vendor who'd originally sold her G.O.D. His glassy eyes, his quirky smile. She wasn't entirely sure it was a good purchase, but G.O.D. had proved to be her most valuable asset.

Dario frowned. "I didn't mean to upset you."

Joan patted his arm, trying to reassure him. "I know you didn't. G.O.D. has been the only friend who's really been there for me these past couple of years. I mean, until you, Trian, and Yui. You've talked to him though; he's been in your implants. You know there's something special about him."

Dario nodded to that. "Yeah. I mean, it's a very useful AI, I can give you that. I don't understand your devotion. It's pretty intense."

"Yeah, it is," Joan said. She paced around the room and back to him again. "And that's why I have to do this. I promised him I would. I have to take care of him like he took care of me when I needed it most. I know Commodore Zhang isn't going to like it. The Council of Ministers wants a hero to go on the media, help them with public relations, but that's not me. I go it alone, mostly alone at least."

Dario tensed at her last words then, and Joan could see it hurt him. "Is that your plan then?"

"What?"

"To go it alone," Dario said. His eye implants seemed to focus in on her, meeting her with more intensity than any natural eyes she had ever seen.

"Well, yeah. It's not like the Star Empire will give me a crew or a strike team to help me with this. Even though they paid me well for the mission—or at least say they're going to, it's not like I can afford mercenaries."

Dario's sadness turned to indignant anger. "I'd go with you."

Joan bit her lip. "I can't ask you to do that. For the same reasons you said I should probably not go myself."

"You can't control me, Joan, and I'm not some person to be held in protection. I'm my own person."

"I know that," Joan said.

"Let me come with you." Dario looked downward at the metal floor. This time, he took both of her hands into his. "I want to help you. I want to be with you. Can't you see? There's nothing for me here. I've left my company, the job I was supposed to do for the rest of my life, and the people I was supposed to interact with until I retired. There's nothing for me out here. Nothing except for one thing. One person. I… I love you, Joan Shengtu."

Joan's throat went dry. She stared at him, frozen, words escaping her. She knew he'd had feelings for her, but love? Was this the way people talked about these things? It felt like a cheesy holovid. Except for the fact that her stomach tightened and she couldn't breathe. What could she say that could compare with his heartfelt words?

The room felt like it was closing in around her. She had nowhere to go, nowhere to escape. She couldn't even think of an excuse to extricate herself from the situation.

But why should she? Something in the back of her mind nagged at her. This man had been there for her every step of the way. When he'd met her, from when he'd thought she was just another corporate employee and even through when he found out the truth of who she was, he never hesitated. He had exactly the kind of loyalty Joan had expected from her unit back when she was in the Navy, when they'd betrayed her, ratted her out to lighten their own sentences for theft.

That's why she was so scared. She'd never allowed herself to fully rely on someone else since then. Over these past few weeks, however, she'd had to rely on Dario. He'd saved her multiple times.

Joan wanted to save him, too. Truth be told, she couldn't bear the thought of taking off without him. Why was she fighting it? She didn't have to be without him. He was here, offering himself freely to her. Joan pressed forward, standing on her tiptoes to give him a gentle kiss on the lips. She lingered there longer this time than their first, not in any rush to be anywhere else. "I love you too," she finally confessed with her lips so close to his.

She dropped from her tip-toes and rested her head against his chest. His heart beat quickly. G.O.D., if he were here, would no doubt make a comment about his vitals. This did mean that she would have to wait to leave until the powers that be were done investigating Dario, that it may take a little time for her to be able to help her AI. That was okay with her. As long as Dario went with her.

Joan's admission had relaxed Dario considerably. He seemed

much more at ease now, elation all over his face. "So, where do we start?" Dario asked.

"With a plan." Joan led him to her room's terminal so they could begin.

ACKNOWLEDGMENTS

First, I would like to thank everyone who believed in this project, which started by talking about the great card game, Star Realms, at a bar outside of San Diego Comic-Con in 2014. I wanted to bring this world to life and talked to my wonderful publisher, Katie Cord of Evil Girlfriend Media, about my dreams of the Star Realms universe before bringing the idea to the awesome people at White Wizard Games: Darwin Kastle, Rob Dougherty, Debbie Moynihan, and Ian Taylor. This book couldn't exist without you and your game that's brought immense joy to my family and me.

Next, this book couldn't exist without all the people who have pushed me along in writing over the past decade: Dario Ciriello, Setsu Uzume, Herma Lichtenstein, Aiden Fritz, and Emily Sandoval for reading the, as of this writing, unpublished books that led to this point. Jan Schroeder and Katie Baker have been a huge help as well in that regard. Todd McCaffrey has been a huge source of encouragement for me to keep going. Then all of the teachers in my life who have been invaluable to my writing, starting with Sarah Tuuri who first assigned me creative writing in high school, and especially Jody Lynn Nye for her incredible instruction at DragonCon 2012.

Much love to the Star Realms Fan Created Community Facebook page and all its members, as well as the Megahaulin' podcast. You guys have kept my interest in the game at an all time high throughout this whole process. If I ever end up playing you, please let me have Brain World and The Ark.

Jennifer Brozek has been the best editor anyone could ever hope for. Thank you for your patience as I took my time to deliver this, and for honing in the manuscript and pushing me to be better. You've taught me a tremendous amount and I hope to continue to learn from you in the future. Shout out to Sarah Hendrix-Craft for your keen eye on the edits as well.

Finally, much thanks to my family, my parents, and especially my wife Samantha for letting me go hide for hours on end to make up pretend people to shoot wordy space ship lasers.

Jon Del Arroz
Danville, CA 2016

ABOUT THE AUTHOR

Jon Del Arroz began his writing career in high school, providing book reviews and the occasional article for the local news magazine, *The Valley Citizen*. From there, he went on to write a weekly web comic, *Flying Sparks*, which has been hailed by *Comic Book Resources* as "the kind of stuff that made me fall in love with early *Marvel* comics." He has several published short stories, most recently providing flash fiction for AEG's weird west card game, *Doomtown: Reloaded*, and a micro-setting for the *Tiny Frontiers* RPG. *Star Realms: Rescue Run* is his debut novel. You can find him during baseball season with his family at about half of the Oakland A's home games in section 124.

Made in the USA
San Bernardino, CA
06 January 2017